Praise for the Novels of Deidre Knight

Red Kiss

"This is a sensual, action-packed, steaming-hot romance! Filled with demons, gods, immortal warriors, and unique world building, *Red Kiss* will leave you begging for more."
—Armchair Interviews

"Ms. Knight did a wonderful job blending the old-world sensibilities with the modern age."   —Eye on Romance

"*Red Kiss* breathes life into some of history's most amazing men, gives them new purpose, and spins a captivating web of honor, deceit, and the overwhelming power of love."
—Darque Reviews

"A sensational story that packs a ton of heat, action, and fantasy into its pages, *Red Kiss* is an enthralling read you just can't miss!"   —Romance Reviews Today

"A must-read for any romantic at heart."
—TwoLips Reviews

"The women are strong and the men are hot! Deidre Knight really knows how to steam up a cold night."
Fallen Angel Reviews

"A terrific tale that once again will have readers believing in the Knight world, where gods and immortals intervene in the lives of expendable humans."   —*Midwest Book Review*

"Just as action-packed and passion-filled as the first one. Definitely a must-read!"   —Fresh Fiction

"Deidre Knight has outdone herself with *Red Kiss*, a novel that will rest on our keeper shelf."   —Single Titles (5 stars)

"Knight's expertise at combining sensuality and pulse-pounding action is on full display. Make room for another 'Knight' on your keeper shelf." —*Romantic Times* (4 stars)

continued ...

Red Fire

"Knight expertly blends scorching passion, gritty danger, and a wildly creative plot in *Red Fire*, the first in an edgy new paranormal series." —*Chicago Tribune*

"Exciting . . . a fantastic series." —Romance Junkies

"An incredible tale populated by only the most incredible characters. . . . Fast-paced, emotional, riveting . . . I promise you'll love it!" —Romance Reviews Today

"What an exciting beginning to this new Gods of Midnight series! Very well-done by the talented Deidre Knight. I loved it!" —Fresh Fiction

"Knight provides an intriguing new twist to both Greek mythology and legendary Spartan warriors with this searing new series." —*Romantic Times*

"Scorching-hot with a pace that never lets up."
  —*New York Times* bestselling author Christina Dodd

"White-hot immortal warriors, heart-pounding romance, and thrilling action. It doesn't get any better than this!"
  —*New York Times* bestselling author Gena Showalter

"Deidre Knight has created a fascinating world of gods, demons, and immortal warriors. I can't wait for more!"
  —*New York Times* bestselling author Angela Knight

"Hot Gates, hot men, myth, and magic in modern day . . . sign me up for more Gods of Midnight!" —Jessica Andersen

"A fantastic and riveting new voice in paranormal fiction."
  —*New York Times* bestselling author Karen Marie Moning

Parallel Desire

"[A] wonderful book . . . [an] outstanding series."
—Affaire de Coeur

"Twists, turns, and . . . scintillating romance."
—ParaNormal Romance

Parallel Seduction

"Intriguing . . . there's never a dull moment in this terrific series!" *—Romantic Times*

"Deep emotion, fast-paced action, characters who come alive, and a plot full of surprises."
—Romance Reviews Today

Parallel Heat

"Powerfully sensual and mind-blowing . . . a hot romance . . . a great paranormal." —Romance: B(u)y the Book

"Once again Knight explodes with another compelling page-turner . . . one heck of a riveting, sensual ride."
—The Best Reviews

Parallel Attraction

"This book swept me off my feet. A fantastically original, smart, and sexy adventure."
—National bestselling author Susan Grant

"At times humorous, at others heart-wrenching, but always compelling."
—*New York Times* bestselling author Gena Showalter

Red Demon

A GODS OF MIDNIGHT NOVEL

DEIDRE KNIGHT

A SIGNET ECLIPSE BOOK

SIGNET ECLIPSE
Published by New American Library, a division of
Penguin Group (USA) Inc., 375 Hudson Street,
New York, New York 10014, USA
Penguin Group (Canada), 90 Eglinton Avenue East, Suite 700, Toronto,
Ontario M4P 2Y3, Canada (a division of Pearson Penguin Canada Inc.)
Penguin Books Ltd., 80 Strand, London WC2R 0RL, England
Penguin Ireland, 25 St. Stephen's Green, Dublin 2,
Ireland (a division of Penguin Books Ltd.)
Penguin Group (Australia), 250 Camberwell Road, Camberwell, Victoria 3124,
Australia (a division of Pearson Australia Group Pty. Ltd.)
Penguin Books India Pvt. Ltd., 11 Community Centre, Panchsheel Park,
New Delhi - 110 017, India
Penguin Group (NZ), 67 Apollo Drive, Rosedale, North Shore 0632,
New Zealand (a division of Pearson New Zealand Ltd.)
Penguin Books (South Africa) (Pty.) Ltd., 24 Sturdee Avenue,
Rosebank, Johannesburg 2196, South Africa

Penguin Books Ltd., Registered Offices:
80 Strand, London WC2R 0RL, England

First published by Signet Eclipse, an imprint of New American Library,
a division of Penguin Group (USA) Inc.

First Printing, June 2010
10 9 8 7 6 5 4 3 2 1

Acknowledgments

Big shout-outs and thanks go to Angela Zoltners for all her insights and assistance. To Pamela Harty for always guiding me wonderfully. To Christina White, such a nice Greek girl! To my new friend Kathaleen Cassody for knowing what the Iraqi desert would be like at night and what a marine might say if he wanted someone to move quickly. And especially huge thanks go, as always, to my children and husband for their love, nurturing, and encouragement as I wrote this book.

Prologue

More than twenty-five hundred years ago there was a land where the bravest, most valiant warriors were hammered like bronze, forged into human weapons by years of rigorous training and sacrifice. These men were noble, heroic, and stalwart, they would willingly give their lives for their homeland and face down even the most terrifying enemy. Their home, called Sparta, lay nestled deep in the rocky heart of ancient Greece. Its people were private and plainspoken, their lives austere. The men made a life of war, always eager for the next battle.

Then there arose a threat of epic proportions, a Persian force numbering in the hundreds of thousands. The Spartans' Greek neighbors to the north reported that this Persian war machine had trampled entire villages, left forests devastated, the land ravaged and scorched, and that their ranks numbered more than the stars in heaven. Unbeknownst to these mortal soldiers, a much more sinister force stood behind the enemy's massacres. Djinn demons, on their own quest to carry darkness into the souls of mankind, drove the bloodlust of the Persian forces and influenced the outcome of the battles.

When this invading Persian army came, they seemed invincible. The Greek forces allied against them, but could not halt their advances. The Greeks were desperate for more time to plan and strategize since it was their only hope of stopping the Persian hordes. One man, King Leonidas of Sparta, announced that he would provide the necessary delay. That he would lead his three hundred most elite officers to make their stand against the invaders at the narrow spit of land known as the Hot Gates.

Thermopylae.

This pass, an opening wide enough to accommodate only

a few men fighting side by side, would be the stage. There Leonidas and his Spartans would bottle up the Persian forces, using the Gates themselves as an advantage to limit the power of the Persians. They would fight to the last man in order to restrain the enemy for as long as they could— even until the very last Spartan lay dead. These three hundred would give up their lives for Sparta and Greece, for duty and loyalty, for homeland and family. And for a hero's passage to heavenly Elysium.

And so it was that for three sweltering August days this courageous, stubborn king fought alongside his crimson-cloaked warriors. Leonidas made no distinctions among them. All were soldiers, equal in battle, and all would drink from the cup of death as the gods decreed. Beside him, his senior captain, Ajax Petrakos, led charge after charge. Together they blocked the pass, warring with swords, shields, and eventually nothing but their bare hands.

The king and his soldiers never relented, never backed down, and, on the third day, when the burning sun began to slide behind the mountains that marked the pass, only a handful of Spartans remained standing. It was then that the final moments came, and one by one the last of these Spartan warriors, inseparable in life, fell together in death. With their passing the battle was lost, but their Spartan duty was fulfilled.

Captain Petrakos was the first to awaken facing the River Styx, that boundary between mortal life and the mystery beyond. Next his servant Kassandros materialized beside him, the two linked together in death as they had been in life. One at a time, other Spartans appeared out of the mist: Ajax's brothers, Kalias and Aristos; then Nikos and his fellow warrior Straton. And finally their beloved King Leonidas, battered, broken, and mutilated from battle, yet standing tall among their ranks. But an unexpected being also emerged from the mist to stand beside their king. One beyond the warriors' imaginings. Before them stood a towering golden god wearing a proud smile upon his face. It was none other than Ares, the lord of all Spartan soldiers, their god of war.

Ares had come to present an offer, one final choice, as the seven warriors stood at this place between life and death. They could lay down their swords and move on to

Elysium and the afterlife that awaited them, or they could turn back to the world, take up their arms once more, and become immortal protectors of mankind for eternity.

They would fight every form of evil that threatened humanity, becoming ageless battlers of demons and fighters of wars. They would serve under Ares, in the name of mankind. With the deity's offer, these warriors could ensure safety for their families, for Sparta, and for the sons and daughters of Sparta for centuries to come. In their immortal form, each man would possess abilities akin to those of the gods. They would be stronger than before and in the heat of battle could assume the form of hawks, with the flight, lethality, and grace of these warrior birds. They would become dark angels, saviors of the night.

The will of warriors was in their blood and in their souls, and they knew in their hearts that it was a noble quest. But it was a noble quest for a capricious god. Still, they would have followed their king to the ends of the earth, to Hades itself if he asked it of them. And when they looked into his wise eyes, they knew his decision had already been made.

Leonidas did not beseech them; the choice lay with each man alone. But these were men born and bred to fight for the glory of war. Their duty, honor, and love for one another bound the warriors in unspoken agreement. One by one, each of the seven men drank from the River Styx, binding their immortality and their vow.

There was no time for second thoughts and no place for regrets. The seven Spartans, now the immortal protectors of all mankind, turned away from what might have been and bowed down before the voice of war.

Chapter 1

Maybe Super Mario Cart would've been a better starting point. Or perhaps Pirates vs. Ninjas Dodgeball. Anything else, Ari decided, would've made a less frustrating introduction to the world of Wii than Dance Dance Revolution.

Especially for King Leonidas, Ari's immortal commander, who happened to be well over twenty-five hundred years old, and a gamer virgin until tonight.

Ari was about to suggest a change to his newbie pupil when the Old Man glared at the flat screen, releasing a shocking string of obscenities. The ordinarily quiet Spartan might have been facing a legion of bloodthirsty Persians; the aggression in his dark eyes was that fierce.

"Uh, sir?" Ari ventured, struggling to tune out the game's tinny disco music. "This is supposed to be entertainment. Not warfare."

Leonidas didn't acknowledge him, only narrowed his eyes when loud booing began pouring forth from the television set. Oh, gods above, this wasn't going to be pretty. Nobody, not even an electronic device, *booed* King Leonidas of Sparta.

Ari decided distraction was in order. "It's like battle drills, sir. Fancy footwork; that's all."

Leonidas barely grunted in reply, and Ari began reaching for the Wii remote his king still held in a viselike grip. "Let's try a slower song."

"*No*," Leonidas answered in a low growl, drawing the word out like a slow peal of thunder—and Ari burst out in loud, admittedly disrespectful, laughter.

He just couldn't help himself; there was such raw pride and fierce determination in the way the Old Man said it. So, hell yeah, Ari laughed, and so did Nikos from his position at the bar. And when grumpy Nik got rolling, it was such an unexpected outburst that even solemn Kalias joined the action. Which was really saying something because Ari's eldest brother wasn't exactly a blinding ray of sunshine himself.

It was a real *Give a Pig a Pancake* moment, to quote the children's book—which Ari actually owned, 'cause he liked kids' humor—pure and basic. All the brotherhood knew the book, too, because the day Ari had bought it, he'd followed them around reading from the thing, claiming that the pig made him think of the scrappiest of them all, Straton. Or, really, that the pig reminded him of their whole immortal brotherhood—if one did something, the rest of the cadre invariably got in on the action.

So, watching the lot of them begin to lose it in the face of their king's disintegrating Wii composure, he just couldn't help blurting out, "You know, if you give a king a pancake ..."

Which most decidedly did *not* help the situation.

Neither did the wine they'd all imbibed during dinner a few hours earlier.

Tonight marked two months since they'd defeated Ares at the River Styx—as well as the fact that they'd not heard from the bastard god ever since—so they'd laughed. Drunk uncut red wine from goblets. Celebrated their liberation from eternal servitude to Ares. Gotten uncharacteristically giddy, tossing back quite a few of those overflowing goblets.

Everyone, that was, except Leonidas, who'd seemed as reserved as always, maybe even more so. Ari suddenly wondered whether his king's current fury with the flat screen had little to do with dancing or electronic games, but instead signaled something much more serious.

He approached Leo again, gentler this time. "Sir," Ari tried, "really, I know you said you *like* Donna Summer and all, but this is a little advanced for a beginner. Maybe we should try something under a hundred beats per minute."

"Aristos," Leo replied, "are you intimating that I'm too *old* to maneuver within the confines of this modern gymnasium?"

"This isn't the Agoge training ground, sir. Nobody's running sprints or wrestling nude."

Ajax cut in. "I might, if Shay'd ever get back from the store."

Leonidas ignored the other warrior, still attempting the movements. "You find me too ancient minded to keep pace in this game the rest of you have mastered?"

"Not at all, sir." Ari gave his king a solemn bow of respect. "I'm just saying that the people who created this game are perverse little fuckers who enjoy giving humans migraine headaches and vicious eyestrain. Our prank is up, my lord. Ari lowered his voice in a confessional tone. "None of us know how to make this damned machine work."

Their commander stopped dead at that, staring at him without blinking, and would have undoubtedly continued to do so for an indefinite amount of time, except that the house phone rang over on the bar.

"Someone's calling," Ari announced in an overly bright voice, thanking the Highest God above that he'd been saved a dressing-down for insubordination.

He instantly regretted that he'd ever considered this particular caller his savior. In fact, the woman on the other end of the line was more like a messenger straight from Hades itself.

"Cecilia," Ari mumbled into the phone, "I've already told you. Plenty of times now. I'm not coming."

She released a long feminine sigh of frustration. The woman was a perfect Southern lady, even when annoyed. "Then put Emma on the line," she said. "Perhaps my daughter can knock some sense into that thick head of yours. And if she can't, then maybe River will. You do still listen to my *son-in-law*, don't you?"

River. Consummate warrior. Shape-shifter extraordinaire. The best pal he'd ever had, in any century. And, as of very recently, husband to Emma Lowery, a human medium who heard voices from beyond the grave—sometimes the source of those words was even heaven itself. It was a talent she'd inherited from her mother, the same woman who currently sniffed her delicate but unmistakable irritation on the other end of the telephone line.

For weeks now Cecilia had been calling, urging him to visit her brownstone in downtown Savannah. She had a message for him, she claimed, from a dead woman; not such an outrageous assertion, considering Cecilia's abilities. It was the identity of said dead woman that troubled him greatly.

He clenched his teeth, counting silently to ten in ancient Greek, then replied, "Emma's not down here."

"Down *where*, Aristos? Hades? Because surely you must be in hell right now, what with the way you're ignoring poor Juliana's spirit."

He groaned. "Nothing pitiful or poor about that woman, dead or alive." He visualized Juliana's deep red hair, the way the auburn hue had once shimmered and changed color when reflected in the candlelight, almost as if it had a life of its own. Now, more than a hundred years later, she remained the most vital, strong woman he'd ever known. "Trust me; nothing about Juliana ever needed my pity."

Or my love.

"She suffers, Ari. Because you refuse to come, refuse to let me share her message, she is in torment. Doesn't that matter to you? You once told me you loved her more than any woman you'd ever known. If that's true, how could you keep her in such agony?"

"I never said that I *still* love her." He swallowed, rubbing a hand over his chest. His heart felt as if it might explode, it was beating so rapidly. He swallowed again and whispered, "I loved her, and she died. End of story. Has been for a very, very long time."

"True love never dies, Ari. Neither does the human spirit." She laughed gently, knowingly. "But you're already well aware of that fact."

He pressed his eyes shut, wincing at the verbal blow. No, despite his ridiculous assertions, his love for Juliana had definitely never died . . . nor had his anger at the why and *how* of that death. A throbbing pain began at his temples, accompanied by a tight burning sensation much like the one in his chest. Oh, his deep, tormented love for Juliana was very much alive; after all, when one has roamed the earth for more than two thousand years, what are a mere hundred of them in the overall scheme of things?

"Her love for you is as vibrant as it ever was. Surely you feel that now . . . every time I call."

Ari stalked to the far side of the small kitchenette. If

any situation in his life had ever called for privacy, it was definitely his current distress over Juliana. No wonder he'd never told River or any of his other Spartan brothers about her. He couldn't have handled the ball busting they'd have dished out—not about her.

He faced the pine-paneled wall of the kitchenette, studying the swirled grains of the wood, how they seemed like eerie faces staring out at him. The thought forced him to look away.

"You hear all kinds of voices, Cecilia," he answered. "You might even be channeling some demon who wants to infiltrate our camp, or some other spirit, or—"

"God himself?" she supplied demurely. Which could be true: Cecilia was descended from the oracles of Delphi, as were Emma and his own brother's wife, Shay Angel. That line of women definitely heard the words of the Highest God and translated them when required.

Ari forced a laugh that he didn't feel inside. "I doubt *He* would claim to be a dead society woman from Victorian-era Savannah, don't you?"

"You don't dare to believe."

"Oh, I believe, Cecilia," he said, thinking of all that he'd observed while hanging around Shay and Emma and Cecilia herself. Not to mention the centuries he'd lived, the supernatural battles he'd waged. He definitely, truly believed. That wasn't the problem in this situation.

"I know exactly what you Daughters of Delphi are capable of. And I know that Juliana was your great-aunt, so I have no doubt that she could somehow revive her spirit long enough to conjure something, anything, for me."

If she ever truly loved me.

"You're afraid. Of her, your feelings . . . of what she might say." Cecilia released a disappointed-sounding sigh. "And here I thought Spartans were the bravest men to ever roam the earth."

Oh, no she didn't, he thought, and was preparing an appropriate verbal takedown when she spoke in a lower, more intense voice than she'd ever used with him before. And the hair on the back of his neck instantly stood at attention in response.

"She gave me proof," Cecilia said.

His palms began to sweat. "What do you . . . ?" He rubbed

his forehead, trying to calm his racing thoughts. "You can't possibly have proof. She's been dead since 1893, Cecilia."

"You of all people shouldn't argue about the perversities of immortality and the beyond, Aristos Petrakos."

She had him there, and they both knew it. She continued. "Did you not die yourself once? More than two thousand years ago?"

"I'm not like Juliana. I made a bargain." He thumped his chest as if Cecilia could see him. "Not saying it was a good one, but that's beside the point. I made a deal with a devil, and that's why I'm here, still treading life when I'd rather—"

"I have solid proof that Juliana's spirit is right here in my house. You *know* that this was her home; why wouldn't you believe that she's here?"

Because long ago she killed our love? Herself?

"She's running out of time, Aristos."

The words hit him like a wall of ice. Cecilia was right—he was a coward when it came to Juliana Tiades. But his heart had been far too broken, and for far too long, to risk opening it again.

"I'm sorry," he said at last, and ended the call.

The kitchenette was secluded from the rest of the downstairs, but Ari could still hear the whoops and hollers from his compatriots playing Wii in the adjoining recreation room. With a groan, he leaned his full weight against the stainless-steel refrigerator and doubted everything. Himself. The newly acquired power in his body. His decision to ignore Cecilia and her persistent calls.

What if the eccentric woman was right? If Juliana was truly reaching out to him, then he was turning his back on her.

It was as if a million voices scrambled for attention in his mind, and he wondered how much of that confusion might be a result of his recently acquired "abilities." Or power. Or curse. Whatever you wanted to call it, he had undergone a tremendous change in the past two months, all in the name of brotherhood and friendship.

River had wanted to become mortal in order to live a normal life with Emma, so Ari had made a new bargain, this time receiving River's own mantle of power in a supernatural exchange. No small thing, considering Ares, god of war, had seeded the powers of life and death inside his best friend. As a result, Ari was now packing a supernatural Smith & Wesson, so to speak. He bore not only his own power, but River's as well now, and that was one helluva dangerous brew, considering that River's gifts had often left him torn between violent madness and raw sexual aggression.

Ari bowed his head, burying it in both hands. The energy in his body felt alive tonight, his soul on fire, even more so after talking to Cecilia. In fact, the cool, metallic surface of the refrigerator only pointed out how heated his body had become.

A firm hand clasped his shoulder, startling him; he looked up to find River's concerned eyes fixed on him. "Why does my mother-in-law keep calling you?" his friend asked, grip tightening. "And why are you avoiding her?"

Ari sighed; he really wasn't ready to confess all, not even to his best friend. Then again, River might already know the bitter details of his past with Juliana, at least if Emma had shared them with him. Ari knew enough about husbands and wives, especially newlyweds, to realize there weren't usually any secrets of consequence between them.

Ari had never told any of the brotherhood, not even River, about his time during that mission in Savannah. Or about the society woman he'd loved and wooed during those sultry summer months of 1893. He'd certainly not shared the details of her death, or how he'd grieved for her—or for how blasted long. He'd told no one until that day at Cecilia's home more than two months ago, when she'd blindsided him with a faded photograph of Juliana, he standing at her side. Emma had been with him when he'd seen it, and he'd not thought it fair to ask her to keep secrets from River.

"We never keep secrets, friend," River prompted as if reading his thoughts. "Emma's obviously aware of whatever this is about, but she told me to talk to you. She wouldn't betray your confidence; you should know that."

Ari groaned, wishing that he could dematerialize and land somewhere very far away. At least Emma had kept silent until now. "River man, look," he said quietly, "just let this one go."

His best friend's answer was to give him a hard shove in

the chest. "You bullheaded idiot. You've been moody for weeks, alternating between being a total smart-ass and a depressed moron. Something's obviously bothering you, and I'm figuring it has to do with Cecilia's calls."

"We both know that's not the only change in the past few months," Ari said meaningfully.

River frowned in obvious concern. "Are you referring to the power exchange? Are you having side effects?"

Ari stared at the floor, wishing he'd kept his trap shut. What was it about River Kassandros that always made him blab the private shit? Well, not quite always. River had never caught even a clue of what the original Savannah mission had done to Ari.

Ari shrugged noncommittally. "Maybe . . . I dunno."

River stared at him, hard, as if he could penetrate Ari's mind with that single glance and know the truth. A truth River surely realized Ari would never own up to, not with the way they always watched each other's backs. If River learned that their recent trade had begun to play havoc with Ari's mind and soul, he'd go to Leonidas, the Oracle, and anyone else he could think of. All the way to heaven or Hades itself to reverse their situation, and Ari wasn't about to allow that. Not when River finally had a happy, secure life; a free one, after millennia as a slave and berserker.

"Dude, how's 'bout bugging out of it, huh?" Ari tried to laugh. "I'm cool. No worries. Everything's copa-fucking-cetic."

River glared at him. "So it *is* the power you assumed. Obviously, you're having a hard time managing it."

Ari groaned and bit back what he wanted to say, which was that the timing of the whole thing was the real bitch. Juliana reentering his life at just this moment was an added complication to an already brewing shit storm. Every time Cecilia called him, the energy in his body screamed its defiant rebellion a little more loudly.

Ari shifted under River's intense study, but his best friend didn't back down. "If it's the power," River said, dark expression intensifying, "then you need to talk to me. I had to shoulder it for more than twenty-five hundred years—"

"You think I don't know what you fucking lived with?" Ari barked bitterly, both hands trembling violently at his sides. "Guess what, *brother*? I'm living with it now."

River's usually warm eyes widened, his suspicions clearly confirmed, and then his entire expression became very sad. "Ari," he murmured, grief in his voice. "Oh, gods, Ari, I'm so sorry. I'd hoped . . . believed the current would be different inside of you."

"Why would it? Because I'm a bigger jackass than you?" Ari tried to laugh, but River's expression only grew more somber.

"Because you are a better man than I," he said seriously.

"That's bullshit, and you know it. If anything, I'm far too rash, rude, and blundering to deserve what you gave me. The power of life and death? Inside of me?" He pointed at his heart. "What a joke. I'm such a perennial fuckup, even my younger brother outranks me."

River shook his head with slow intensity. "You're not yourself, and comments like that prove it. You've always been one of our bravest, most valiant warriors. That's why Ares chose you after Thermopylae."

"Why did *you* choose me, anyway?"

River seemed to think about the question, looking off to the side for a long, pensive moment. Finally, his gaze slid back to Ari, eyes bright. "There was no one else I'd have trusted. Not to remain uncorrupted by so much power." River blew out a guilty sigh. "But I should have thought harder about what it might do to you."

Ari seized his friend's arm. "I don't regret my decision," he rushed to say, but knew his reassurance was too late. "River, I promise. It's not like this all the time. Not even a lot of the time. It's this thing with Cecilia, how she won't leave me alone . . ."

"Her calls upset you, and you experience a power surge," River finished knowingly.

"Yeah, it's like an explosion, beneath my skin, down in my muscles." Ari lifted his heavy forearms, flexing them in the air. "Like a grenade goes off inside me." He thumped a fist against his chest. "Right down in here . . . some fucker pulls the pin, and it just explodes."

"Trust me," River said. "I know that feeling. Unfortunately all too well."

Ari nodded, studying his best friend's face. So familiar . . . and yet so very different since their fateful trade. There was a peace in River's eyes and facial expression that had been lacking throughout their eternal years together. Ari shivered, wondering whether his own features had changed for the worse, whether the weight of what he'd accepted had transformed his appearance.

As if in reaction, a jolt of electricity sizzled through his fisted hands, and there was an answering explosion from the other side of the room.

"Damn it, Ari!" his big brother, Kalias, cursed. "That's the third Wii you've fried this month."

He gave his brother the middle-finger salute, even though he couldn't see it from the next room. "So bill me, Kali*ass*," he shouted irritably.

And instantly felt the burn inside his body intensify tenfold.

River clearly saw that change, because he cuffed Ari by the neck, hauling him toward the stairwell. "Move out," River commanded.

"Why?" Ari wrenched out of River's grasp. "Where the hell are you taking me?"

"Cecilia's. We're going to deal with whatever the problem is," he announced, shoving Ari forward. "And you're going to tell me the whole story. *Now.*"

Chapter 2

The wind atop Olympus blew warm and brisk, whipping Daphne's hair across her eyes. She stepped onto the stone portico that led to her brother's palace, one of the most elaborate of all the gods' homes, situated just below the mountain's peak. From within, sheer curtains billowed in golden invitation.

Ah, brother, your beauty is always so deceptive. Even your palace lies for you.

Normally she preferred leather and miniskirts to the traditional white gown she'd donned for this familial visit, but things were tense enough with Ares right now. She didn't need her fashion choices pointing out that he no longer controlled her destiny

She entered the throne room, following one of her brother's female servants; the woman was practically nude, clothed only in links of delicate gold chain and a diaphanous skirt that hid nothing. Ares rose from a velvet settee and greeted Daphne, drawing her uncomfortably close.

"I see those grimy Spartans haven't corrupted you yet, sister. At least not fully." He pressed his nose against the crown of her head, inhaling her scent. "Or perhaps you merely bathed before entering my presence. That would account for the aroma of lilacs."

He slid one arm about her waist, walking her toward his throne. It was a monstrous, ornate slab of gold that he'd commissioned some age or two ago, engraved with images of homage and victory. They were his usual self-adoring fare: Ares astride his stallion; Ares borne aloft a shield; Ares being lavished with maidenly kisses.

He stroked a warm hand down her forearm, lingering far too long, and she jerked free as if scalded.

He censured her with a dark warning. "Not very grateful."

"And for what should I be grateful?" she spat. "My centuries of captivity at your hand? The millennia of control, when you kept me invisible to the man that I . . . that I . . ." She bit back the rest.

Ares laughed mockingly. "*The man that you love?*" he finished in a singsong falsetto, fanning his chest. "Oh, flowers and sonnets, how touching," he chirped, then frowned as if tasting something noxious. "By all of Olympus, love makes me *sick*. The emotion is a weakness, a blight. How disappointing that my own offspring should be the keeper of it."

Ares had very little respect for his son Eros. In fact, she wasn't sure how many years had passed since he'd even bothered to see the playful, amorous god of love. Her brother twisted his face nastily. "I blame Eros's existence on Aphrodite. The weakness in her bloodline sired his foppery, not me."

"He is your own son." Daphne shook her head angrily. "You should care for your family, have some decency of feeling. Not torture and neglect us."

"I have never neglected *you*, Daphne," he answered in a tone that sounded almost sincere. "And we both know how much I care." The last words dripped with double entendre, but she ignored their lascivious suggestion.

"If you truly care for me, Ares," she rushed to say, stepping near him, "then *show* me. Make your words true."

He did not reply, simply studied her with obvious interest and then gave a half nod.

She continued, daring to hope that her brother might display some compassion today. "Do not harm the Spartans," she asked, bowing her head. "My lord, please. Do not seek revenge upon Leonidas or his immortals."

She dared to look up, meeting Ares' tawny-eyed gaze, and he laughed, tossing his head back as if she'd just made a delicious joke. "Oh, dearest Daphne, you charm me still. Even now, after all that's transpired between us, you captivate me. How naive you are," he said at last. "And how pitifully, shamefully in love you remain with that brittle old king."

She chafed at his description of Leonidas as "old," just as she hated it when the warrior described himself that way. Leo had been only thirty-five at Thermopylae, and the immortal years didn't show in his features. He bore no significant lines on his swarthy face, no gray in his curling hair and beard.

She defended him softly. "Leonidas is not old. He is immortal."

Ares mounted his throne, lounging in it with an affected, languid posture she knew was meant to intimidate her. "Our father may have granted you freedom, sister, but he issued no such orders regarding the Spartans. They will be brought to heel for their treasonous rebellion."

She slid to her knees, assuming the most humble, beseeching posture she could manage. Tears burned at her eyes, but she didn't care how pathetic or subservient she seemed. Not with Leo's life suspended in the balance; not when she might be the only one who could save him from her vicious brother. "I beg of you, Ares. Please. Spare them . . . him."

"On your knees before me, Daphne? After so many years? That is the right place for you." He shifted slightly on the throne, leaning forward so that their eyes met. "But it does not change the Spartans' fate. I am only beginning to toy with them, sister. Only beginning to reveal the cracks in their pitiful foundation. Your precious king? I suspect he's feeling a bit *older*, recently. And older still with every passing day."

She wrestled to keep her voice calm. "What do you mean?"

"Oh, I'm sure you will learn soon enough. Perhaps it is your beloved you should ask?" Ares studied his fingernails absently. "He already suspects the truth."

She felt her blood run cold, her skin prickle with dread. Hadn't Ares mentioned something similar, that day by the river two months earlier when he'd wrenched her away from Leonidas, forcing her to become invisible to him again? What had he said then? She tried desperately to recall the god's exact words.

"I cannot ask him." She shook her head slowly, maintaining a steady gaze on her brother's cruel face. "Leonidas and I have no relationship. Not anymore."

She'd ended their relationship after the battle in Hades, fearing that Ares might use their love as an excuse to hunt the king down. And she'd cried herself to sleep every night since.

"Oh, come now." Ares licked his lips as if tasting the remnants of a delicious fruit. Rising from the throne, he took her hand, pulling her to her feet. "You are finally visible to your noble king, just as you prayed for over the past thousands of years. Surely the nubile bloom of love has not wilted already?" He pressed a hand to his lips in a feigned display of shock. "Or, perhaps it is the brave *commander's* rose that has wilted? Is the old man unable to satisfy you, dearest Daphne?"

She reached to slap him without thinking, furiously defending Leonidas against such a rude insult—and their broken relationship against the cruel slander. She'd have been at Leo's side right now had she not been protecting him from Ares' jealousy and vengeance.

As her palm nearly connected with Ares' cheek, he seized her wrist, twisting it harshly. "I wouldn't do that if I were you, sister."

"Half sister." She squirmed in his grasp, desperate to be free, but he spun her hard against his chest.

He pinioned her close, and a long lock of his golden, silky hair fell across her cheek. "Oh, Daphne, you are my greatest disappointment, don't you see? Not the Spartans. Not even your precious Leo. You."

He brushed his lips against her ear, his breath smelling like overripe wine. "And it is because of your disobedience that the Spartans will—no, they must—be punished." His wet mouth grazed her cheek. "And it is because they turned upon me that they shall be eliminated."

Then, with a harsh shove, he sent her sprawling out of his grasp and across the polished floor. He barely noticed, railing at her furiously.

"Consider their pitiful human frailties! The way they moon and long for love as if they did not have the very power of the *gods* in their blood," he thundered, raising a proud fist toward the peak of Olympus. "I made them lords among men, sired by my eternal power!" He lowered his voice contemptuously as he paced the floor. "I made them glorious. Far more glorious than they'd been at Thermopylae. The fools. They could have had any lover they craved, any creature they lusted for . . . male or female, human or immortal. Oh, but even *that* was not noble enough for your—"

Ares pulled to a full stop, the rest of his sentence dying on his lips. He smiled in cryptic amusement, as if he hid the cleverest of secrets.

She stepped toward him, knowing instinctively that his clever secret was dangerous, deadly. "For a god, your thoughts certainly wander, my lord."

"My thoughts are as strategic and precise as ever." His calculating tone chilled her. "Especially regarding your old king."

"Please tell me what you intend to do. To Leonidas. The Spartans."

He answered by raising both arms, a cyclone forming between them, whipping at her gown, tearing at her hair. The wind intensified; the floor beneath her feet seemed to split wide-open.

"You must . . . tell . . . me. . . ."

Her outcry was already lost in the grist of time and changing space, and then pure darkness engulfed her.

Chapter 3

A ri had survived more battles than he honestly remembered. Had died and been brought back to life after what was arguably history's most famous conflict. Yet throughout that long, eternal tide, he'd never actually found himself at war with a *literal* battlefield.

Until now.

Standing on the opposite side of Savannah's West Jones Street, eyeing his quarry, he reminded himself that the four-story brownstone was nothing more than a physical structure. A dwelling that had stood for more than one hundred years, a brick-and-mortar home where Emma's mother happened to currently live.

But it was hers, another voice argued. *You courted Juliana inside those same walls.*

No wonder he could practically feel his knees knocking together. The reaction was enough to make him duck his head in shame: he, a brave Spartan warrior, one of Leonidas's most daring and bold, felled by a *woman*. And a dead one, at that.

The live oaks along the street created wavering shadows in the dark, mirroring his mood. Their limbs swayed overhead, as if reaching toward the heavens themselves. A gale had hit the barrier islands earlier in the evening, causing sudden surges of wind as a hurricane built strength much farther off the coast. Not unusual weather for the low country in late October, but the heavy, sporadic gusts of wind haunted him nonetheless.

It had been on a night much like this one that he'd seen Juliana for the last time. They'd thought it a simple storm that late-August night, the sweeping, sudden breezes pleasant after weeks of blazing heat. How wrong they'd all been, he especially, and about everything he held true.

Suddenly it was the twenty-first century again, Emma shoving him in the center of his back. "Come on, Ari," she scolded. "Get it over with. You've spent two months avoiding this moment."

He grunted at her. "Yeah, Lowery, Juliana may be your great-great-aunt, but it's not *you* she wants to talk to."

"Why so scared, big guy?" Emma moved in front of him, staring up into his eyes. Much as he adored the woman, he could've done without the familial game. *Blasted heredity*, he thought, trying to avoid the ethereal blue of her eyes that were so much like Juliana's own as she continued. "You've faced down legions of Persians, battled demons and Olympian gods. What could ever intimidate you?" She gave him a playful slug in the arm. "Huh, Petrakos?"

"Uh, maybe one little fact." He widened his eyes dramatically, raising his voice. "That Juliana's a freaking *ghost*? Nothing like getting a phone call from the dead to shake things up a little."

Emma waved him off. "Puh-lease. It's my mama who's been calling you, not Juliana."

"And who keeps on calling me, persistent female that she is." He dropped his voice lower, muttering, "Must run in the bloodline."

"Heard that. But you know you love me." Emma linked arms with him, undaunted. Hers was truly a brave, conquering soul. From the moment he'd first met her on Tybee Island two months ago, they'd been good friends. Probably in large part because of how much she loved River. Best friends by proxy, and all that.

He resisted her tugging grip. "Hold up. Really. I'm still not so sure about all this."

River appeared on his other side, the pair of them bounding him like the bun around some highly reluctant Oscar Mayer wiener. "Ari, man, what's the harm in just hearing what Juliana's got to say?" River gave him a shove of his own, and Ari had to admit, the duo took newlywed tag teaming to new levels. He also knew they were only here, shoving his ass toward the cobblestone street, because they loved him. Best friends were funny that way.

"I think we already covered this problem in the car." Ari sulked, keeping both feet rooted to the sidewalk. He really was not going to take another step closer to that soul-sucking pit of a brownstone across the street. This was as close as he cared to get.

During the drive over, he'd given River and Emma a highly abbreviated account of his affair with Juliana, leaving out all the maudlin pain and heartbreak parts. He just couldn't go there with either one of them, not tonight. Even though he'd played his cards close, there'd been a moment in the car when he suspected River understood far more than he was letting on.

River scowled up at him. "I thought you said you'd loved the woman."

"Yeah, but Juliana isn't exactly someone I've been hoping to hear from, like an old friend looking me up on Facebook. Got it?"

River smacked him on the back of the head and started across the street. "Aristos, troops are rolling out. Man up or pussy out."

The words hit Ari in the gut like a battle charge—just as River had known they would. A challenge to his bravery and manhood motivated any Spartan into action.

"Fine," Ari groused. "But if it gets too weird, I'm out of there."

"Aristos! You've come to see me at last." Cecilia Lowery, smelling of perfume, patted his cheek affectionately. "About time, too. Juliana is proving to be quite . . . persistent."

Ari shivered at the statement but didn't let on that he was afraid of what Juliana might want to say. "Yes, ma'am. Sorry about the delay."

He heard Emma laugh as she followed him inside the house. "Such a polite young man," she muttered under her breath.

He turned and gave her the evil eye, mouthing the words *shut up*.

He couldn't help it if he talked trash to demons but grew polite around his elders. He'd have thought Emma, with her Southern manners, would appreciate that he'd been raised right.

As the trio filed through the main doorway into the hallway, Cecilia kissed her daughter and then embraced River, her new son-in-law. Words were exchanged, but Ari didn't hear them; he was too focused on the skin-tingling energy that swept across his entire body the moment he entered the house.

There hadn't been this kind of palpable electricity when he'd last visited the house more than two months ago. He'd come here with Emma then, shocked to realize that she was Juliana's great-great-niece. Yeah, there'd been that cryptic communication from the spirit realm, the one where Cecilia brought out their family photo album. It contained a sepia print of him and Juliana standing together at a party in this very house, a photograph taken back in 1893. Juliana looking eternally beautiful in the high-necked Victorian dress with its intricate lace. He in that ridiculous suit she'd loved so much, the tailored one with the vest and shiny brass buttons he'd always thought might pop loose at any moment because of how big he was.

Now he kept that photo in his bedside table drawer, battling the urge to pull it out almost every night before sleep. And every morning when he woke. And anytime he went in the room to so much as change his socks. The damned picture burned a hole in his consciousness, creating a compulsion for Juliana that seemed to intensify with every passing day—and every new call from Cecilia.

"I'm supposed to give you this photograph," Cecilia had told him at the time. He'd been blindsided enough as it was, but then she'd lobbed an even more powerful mortar—she'd asked whether he'd loved Juliana. Talk about being set up from the other side of death's veil. He'd admitted the depth of his feelings for Juliana, confessing that he'd loved her more than any other woman he'd known throughout his immortal years. Including his onetime wife back in Sparta, although thankfully none of them had pressed *that* point.

He'd had a question of his own in return, had been burning to know—was it Juliana herself who'd supplied Cecilia with the question about his affection? Unfortunately, at that time Cecilia couldn't respond with certainty.

However, in the days and weeks since that visit, Juliana had asserted herself more specifically to Cecilia, wanting Ari to know that she was the one who'd reached out to him that day. Not only that, but she'd continued summoning him through Cecelia to this very house—this same parlor that they now gathered in—ever since. A parlor that remained eerily similar to how it had been when Juliana owned the brownstone.

Sure, the times had changed: No more Victorian furnishings filled the high-ceilinged room; no more Chopin wafted from the music room down the hall. Beneath the new furniture and well-kept rugs, however, his imagination easily supplied images from his past—the way the rooms had appeared back in 1893. The year of his torrid love affair with Juliana Tiades.

"Have a seat, why don't you, Aristos?" Cecilia urged in a warm tone, indicating the large sofa. Emma and River found spots on the smaller settee across from him.

Ari complied, sinking deep into the plush cushions, and wondered how fast he could beat a retreat if things grew too bizarre. Nervous and unsettled, he raked a hand through his nearly shoulder-length hair. He'd grown it longer in the past month, as he always did each year when fall approached; by midwinter it would fall loose across his upper back.

He fixed his gaze on the antique rug beneath his boots, feeling jumpy and eager to leave. That same burst of electric energy that he'd sensed the moment he entered the hallway kept buzzing all over his body, wrapping about him, working to burrow beneath his skin. Which wasn't just disconcerting, but annoying as hell, too, because the fiery sensations were affecting him intimately. Far *too* intimately. Arousal speared him low in the groin as if someone were actually touching him there, and he felt his cock stir and twitch in reaction.

Was it Juliana seducing him that way? Hell, was she with them even now, having a laugh by pleasuring him while none of the others could see?

With a rough, commanding growl, he shifted on the sofa, moving his legs so he could subtly adjust himself. *It's not like you ever touched me there while you were alive*, he thought, speaking to Juliana inside the privacy of his own mind. *We never wound up getting anywhere near that close.*

Although they'd planned to, he thought, shivering—and very aware of another tantalizing, slow stroke between his legs. Why would she be teasing him sexually now? Maybe she was out to prove a point: that she could still turn him on, make his whole body come alive with yearning for her.

Stop manhandling the goods and leave me alone, he warned mentally, not sure whether mandates worked with ghosts, or whether the spirits could read minds and thoughts at all.

"She's here," Emma said suddenly.

Yeah, no fucking kidding, he almost replied, shifting his long legs again and willing his full-gun salute to sag before anyone else noticed.

"I feel her spirit moving about the room." Emma looked up toward the ceiling, and then her gaze tracked back and forth, almost as if following a fluttering butterfly.

Like her mother, Emma was a highly gifted medium, one with the ability to hear the spirits, as well as sometimes see and smell demons or specters from the spiritual realm.

"I sense her, too," Cecilia agreed, her voice trilling with enthusiasm.

Ari glanced up and found both women staring at him, but he hadn't expected the slightly wide-eyed expression on Emma's face. She appeared panicked, threatened. He'd seen a similar look in her eyes during their recent showdown with Ares by the River Styx.

River picked up on her reaction, turning toward her in concern. "What is it, Em?" He slid an arm about her shoulders, drawing her against his side. "Are you all right?"

Emma swallowed visibly, nodding. "Juliana says . . . she's glad that Ari has us as his friends." She glanced at River. "That you, especially, are a true, kind friend, and he deserves that . . . needs that." Emma's voice had a distant, slow quality to it, as if she were on the telephone, repeating what the person on the other end of the receiver was saying. In a sense, that was exactly what she was doing, only in this case she was listening in on a party line from the other side.

Ari tensed against the sofa, torn between wanting to bolt and needing to move closer to Emma as she spoke.

Emma locked gazes with him, her pale eyes blazing with otherworldly energy. "Juliana says that she waited for you. That you never came back to her." She tilted her head, eyebrows lowering as if she was straining to hear the words. "Juliana says she kept waiting here, but you were gone." Emma's gaze focused on him, eyes brimming brightly.

Panicked at the sudden change in inflection and tone that Emma had assumed, Ari stood. "What's going on, Em?"

She pressed both hands against her temples as if in pain. "I believed you loved me, Aristos. That you understood how deeply I loved *you*. Surely you knew my heart; I was very clear about my feelings. Why did you wait such a very long time to return to me?"

Oh, shit. Juliana realized she was dead, didn't she?

He began to tremble like crazy, feeling that fiery energy blaze all over his body. His face flushed, his arousal magnifying sharply, and he started pacing in short strides in an effort to walk it off.

One more time she repeated the plaintive question. "Why did you not return to me, Aristos?"

He rounded on Emma, staring at the regal countenance of Juliana herself. Not literally, but the words and timbre of voice coming from Emma were no longer her own. And years of pent-up grief, and heartbreak, and longing, welled up inside of him; he couldn't hold back the torrent of feeling.

"Why didn't I come back for you?" he cried out, not trying to censor his reaction. "Because you were long gone! Damn, I was hardly gonna hang around after that."

Emma jerked back on the sofa as if he'd slapped her, blinking in stinging reaction. "This manner in which you speak is unfamiliar to me. I don't understand these coarse words. When is this time?"

Oh, double, triple shit. What am I supposed to say to that one?

"Uh, Emma?" Ari tried, never taking his gaze off of her. "You in there still? Emma, I think I need . . . a little help."

Cecilia moved to his side very quickly. "Aristos, listen very carefully to me," she said, leaning up to whisper in his ear. "You don't have to tell her how long she's been gone, or how she died. She does not seem to understand her fate."

"She knows who you and Emma are, and that I'm

here. . . . Why doesn't she realize when she . . . *you know*?"
he hissed.

"Juliana's perceptions are not grounded in time and
space. Some facts are clear, others very murky," Cecilia explained in a low voice. "Be cautious with her."

When Ari gave her a desperate glance, Cecilia added,
"If she's confused about her past, actual details might upset
her."

He nodded and was about to attempt a bland, open-
ended answer to Juliana's queries, when Emma cried out.
She doubled over, pressing both hands against her temples
with a moan. River knelt down in front of her immediately,
murmuring words that Ari couldn't make out. The buzzing
energy in his own brain had become much louder, deafen-
ing, until it blocked out all other sounds.

Emma looked in his direction, her dazed eyes filled with
anxiety. "Juliana's pushing at my mind. She wants to enter
me, speak through me . . . touch through me. Before, I was
only repeating her words, but now she's trying to force her
way into my mind and body."

"Just tell me what she says. I can't deal with anything
more, Emma."

He bolted as far away from Emma as he could without
leaving the room, backing toward the fireplace. The posture was his military default—the need to secure his rear,
positioning himself where he could see and thwart any impending attack. Current events definitely felt like one hell
of an assault.

Emma wrapped both arms about herself as if hoping to
bar the ghostly spirit from invading her body. "She's too
strong, Ari. She's insisting, and . . . she needs to see you. To
touch you. I can't keep her out."

A cold chill chased down his spine as if he'd just been
blasted by an arctic wind. His whole body trembled; he
shivered like Emma herself was doing. He backed up another step, the fireplace mantel jabbing into his back.

Emma's head lifted once again, her pale blue eyes—
ones that were identical to those Juliana had possessed—
locking on him with a vibrant, magnetic gaze. *Emma's not
the one looking at me anymore*, he realized.

Only one woman had ever studied him with that kind

of fire blazing in her rare gaze. Juliana Tiades. "I think I'm losing it," he muttered, rubbing his sweating forehead, but nobody seemed to hear.

With a regal sweep of her right hand, Juliana rose to her feet, standing tall and confidently proud. The refined posture was hauntingly familiar, just as Emma was hauntingly gone from her own body. Ari jerked backward, the mantel pushing hard against his spine. Nowhere to run, nowhere to hide, and Juliana continued walking toward him, that graceful glide the same as it had been more than one hundred years ago.

Their gazes locked across the small space that separated them, and it was as if words passed between them. Volumes of unspoken syllables that he'd never had the chance to murmur in Juliana's ear; hundreds of excuses that she hoped to offer him as to why she'd taken her own life the day after seeing what he truly was. The harsh truth of his immortal nature, black wings and all.

"Stay back." He pointed an accusatory finger. "I don't have anything to say to you. The only reason I'm here is so you'll leave me alone."

Juliana seemed unaware of his anger, his bitterness. She practically sailed toward him, a lovely smile filling her face, one that hinted at intelligence and amusement . . . and absolute joy at seeing him again after so many decades. That expression was one he'd seen many times before, one that couldn't have been imitated by an imposter. The reality of it broke down every argument he'd been trying to wield against her.

Juliana was smiling at him; Juliana was moving closer; Juliana had found him through an intricate maze of death and time.

"What are you doing here, Jules?" he whispered, throat so tight he could barely speak.

She seemed briefly taken aback, standing slightly taller. "This is my home. Need I explain my presence in it, Aristos?"

Ari's patience boiled over. "Woman, this isn't your home. It hasn't been for a long damned time." Then he remembered Cecilia's explanation that Juliana didn't fully understand her current predicament—that she knew some facts but was oblivious to others. "I mean, you don't belong here now," he added a tad more gently.

She frowned back at him, eyebrows drawing into a tight line. "Well, sir, one fact has not changed since I last spent time in your presence," she announced indignantly, a hand fluttering against her breastbone. "You remain sinfully handsome, dangerously so, and you still lack the fine manners of my own age." She glanced about her in sudden surprise. "What year is it incidentally?"

Chapter 4

Ari kept wide eyes on Juliana, torn between wanting to get as far away from her as possible—and rushing to hold her again. Whether it made him the worst kind of lovesick fool or not, the latter reaction was winning like a backroom card sharp.

She smiled up at him, a faint blush coloring her cheeks, a reaction he'd observed numerous times during their courtship. Juliana had been unexpectedly shy with him on occasion, despite her conversational charm and poise. She'd often flushed at what he considered to be innocent compliments, or the briefest touch of his fingertips against her hand. She might have maintained an elevated position in Savannah society, but that formality had dissolved in his arms. The first time he'd kissed her? Oh, she'd blazed like an inferno, her face turning as red as the hair atop her head. That uncensored reaction, so naive, had charmed him completely.

It might have even caused him to fall in love.

The familiar russet heat infused her face now; for a moment, the physical limitations of eternity and death melted away. Emma was no longer their bridge, and Juliana was truly alive again, near enough that he could hold her, stroke her hair, murmur in her ear, because she was real, vital. She stood in front of him, obviously expecting him to say *something*, when he could only gape like the ill-mannered idiot he'd always been in her presence.

Except she *wasn't* real; she wasn't even physical, he reminded himself. The only reason she was here like this was because she'd overrun Emma's resistance.

"Juliana," he ventured carefully. "You've taken over my friend's body. You can't do that. Not without asking permission." Was that even how a channeling relationship worked? Was it like borrowing someone's car or shoes—like when he pinched Nikos's Harley without *quite* getting the okay?

She peered up into his face. "But I want to be here, with you, Aristos."

His eyes watered suddenly, forcing him to look away. "You've got to leave."

I need you to leave here because I can't deal with these feelings again. He was just too frightened of the swirling emotions roaring through him. "You can't possess Emma's body. She's my friend. You can't use her, no matter what you want."

Cecilia barricaded that emotional escape route by piping in. "Juliana could never have gained control or access not if Emma weren't willing."

Blasted mediums, he thought. Blasted friends who forced you to face things you'd just as soon keep running from.

Juliana moved much closer in that elegant way of hers. The familiarity chilled him, angered him—and made him hope. That was the most maddening reaction of them all.

"Aristos?" she said. "I asked you what year it is."

He cut an inquiring look toward Cecilia, panicked. If he wasn't supposed to answer these questions because they might upset Juliana, then what was he supposed to do instead? Lie? Tell her it was still 1893?

"Go on." Cecilia nodded encouragingly, leaning forward from where she sat on the sofa. Beside her River watched, and his calm reaction lit a fuse inside Ari. How could the guy look so placid when his wife was sharing skin space with their very own version of Linda Blair? "Talk to her, Aristos," Cecilia pressed.

"About *what*?" he roared in frustration, tossing his hands into the air.

"What do you wish you'd said? If she'd stayed with you? Whatever's been in your heart and mind, this may be your only opportunity."

He'd never gotten to tell Juliana good-bye. Or how much he loved her. A love that came from this strange, mystic place in the core of his being, one that he'd never known existed before he met her. He'd never had the chance to acknowledge that feeling, the full scope of how it had consumed him from almost his first sighting of her.

In the end, he'd not gotten to say perhaps the most important words of all—that he was sorry for being a creature so dark, so disturbing, that it had driven her to take her own life rather than face what he was. But those confessions were smothered in layers upon layers of anger over one true fact: She'd given up on them, never let him explain what she'd seen so long ago.

He began hyperventilating slightly as Juliana moved right up into his space. She had him cornered against the fireplace. Her eyes shone brightly, filled with the same vivacious energy she'd always possessed.

She lifted a porcelain-delicate hand toward his face. "Aristos?" She sounded uncertain, vulnerable. Almost sad. "I was so certain you would want me, or at the very least show some joy at my return. Are you not happy to be here in my home?"

His skin prickled with electric tension. "It's not your home anymore, woman."

Those intense blue eyes grew sharp, almost irritated. "My father built it for me. You *know* that."

"A long time ago. Long, *long* time ago," he added, hoping she'd catch the hint.

Her eyebrows knit together in apparent confusion, and he swore that they changed color, becoming auburn briefly. He blinked, sure it was the spell of the moment, the spooky unnaturalness of it. He searched Emma's face, ignoring the fact that she'd temporarily vanished from her own body, seeking some physical sign of Juliana. It was like that moment when a lit candle suddenly catches a gust of wind. The flame gutters. *Light . . . dark. Dark . . . light.*

They shared the same blue eyes, color of the Aegean, with the same long, thick lashes.

But then Emma's dark brown hair seemed to flicker, too, morphing into auburn. Emma still stood before him physically, but in the spiritual realm, he could see the blurring of their identities.

"She's . . ." *Consuming Emma*, he almost warned River and Cecilia, but he doubted that was true.

Juliana anticipated his concern. "Emma is safe," she whispered reassuringly, reaching for his hand. "She's allowing us this moment." Juliana released a slow breath, shutting her eyes, and he was looking at Emma again. This was still her body, after all, and with her eyes closed, Juliana's powerful, insistent spirit seemed to vanish.

It hit him then that the reason he'd become certain he was truly interacting with Juliana was because of their eerily similar eyes.

Yes, she carried herself elegantly, more fluidly than Emma did, with her modern, athletic grace. Still, without Juliana staring out at him, he could almost imagine that he'd dreamed the whole thing up. Until the thick lashes fluttered open and that coy half smile he'd fallen in love with formed on her lips once again.

And damn the stubborn woman, she slid a warm palm against his chest, resting it over his heart. The warmth of that contact, the soft flesh pressing against his own skin, searing him through the thin cotton of his T-shirt, swamped him totally. Desire, yearning, need—it all washed over him like high tide.

"Don't." He covered her hand, honestly intending to move it. Only he didn't; he cradled it even closer.

"I was going to tell you what Emma just whispered to me."

"Whispered how?" He shoved her palm away from his chest. "So you're in total control of Emma's body now? She can't speak for herself?"

"Ari, we are as one right now, Emma and I. You already *know* that." She searched his face for permission to continue, and when he didn't interrupt, she went on. "She says, and I quote, 'I saw how you reacted to the photograph, what it meant to you.' " Juliana peered up at him, obviously expecting him to explain about the photo. He gave a nasty glare in return, forcing her to look away as she continued sharing Emma's message. "Emma says . . . 'Let me give this to you, Ari. You've given so much to River and to me. Now it's my turn.' "

The reality of the moment slapped him hard, ripping the pin off yet another emotional grenade. This was Juliana; he was being given some perverse second chance with her, if only for this moment. But did he want one? Could he trust her or the opportunity or even his own desires?

Panicked, he threw a glance at the parlor door. He could still get away, beat a fast, strategic retreat. But he was blocked by Juliana, who stood so close that he caught the scent of jasmine off her skin. Em never smelled like jasmine; she smelled like lemons and fresh air.

He began hyperventilating in earnest, rubbing an open palm over his heart. It seemed the little fucker might detonate at any moment. "Shit, I've got to get outta here," he blurted, feeling cornered, unable to breathe. He moved around her, toward the far side of the room, hating the caged feeling that came over him. "I really need to go," he repeated, plunging his fingers through his hair. He would've sworn the floor beneath him shifted. It had to be his new power; the energy must be reacting to the high emotion of the moment, gyrating inside of him.

Juliana was right behind him, her hand instantly placed against his lower back, reassuring and kind. "You are so frightened," she whispered, planting her other palm against his belly. Heat shot straight to his groin, a rolling wave of sensual reaction at being touched so low on his body. It had always been that way, damn the woman. She so much as blinked, and his cock went to full mast.

He wrenched out of her hold, backing toward the parlor door. "This whole setup is just a little too much."

She studied him in concern. "I don't recall you ever being afraid, and especially not of me. Is that why you never returned?"

He rounded on her. "You really want to know why I never came back, Jules? You so sure about that? Because some things," he said, looming over her, "are better left dead and buried. Know what I mean?"

Her expression grew pained, her eyes shining brightly. "I've waited, for such a very long time, but you never came. I need to know why."

"Because I wasn't the one who left!" He threw his hands into the air. "You did."

Juliana poked a long, delicate finger at the center of his chest. "Explain yourself, sir. With all that we once shared, why would you toy with me now?"

It took a serious pair of balls for the woman to get indignant with him, and it set off another physical chain reaction inside his body. That familiar shaking took hold, his hands trembling at his sides; a roaring noise reached a crescendo inside his brain. Vaguely, he was aware that several lights in the room snuffed out with a crackling staccato of electricity. His power was starting to ramp up way too fast, was overloading, but he could hardly harness it now.

He ignored all the warning signals, seizing her arm tight. "Juliana, you asked me what year it is. Why don't *you* answer that question?"

She shook her head slowly. "I find it difficult to say. Eighteen ninety-four, perhaps? Nincty-five?"

He made the sound of a game-show buzzer. "Wrong. Now for the daily double." He was being cruel but couldn't seem to stop himself. "Juliana, are you *alive*?"

"Aristos!" Cecilia leaped to her feet. "Watch yourself. Her soul's peace could be at stake."

Ari barely heard the woman's warning; he was too focused, too far gone. "Answer the question, Jules."

"I'm ... not sure. I persist. I wait for you. . . ." Tears filled her eyes. "I always wait."

"You are *dead*. You've been dead for more than a hundred years. That's your clue."

She worked a hand at her brow, appearing troubled, but said nothing.

"What—you forgot?" he said loudly. "Gee, here you stand in someone else's body, wearing clothes you've never seen before"—he reached in his back pocket and whipped out his cell phone, shoving it into her palm—"holding technology you never knew existed." He hit his forehead with the heel of his palm. "But, yeah, I guess it really is good ole 1893—huh, Jules?"

The phone fell from her grasp, clattering on the hardwood floor. She wavered on her feet, tears streaming down her cheeks. "Yes, yes, of course, you're right." She swiped at the dampness on her face, staring down at the carpet. "I know you're right. I shouldn't have become so carried away."

Ari nodded vigorously. "Damn straight, woman. Glad you're catching on to current events. Next thing we know, you'll be on Twitter."

"Twitter? Like a bird?" she asked in a soft voice. "Like a little bird?"

The question killed him, nailed him right between the eyes. So did the rush of her tears. "No, Jules," he murmured, ashamed. "Not like a bird."

He caught a glimpse of memory then, of her pure joy

when a robin had made a nest outside her front door. She'd shown him, childlike wonder on her face and in her eyes as she'd leaned over the railing to watch.

He reached for her cheek. "I'm sorry. God, I'm so sorry."

Those tears kept washing over her face like a slow, depressing rain.

And he felt just as depressed, like a real shit. What sort of man bullied a ghost to the point of tears?

But she had always, *always* given as good as she got. She slapped his hand away, her voice stronger, her posture resolute. "You must have always hated me," she declared harshly. "I must have completely misunderstood your feelings. You were certainly no *little* bird, were you?"

His wings had been mammoth, dark, threatening. What must she have thought the moment she'd first glimpsed them?

He took several steps back, smarting. "Oh, I think you understood my feelings very well—no wonder you ended things. And, hey, not like I can blame you." He shrugged sarcastically. "I've always been a jackass, in love or out. Just ask any of my brothers."

"I never met your family. You told me nothing of them. Yes, surely I was deceived as to the depth of your affections."

River moved into his peripheral vision. Only then did Ari realize the erratic way he'd begun walking the floor, in a kind of zigzag, jerking pattern. River, on the other hand, hadn't missed a thing. He stepped in front of Juliana, forming a barricade of sorts with his own broad-shouldered, sinewy form. Ari wondered whether his friend had begun to fear for Emma's safety. "I'm okay. She's okay," he muttered.

"It's all my fault," Juliana said, leaning around River. "I had thought you would be happy to see me once again after our long separation."

"Happy? Did death make you crazy, woman?" Ari jabbed a finger in the air. "I stayed behind. I had to mourn. Now I'm supposed to be thrilled that you've come popping back into my life like something from a bad episode of *I Dream of Jeannie*? Well, keep dreaming." Then he growled in frustration, turning toward Cecilia. "Now do you understand why I kept ignoring your calls? This little reunion was never gonna go down well."

"*I* don't understand," Juliana argued, still leaning around River. "I would never have left you."

River lodged a palm on his shoulder. "Take it down a few notches," he cautioned. "Come on, brother, ease off."

Ari nodded obligingly, dragging in deep breaths and releasing physical tension until River seemed satisfied and backed away. Then, turning to Juliana, Ari moved much closer. Until he could feel the heat radiating off her human body. See the lifting arch of her auburn eyebrows, the flecks of unexpected gold in her blue eyes, the occasional blond strands in her otherwise russet hair.

"Well, Miss Juliana Tiades," he said. "If you want to put a fine point on it, you left me by dying. You couldn't get away fast enough once you saw what I was. I revolted you," he told her in a seething voice.

How dare she fucking forget the way they'd ended? How dare she not understand his pain?

"No, sir. No, indeed. I always found you overwhelmingly handsome, more beautiful and fine than any other man in Savannah." She smiled despite their angry exchange, as if their past was suddenly immediate, right before her eyes, no passage of time separating events. "The way you dressed, you were so proud. All the ladies watched you, and you knew it. You drank it in. But you only had eyes for me," she added dreamily, looking up at him. "And I, sir, was most fully consumed by you."

"How can you not remember? Not our courting, not the parties. Not this room." He waved a hand all about them, and then he slammed a fist against his chest. "But *me*. Juliana, you saw me." In reaction, he felt an itchy, burning sensation crawl along his spine, the first prickle of feathers piercing his skin, and prayed he could stave off his transformation. "My . . . wings," he gasped. "I allowed you to see my wings."

"Because you were an angel," she murmured, eyes widening in memory; then that blush hit her cheeks again, a reaction he didn't bother trying to understand. "So beautiful. So exotic. Oh, I wanted to touch your wings; that was my very first thought. 'Will he let me touch them if I promise to be gentle?'"

"You're lying. The moment you saw my changed nature, you turned away."

She shook her head. "That's not true! Something happened." She pressed fingertips against her forehead. "Something . . . someone. I don't know. Why can't I recall what it was?"

"I bet you'll remember this." He yanked her flush against his chest, lowering his head; he wanted to be cruel, wanted to force her to recall how she'd hurt him.

He covered her mouth with his, thrusting his tongue past her lips aggressively. Punishing her for his own years of grief by taking something she wasn't ready or able to give. He plunged his tongue deep into the warmth of her mouth, wrapping his arms about her back.

He would teach her, show her all that he'd suffered. Only he'd forgotten the most crucial lesson of all: how just one kiss with Juliana Tiades could level him. The moment she wound her hands through his hair, opening her mouth completely to him, he knew that he was free-falling straight into hell.

His hair was as silky and thick to the touch as she remembered—only he wore it longer and there was more of it to run her hands through. And Juliana could feel him, truly feel him; the warmth of his flesh, the heat of his skin.

She was alive! She was actually in Aristos's arms, touching him again after so long.

She moved her fingertips across his jaw, stroking that familiar bristle of beard growth. His mouth tasted like fine red wine: She could get drunk on him, just as she always had. She moved in his embrace, slid closer, pressing her breasts against his muscular chest. Was it even broader, thicker than before? The strength of it caused a warm, tingling sensation between her legs, a feeling she'd not had in a long time. Dampness grew there the longer he kissed and held her.

His hands were in her hair, too, winding all through it. His tongue moved into her mouth, pushing against hers. Angry? No, needing. They had always needed each other; she had never stopped needing . . . this. She wrapped her arms about his neck, drawing him even closer.

Ari's tongue swirled deeper, teasing her, tempting her.

She kept her eyes closed, lost in him. In the sensation of being alive. She had always believed he would come back for her, and maybe it had taken a few more years than she would have liked, but he finally had.

She clung to Ari even harder, tears burning beneath her closed lids as he kissed her with increasing ardor, one hand sliding along her lower back, teasing. Seeking gifts she'd never given him in life.

But this body wasn't hers; the moment wasn't real. A sob built inside her chest.

She ran her hands across his shoulders, thrilling at the thick bands of muscle, powerful as always, as strong as oak. She'd always known this man would protect her from any destructive force, any soul that sought to harm her.

In a last desperate surge, she deepened the kiss. Ari's hands were all over her back, and he pinioned her even harder against his own body. Then, with a gasp, he tore his mouth away from hers, murmuring, "I always wanted to believe you were mine."

She felt his tears then, salty as she pressed her mouth closer, needing to kiss him again.

She didn't see the furious fist coming, not until it connected with Ariston's jaw, knocking him back against the wall with a loud, snapping sound.

"River!" She heard the word bubble past her own lips. "Stop it; that's Ari you're hitting." Juliana touched her mouth, only to remember that it wasn't hers at all, nor was the body. Nothing was real, not even those arousing, sensual kisses.

Nothing was alive, or true, except one thing. Aristos—and her love for him. That had never ended, she thought, drifting out of Emma's skin and up toward the ceiling.

Weightless, nothing. *She* was nothing . . . but dead.

Chapter 5

For some reason, Ari thought vaguely, he was floating. One minute he'd been kissing Juliana; the next, everything had gone black. Now he seemed to be as unmoored from physical reality as Juliana had been.

Where had the slamming pain in his head come from? He rubbed a hand across his aching jaw, unsure about the source of the godsforsaken pounding in his skull. Blinking slowly, he finally focused on a familiar, concerned face.

Emma. Emma was leaning over him, looking into his eyes and stroking his hair. "He's coming around," she announced, appearing relieved.

Someone had punched him, knocking his blasted head against the wall—hard. "Who clocked me?" Even talking was a problem, creating an answering swell of nausea in his belly.

River appeared in his line of vision, kneeling beside Emma. "You were kissing her," he explained guiltily. "What else was I supposed to do when my best pal had his tongue halfway down my wife's throat?"

Ari groaned, the room wavering like a gyroscope. "I wasn't kissing Emma. I was holding Juliana." He tried sitting up, but his pounding skull and the answering roll of nausea forced him back down.

Thank God someone had thought to wedge a pillow beneath his throbbing head.

He'd been kissing Juliana, and it had felt . . . disturbing. Arousing. As if time did not exist at all. Panicked, he glanced about the parlor for some sign of her, almost expecting to see her tall, willowy form looming over him.

"Where is she? Where did Juliana go?" He gestured toward his chest. "I had her in my arms, damn it."

Emma continued stroking his hair very gently. "She was never here, sweetie. Not physically."

Ari sank deeper into the pillow with another groan. "I know, I know, but I need to apologize. I was such a nasty bastard. She's got to be here still."

"I no longer sense her presence," Cecilia answered, staring down at him sympathetically. "With a kiss like that, I'm amazed that you stayed away from here five minutes, much less two months. *That* was your proof."

"And you wondered why I slugged you?" River muttered.

Ari looked up at Emma, who continued petting his hair in a soothing gesture. "Em, you knew the score, didn't you? That I wasn't really kissing *you*, right?"

Emma's blush told him everything; so did the way she glanced away, her hand pausing against his temple. "I . . . well, I was still in there," she said. "It was my body, you know?"

"I wouldn't put the moves on my best pal's wife." He scrubbed a trembling hand over his eyes. "Wouldn't do anything to hurt you, Em."

River folded his arms across his chest, unyielding. "From my position, can I just say that it appeared you wanted to swallow Emma whole?"

"That wasn't bloody well my fault, was it?" Ari shot back.

"O-kay," Emma said. "He's speaking with a British accent now. That's just . . . weird."

River turned to Emma. "We lived in the British Isles for years," he explained, then bent lower, peering down into Ari's face, concerned for real. "Seeing stars? Room spinning?"

Ari studied the rotating ceiling, swallowing down the bile that filled his throat. "Vertigo. Really bad case of vertigo."

River sighed, and this time he was the one who began stroking Ari's brow. "I'm sorry, buddy."

"For hitting me like I was a piñata?" Ari asked, vaguely aware that his words remained precise, accented as if he were a West Londoner.

"No, Aristos." River sighed again. "For giving you what appears to be a concussion."

Ari groaned as another wave of pain rolled from his

skull to his stomach. "So fix it. Do your thing." River had healed them all of stab wounds, sword slices, and even ingrown toenails. A concussion was small-time stuff for the man.

River leaned back on his heels, shaking his head. "Definitely a concussion. You've forgotten that I can't heal you anymore. I gave my power to you, remember?"

Ari closed his eyes. "My best friend gave me a concussion, and I have no idea how to heal myself. Bloody brilliant."

Emma resumed stroking his hair, her gentle touch at least somewhat comforting. "Ari, do me a favor? Please use your normal *Greek* accent. The whole Brit thing is starting to wig me out. I need to know that you're all right."

"This from a medium who just channeled a dead woman? You're hardly a reliable judge of the bizarre."

"Ari, please," Emma tried again. "Let us know that you don't have some kind of serious head trauma. Okay? Talk like you."

Ari cleared his throat and tried to think like a Greek man. All that came out of his mouth, however, was a string of atrocious Greek curses, followed by the keen desire to punch his best friend in the nose. Retaliation, Spartan style.

River placed a comforting hand on his chest, laughing. "Thanks, Petrakos," he said. "There are times I'd like to do the same to you myself."

To that smart reply, Ari only cursed more rudely, calling River every profane name in his ancient Greek dictionary. Ari noticed something then, a nifty little fact that hit his awareness on a twenty-second delay. Emma's eyes had grown surprisingly wide, as if she actually understood his foul accusations.

Ari sat up, swatting at the stars that swam in front of his eyes. "What?"

"I guess you've forgotten that River's been teaching me Greek."

River grinned. "It's fun to coach her on the nasty bits."

"Fucking awesome," Ari said, sliding back down onto the pillow.

"Maybe Sophie can help him," River volunteered.

"Yeah, she fixed Sable," he groaned. "She got rid of those spikes . . . the ones Ares put on his body."

"Not all of them," Emma corrected. "And she hasn't figured out how to use the ability again."

"Get . . . me . . . Sophie," Ari ground out. "And some ibuprofen. Stat."

Juliana blew down the street, struggling to gain some kind of physical anchor. One moment, she'd been rooted inside of Emma; the next, that fist had knocked into Aristos—and she'd been released, unable to remain inside the woman. She'd been discharged against the walls of her own brownstone like inhuman scattershot.

She'd hurled through the air and dimensions, nearly landing on the sidewalk outside, but then the wind had gusted, catching her in its tumbleweed hold. Until the low branch of a live oak had snagged her ghostly hair, capturing her like a wayward butterfly. Hers was an in-between state, not quite physical, not fully spiritual—enough that a low-borne tree could trap her, even though she wasn't visible to passing mortals.

She clung to that branch, which was like a protector, resisting the wind's force lest she end up blocks away from home. She had no idea how long she'd been tangled up in the limb's fragile grasp, and kept praying that she hadn't lost her own hold. The one she had over Aristos, her true love.

And still that wind blew, thrashing her thin essence, beating her against the trunk of the old live oak.

She hated stormy nights; they brought back painful emotions. A night like this one had spelled the end of her relationship with Aristos, but she could never seem to recreate the details, only the physical sensation of the wind. And that heavy, crashing water, waves upon waves of it.

Ari obviously knew she was dead—he'd proclaimed as much. Why was it that she so often forgot the fact? Perhaps because she did not want to accept that fate, but even so, her mind and memories fluctuated. Sometimes, as she stared about Savannah, she *knew* this was not her own time. The physical proof assaulted her undeniably: the very fast carriages, lit by the odd lanterns at night. The hard, darkly paved streets. The women hurrying past without proper escorts, never seeing her and dressed as Emma had been tonight, in men's attire.

Other times, she saw nothing, lost only in a circular maze of memory, reliving her final moments with Aristos. How could he believe that she would ever, in any lifetime or place, have left him willingly?

On any other night, she'd have simply let nature have its forceful way, would have landed wherever fate dictated and then worked her way back to West Jones Street. But not this time, because then she might miss seeing Aristos when he left the brownstone. He'd be walking down those steps soon, just as he had the night they'd first met.

But this next sighting of him might be her final one, for certainly their last encounter had not gone as she'd expected. He had been so furious with her, a reaction she never could have anticipated.

I am naught but a dead woman, she reminded herself. *That is all he thinks of me. He believes that I abandoned him, found him horrifying.*

Oh, but his wings had been *mesmerizing*. A welcome explanation after a courtship where she'd known he wasn't human but never learned enough about what he *truly* was. Until he'd landed on her balcony the night when they had planned to give themselves to each other. She'd known nothing yet understood everything about him in a moment.

He was far more glorious than she'd even imagined. With that, another voice ripped into her memories, one that didn't belong to Aristos, but she could not hear it clearly enough to identify the speaker. Closing her eyes, she forced herself to recall what had happened next. She could see Aristos, there on her balcony, waiting, and then . . . Someone had blocked her from him; someone had pulled her back as she'd gone to open the French doors.

Ari! Ari, help me.

She'd cried out to him, but he'd already been turning away, believing her terrified of *him*. Yes, that was it! But who had been in her room that night, and what had that person done or said to keep her from Ari, filling her with such terror that he would forever believe she'd rejected him?

Oh, why could she not remember? She worked at the memories, trying to unravel them as she twined her insubstantial fingers through the branches. But no matter how hard she puzzled over them, the memories remained as vague as a river mist.

Chapter 6

Eros dipped his red-feathered quill into the inkpot; smiling in anticipation, he began scrawling conjured words of romance upon the parchment. His pen moved quickly, yet even so, he could not keep pace with the agile movements of his sensual imagination.

Dominick slid a palm against Adrianne's ripe, swelling flesh, his fingertips alive with need, he wrote with a flourish. *Moving his mouth lower, dangerously so, Dominick brushed a kiss upon his beloved's mound, urging her aggressively, tantalizingly, hungrily . . .*

He hesitated, frustrated by his inability to convey the eager passion he felt thrumming in his god's veins. *Too many adverbs; not precise enough.*

He tossed down the quill in disgust; he, lord of all love, reduced to this! Penning a dull, lifeless imitation of what he could easily create with one strategic aim of his bow, all because of a dare his father had issued. *No, not a dare,* he thought, *a test of strength.* His father had wagered that Eros could not go a month, much less six, without creating passion between mortals.

Dominick and Adrianne weren't even well written, much less a reflection of his true skill. He'd only begun scribing their imaginary courtship as an outlet of sorts, a salve to the heat of his unanswered addiction. As proof to Ares that he lived off more than love and lust and tupping.

His father had sworn such discipline impossible. "You are obsessed," he'd scoffed. "You have no other outlet for slaking your need than to meddle in the affairs of mortal hearts."

Ares despised what he, his own son, treasured. Love, in all its giddy, charming sensation. Although Eros did not limit his craft to sensual love. He dispensed doses of brotherly affection; enjoyed occasionally besotting wayward fathers with their deserving offspring; adored creating bonds between fellow soldiers. One particular favorite was sorority rush season, weaving those bonds of deep sisterhood between young women, the kind that lasted lifetimes.

Yet courtly love, in all its forms and enthrallments, remained Eros's true intoxication.

His father could never appreciate such rarefied gifts.

Eros had been born of the war god's loins, his mere existence a cruel twist of Olympian fate. A fate he could never change because his bow had no impact upon any deity. Otherwise, he would have sighted his most powerful arrow upon his own father, seizing his greedy affection. Alas, his mighty aim was impotent within his own family.

So here he was, climbing the walls of his palace, waiting for some sign of his father's approval. It was enough to bring on madness, Eros thought, despising the quiet that filled his normally lively home. A dulling dust had crept over the place during these past months. Crimson arrows and bows hung useless in his corridor, quivering every time he came near, practically begging to be put back into service. Those weapons of love missed working their magic almost as much as he did. He'd tried explaining the details of his recent pact to them, but his living arsenal never had been much on patience.

But they were very high on loyalty, a bond that went both ways. Eros had found them, a battalion of castoff soldiers cursed by his own father's hand, transformed to standing stones, forever overlooking the Straits of Salamis. Ares had left these mighty men of valor, these Greek fighting warriors, lifelessly observing the battleground, unable to defend their beloved homeland.

Eros had taken pity upon the soldiers. Knowing firsthand how cruel his father could be, he'd transformed and conscripted them into his arsenal. They held rank and name, as they had in life, and he hoped that perhaps one day Ares might be persuaded to return them to their human state—a power he himself did not possess. At the moment, his arsenal did not understand the wager he'd made with his father. He pitied them, hanging uselessly in the hall of weapons; they surely felt as if they'd been turned to stone again.

Eros understood the sentiment, that deathly pall of uselessness.

That was where Dominick and Adrianne had entered into his affairs. Although imaginary, they at least provided some outlet for his talents. He'd hoped that, like the dossiers he had always maintained on his pairings, imagining their amorous intersection would give him purpose. He stared at their insipid tale upon the scroll, and despite himself, a thrill charged through his veins. Creation. Love. Seduction. Ah, it was only on the page, but it mimicked the real-life wicked rush.

He blew on his latest passage, urging the ink to dry. He wondered when his hard-won temperance would earn his father's favor.

"Still trying your hand at verse?"

Eros started, turning over the inkpot, his hands and arms becoming drenched in crimson color. "Father. You were not expected." He struggled to sound composed, even as he dripped ink ingloriously.

Ares stared down his nose. "We wouldn't want you to appear drenched in blood. Not like a real warrior; then again, perhaps you've put those arrows of yours to legitimate use at last."

Eros blotted at the ink, but it only smeared into a greater mess.

His father sniffed. "Go clean yourself, boy."

Eros's face flamed hot. Neither of them ever aged, and although he was this god's son, he hadn't been a "boy" in many millennia. Still, he found himself muttering, "Yes, my lord," as he hurried toward the bathing rooms for a towel.

When he returned, Ares was reading from his scroll, sneering at Adrianne and Dominick's tale of mortal love. "What a waste," his father declared, dropping the parchment back onto the bed as if it were a lethal snake.

Eros quickly rolled it up, trying to blot away the remnants of spilled ink. "You know my gift must find an outlet, father," he explained, hating how nervous and jittery he sounded. "It has been months since I worked my own arrows to any romantic effect."

"Months, and yet the mortal populace moons and sexes onward, no end to their need for love." Ares wandered toward a large Delacroix canvas that hung over the bed, one with surging bodies twined in an orgasmic, voluptuous display. "If it were me, I'd begin questioning my relevance, seeing as how humans carry on quite well without you, Eros."

"It is their way. I did not sire the need in them. That came from the Highest."

"Don't mention *Him*."

"Merely stating, father, that you cannot blame me for the existence of the emotion."

"But for its many permutations and lasting effect . . . clearly you have no significant relevance. Even you must realize that after so many months of abstinence."

For some reason, Eros thought of the arrows and bows hanging in his hall of weapons, how the god before him had taken that battalion of brave men and robbed them of everything, made them useless.

And had always wished to do the same to him.

"So what inspires your visit, Ares?" He kept his voice chilly, refrained from calling the god by either a worshipful title—or a familial one.

Surprisingly, the deity smiled. "Well, well. A spirit of rebellion has been birthed in my son after all this time? Perhaps self-denial has toughened you as I'd hoped."

Eros held his tongue, waiting. There would be more. There was always more whenever his vain father spoke, and often much was revealed because of Ares' insane self-adoration.

Glancing up at the painting again, Ares narrowed his eyes. "One must admire the intense passions of these humans, son. And for that, I do give you long overdue credit. Imagery such as this, well, it almost reminds me of battle . . . the thronging bodies, the need for domination." He pivoted, facing Eros again. "I believe I've been overlooking the possibility for a critical alliance."

Eros's heart thundered at the words. Alliance? Did his father intend to extend some sort of partnership or approval? He'd waited, for so many millennia, waited and hoped that one day some other mystery of love would bring his father here, compel him to love his own son as he should.

He swallowed. "What . . . partnership do you have in mind?"

"Ah, not a partnership, per se. A joining of our skills for battle. Intrigued?" Ares lifted a golden eyebrow, smiling openly.

"Absolutely, father." He nodded vigorously, not listening to the doubts that tried to surface in his mind. The urgent reminders that Ares was a bloodthirsty, craven god and not to be trusted. "I am eager."

Ares extended a hand, ready to shake on the arrangement. "I suppose even fighting with me is better than sitting uselessly in the palace all day."

His father's hand was there for the taking; a bargain; an alliance. For one last moment, Eros hesitated. "This is love spelling you want from me, correct? I do not have the skills of warfare and battle that you trade in."

His father's smile grew blindingly bright. "That is precisely what I want from you, Eros. Your divine skill with love's bow and arrow. Strategic, powerful, relentless. You will be a welcome addition to my current fight."

The desert was balmy at night. Eros remembered that much about Iraq during late October, although he'd not visited the bleak, sand-burned land in almost a year. There hadn't been much love to make or conjure in this forsaken place, not for a while.

He reminded himself of the reason that he'd traveled here tonight. After so many, many millennia, his father needed him, wanted his help. That assignment had led him here, the first phase of his quest, part of a much larger and overarching assignment. Once he found his quarry, he would take her to Savannah. The rest of the pieces would fall into place then.

Layla. Layla Djiannis. She was the one he sought here in the heavy blanket of darkness. When he'd stared into the cascading pool, the heady waters that often revealed intimate love and relationship knowledge, hers had been the first face that he'd seen; he'd also quickly grasped the multitiered mayhem she could cause in the arena of love. At least for his father's targeted group. Layla, it appeared, could solve quite a few problems on Eros's behalf, not least, helping him earn his father's long-denied approval . . . and all in the name of love.

*   *   *

Sable kept to the shadows along West Jones Street. Clomping his centaur's hooves on the uneven cobblestones angrily, he castigated himself. As he always did upon returning to this piece of human land, night after cursed night.

Why, by the name of every unholy thing, was he—a Djinn demon—lurking around a mortal's home? And not even because he hoped to consume this particular human female, as he should have done months ago, but out of some paltry need to—what? Protect the annoying, compassionate little bitch?

Disgusted by his ongoing obsession with Sophie Lowery, he galloped down to Whitaker Street, vowing never to return in search of her again. As he reached the intersection, however, he found himself unable to continue, and instead cut a turn, heading back to the brownstone where she lived. He would wait, hidden as always, until he saw her arrive, reassured of her safe return.

Just once more, he promised himself, hissing in revulsion at his inability to stay away. He blamed the mortal for the alteration in his otherwise robust and hateful demonic nature. If she'd not healed him, not taken those hands of hers and ... He flinched, closing his eyes and battling away the memory of her soft fingertips moving across his chest.

A thin, feminine cry pierced his consciousness, and he glanced down the street. *She* was back: that damned apparition he'd been seeing ever since he started lurking around Sophie's house two months ago. The same one who always nodded politely every time they met, as if he wasn't half-covered in horned protrusions, and his body, once winged and beautiful, now cursed into the gruesome form of a centaur.

Yet no matter how rude or insultingly he treated the spirit, she never ceased to be horribly gracious. He shivered, keeping his distance now, but oddly enough, she seemed unmoving tonight. Normally she floated along the street, head held high. Didn't she realize that she was dead? He'd even tried, once, to point out that pitiful fact. All in the name of helpful cruelty, of course, but she'd maintained her poise, smiling up at him.

Tonight she seemed to have become tangled in the branches of an oak. For a moment, he stepped forward to help her, but then started to laugh. He owed kindness to no human, dead or alive. *But she's one of them*, an inner voice murmured. *She's like Sophie.* With the same annoying, beautiful, cursed blue eyes.

He slid back into the shadows, concealing himself. Why by Ahriman or Zeus or any other deity did his path keep colliding with Daughters of Delphi? *Well, you fool, perhaps because that same blood—piddling trickle that it is—flows in your own half-demon veins.*

Perhaps *that* was why he'd been susceptible to Sophie, allowing the skinny imp of a mortal to approach him right after that recent battle when he, along with the Spartans, had taken up arms against Ares. Perhaps that was why he'd actually allowed that particular Daughter to touch him. To heal him. To take on some of his pain.

He frowned at the memory, torn between fury and revulsion, but much as he hated the fact, he did rather owe Sophie. Because of her, he bore only half as many of the hideous horns across his body as he'd had before she'd laid her warm hands upon his body. Not that he'd asked for help, not that any Djinn worthy of the name ever would.

He sighed. And so he found himself here once again. Night after night, out of some—he spat over his shoulder in disgust at the thought—obligation. Had he lost his demonic mind? He should trot on down the cobblestone street and find a soul to suck dry. Locate some depressed art student to siphon, mainlining their suicidal tendencies like the pleasing, heady drug such emotion truly was. His mouth curved upward in a smile at the thought, but another urge snuffed it out.

Shame. When had he ever felt shame for his wicked desires?

Never. Until Sophie had touched him.

He blamed her. All her fault, all her problem, and now his burden. As if in reaction to the litany, that smooth skin along his chest grew warm, the place that had been littered with aching horns until she'd healed him. Every time he thought to turn back to his basest desires, his simplest needs, his chest grew hot—as if she were touching him all over again.

Damn it, Sophie, he thought, glancing up and down the street. It was late and getting later. Didn't she know that creatures like him existed? That they lived to inspire rape and murder and every depravity that existed in between?

She should be back by now. What of those blasted cats she fostered, each with its own special name that she'd given it? Someone should be feeding the pests. Her potted daisies—had she even thought to water them today? He hated the small kick of concern that flooded into his sinister heart.

"Sophie," he said on a growl. "You should be more careful. If something happened to you . . ."

He could not, would not, let himself finish the sentence. Instead, he forced his way farther into the shadows, ensuring that if she should come whistling around the corner, swinging her thin arms, she'd not discover him. Even with her gifts, he still knew how to hide in the mid-dimensions, and so he moved into darkness.

Suddenly, the sound of feminine voices echoed down the quiet street. Remaining concealed, he peered outward, wondering whether Sophie approached, perhaps with a friend.

But it wasn't Sophie's voice, he realized, and the second female was *not* a friend. Not of the Daughters themselves, and certainly not of the polite spirit who currently stood engaged in eager conversation with her. Far *too* eager, he thought with a twisted smile, considering the danger that little ghost now entertained.

Layla Djiannis. In the Americas. What an interesting twist of fate, and a useful bit of knowledge. What mischief did his dark cousin wish to make here in Savannah? And with his friendly little ghost, no less?

Yes, most intriguing indeed, he decided, easing farther into the shadowy spaces.

Chapter 7

A ri awoke feeling like a jackhammer was going to town inside his skull—and still under the spell of that erotic, disturbing dream. The one where he'd been lying in bed, Juliana slowly massaging his entire body, unfastening his pants, untying his freaking Nikes. And that last bit, with the cross-trainers? It had actually been sexy as hell.

Because that was how Juliana had always affected him, in any century.

By so much as glancing his way, she'd turned him as stupid as one of the turkeys that roamed their new property, following him around like he'd adopted the damned things.

And if she flirted or, gods help him, allowed her hand to graze any portion of his *clothed* anatomy? He'd thrown wood like a Major League Baseball player up at bat.

Rubbing the sleep from his eyes, he groaned, "Juliana, why are you so determined to mess with my head?"

"I'm sorry, Aristos, but I don't know exactly what you mean."

She was right here, in his room, gazing down at him on the bed.

"Holy shit, Jules!" he shouted, scooting as far back against the headboard as he could. This wasn't Emma channeling his onetime love; this wasn't some spirit whispering in his ear. No, this *was* Juliana, in her physical body, dressed in that pale blue, lace-collared gown that he'd always particularly loved.

He pointed numbly. "That . . . that dress. You're wearing our dress."

She smiled, brushing her fingertips over the bodice. "I remembered." The words were sensual, flirtatious.

Her hair was swept high off her neck, delicately curling

tendrils falling free across both cheeks, and her face was flushed. *Alive. Not dead.* Here, now, having the gall to blush. Her clear blue eyes were wide as if amazed herself at being alive again.

"I don't know how you got here . . . ," he began, but she didn't seem to hear. Instead, she sank onto the edge of his bed, settling so close that the physical weight of her graceful body pressed against his thigh.

She was no ghost; she was a woman. His woman, or at least she had been, and she'd come back. Somehow, someway, the infernal female had found a loophole in eternity, chasing him all the way to the compound—a zone that Leonidas kept warded so that no supernatural creature ever got behind the wire without permission. Which only made her sudden presence that much more impossible to understand.

"So how are you here? What did you do? What devil did you bargain with?" he blustered.

Ignoring his questions, she touched her face with child like wonder and then stared down at her palms in surprise. "I really am here, aren't I?" Leaning forward, she lifted those same hands to his own face, slowly stroking his scratchy beard growth, drawing one fingertip down the length of his nose, outlining the faint scar beside his right ear. "You feel exactly the same," she declared, tears filling her eyes. "I never thought I'd touch you again, not with my own hands."

Without analyzing, without trying to make sense of the unnatural moment, he drew her into his arms, clinging to her as if to life itself. "Jules," he murmured against the top of her head, drawing in her scent. He bunched the back of her dress within his hands, desperate to feel and prove that she wasn't an illusion. "Jules. Sweetheart. My love. How is this possible?"

Wait. How was *this possible?*

With a rude shove, he pushed her out of his grasp, nearly knocking her off the edge of the bed. "You're not right. This . . . this reunion . . . isn't right." He shook an angry finger at her. "People die, and they're dead! *You* are dead."

After River and Emma had lugged him home with that concussion, they'd stuck him in here, planting a remote in his hand and putting on the DVD of *Gladiator.* Then they'd told him not to fall asleep, not until Sophie could come heal him. But what had he obviously done? Oh, just the one thing you should never do when you have a concussion. Zonked out. No wonder he was hallucinating.

He clutched his head. "*Skata*, I've got to be dreaming or I'm truly screwed in the skull. You can't be here, not like this."

She reached out a very physical, very warm hand and stroked his arm. "You held me at my house tonight, so you know that I'm real."

"That was Emma!" he thundered. "And it was *her* body you hijacked so we could do the tongue dance. You weren't ever there, not really."

Juliana cocked her head, studying him. "I don't understand these words. Hijacking. Tongue dance," she repeated uncertainly. "Is that the latest trend from New York City?"

"Kissing!" he shouted, climbing down the length of the bed and out of her grasp. "We were kissing!"

Her expression brightened. "Oh, that. The French style of affection. I never thought of it precisely as a dance before." She seemed amused, watching him scramble away from her. "You shouldn't move, Aristos. Not with a head injury."

"And how do you even know about that?" He eyed her warily.

"Because our tongues were . . . dancing . . . when your friend—River . . . is that his name? When he punched you into the wall." She frowned. "That, unfortunately, ended our 'dance.' Until now, when I've found a way back to you. One that will last this time. And so shall the . . . tongue dancing."

All he wanted was to put as much distance between them as he could manage without screaming and fleeing the room like a serious pansy. "Let me teach you another phrase, one I learned from a friend of mine. That dog," he said ferociously, "ain't gonna hunt."

She rose from the bed, following him toward the bedroom door, where he'd flattened himself. With the crook of her finger, she beckoned him. "Ari, come back. I need you. . . ."

Never taking his eyes off of her, he bellowed River's name, then Emma's, and when he didn't get an answer, he tossed in Ajax's. Dead silence answered him. Great, he was supposed to be laid up in bed, recovering from his own best bud's sucker punch, and they were off doing gods knew what. Anything other than, it seemed, watching his back.

Maybe it was realizing that his nearest and dearest had left him unprotected right when he needed it. Or maybe it was that small voice inside his mind—the one whispering that Juliana was alive, here, back in his life. Really, it might've been the wicked hard-on he'd developed just from staring at the woman, his body reacting as if they'd never spent time apart. As if time didn't exist at all.

Whatever the cause—the roiling heat in his body, the ache in his groin—all of it coalesced in a heartbeat. He stormed toward Juliana, furious. "What happened to ending it all?" he shouted. "What happened to leaving me?" Then, lowering his voice into a seething, livid tone, he asked, "What happened to you being *dead*?"

He was furious, off the chain without a moment's warning. His entire body shook just like the windowpanes currently did from the gale-force winds raging outside. She opened her mouth to reply, but he cut her off, raising his voice over the riotous buzzing noise inside his head.

"No, I don't believe Juliana would've changed her mind about that," he said coldly. "She made a final decision, and it didn't include spending another moment near me. I was so repulsive, she had to leap into the Savannah River during one of the worst recorded hurricanes in history."

He pointed toward his large bedroom windows, the ones that overlooked the farm's sweeping pasture. They groaned as if to underscore his fury. "Speaking of which, maybe you could try for a repeat performance. We're in for another whopper of a storm this week."

She shivered visibly, casting an anxious glance toward the panes, but he seized both of her thin, strong arms. "You see, we were in love. But my love . . . was a poison for her. I was a poison that drove her to suicide."

Tears brimmed in her eyes as she let him throttle her like some rag doll. "Why won't you fight?" he growled bitterly. "Slap me. Denounce me. Fight back!"

She began to cry, her delicate shoulders shaking. "I'm sorry. I'm so sorry that . . . you don't understand. I have to explain, have to understand what happened myself. No matter how hard I try, I can't remember. But there is one fact, Aristos. One unwavering truth—I loved you. I still do. . . . I have always loved you."

He yanked her flush against his body, pinning his left forearm across her back, preventing her potential escape. "What are you, woman? Some kind of demon?" he demanded hotly. "A ghost?" He cupped her jaw roughly, forcing her to look up into his eyes. "You can't possibly be the same Juliana I once knew. So you tell me right now. What are you, and who sent you here?"

He knew he was being brutal, handling her as if she were a soldier, not the sophisticated, beautiful woman she'd made herself appear to be. Then again, whatever she actually was, it sure as *hell* wasn't delicate. It probably possessed horns and fangs and scales when in its true form; he'd lay honest money on that. He tightened his hold on her jaw, shoving her back against the wall, pinning her there by the collarbone.

"Aristos," she whimpered, squirming beneath his harsh grip. "You're hurting me. Please. Please, just let me explain."

He sniffed at the air, expecting the scent of sulfur or decay, but swore he caught only the fragrance of jasmine. "Stop with the crap," he insisted, sliding his hand lower beneath her chin, keeping her face tilted upward. "Stop with the lies, creature. Reveal your true self. *Now*."

She blinked up at him, and his heart clenched with a painful sensation. Those haunting, alluring eyes. Oh, by the very Highest God, he'd never forgotten them. Whatever this entity was, it was doing a marvelous job of mimicking his Juliana. His very dead, forever-lost-to-him, ghostly Juliana.

He gave his head a shake, dropping his hand from her chin. "Do you have any idea what I'm capable of? What me and my kind do to the likes of something like you? I'll give you kudos. . . . You've sure got a whopping pair on you." He forced a laugh. "I'm betting you're not even female, whatever the hell you are."

"I never knew what *you* really were, Aristos. That night when you came to me, and I saw your wings—"

"Shut up!" he barked, clasping at his pounding head. No way would he let this thing taunt him with his own memories of that horrible night. The image before him now was false—cruel, wrong in every way.

But her ethereal, lovely blue eyes fixed on him again, widening slightly. "Why can't you believe that it is me?" She leaned closer, sounding frustrated. "I promised to find a way back to you. I promised, Aristos. Do you not believe Cecilia, who proclaims me to be true? As does your friend Emma."

"They're deceived," he hissed. "They don't know demons like I do. They don't know Juliana Tiades like I do." A stabbing pain of anguish hit him hard, spearing him through the chest. He realized then that his fury at the entity wasn't even about what it was—he encountered demons and destroyed them on a near-regular basis. No, it was about everything this illusionary being *wasn't*. "You're not her. I'd know if you were. You'd . . . feel the same."

"Yes, I have changed. But you've changed, too. A hundred years is a long time."

Her words caught his attention. "What do you mean exactly, that you've changed?"

She gave a diffident shrug. "Certain arrangements were involved in regaining a physical form. Nothing significant."

"Oh, just hurdling across this little thing called eternity. One minor detail of getting your body back, and poof, you're here with me again."

She frowned. "A guide helped me find my way here, to you—to this very room. A kind female spirit who saw how deeply I love you, still, after all these years."

He laughed darkly, shaking his head. "I know way too much about the kinds of deals you gotta make in order to come back from the dead, and it's never that easy."

"Is that why you appeared that night . . . winged?" She cocked her head, studying him with wide eyes. "Because you really are an angel?"

"Sweetheart, I'm definitely no angel," he muttered. "In fact, I might be the very devil himself."

"There is no darkness in you. I was always sure of that, even though I never knew what you were." Juliana reached a hand to his chest, splaying her palm over Ari's heart. The fucker was slamming like a Gatling gun, a tempo that only increased with every moment beneath her gentle touch.

"Yeah?" He snorted. "Well, I don't know what kind of

bat-shit crazy thing you are, either, woman! But I sure as bloody hell know you're not my Jules."

She smiled, a lazy, slow reaction that had him growing rock hard inside his pants all over again. And that look, that smile, *was* pure Jules. It was her flirtatious look, her pleased one. She'd always glanced at him just that way whenever he made her feel beautiful. He'd recognize that look in any city, on any continent. And definitely in any age.

He tensed, struggling to process his conflicted emotions, but took just one slight step closer.

She rubbed her neck. "I was always yours. There was nothing, absolutely nothing that I wouldn't have done to find my way back to you." She patted her chest imploringly as if she were offering up her soul as collateral. "I am truly alive again now, eager for your love." She looked down right then, her gaze lingering on his tight groin. "Eager for all of you, Aristos. At last."

Ari's entire body began a free fall right then, a headlong dive into an intoxicating mix of power and arousal. His spine began to burn and prickle, and he knew it was only a few heartbeats before his wings emerged of their own volition. He had no control over the rapid, unnerving transformation that came over him in that moment, just from being near this female.

He blinked, but his eyes were on fire, blazing with blinding white light that reached toward her like moonbeams. "Only a demon could call forth my power this rapidly," he declared, his voice harsh and tight. "Only the darkness would summon my Change."

The prickling of his feathers pierced the skin along his spine, and he barked out a cry, feeling trapped by his clothing, knowing it would be shredded if he couldn't halt the rapid alteration in his shape-shifter's body.

Desperate, his back and shoulder muscles aching from the transition, he yanked at the edge of his shirt, dragging it over his head until he stood before her, bare chested. He pressed a hand behind his back, wincing, and practically held his breath in expectation. Juliana stared at him, eyes wide in . . . wonder. It wasn't an expression of horror or disgust on her face; she appeared amazed.

"Is this how your wings emerge?" she whispered hoarsely. "Do they . . . sprout? Along your back?"

He swallowed hard, nodding, feeling the heavy, dragging sensation of wings form along his spine.

"Oh, I so want to see them! Up close this time," she said, beaming at him.

As opposed to *last* time? When Juliana had gaped in horror at the truth of what he was, a man who bore dread wings upon his back? An eternal warrior capable of flight and transformation, part human, part hawk when changed?

No, he thought, battling the urges inside of him, trying to retract the emerging wings. *No, you must resist her dark effect! This isn't Juliana. She never wanted this part of you— she reviled it.*

He palmed himself, giving his length a rough, cruel yank through his jeans. "I'm halfway to orgasm with a demon," he hissed. "But I won't let you finish this job, creature."

Reaching to the floor, he snatched up his discarded T-shirt and yanked it over his head, retracting his wings as he did so. "Gonna get this dog-and-pony show back under control," he said, grabbing her by the upper arm.

"What are you doing?" she demanded as he yanked her toward the closed door of his bedroom. "Are you taking me somewhere?"

She dug her heels into the carpeted floor. "A gentleman would declare his intentions, sir."

He opened the door to the hallway, hauling her along with him. "*Madam,*" he warned her, "I never have been and never will be a gentleman."

Chapter 8

"Go on and tell me," Ari announced, still clutching "Juliana" by the arm, twisting his hold violently. "Just say it." He glanced between Nikos and his own brother Ajax, bobbing his head. Waiting for the confirmation of what he already knew but needed to hear from their lips.

Both men sat at the glass-topped kitchen table, eyeing the female he held manacled in his grasp as if she were a specimen of disease. Or an alien that had suddenly flown into the room, complete with green skin and bug eyes. "Come on, brothers. Tell me."

Nikos pointed at her. "*Who* is that?" he asked with slow, meaningful precision.

"And what is she doing here?" Ajax tagged on impatiently.

Ari waved a hand between them. "Stop trying to sound reasonable, and tell me what I already suspect."

Ajax kept his eyes on the female. "Tell you what, you *malaka*?"

"That I'm still under the influence of my concussion."

Nikos stepped forward, black gaze moving up and down Juliana's form. "She's not dressed right."

"I beg your pardon?" she asked tartly, standing a little taller.

"He means, for this century," Ajax clarified.

Ari maintained his hold on the female, even as she squirmed in his grasp. "So you see her, too? It's not just me?"

"Yes. There is a woman standing in our kitchen," Nik confirmed. "Who appears to have emerged from the past? From the Victorian era, it would seem, based on the clothing."

Ajax jumped out of his chair and smacked Ari on the

top of the head. "You *pousti*, what the hell kind of mess have you gotten into now?"

Ari slapped his brother right back. "Watch the concussion. Besides, you're the *pousti* in our family."

Ajax volleyed the macho shit right back. "I'm married. When's the last time *you* got any?"

"Almost did tonight," Ari muttered, wishing that, for once, he wasn't outranked by his younger brother. He dragged the woman toward the table, shoving her down into one of the chairs as if she were a felon. Not sexy as hell; not a dead ringer for Juliana.

Dead ringer. He castigated himself. *Loaded word choice.*

Ajax, of course, missed nothing: not one iota of emotion or subtext, thank God. His brother, then captain, stalked toward the female, glaring suspiciously. "So," he said, sidling onto the edge of the table beside her. His tone was almost friendly, but Ari knew better—his little brother was a master interrogator. "You apparently have a way with Aristos, no?"

The faux Juliana looked up into his brother's eyes. "You're obviously his brother."

"Bingo." Ajax did not bother looking impressed.

She brushed long fingertips across her brow, smiling. "A fine bloodline you Petrakos brothers share," she observed, cultured Southern accent more elegant than ever.

Ari scowled, hating the fever that hit his groin in automatic response to Juliana's voice.

And hating even more that his idiot little brother appeared . . . ever so slightly . . . charmed, that lopsided, arrogant smile growing wide. "Thank you." Ajax inclined his head. "Nicely played, whoever you are." Then he cast Ari a stern, judgmental glare, saying nothing.

That chastising glance set off yet another grenade inside Ari's chest, and his whole body shook with fury. "You arrogant *kolos*," he bellowed at his brother. "She's the one you should be blaming, not me."

Jax folded both arms across his chest, still poised against the table's edge. "She didn't violate our long-standing rules and protocol," Jax said smoothly, his commanding officer's tone more than grating. What a superior-officer prick. "We don't bring outsiders behind the wire. You know that. The compound is off-limits to unapproved mortals."

"Newsflash! I didn't *bring* her here. She popped into my bedroom while I was convalescing." Ari forged onward, ignoring the charming smile his brother offered the female he himself held rooted in the chair. "Besides, she's not our biggest problem, boys," he declared.

Ajax's dark eyebrows cranked upward to his hairline. "There's actually something bigger than your current protocol violation?"

"Wake up, Jax-ass." Ari anchored his captive in the chair; she tried to look up at him, but he pinned her against the back of the seat. "This little chick ain't human. Not even close to mortal." The Spartans stared back at him, dumbstruck, right as Mason and Jamie Angel entered the room. The brothers were fifth-generation demon hunters and really knew their way around the evil and the undead. If there was any pair of humans he'd ever welcome in a supernatural hoedown, it would be the Angels.

Ari nearly kissed them out of sheer relief, pointing down at his prisoner. "See, guys, we were just having a little discussion that I'm hoping you can straighten out. I was explaining to my fine Spartan warriors that this is no lady; this is—"

"A demon," Mason finished, hackles rising like some alley cat confronted with a Doberman.

Ari gestured toward Juliana with an "I told you so" wave of his hand. "See? Bigger problems, men." He leaned down over the creature's shoulder, voice rising in a crescendo. "Yeah, demons wandering into our *bedrooms* while we *sleep*!" he roared. "Always wanting to get inside our pants! Totally everyday thing, right?"

"Aristos, I fear that since I last spent time with you"— Juliana hesitated with embarrassment, clearing her throat, and then steadied her gaze on him—"you might well have lost your mind."

Jamie propped himself against the door with a low whistle in response to that remark. "Well, if it's a demon, it's a mighty sophisticated and refined one."

Jamie and Mason exchanged a glance, but Mason still had that spooked, hair-on-end expression. Ari had never seen the human react so strongly to a supernatural situation before, not even in a demon fight.

"I'm telling you"—Mason pointed a finger at her, jabbing at the air—"that's not human," he said in an eerily disconnected voice. "Not even close."

His brother, Jamie, reached to the pistol he had holstered at his hip. "So you wanna finish her, or should I, Mace?"

But Mason stood paralyzed, eyes as wide as full moons. "Jamie, don't go near it. Nikos," he called out in that oddly disconnected voice. "Nik? Get far away."

Ari didn't understand why Mason would specifically single out Nikos with that warning, and he looked toward the warrior, who appeared equally confused.

"Mason," Nik answered in a calmer-than-usual voice, "is there something different about this one?"

But Mason didn't answer. The tough-ass former marine, the stealthy demon killer, nearly sprinted out of the room.

"Yeah, I'm pretty much thinking Mason's reaction proves my point." Ari eyed the beautiful-looking creature with even more disdain. "So, go on, Jamie. Finish her off."

Jamie holstered his weapon, staring out the window as bright lights arced through the blinds. "Not just yet. Let's see what Shay says; she just pulled up. She's got no preconceived notions about all this, and my sis can spot a demon as well as any of my most talented Shades."

The Nightshades, or Shades for short, were a band of paramilitary demon fighters, led by Jamie Angel. All three of the Angel siblings were fifth-generation hunters, inheriting the family biz, so to speak. Shay bore a double legacy— the demon sight that she inherited from her father and her lineage as a Daughter of Delphi, which made her one of the Shades' most potent weapons.

Shay came in the door, calling out to Ajax. When she rounded the corner into the great room, she pulled to an abrupt halt, staring right at Juliana.

Ari almost blurted, "See! Told you!" when he saw a shocked, wide-eyed expression overtake her.

"Okay," Shay announced, gaze fixed hard on Juliana. "That's just wrong."

"You know what she is?" Ari asked, half-triumphant, half . . . something he didn't want to acknowledge. But it felt a whole lot like heartbroken.

"No, but that's just some seriously wrong fashion." Shay eyed Juliana warily. "And who is she? What happened to the no-outsiders-allowed club rules?"

"Is she a demon or not?" Ari blurted. "On the soul train or off?"

Shay narrowed her eyes on Juliana, seriously studying her. "Honestly?" she said at last. "I'm not sure *what* she is."

"What's up with you, Angel?" Nik asked, forcing a casual tone. "No stomach for the smell of sulfur this late at night?"

Mason Angel never fled fracases with demons; in fact, his appetite for destroying evil entities was a downright compulsion, one that had him patrolling the streets of Savannah on a nightly basis.

"No, I'd say *retreat* isn't in your vocabulary," Nikos added.

For a long moment, Mason didn't even seem to hear him, and then slowly turned his gaze upward, gradually focusing on Nik. But not really. From what Nik could tell, the former marine was anywhere else but out here on their downstairs patio. By the looks of things, he had a feeling Mason was much closer to the Sunni Triangle of Iraq.

Dropping to his haunches, he tried to get a bead on the human's status, but Mason had shut down. Totally. That same thousand-yard stare he'd gotten in the kitchen still haunted his green eyes.

"Mace, come on," he encouraged. "You do demons all the time; you destroy them without hesitating. What's so different about this particular one?"

Mason only stared ahead of him, until Nik reached out and touched his hand. "*Mason*," he whispered roughly. "Come back to me."

Mason jolted instantly. "Did you say something?"

Nikos leaned in a little closer, still squatting but working to meet Mason's eyes. "Talk to me," he urged softly. "You and I . . . we're always good that way, right?

Mason's green eyes were no longer distant, but alert and locked with Nik's. "You don't have to treat me like a pussy," Mason said, playing it tough. But his eyes. His eyes begged Nikos to fix whatever had come unhinged inside his mind, his soul. "I don't need a psych evaluation."

"No Dr. Freud here."

"Yeah, you've probably done time on the guy's couch,

long as you've been alive," Mason muttered, a hollow attempt at humor that Nik wasn't about to let distract him from the real issue.

Nikos nodded, saying nothing at first, then, "You have that look. The one you had when I first met you ... the one I've observed in a lot of men over the years. Men who've seen too much, fought too long."

Mason's eyes drifted shut. "Nik, tell me I'm okay. Tell me I'm still here," he murmured. "Tell me I'm still tight."

"You're right here with me. Totally lucid."

Those green eyes opened again, filled with a kind of terror that Nik had never seen in the man before. "Because that ... thing? It spooked the hell out of me, dude. It was ... Oh, shit, I'm losing it. Losing my fucking mind! Just when I think I'm all glued back right—when I think you've helped me square away my loose shit—it all falls apart. Like out of the blue, something blindsides me."

Nik didn't know what Mason meant, but he nodded as if he did, realizing that the mortal needed him to be rock solid right now. He'd learned that about Mason over the past six months: that stability, security, those things were worth more than gold to him. "Well," he said after a moment, "you weren't exactly expecting a demon in our kitchen. So you *were* blindsided."

"I'm not talking about that."

The problem was that Nik really had no idea what Mason was talking about. "Then explain," he said laconically.

"It was her eyes. The look in them. For a moment, she stared at me, and I swear it was like . . ." Mason raked his hand over his scalp again, back and forth as if trying to soothe his troubled thoughts. "Forget it. It's fucked."

Nikos leaned forward and took a risk, the sort he rarely had the guts to try with Mason: He slid a palm onto the other man's thigh, resting it there. "Tell me. Say it."

Mason looked down at Nik's hand as if it were a disembodied object, as if he wasn't sure how it had even arrived on his leg. But Nik went on instinct; Mason needed reality, needed connection, so he didn't move.

"It was like, for this split second, that woman—demon, whatever—her eyes changed. They became ... hungry. For me. She looked at me like she wanted me."

Nikos almost laughed, as inappropriate a response as it

would've been. Because he certainly understood looking at Mason Angel and wanting him. He probably did that at least ten times a day. Nik nodded for him to continue. "Go on," he urged, keeping his palm steady on Mason's leg, afraid any sudden movement would send him running for emotional cover. "Tell me, Angel."

"I haven't seen a look like that since . . ." Mason's eyes closed again, and he gave his head a shake. "Fuck. I *am* losing it."

"Where've you seen a look like that before?" Nikos insisted, desperate to keep Mason open and alert.

Mason only mumbled, "Forget it, dude. Just forget I ever said anything."

"Do you still think she's a demon?"

The human shrugged, slowly opening his eyes. "I'm not sure of anything anymore, Nik," he whispered, sinking back heavily into a chair. "Not even me."

Chapter 9

"Well, now that we've managed to clear half the crew out, maybe you'll tell me exactly what you are, hon." Jamie Angel smiled like a perfect Southern gentleman, leaning one hip against the dining table. "My brother, Mason, clearly thinks you're a demon, and my sister . . ."

Shay shrugged in response, folding muscular arms across her chest. She'd been fighting demons on an almost daily basis recently, and it showed in her strong, honed physique. "Jamie, really?" she said. "I got no clue on this one."

"My sister's obviously not sure what to make of you, either." Jamie lowered his voice to a gentle timbre. "So why don't you just tell me all about it, sweetheart."

Ari felt no such gentle tendencies. Not when the imposter looked up at him, those beautiful, thick-lashed blue eyes almost more than he could handle. Gazing back at her, his whole body reacted—his groin, his heart, his mind.

No! he tried telling himself. *Even if she is Juliana, she left you. Gave up on your love!*

Flexing first one hand, then the other, he hated the buzz saw of electricity that kicked on inside his head. And his skull still hurt like a mother. He recalled his concussion then, that fact resounding in his head like the second boom from a mortar, the one that was much more dangerous than the first.

"Aw, damn it all," he muttered as the room grew swimmy and dark. "Who hit the lights?"

Ajax was instantly at his side, helping him to his seat. "Come on, big bro, let's go sit down."

Shay followed Ajax. The married duo always seemed to move as one, and as Jax helped him into the chair, she handed Ari a damp cloth. "Here, press this to your forehead," she urged, and he complied, leaning his head back.

The cool wetness eased the thundering tempo in his brain slightly.

"Who is this female impersonating?" Ajax asked bluntly.

Ari heard a delicate sniff of feminine indignation from beside him. "Apparently manners do not run in the Petrakos bloodline."

"I was in love with her," Ari explained, holding the cool cloth against his eyes. "Here, in Savannah. Over a century ago. She's been dead ever since."

And so have I, he thought. *So have I.*

"I am very much here now, sir," the female said tartly. "Do not speak of me otherwise."

He peeled the edge of the cloth away, ready to give her the evil eye, and saw that Emma was walking into the kitchen, River right behind her.

"Nice of you to finally show up," Ari groused, noting that both of them had wet, neatly combed hair.

A cozy shower together; even lovelier. Or maybe a long, sensual bath in each other's arms?

The heat that had been lodged in his groin all night long hit overdrive as an image of hauling Juliana out of her chair and off to his own posh bathroom danced through his mind—of her bare body gleaming with droplets of water, his dark hands all over her porcelain skin. Maybe pulling her into the glass-walled shower, where he'd lather her up, drop to his knees . . .

"Oh, my God!" Emma cried suddenly, eyes still locked on the Juliana imposter. She pointed, turning toward River in explanation, then jabbed her finger significantly. "That's *her*. That's Aunt Juliana, in the chair. That's my great-great-aunt."

"Actually, Mason doesn't think she *is* Juliana," Ajax corrected. "He says she's a demon. One masquerading as your dead relative."

"Hey, wait!" Ajax looked at Emma. "Was she *Shay's* great-great-aunt, too?"

Emma nodded, frowning as she swept her gaze up and down Juliana's form. "Yes, Juliana was our great-grandmother's sister." She hesitated, gesturing toward the woman. "I'm sorry; not to dispute my cousin's word—I mean, Mason's really good at what he does—but that *is* Juliana. She has the same spirit I channeled earlier tonight. I sense it."

Ari's head only pounded harder as the group talked over one another, debating whether Juliana was the real deal or not. He rubbed his temples, almost daring to hope Emma was right, but his heart clenched at the thought, even as it tried to embrace the possibility.

She had broken him, with both her rejection and her death. Now, if she truly *had* returned? How could he ever trust her again, much less risk his heart?

He groaned. "My head, gang. Is Sophie coming? She gonna heal me or what?"

Emma moved to his side instantly, pressing the cool cloth against his brow again. "I couldn't reach her for a while, Ari, but she's on the way now. She'll take care of you."

He noticed that "Juliana" was watching the action very closely, blotches of color staining her cheeks. The little hellion had the nerve to be jealous? And of Emma?

"So Juliana was a Daughter of Delphi, too," Ajax resumed, sounding as if he were a hound chasing down a fox's trail. "Like you, like Shay. The gifts came down through the female bloodline, correct?"

Emma nodded, gaze locked on the woman she clearly believed was her great-great-aunt. "All the way back to ancient Greece. It's in our family journals; the exact lineage is traced."

"Your point, Jax?" Ari asked, dropping his hands to the table. At that exact moment, "Juliana" spread her palms openly in front of her, causing their fingertips to graze. It was like being touched by wildfire, Ari's entire body tensing and electrifying in response. For such a simple touch, it sure incited a complicated, intense reaction.

His brother kept talking, oblivious. "Well, as a man who happens to be married to a very powerful Daughter of Delphi," Jax said, "I've learned they're capable of quite the supernatural feat. Channeling the Highest God, seeing the future, hearing the dead . . ."

Ari turned to look up at his younger brother. "Again, Jax, get to the point." He knew he sounded raw and irritable, but physical awareness of the female beside him was starting to burn a hole in his consciousness.

Ajax smiled slowly, a warm, genuine expression that reached his eyes. He bent over Ari's shoulder, his voice so low that only the two of them would know the secret. "Brother of mine, I'm suggesting that you might be sitting beside your one true love." Jax paused, letting those intense, meaningful words sink all the way in. "So close, Aristos, that you could turn and kiss the lass if you wanted."

Then Jax straightened up, raising his voice for the whole group to hear. "There's only one way to confirm the woman's identity for sure that I can think of, and that's to summon a very old, dear friend of mine. Of ours."

Oh, by the Highest, Leonidas would think she'd come of her own volition, Daphne thought, afraid to even breathe. Ares had spun her through the dimensions, torturing her as she hung in between for what felt an eternity—but was probably only a few hours. Now she'd landed gracelessly in the king's intimate chambers, clearly her brother's notion of a cruel joke. Or a dangerous temptation.

Leo was unaware of her silent arrival, kneeling before a makeshift, candlelit altar, lost in prayer. His head was bowed, one hand pressed over his heart, quiet and earnest words spilling past his lips. She closed her eyes, willing herself to vanish or move through the heavens without lifting so much as a pinky, but she couldn't bring herself to leave the man she loved.

"Highest Lord, Father of all, guide our steps. Lead us from the path of evil. Protect us from the arrows that fly by day and by night," he prayed, but then his words simply faded to nothing. With an anguished groan, he rubbed both palms over his face. "Highest, what is she, this woman I love to the point of distraction? A goddess? Half a goddess? And what are these gods, when you command them all?"

Leonidas kept his face buried in both palms, moaning low in his throat. "I've never wanted anything for myself. Not glory, not handsomeness, not even immortality. But this Oracle, this mystical Daphne . . . I want her to the point of madness."

Daphne stifled a gasp, eyes wide and fixed on Leo's profile. In the candlelight, his dark skin and hair appeared to glow with otherworldly power. As if the fire crowned him somehow, making him shine from within, reflecting all the noble goodness and heat she always felt simmered inside his quiet nature.

He let his hands fall away then, and she saw what his palms had concealed: Tears shone in his brown eyes. "God of all, Highest of all, who is this Daphne, the one I love so fiercely?"

She could not keep silent, not now. "I am just a woman, my king," she whispered, barely able to find her voice, "A woman in every way."

He jolted, whipping his head in her direction, pinning her with a severe gaze. "I thought you would not return," he said without blinking. "You said that you would not come to me again." The words were almost an accusation, with undisguised pain behind them.

It took everything within me to stay away. Required strength I never knew I possessed.

That was what she ached to cry out, but didn't dare. The moment Leo understood how easily he could have her—fathomed how deeply she would always love him—she'd no longer be able to resist him. Those long-pent-up emotions were so strong, if they ever gave way, she knew that she and Leonidas would be swept up in the roaring tide, no turning back.

And they could never have a relationship like that. Not any relationship at all ever again. Because if they did, then Ares would not rest until he chased Leonidas to the ends of the earth. Her brother would hunt and destroy Leo for one single reason: his own raging jealousy.

If he hadn't targeted him already, she thought in alarm, recalling the veiled threat he'd made about Leo's immortality.

Slowly Leonidas rose to his feet, favoring his right knee briefly. That old war injury that had never stopped causing him pain, she thought, feeling a sharp, sympathetic ache in her own right knee. "No answer for me . . . Daphne?" He whispered her name with more fever and intensity than anything else he'd said so far. As if just using it after not being allowed to know it for so many years was something of a prayer in its own right. Then he repeated it, dropping his voice into a lower, huskier timbre. *"Daphne?"*

She flattened herself against the door to his chambers. "I wasn't spying. I really, truly wasn't spying, my king."

"I never accused you of it." He took several slow steps toward her, head tilted down slightly so that his gaze fixed on her with a focused intensity. "I merely pointed out that you'd said we could not see each other anymore. That you would not come to me except as your duties required. Are you here with a prophetic word now?"

She swallowed and shook her head.

He smiled, the harsh scar that split through his lower lip twisting his mouth into a rough expression that she always found oddly beautiful. "Somehow I thought not."

She placed her palms flush against the door, half thinking she should teleport, and half wishing that he'd sweep her into his strong arms. "I didn't come here, my lord."

"You're here now."

"I . . . I was sent. Thrown here, I mean. Well, teleported against my will."

He stopped right in front of her. Only a minute distance separated them; he stood so close that she could feel the warmth of his breath, smell the tantalizing, musky, male scent of his skin. His eyes flickered for a moment. "Ah, so the only way you'll visit your king now is against your will?" he asked, lifting one thick eyebrow. "I suppose that should surprise me."

She flinched at the words, splaying both palms against his chest in an involuntary response. "My king, don't say cruel words just to spite me."

He stared down at her hands, distanced from the physical intimacy. "You heard my prayers."

"Yes."

He was quiet a long moment, then: "You know how I feel."

"You've always known how *I* feel, my beautiful king. At least, ever since you could see me. I hope you have."

He shook his head, gaze still averted. "I'm not sure how you ever felt, Oracle. I have not seen you in two months. You come and go at will, and every time you leave, I swear you only possess me more." Slowly he lifted his own hands and covered hers against his chest. "I want to be angry. I try to be, but now that I see you? Now that I feel you here, so close against me, all I want is to make love to you at last. For hours and days, I yearn to hold you in my arms, like this. Yet closer."

She felt her face grow hot beneath his inspection, in reaction to his words. "For a quiet man, you speak very plainly, Leo."

His dark gaze, nearly black with desire, met hers, but he said nothing. It was his eyes that spoke everything in his heart, wove poems and epics in the air, all without uttering a syllable.

When at last he did speak *aloud*, the words were husky and low, his tone more overtly sexual than she'd ever heard from him. "I've already taken you hundreds of times in my thoughts and dreams."

She felt her entire body surge with fire and need, the sensation so strong that she had to lean into him to keep steady. "Then you must be eavesdropping on my own dreams," she admitted, leaning her cheek against his chest. His heart beat rapidly, the rhythm a vibration against her face.

He placed a steadying hand against her lower back. Her gown was open there, and the sensation of his masculine, warrior's flesh meeting her own smooth skin shredded whatever was left of her sanity. "You want me, too," he said on an exhale. "You still want me." The obvious relief in his tone wrenched at her heart.

With both hands, she cupped his bearded face, tugging it downward so she could kiss him. Slowly she brushed her lips over his, determined that it would be a brief touch, and whispered, "I only stay away so my brother won't hurt you. Always know that, love."

He frowned, the scar in his lip blanching white. "But losing *you* hurts me. That you're not here with me all the time, that I can't hold you . . ."

She kissed him again, felt his mouth opening, how hungry he was to taste her. He pushed his hips against her, pinning her against the door, deepening what had begun as a tentative, gentle kiss. His hands raked into her hair; his body surged against hers; their tongues intertwined, the wet heat of him almost more than she could resist. But an image of Ares' cruel face flashed in her mind, and she pulled back. "If I let myself love you . . . my love will kill you. Ares will kill you."

He dipped his head low, moving in to kiss her again; she felt the bristling tickle of his beard against her cheek.

"I'm immortal, Daphne." The words were a rough, low pledge.

She instantly thought of Ares' threats, the implications that Leo had begun to age, that his transformation would take hold quickly.

She pushed against his chest, determined to protect him. "No. No, Leo. This can't happen."

"There are only two of us here," he growled, cupping her face roughly and tilting it upward until their eyes locked. "We are the ones who decide our future."

She couldn't fight her tears: They welled from deep inside her soul. "I wish that were true, but if you died again, Leo," she whispered, "I would die a thousand times with you. You must live. Above all things, above all my own needs."

His muscular arms seized her about the waist, and he cried out her name with such anguished strength, she nearly stayed with him forever.

Until she saw the only proof that could ever keep her away.

A few strands of silver glinted in his beard, gleaming lustrously by the candlelight. Leo's beard had always been dark, nearly black, without a single graying curl.

Until now.

She lifted her fingers and outlined the few silver hairs, finding them oddly beautiful, while hating them at the same time.

"What, Daphne?" he asked, capturing her hand against his face. "What is it that you see?"

She swallowed, shaking her head. At that exact moment, there was a loud rapping on the door behind her back. She startled, leaning into Leonidas, and he wrapped her close. Clearing his throat, he called, "Yes?"

"My lord, pardon the intrusion." It was Ajax's deep voice, just on the other side of the thin barrier that separated them from the hallway. "But you are needed, sir."

Leo only nuzzled her closer, locking a protective, proprietary arm about her. He did not intend to relinquish her now that she'd returned, not ever, and she knew it in that moment.

Neither of them spoke for a long, suspended moment, only the sound of their breathing filling the silence. If they parted, if they stepped out of each others' arms, would they ever be together again?

"Sir, we require the Oracle," Ajax added when Leo did not reply. "We thought, perhaps, you might be able to summon her."

Leo's arms tightened about her, and she heard him swallow. At last he called out, his voice falsely bold, "Understood. I will need enough time to . . . to summon her."

There was a pause, and then, "Yes, sir," and the sound of footsteps retreating on the hardwood hallway.

Daphne's eyes locked with Leo's in the ensuing silence, as each studied the other. Memorized the shape of a lower lip, the way a mouth quirked at the edge, the outline of a brow. But despite Daphne's attempt to burn Leonidas's full visage into her soul, one facet of the man's appearance blazed brightest of all.

Her gaze went to it now, even as she fought to pretend it was not there: silver. The silver hairs in Leo's dark beard were virgin. Brand-new. And they betrayed a tragic truth, fulfilled her brother's threat with alacrity.

He touched his beard, rubbing his thick fingers over it curiously, gaze locked on her. "What do *you* see?" he repeated hoarsely. As if he already knew. As if he'd already glimpsed his fate himself, perhaps in the mirror that morning.

Silver washed through her vision, blinding her, poisoning her deepest soul. Because now she knew what Ares had been hinting about in his throne room. That Leonidas, brave king of Sparta, protector of Greece and eternal humanity, her only love, was aging. And that meant . . . he was also slowly dying.

Chapter 10

They had moved from the dining table to a very large, high-ceilinged room that, with its slanted angles and windows, reminded Juliana of a church. She'd heard them call it "the great room" as they'd directed her within.

A balcony ran the length of the upper portion, a kind of catwalk that apparently led to more rooms farther down the hallway. She stared upward, surprised by how basic the ceiling looked, not adorned by intricate tiles, nor painted a vibrant, rich color. Had architecture become uncommonly plain and massive in the past hundred years? And obviously electricity had won the war against oil and steam, as every light she'd seen so far was electric. There would be much to experience and learn in this century, she decided.

Slowly she lowered her gaze and counted the other people in the room. Apart from Emma and Shay, there were seven men, almost all of whom were massively built, although Aristos had to be the biggest among the group.

She sighed, sinking back against the cushions of the long settee; Ari sat beside her, and she realized that apart from him, she was surrounded by strangers. Well, mostly so, since River and Emma didn't quite fit into that category. Still, with the others offering her a mix of curious, indifferent, and cold glances, she felt inspected, as if she were on display at an exhibition.

Ari never even looked in her direction, but instead faced forward, eyes fixed on an unseen point, back as straight as a rod. Folding neat hands in her lap, she stared straight ahead, too, attempting conversation. "For whom do we wait?"

No answer. No reaction whatsoever. His unresponsiveness perturbed her greatly.

Why wouldn't he at least acknowledge her? Offer some encouraging or polite word?

Apparently, pretending that she didn't exist was his current strategy for dealing with their unusual situation.

Fine; he wished to wage war of indifference? Then she would match his every maneuver. Except . . . the longer they waited, the others chatting easily around them, the more his enforced silence became a war of attrition, wearing down her attempts to stay calm.

What if he tosses me out to the street? Perhaps he won't have me at all. She suddenly worried, chewing on her lip. *I have nowhere to go, no idea how this new world operates.*

The possibility that he would reject her outright had never even entered her mind when she'd made her choice earlier tonight. She had thought only about making Aristos hear the truth of the night she died. But now, here with the man she had never stopped loving, seeing such harsh lines on his face, she began to doubt in earnest.

A deep, hollow loneliness filled her right then, such a powerful sensation that she had to blink back tears. Because she wanted to go home with a raw, childlike intensity. Wanted to be back in her own bedroom near her own things, smelling a familiar world, but that world was as lost as she'd been until just a few hours ago.

She pressed her eyes shut, struggling to tamp down the homesickness. *I have no home. No time. No mother upon whose shoulder to cry.*

And, apparently, no man who loves me.

She frowned, staring down at her hands, kneading them in her lap. Then she stopped, studying her pianist's tapered fingers, noticing for the first time that her left hand was bare of the ring she'd always worn, a cameo of a Roman warrior and his bride. It had been a gift from Ari on her twenty-sixth birthday, instantly becoming her favorite piece.

"Whom are we expecting?" she tried again, leaning against Ari. She needed his solid, physical reassurance. He jerked away as if she'd pressed a hot poker to his skin. "I'm not poisonous, sir," she huffed.

He began tapping his bare right foot, his knee jerking up and down. "Hey, Jax," he called to his brother on the other side of the room. "How long did the Old Man say he'd be? When's he gonna come?"

"'Soon' was all he said. Maybe it took a while to summon her?" Jax shrugged. "I don't know."

Who was this "Old Man" and who was the "she" involved? Juliana wondered. More important, how would
their opinions impact her fate?

A bald man sat in the far corner astride a straight-backed
chair that he had turned backward. His shiny, smooth
scalp had several ugly scars upon it, which only added to
his menacing appearance. When he looked up, their gazes
locked briefly. "He will come soon enough," he said, and
she shivered.

That man, she noted, was frightening. She could have
sworn she heard a slight growl emanate from his corner, as
if he were a caged beast.

"Straton, dude. Just asking," Ari replied.

Straton was a Greek name as well; it seemed that all
the men gathered in the room shared that bond. Perhaps
they'd also defied time itself, like Aristos, which puzzled
her as always.

She voiced the question aloud, vexed. "What *are* all of
you?"

Ari, of course, remained as silent as a Sunday morning.

"I won't be vanishing simply because you choose to
ignore me," she warned him quietly, leaning closer so he
could hear. He cut a sideways glare at her, and those eyes of
his—their dark depths were pools of very intense emotion,
revealing the truth of his mental state. She could practically see heat and anger and passion swirling in his gaze.
No, contrary to what he'd wanted to make her believe, he
was not unmoved by her presence. The furthest thing from
it, in fact.

That realization caused every one of her fears to flee;
her heart soared like the winged creature she knew him
capable of becoming.

She touched his hand. "Aristos, perhaps you could talk
to me," she encouraged gently. "Realize that you don't
need to be so . . ." *Afraid. Heartbroken. Confused.* Dozens
of words came to the tip of her tongue, but she was certain
that every one of them was wrong. "So . . . uncertain," she
added at last.

She tilted her face upward as she studied his profile.
That long, aquiline nose was still perfect, still beautiful. So
were his high cheekbones and dusky, Greek skin.

She reached a hand to his cheek, not caring if he swatted

it away. "Your skin is still so beautifully dark. Remember when I told you it was the color of ripe walnuts?"

"You tossed one of the blasted things at me from across the table, and it pinged off my forehead," he said.

He'd laughed, eyes crinkling at the edges. Small lines had appeared, betraying his age. He'd been thirty-two then, in visible years, at least, and not aged at all since.

"I believe you were embarrassed. That's why you cracked the nut open with your bare hand, hoping to regain your dignity."

"I was always trying to impress you," he said, then closed his eyes, wincing at the vivid memories. "Oh, Juliana. Please . . ."

He'd called her Juliana! He did believe, or at least he'd responded to the shared memory. She pressed on, brushing the backs of her fingertips down his jaw. "You always wore such fine suits when you courted me. I loved your silk vests, especially that crimson one. Remember? And your fancy pocket watch, the one with the gold-coin cover. It was so flashy, my mother hated it, which only made you display it more frequently." She felt his cheek quiver with the hint of a smile, and she stroked his face again.

"And that black felt derby . . ." She sighed. "No man should look so sinfully beautiful in a hat."

"Jules, please," he begged again. This time, he'd used her pet name! She was reaching him, making him understand.

He forced her hand away from his cheek, their fingertips grazing briefly. A flare of heat moved up her arm at the intimacy, and she started to reach for him all over again. This time he clasped her hand, holding it in his. "Please don't touch me, okay?" he asked gently, his eyes pleading with her as he slowly released her hand from his grasp.

"Earlier, you seemed quite happy to be physically close to me," she reminded him.

"I was."

"Why can't you still feel that joy?" She patted her chest. "I am *me*, Aristos, and I am here. You can feel my beating heart if you wish, feel the pulse at my wrists. I'm no spirit or illusion."

He pivoted, seizing hold of her upper arms. "Don't you understand my hesitation, woman?"

She bit her lower lip, shaking her head slowly. "No. I don't understand, not at all."

He tightened his hold, bending lower so that only she could hear. "I don't dare hope, don't dare believe that you've found a way to come back to life or whatever it is you claim you've done," he hissed. "Can't put my faith in it. Don't dare even think that you *are* Juliana and that . . . that . . ." He panted several heavy, hot breaths against her cheek, and then added thickly, "That you've come back to *me*.

"Because you left me once before," he admitted on a barely spoken whisper. "I can't face losing you again."

"You'll soon see the truth. That I never wanted to abandon you," she promised. "You will." He released his hold on her, but she needed him close, the heat and scent of him. She loved the way his silky hair tickled her face, and she drew in his scent deeply. Whatever had happened in their past, she was certain of one thing: She would never repeat the mistakes that had led to their separation. And she would never, at all costs, hurt him again.

She leaned her cheek against his shoulder, and this time he didn't shove her away or try to shake her off. She sighed, relishing the feel of his comforting, strong warmth, tucking her hand through the crook of his arm. Even in her own time, at the height of her independence and youth, she'd found him the most stable, reassuring presence she'd ever known. It was part of why she'd fallen in love with him: that he could regale her with bawdy jokes and wordplay, then reveal himself to be such a gentleman. The unexpected juxtaposition had beguiled her, as had the way he could become unexpectedly tender at the oddest moments.

The only uncertainty he had ever created in her heart was his refusal to answer her questions. *What are you, Aristos? With all that we've come to share, surely you would trust me with your secrets now*, she'd told him on their final day together. It had been lunchtime, and she'd had no inkling that midnight would bring their very last moments together.

He'd cupped her cheek, murmuring in her ear, promising that his heart belonged solely to her.

She'd leaned against his chest, comforted by the steady, calm rhythm of his heart. By its firm, dependable beat. *It frightens me sometimes, these mysterious errands of yours, the way you vanish for days,* she'd told him.

I keep you safe by keeping my nature secret, my love, he'd said, showering her with kisses. Along her ear, down to her nape. *Juliana, this feeling for you ... I need to have you fully. For always. I shall tell you everything, I promise. In due time, I will tell you these secrets.*

Then I shall be yours fully, she'd said. *Tonight. Come to my balcony at midnight...*

And she'd meant it; but had he ever intended to color in the canvas of his identity for her?

She pulled away, sitting tall beside him. "You are not the only one with questions, you know."

He cocked an eyebrow, drawling, "What's that supposed to mean?"

She lifted her own eyebrow, mirroring his expression. "Or the only one who's defied death, for that matter."

He opened his mouth, clearly about to sputter some argument in reply, but was interrupted by the sound of voices from the hallway. "That's probably them." He leaned forward, trying to see around the corner. "Daphne and Leo are going to get to the bottom of this sinkhole. Or perhaps I should say sink *hell*, considering where you come from, huh?" he laughed grimly.

A petite, dark-haired young woman with wild curls entered the room. "What's going on, guys?" she asked, dropping a ring of keys onto the main table. They clattered into a heap, and Juliana marveled at their strange shapes and sizes.

Emma walked the girl forward. "Sophie, meet *Juliana* ... ," Emma said, emphasizing her name significantly. "Juliana, this is my sister Sophie."

Juliana stood, extending her hand politely to yet another great-great-niece. She blinked at the shock of it all.

Sophie's clear blue eyes widened. "You mean like Mama's ... ahem ... *friend*?"

"Yes, she's also our great-great-aunt," Emma agreed.

She took Sophie's hand in her own. "It is delightful to meet you, Sophie."

Sophie smiled up at her. "I bet Ari's a happy guy tonight." She looked in his direction, raising an eyebrow at his gloomy expression. "Then again ... maybe not so much."

Juliana glanced away from the group, noticing something she'd missed before. Hanging over the fireplace mantel was a large, vividly colored photograph—much more detailed and clear than any she'd ever seen in her own time. "How lovely," she observed, walking closer to it, instantly recognizing the subject.

"Thanks. I took that one," Sophie explained. "I gave it to the boys here so the walls wouldn't be so . . . uh, *Spartan*."

The Spartan reference seemed to be some sort of private joke among the group, because Shay laughed, nodding in agreement.

"The Angel plantation. Ah, I remember the parties there." Juliana sighed dreamily.

"That's my family's place," Shay said, and Juliana turned in surprise.

"Are you part of the Angel clan?" she asked.

Shay nodded. "Yep, and so's my brother Jamie." He gave a wave from where he sat sprawled in one of the club chairs by the fireplace. "And our other brother, Mason, is, too." She looked about the room. "Where'd he go, by the way?"

Ari rolled his eyes. "He fled the hellmouth."

"Mace got spooked by our lovely . . ." Jamie Angel coughed into his hand, clearing his throat. "Well, by Ari's visitor."

"So, you must've known some of our ancestors," Shay observed with interest.

Juliana smiled, recalling the glorious galas the Angels had once hosted. "Actually, I was courted by Demitri Angel."

Now, this comment, Juliana realized a heartbeat too late, captured Aristos's interest completely, and not in a positive way. He leaped to his feet and said, "You didn't date anyone else but me."

Not that she wanted to upset him, but his jealous outburst gave her the greatest hope she'd felt since arriving. "Actually, Aristos . . ."

Jamie cut her off with a loud, rolling laugh, trading a look with his sister. "Whoa, ho, Petrakos," he said, giving Ari a smug look. Then he laughed even harder.

"What's so godsdamned funny?" Ari barked.

"Just that apparently your number one girl there"— Jamie kept laughing—"had a thing with my great-grandfather."

Chapter 11

"My *girl* did not have a thing with your great-grandfather," Ari contradicted with a snarl. He shook his head, muttering, "Just like a demon to try to incite a mutiny among us, turn us against each other."

And make me jealous as ever-living hell.

"Jules would have said something." He stared at the ceiling and blew out another breath. "*She* would've told me."

"*I* never told you," she corrected, "because *I* knew you'd have reacted precisely as you are now! By displaying a terrible jealous streak. You always were so possessive." She had the audacity to seem pleased with herself, as if eliciting this reaction was a true romantic achievement. "It's a flattering compliment, of course," she added with a sweet smile, "but I truly do not wish to upset you with long-ago details."

He grew wide-eyed. *Long-ago details?* Hell yeah, he was worried about petty bits of history—like why she'd killed herself, why she'd not loved him enough to live. And now this? That she might have loved another man was almost more than his battered heart could handle.

A thought hit him right then. "Is that why you walked into that storm? Because you actually loved another man?" His hand formed into an involuntary fist, and when Jamie laughed again, he had the urge to punch him, use him as a proxy for his own great-grandfather.

"We already discussed the storm." She paused, glancing self-consciously about the room. "As for my affections for you, I think you've seen tonight that they have never once wavered."

"Okay, okay," he said, and began pacing the room, ignoring the way the cadre watched, and especially—most especially—that Shay and Emma seemed to be elbowing each other and making eyes over the whole thing. "So, if Demitri Angel courted you, what exactly went down? What was involved with that sort of thing, and how much of it went on, precisely?"

"Aristos." Juliana lowered her lashes slightly, glancing to the side shyly. "These are very personal questions for such a public gathering."

"You're saying something actually *happened* between you two?" He gaped at her, feeling as if she'd just taken her neat little high-heeled boot and kicked it into his gut. "You and Demitri had an . . . an . . . affair?"

She folded arms across her chest with a satisfied sniff. "So you *do* believe I'm Juliana. Why else would you be jealous?"

Of course he did. That fact had become patently obvious to him in the past minutes, the way he wanted to throttle a dead man for having taken any interest in his Jules. Still, he was angry and confused about basically everything at the moment, from her reappearance in his life, to her unexplained suicide, to her rejection of his winged form. Those tumultuous emotions fired at him like thousands of enemy arrows, aimed right at his heart, and he without a shield of any kind.

Juliana stared at him as if still expecting confirmation of his faith and belief in her, but he refused to answer, not until he at least learned about her past with this Demitri. He stormed over to the other sofa, where Ajax and Kalias sat, wedging his way between them until they made room for his massive form.

Jamie piped up, grinning. "Tell me about him. About Demitri."

All this time and he'd believed he was her only love, the only man she'd ever even kissed.

"Demitri and his father were unique—as odd as my own family. No wonder . . ."

"What?" Ari demanded impatiently. Something really must have happened between her and this Demitri. A thick river of jealousy began roaring inside his veins. He hated the idea that Jules had ever been courted or charmed by any other man besides himself. She'd never mentioned anything about a Demitri Angel.

"If he's their great-grandfather, and you're their great-great-aunt, wasn't that a little too cozy-close?"

The jealousy bloomed hotter, stronger.

"In fact," he pressed, "wasn't it fucking illegal?"

"There was no connection between my family and Demitri's at that time," Juliana explained. "None other than . . . how shall I put it? Our rather unique talents with the spiritual side." Juliana lifted her chin proudly, turning toward him. "It was the winter before I met you when Demitri made his feelings known to me."

Ari's eyebrows cranked downward. "What did that man do? Put the moves on you?"

"Nothing happened between us. I told him no."

"You told him no," Ari repeated numbly. There were only two questions a woman said no to, and only *one* of them was routinely asked in the Victorian era. "You turned him down," he said, much louder.

"Of course I turned him down," Juliana said with a light laugh.

Ari couldn't hold back a very heavy sigh of relief. "You didn't accept his proposal," he said, still needing to reassure himself that the Demitri threat had never been real.

"My great-grandfather proposed to you?" Shay and Jamie blurted almost simultaneously.

"It appears," Juliana said with a smile, "that our unique bloodlines were always destined to join, just not by my marrying Demitri. He said that ours would be a powerful connection, with his ability to see demons and spiritual creatures, and my own prophetic abilities. He believed that we were meant to . . ." She tapped a finger against her brow. "Battle evil itself. Yes, that was how he phrased it. Unfortunately, I didn't find it a very romantic appeal. And then I met you, Aristos," she said, beaming up at him.

"Tell me everything. Leave nothing to my imagination."

"He came to my brownstone and asked Mother and me to accompany him on a grand tour to Greece. Those months traveling would allow us to become better acquainted. He believed that after that time spent together, I would perhaps acquiesce and agree to become his wife."

Ari stared straight ahead, unable to fight the tide of emotions that assaulted him. The jealousy was morphing into a new, even stronger feeling—one that felt an awful lot like the grief he'd long battled and attempted to deny.

"I said no to that as well, of course," she rushed to say.

"And met you only weeks after. I found you a challenge and a riddle from the moment I first encountered you. Keen mind, irascible behavior, rapier wit. I was fully enamored from that very first night. Utterly besotted."

Ari pressed fists against both thighs. Jules looked down at the gesture, frowning. "Aristos, these things happened a long time ago," she said. "Long, *long* time ago, remember?"

"Those days live inside of me as if they're happening now. They have ever since." Then, plunging his fingers through his hair, he gave her a desperate look. "You never truly died for me, Jules."

"Trust your heart, Aristos," she whispered, eyes welling with tears. "Trust your love for me."

Trust your heart, Aristos. Trust your love for me.

The words began hammering into his skull, driving into his doubts, creating more fear than he'd known in ages.

"Oh, I'm so screwed," he muttered, rubbing a big palm over his scalp. "And my head feels like it's about to explode."

River spoke up. "Buddy, we need Sophie to heal your concussion. That can't be helping anything right now."

Sophie moved toward him, kneeling in front of him. "I'm not sure how my power works yet, Ari," she said, rubbing her palms together and blowing into them. "So . . . here goes nothing, right?"

The pain was completely gone. A warm blanket of light and love and safety folded all about him, tucked as neat as a downy comforter beneath his chin.

Juliana's scent was all over his skin, in his nostrils, on his hair. She was real, alive.

She was not a demon.

She's not a demon!

Ari came slamming awake at the revelation. He sat up, blinking, and realized he'd been sprawled out on the sofa. Conked out. Again.

Sophie squatted beside him, holding his hand between both of her small ones. "I didn't mean to give you an overdose."

He rubbed his eyes. "Of what?" Had they given him drugs? He didn't remember that. All he remembered was

Sophie Lowery rubbing her hands together like a happy little fairy, then placing them on his head.

"My power. I really don't know what I'm doing," she said sheepishly. "Sorry."

"Second time tonight I've been out cold, but at least you didn't make me hurt. In fact . . ." He rubbed his scalp, thrilled to confirm that the pain was gone. "It's gone! The concussion is totally gone." He leaned forward and gave Sophie a sloppy kiss of gratitude on the cheek, then looked around for Juliana. He didn't see her and instantly panicked.

"Juliana . . ." *She is not a demon.*

Somehow, some way, he'd heard that while in that place of healing. He knew enough about supernatural ability to guess it was some echo of Sophie's power coursing through his veins, and she was a prophetess, so wouldn't that mean that the small voice had been right?

"She's with the Oracle and Leonidas in his study," Sophie explained. "And with Ajax."

"*I* should be in there, too," he said, already on his feet. "Why didn't they wait for me to wake up?"

Nobody answered, and there were some uncomfortable, awkward glances between his brother Kalias and Straton, and even River and Emma.

"River man, what's going on?" he asked slowly, looking only at his best friend. "Did something happen while I was unconscious?"

Kalias sighed heavily and stood, walking toward him with his usual military bearing. "Aristos, you're incapable of reaching an objective conclusion in this particular instance."

Straton rose, too, standing beside Kalias; they formed a wall of muscle and strength between Ari and the open doorway.

"The meeting went on as scheduled," Straton said. He always had been his brother's pit bull on the occasions when he needed one.

Ari moved right up, close and personal to the duo. "I was barred."

"Well, technically, no. You weren't even awake," Kalias said with a half smile.

"You're not keeping me out of there." Ari shoved his

hands between both men's shoulders, forcing them apart. "No way am I out of that meeting."

Kalias moved slightly to the left; Straton didn't so much as breathe.

"Listen, Spartan." Ari pushed his chest against Straton's. "You really do not want to get in my way tonight."

"You aren't clearheaded enough to reach any conclusions about this female," Straton replied, unblinking as he stared up into Ari's eyes. He was the stockiest of their immortals, with a thick build that made his chest seem even broader than Ari's own. "Certainly not with your new power. A demigod's strength is hardly familiar territory. You're barely in control of—"

Ari cut him off. "Careful, bulldog."

Straton plowed right over the warning. "We all see what's happening to you, the way you're changing. Don't think River can cover for you from now on," he cautioned icily. As if Ari had sought the power for his own gain or hoped to rule the universe with it.

Ari placed a hand on Straton's waist. He knew the warrior despised being touched, so he did it just to fuck with him, getting so personal and all. "Careful, like I said. Or I just might use this new demigod's power of mine"—he slid his hand a few inches inward, jabbing the center of Straton's stomach with his forefinger—"to fry your shriveled old unmentionables right off."

They eyeballed each other for at least ten more seconds; then Straton finally moved to the right. Ari gave the other warrior a shove with his shoulder as he passed, cursing all the way to Leonidas's study.

So what if he'd just managed to win a pissing match with the shortest, coldest, and most ruthless member of their cadre. That was small-time stuff compared to the battle that awaited him in Leo's study—a skirmish that would determine Juliana's fate. And if those words he'd heard during his dream vision had been correct . . .

Then she was *his* Jules. And if so, it was going to be a serious issue if the Oracle didn't vouch for her. What would he do then? Take Juliana on some road trip right out of a Tim Burton movie? Marry his sophisticated, beautiful corpse bride?

Nah, nothing about her looked freaky or morbid. She

appeared, as a matter of fact, exactly as his sweet Jules always had, which begged a totally new question, one he hadn't dared entertain throughout the evening's chaos.

What exactly was he supposed to do with a Victorian-era socialite who'd chased him right out of her grave in Bonaventure Cemetery?

Chapter 12

"About time you came glowering in here, Aristos," Daphne said, smiling despite the Spartan's dour expression.

The warrior glanced about Leo's library, clearly searching for Juliana. Daphne walked toward the big man, extending both hands. She'd managed to conjure her usual Goth garb for the meeting, not wanting any of them to know that she'd been in Leonidas's chambers when he "summoned her."

She'd excused herself to his bathroom and, in a whirling flash, discarded her Olympian gown in favor of a leather mini and thigh-high boots. Her hair was spiky and short again, streaked with the cobalt blue she knew Leo adored. Of course, he seemed to treasure her in whatever form she came to him, whether that be a golden gown or plain street clothes. He loved her, a fact that should have brought comfort but only created more anguish in her heart.

As she'd emerged from the bathroom, he'd given her a wistful smile, brown eyes filled with longing. "I'd rather hoped to spend all evening with you."

She'd tried to appear stoic. "We will always have our duties, my king. I see no way around that fact."

"At times," he'd answered just as stoically, "I wish to be an ordinary man."

They'd fallen silent then, having already bared their hearts and souls. And, really, what more could be said when they had no future together? They'd walked to his study like true warriors, shoulder to shoulder and resolved. Ajax had entered with the young woman, explaining Juliana's history until Ari had interrupted by storming into the room.

"Have you prophesied yet?" Ari asked as Daphne gathered his hands in her own.

She gave him a reassuring squeeze. "No need to worry." She smiled up at him, noting the anxiety in his eyes. "Ajax already told me all about it. *All* about it." She winked at him, but Ari never noticed. He was too busy glaring at his brother.

"What'd you say, huh?" Ari pointed an accusing finger at Jax.

Ajax shrugged innocently. "The facts are always helpful when asking for our Oracle's time."

Juliana's auburn eyebrows quirked together. "Oracle? As in . . . Delphi?"

Daphne bobbed her head. "I'm a . . ." She sought for the best way to put it, not sure exactly how much Juliana knew about their unusual group. "Daughter!" she finished brightly. "Like Shay and Emma and Sophie."

Juliana smiled in obvious understanding. "Like me. I'm a Daughter, as well."

Daphne smiled in return. "Exactly. My particular gift is hearing the words of the Highest God. He guides these . . . uh . . . men through me."

Ari cleared his throat. "So, not to rush you or anything, my lady, but how's this gonna go down? I'm . . . well, I want to know if you think she's the real deal or not."

"Eager, are you?" Daphne teased, recalling Ajax's description of Ari's intense resistance to Juliana.

Ari glanced away, looking sheepish. "I need to know who she is."

"Oh, but I believe you already do know." Daphne settled into one of the chairs facing Leo's desk. "Still, expediency is a good plan."

"You're ready?" Leo asked gently, facing her. He, more than any of the Spartans, realized the great toll her prophesying always demanded, both physically and emotionally. By positioning himself so close, he was offering his own protection and strength.

She smiled at him gratefully, closing her eyes. "I shall begin."

At once, a great force began pulling at her, dragging her under as if she'd been caught beneath a massive wave. She felt herself tumbling, falling into a whirlwind, and rose into it, standing tall and reaching out her arms.

Suspended before her, she could see golden, shimmering words. With both hands, she outlined the letters, true joy filling her being.

"Juliana Tiades lives again," she said, speaking the words beneath her fingertips. "She is good, not evil. Her soul lives forever; her body lives anew."

She swayed on her feet, feeling weaker, and then strong arms rescued her. *Leonidas, my love*, she thought, and the words she'd been touching were gone. She tried to open her eyes, leaning into the king, but that dragging darkness pulled her farther down.

Then a second prophecy materialized, a more threatening one, and the words gleamed like a banner all around her.

Slowly, she began translating the message. "The Daughters of Delphi must gather . . ."

Ari strode to the window of Leonidas's study, bracing his hands against the dark wooden frame. Books towered to the ceiling, and he wished only to find some answer on those pages. Correction: an answer he liked.

"Aristos, the words come from the Highest himself, and He has verified that Juliana is, indeed, the woman you knew and loved," the Oracle's musical voice reminded him. He heard a smile in her tone.

Well, she might have thought she brought jolly, happy tidings of love, but he sure as hell didn't feel that way. No, he didn't feel like rejoicing at all.

The first part of their Oracle's declaration validated Juliana. It was the second portion that had been his undoing, stealing away every bit of life that she'd just breathed back into him. In its place, he'd inhaled bone-deep fear. Fear that Shay, with her training as a Deadly Nightshade, would declare Juliana as inauthentic, a demon from the darkest pit.

And no emotion contradicted his Spartan training and discipline more than fear. Which was why he'd separated from the group after Daphne finished her pronouncements. She'd stared up at him expectantly, with that damned joyous little gleam in her elfin eyes, but he'd said nothing. Just walked to the window where he now stood so he could get his shaking body back under his own command.

He continued staring outside now, searching for some answer, some sign, but the storm clouds concealed the moon. He glimpsed nothing except the vaguest outline of the far fence and stables. Pattering rain streaked the dusty glass, the long, dry winds suddenly done. "This tropical storm might get ugly in the next few days," he observed.

"It's tracking off the coast, not hitting shore," Leonidas told him. "But that's not our concern right now. Our Oracle has spoken; have you no response for our lady?"

Ari dropped his head forward, ashamed. He caught the rebuke in the king's words, and he'd earned it. Slowly he turned, facing the others. Leonidas leaned against the edge of his desk, watching him, the Oracle at his side. Juliana remained in the far corner, positioned against the bookshelves with a weary, resigned posture. She had to be exhausted by now.

He gave her a rueful smile. *I believe now. I know who you are.* He did his level best to convey that with his eyes.

She stood taller in immediate reaction, as if energized by his show of faith.

The Oracle twisted a lock of cobalt blue hair around her finger, studying him. "Aristos Petrakos, for many years your younger brother was my only link with all of you. Only he could see or communicate with me—and he is a dear, beloved friend, but he's never been easy." She cast a smile toward his younger brother, who gave a light bow in return.

"And it seems," she continued, facing him again, "that you aren't making this moment easy, either. None of you Petrakos brothers *are* easy, I suppose. Well, except on the eyes, right?"

She waggled her brows conspiratorially toward Juliana. Then, as if remembering herself, she turned to their king with a wide-eyed, caught-in-the-act-of-ogling expression. "My apologies, sir," she blurted, but Ari noticed that Leonidas hardly seemed mollified. In fact, he appeared . . . miffed.

The Old Man never got annoyed at their Oracle, not that Ari'd ever seen. She always seemed to have their commander wrapped about her pinky.

"So, anyhow," she continued dramatically. "My point, Aristos, is that Juliana Tiades"—she walked toward the corner and, looping an arm through Juliana's, led her forward—"is not a demon at all. She's the woman you have always loved."

Daphne smiled up at him, motioning him closer to Jules. "Go on! Take her hand. Show some affection, now!"

Ari smiled at Juliana, almost ready to reach for her. Then he froze, dropping his hand to his side.

"Aristos!" Daphne chastised sharply. "This is not the way to treat one's lady love! You heard my prophecy; you know that the Highest God is blessing your relationship."

"I heard the words." He struggled to avoid Juliana's stare. "But, Oracle, you are our guide. You have always ordered our steps with your words," he argued, hating the way his heart hammered wildly, the trickle of sweat he felt along the side of his neck. "If you say she is legitimate, isn't that enough?"

She gave him a kind, sympathetic smile. "In this instance, my own word is not enough. We must hear from Shay, Emma, and Sophie."

He closed his eyes, the words stampeding through his mind all over again. Daphne had begun in a whisper, swaying back and forth on her booted feet. "The Daughters of Delphi must gather," she'd proclaimed. But then she'd wavered physically, almost as if the words were too intense to be spoken. For a moment, he'd even thought she was going to faint, but Leonidas had been at her side instantly. She'd leaned into him, eyes closed, still caught in her trance.

"I have you, Oracle," Leo had murmured reassuringly. "You are safe with me."

The Oracle had released a high-pitched, eerie cry then, one that made the hair on Ari's nape prickle. "The Daughters of Delphi will separate the wheat from the chaff, ordain the truth. Proclaim Juliana Tiades' nature to be true," she'd murmured in a disembodied voice. "Gather the Daughters. . . . Gather them tonight. In truth there is freedom from the curse of lies and uncertainty. The promise of eternity, of walking in light. The Daughters of Delphi must gather, must proclaim her innocence, and grant freedom . . . or destroy the evil."

They were to declare her innocence or destroy her as a demon? Which one was it?

He'd practically shouted those questions, but then Daphne herself had returned, half collapsing against Leonidas. Leonidas had lifted a bowl of water to the Oracle's lips, very gently.

"Our lady's gift always takes such a toll on her," Leonidas had explained, still holding the drink to her mouth.

"Not to be impolite, sir," Juliana had asked quietly, "but why does your Oracle guide you in all things?"

Leo had turned to Ari in question then. "How much did you tell Juliana . . . before?"

Ari just shook his head. He'd willed their leader to hear his mind, transmitting one phrase: *She knows nothing.*

"No idea about what we are?" their king pressed.

Juliana shook her head, too, obviously frustrated. "Which, gentlemen, seems most unfair, as it appears that you're trying to decide whether to allow me to stay, instead of . . . well, I don't know what you do with demons, but I don't imagine it's very pleasant."

Ari was thankful when nobody even tried to answer. He'd be the one to explain the facts to Jules—no matter which way this evaluation went down. Good gods, he thought, it was like some medieval virginity test, with Jules needing to prove the purity of her spirit and soul.

Juliana spoke after a long, awkward moment. "I told you I'm the one you loved. . . ." Slowly she lifted her eyes, looking at him. Into him, it felt like. "And the one who always loved you."

As if he didn't already feel like a total jerk for how he'd been treating her tonight.

"It's not just on me to decide," he explained lamely. "It affects a lot of people, and . . . yeah, this isn't my call."

"Quite obviously, sir." She stood even taller, maintaining an air of dignity and grace.

He hated himself in that moment, that he hadn't stepped up to the plate on her behalf from the get-go.

Her hair had come loose about her face, and those disheveled tendrils made her appear only more vulnerable. He reached and, very carefully, as gently as possible, began repinning the loose curls. His hand grazed her ear, and she shivered, turning so that her cheek brushed against his palm.

"I'm sorry," he mumbled, and moved his hand away, but she'd have none of that. She seized his big palm, pressing it right up against her face. Closing her eyes, she savored that connection, breathing deeply as if finally being offered water after an endless drought.

"No, no, Aristos. I want to feel you. I need to do so," she said. "Until tonight I haven't been touched by anyone in so many years, and certainly not by you."

"How did you really find me? Come back to me?" That one question still nagged at him and couldn't be denied. "You indicated earlier that you made some sort of arrangement with a spiritual guide."

She glanced away, chewing on her lip. "I believe she was an angel. She wore glowing robes and was the most beautiful woman I've ever seen. Very kind. She had observed my many efforts and attempts at reaching you, the way I've hovered around the brownstone."

"An angel," he repeated, wondering why he'd not seen any such spiritual messengers outside her home earlier tonight. And thinking of all the times he'd prayed to the Highest God about his grief over losing Jules. Perhaps he had finally answered those supplications, which wasn't so hard to believe, not with the spiritual battles of good and evil he'd engaged in over the millennia, and not when Ari knew firsthand that angels were real.

"This angel gave you physical form again?" he asked, his mind whirling with questions.

She gazed up into his eyes. "I'm not sure how she did it, or knew how to send me to your side, but one moment I was . . ." She stared at the floor and in a quiet voice said, "A ghost. I was a ghost just as I've been since my death, and then . . . she transformed me." Jules lifted her hands, staring at her palms with wonder. "I was physical again, and then I was moving through this dark, whirling wind . . ." She hesitated, seeming to search for words. "More of a tunnel? I find it most difficult to describe, how the sensations felt."

"She teleported you," he explained, recognizing the process she sought to describe from firsthand experience, although with their Oracle and Ares, not an angel. "The angel sent you to my side."

She nodded, amazement in her eyes. "First, there was the sensation of being alive again, right there, standing on the cobblestones! And next, the darkness folded away and I found myself in your bedroom." A broad, radiant smile filled her face, her eyes growing bright with emotion. She took hold of his hand, squeezing it. "Aristos, I cannot tell you the joy I felt. My heart and soul triumphed, seeing you there in the bed, alive and real and waiting for—"

He didn't even let her finish; he reached out, folding her tightly within a bearlike embrace. Wanting to use his own brawny body as a shield against anything or anyone who might try to take her from him, ever again.

How she had died, why she'd drowned herself . . . There would be time to solve his questions. Later.

"I need you," he murmured against the top of her head. "I . . . God, I've loved you all these years, just couldn't stop, sweetheart."

"I waited for you—and you finally came back to me." Juliana buried her face against his chest, inhaling as if needing to verify for herself that he, too, was real and alive.

The rush of love and sensation he felt right then was so intense that for one delirious moment he actually forgot the second part of the prophecy. The one that indicated that Juliana would still need validation from the other Daughters.

Very slowly, he released her. "Look, we still need to hear from Shay and Emma and Sophie," he said, but the words sounded halfhearted even to himself.

She blinked back at him, finally turning away. It was all he could do not to pull her back into his arms—to hold her until time itself melted away.

Because he did believe. With his whole heart, he was now convinced that Juliana Tiades stood only a few feet away from him. And that was the problem. Because she'd broken him once before, and now? Feeling her heart beating against his chest, smelling that familiar aroma that belonged uniquely to her? He was falling for her all over again, and hard, because he'd never once stopped loving her. "Yeah . . . ," he said lamely. "Just need to hear what the Daughters all say."

Juliana inclined her head. "Of course, Aristos. I understand," she said, but her blue eyes became very sad, as if she'd sensed the true reason for his hesitation.

Daphne folded both arms over her chest and gave him the feminine once-over. Nothing like being sized up—and snickered at, albeit sweetly—by the Oracle of Delphi.

"What?" he demanded when she just kept on grinning at him with that knowing, goofy smile.

She waltzed across the room, working that leather mini like she expected to be noticed. And maybe she did, he thought, seeing the way the king's eyes flared, locked on her rolling hips like a laser beam. She crooked a finger, beckoning Ari to lean down to her much shorter height. He knew whatever was coming next was not going to make him proud of his actions tonight; nor was it going to be gentle on his ego.

She reached up onto her toes, pressing her mouth against his ear. "I thought you were angry with her. That you couldn't forgive her for dying? And then *that* embrace? Whoa! Smokin'!" She dropped her voice confessionally, eyes sparkling. "Too bad you chickened out."

She was gloating! Their mystical guide, their own prophetess was . . . mocking him.

After reading either his thoughts, or maybe just his indignant body language, she disagreed. "I'm merely egging you toward . . ." She tapped her chin with her forefinger. "Well, let's call it appropriate, gentlemanly action in regards to Juliana."

"Holding her in my arms isn't gentlemanly?"

"Sure, but letting her go that abruptly wasn't." She sighed, shaking her head. "It seems you need a little kick in the buckaroo there, Aristos, considering you're still mentally ranting at her for that one teensy, tiny issue of her death."

He sputtered back at her, embarrassed. "How'd you . . . You can't know that. I didn't say that in front of you or tell you that."

Yeah, as if you stood a chance arguing with the *Oracle of Delphi, who naturally knew all the mysteries of the universe, and your own private mind.*

The woman only laughed, tugging on her faded Oingo Boingo T-shirt. "When I prophesy, I hear lots of things, Ari. I always have."

He could think of "lots of things" he'd rather she not see or hear from inside his mind. Since, of course, it wasn't exactly like he'd had a girlfriend or lover for the past hundred years or so. During a drought that long, there were certain matters you learned to take into your own hands. And often. But that didn't mean you wanted your Oracle glimpsing you in the shower, going to town solo, wishing you had a real woman instead of just your fantasies.

He shook off the embarrassing thought, frowning at a much more real one. "And if Shay or Em or Sophie declare her a demon after all? What then?" Ari flashed on a horrific image: of the Shades taking out Jules like one of their darkest, vilest prey. "Can't you see my hesitation?"

Daphne leaned close again, kissing his cheek. "You have such a huge heart, Ari. Release your fear, and don't worry. The Daughters will concur with my words."

"If you're so sure, then why do you need them?"

"Oh, I don't need them at all. That was the Highest God's instruction." She stroked a long lock of hair back from his face, as tender as a sister or a mother. "Because without them, *you* won't fully believe. There will always be hidden doubt, a place you'll hold back from Juliana, as you did just moments ago."

"You're saying . . ."

She placed a warm hand along the back of his neck, whispering in his ear once more. "You need their validation so *you* can trust again. Your love for Juliana will be tested greatly. I'm so sorry, Ari, but I saw that it will. The Daughters' words will give you strength in the oncoming trial."

He didn't want a trial, not about his feelings for Juliana. Wasn't holding on to his love for her, clinging to it, raging against it—and for more than a damned century—enough of an ordeal? Didn't that qualify as the trial to end any and all *future* ones?

Turning the tables, he pressed his own mouth to their Oracle's ear. "I love her. That should be good enough."

No answer came at all; the fey prophetess only smiled and, oddly, looked at King Leonidas as if that glance were an explanation all its own.

Chapter 13

Eros reached into his quiver, retrieving the captain of his arsenal, Karanos. Immediately the arrow grew hot within his hand—apparently as eager to be back in the trenches as Eros himself was.

Eros kept himself concealed with his god's glamour, watching the unfolding discussion as if it were one of Aristophanes' great plays. He positioned the projectile neatly in his bow, firmly concealed in the corner of King Leonidas's study.

Captain Karanos nearly scalded his palm, making one point very clear: He was ready for battle. Eros patted the warrior, wondering, as he often did, how bold that man must have been when engaged in ancient warfare.

The arrow spun in his grasp, aimed right for Leonidas. The king stood beside his desk, quietly listening, hands clasped behind his back.

"Leonidas?" Eros asked Karanos in surprise. "You wish me to use you against the great king of Sparta?"

Although such an aim would certainly complement Eros's current mission, it was unnecessary. The leader's body was surrounded by a crimson aura, a glow that appeared only when a man had become blindingly intoxicated by love.

Pity, Eros thought, *that I'm not the one who served the elixir to him.*

"He loves without aid of our aim, old friend," Eros told the agitated arrow in his grasp, but Karanos only continued his desperate vibrating, eager for attention.

Suddenly, Eros had a thought, "Are you telling me, brave captain of mine, that you are a Spartan? That Leonidas was your own king?"

At once the arrow grew so hot, he could barely hold it in his palm.

Their long-standing mystery, solved! His arsenal was not comprised of common Greek soldiers as he'd always guessed, but the greatest warriors of all time. Perhaps his army had even fought in phalanx formation beside these very same Spartans, the ones his father now sought to destroy.

"Karanos, if I use you in this battle, know that your arrow shall not bring death," he reassured the arrow, "but it will bring mayhem and chaos. That is my father's plan. Do you understand? I would not ask you to battle your own people. If I must, I will seek another weapon for the coming weeks."

The arrow bristled within his palm, clearly affronted. Eros smiled. "Ah, you are a military man to the core. Duty and honor above all else."

Karanos offered no answer, so Eros returned him to the quiver, listening closely to the conversation unfolding in Leonidas's study.

Slowly, Eros smiled. *Yes.* The Daughters were approving Juliana. They believed her intentions to be pure.

"She's not a demon," he heard the one called Shay Angel say. "But what about Mason's reaction? That should be considered, don't you think?"

Eros frowned sharply, adjusting his tunic. *That* was a complication he could not abide—Shay relying on Mason or considering him a credible authority. What better way to create discord than by turning brother against brother, lover against beloved, and friend against friend. Still, the plan didn't sit well with him. It went against his calling, violated it . . . except he knew it would earn his father's care and respect. For that reason alone, he'd undertaken this mission; for that reason entirely, he was determined to complete it.

Eros reached into his second quiver, the one where he kept a set of female arrows, the chief of whom—a onetime witch—was named Eris. *Confusion.* She was as subtle and coy with her movements as Karanos was strategic. As he cradled her arrow, Eros felt a sensual trembling against his palm. She had always stirred him oddly, he thought, frowning in reaction.

With a whistling shot through the air, the weapon nailed Shay in the arm.

The woman never felt a thing. Although she did pause, staring into space for a moment before continuing. "Mason . . . hasn't been himself for a while now," she said, answering her own question.

Eros's heart grew heavy as he recalled how deeply Mason Angel had once loved. He felt guilty, too, for using that love as a weapon against the human now. Eros's mission and gift was to create love, not use it to cause destruction and heartbreak, especially not in an instance where he himself had worked so hard to fan those flames. Kelly's love, too, had been pure. Yes, he frowned, realizing the compromise this situation represented to his calling.

Still, his ultimate purpose here did involve love spelling and drawing hearts together, he reminded himself. That was the nature of the compact he'd forged with his father. And if working his magic happened to create confusion? Disunity? Eros shrugged the concerns away.

After all, he was the one who'd originally penned the phrase "Make love, not war," so it made sense that he'd serve his father's violent cause by applying his own unique skills. Still, he hated the stab of uncertainty he felt as he glanced between Aristos and Juliana.

He could see the heavy webs of crimson and gold that tangled invisibly between their souls. They were knit together—so tightly that not even death or time had severed those rare tethers.

He frowned as more discussion ensued about Juliana's identity. It was imperative that they declare her legitimate, and he stepped forward, withdrawing the arrow of confusion from Shay's arm.

Don't ask; don't contemplate . . . , he urged, lifting a powerful hand and sprinkling Olympian dust among them all. Even Leonidas blinked, rubbing his eyes. *Don't wonder how she's come back*, he urged the king and those he guided.

Under the influence of his magic, Shay Angel and her cousins all nodded. "She is legitimate. She's the woman you loved, Ari."

But convincing the Daughters was only one part of his task here tonight, and Eros knew it. He raised the arrow of confusion, pricking it between the warrior's shoulder blades. Ari's back muscles gave a spasm, and he began rubbing his right shoulder with a frown, seeming surprised by the sudden pain.

Eros strolled to Leonidas next, repeating the action; the king swatted his arm as if stung by a bee, nothing more. One by one, he wove the toxin among the entire group, until they were fully assured of Juliana's authenticity, welcoming her into their midst with hugs and warm embraces. They were so carried away, in fact, that not one of them thought to ask the most obvious question of all.

Why, precisely, would an angel have resurrected Juliana Tiades from the dead?

"So, what happens now?" Juliana asked softly, leaning against the edge of Leonidas's desk. The rest of the crew had cleared out, giving them a few minutes alone.

Ari raked a hand over his brow. Despite the healing he'd experienced, he still felt weak and unsteady and was glad Jax had volunteered to wait right outside Leo's study. "God, Juliana. I have so many questions and thoughts, I honestly don't know where to begin. What am I gonna do with you now?"

She chewed on her lip. "I'd rather hoped I'd be able to stay here, with you. With the others."

"Jules, of course," he reassured her, and hated the genuine relief he saw in her eyes.

"Thank you, sir," she breathed on a sigh. "Thank you."

"I'd always protect you—you should know that. Always make sure you're safe and cared for." He reached a hand to stroke a loose curling tendril, the auburn burnished beneath the lamplight. "And, gods above, you're still so damned beautiful. This hair of yours, the way it changes colors depending on the light—seeing that always stole my breath."

She moved closer, sidling her hip right against his on the desk's edge. "Everything about you always aroused me. I was so eager to become your lover that night. That's why I want to finally join with you, to share what we were denied before."

He gulped. "Join . . . with me?"

She smiled, such a joyful thing that he felt as if his heart might burst. "Yes, Ari, I want us to become lovers."

Lovers. Not wall-bumping, mindless sex, not palming himself in the dead of night, not even hooking up with some girl at a bar. Had any female ever truly touched his body and loved him? His wife's affection had been a duty. Only Juliana Tiades had ever kissed him as if she meant to take his very soul inside her own.

Lovers. In love, beloved, loving, giving . . . The words played like some tinny, late-night AM radio station echoing inside his head.

She extended a pale, regal hand toward him. "Tonight. I am ready and far more than willing, Aristos. You need only make your move to take me. Shall we return to your bed?"

Not a day had passed, much less a year, when he'd not grieved—all the while naming himself a fool among all men for still loving Juliana Tiades. No wonder his heart now thundered with long-denied hope. "Are you saying that you . . . you really did want me? That you weren't horrified by my wings that night? You . . . desired me?"

She sighed, smiling broadly. "Oh, yes, I wanted you that night, Ari." She had rarely called him by his nickname, the one all his Spartan brothers used. And when she did, she always said it a little huskier than his full name, adding a slightly seductive timbre. As if they were sharing some very intimate secret.

"*Ari,*" she said, "you have no idea how desperately I craved you."

"No, when I came to your balcony," he tried arguing again, determined to resist her. "That look in your eyes . . . it couldn't have been a lie."

"You are incorrect regarding that night's events." She tilted her head upward, meeting his gaze boldly. "And you should know the truth. That I waited in my room until midnight, just as we'd planned. The hours seemed endless, the clock frozen in its progression. I waited and my body burned, terribly . . . so hot all over, so tight until I"— she dropped her voice confessionally, leaning even closer against him—"touched myself."

She took hold of his hand, sliding it down her belly with a significant look, and he felt his groin draw as tight as a bow in reaction to the heat in her gaze and words. "I imagined you touching me with this large, calloused hand of yours," she explained in a low voice. "How it would feel against my skin. I knew there would be a contrast, your roughness . . . My own body was never caressed. Never . . . explored."

She pressed his palm even lower down along her abdomen. "I imagined your fingers, felt them sliding beneath my lingerie. How you would be such a gentleman, yet work at the satin and lace to free me."

He groaned, staring at the carpeted floor, but damn the woman, she kept on. And the erection he'd developed only grew thicker with every word. He shifted his hips against the desk, but the motion seemed only to intensify the tight discomfort of his pants.

"I was clad in pale pink for you, Ari," she whispered. "I'd sent my maid on a special errand, a forbidden one, so that I'd be perfect, a gift that no one else, no man except for you would ever open."

Open. She'd wanted him to open her. The full ramifications of that knowledge hit him like an enemy's bronze shield, slammed him full force with stark, startling reality. He gulped hard, feeling the warmth of her soft abdomen beneath his hand, imagining the wet heat that wasn't much lower. They were separated by her gown, chaperoned by nothing except her own era's fashion.

"Yes," she continued on a sigh, "I wanted your hand touching me here . . . moving between my legs."

He was frozen. Awakened. She urged his hand slightly lower, the expensive linen of her dress shockingly smooth beneath his coarse, awkward touch.

No, he couldn't do this; such behavior was too ungentlemanly with someone like Juliana Tiades. He yanked his hand free, but then she was up close, like a purring, sultry feline, brushing against him without any reluctance. She began stroking his chest, fingertips working against both his nipples, abrading them through the thin cotton of his T-shirt until they beaded beneath the caress.

He moaned an involuntary response, arching slightly, as one of those mercenary hands slid down, coasting across his hard, muscled abdomen, aiming even lower. He bit back a cry as her elegant, graceful fingertips stroked between his thighs. She rubbed, long and slow, back and forth, teasing his thick erection; he braced against the desk, eyes closed. "What . . . are you doing to me, Jules?"

"This," she whispered, leaning up and pressing her mouth against his ear, "was what I needed. *All* of you, Ari."

His name, said in a breathless, husky way. *So fucking arousing.*

He forced himself to open his eyes, to fight this drowning tide, but her gaze was fixed on him, as self-assured and determined as that of any soldier. She would not accept defeat, not in this battle, and his ramparts were overrun.

He was utterly destroyed because he could not pull away, and this woman had broken him the last time they'd held each other this way. That pain had never subsided, but he had no ability to fight this tide she'd already unleashed inside of him.

He didn't have a hope of resurrecting even a frayed shred of discipline against the woman before him. He simply did not possess the strength of will that such resistance required; his Spartan resolve meant nothing as she rose onto her toes and he caught the sweet scent of her skin and hair. Jasmine again.

She's always been the scent of a Savannah garden.

Alive. She is totally alive. There's not the aroma of death or Hades on this woman. I have always loved her; she should be mine.

But she'd never been his, not really. He sagged against the desk and ground his teeth together with an agonized moan. He could not want this, could not hope that she'd returned to him out of love and the desire to be with him.

She had drowned herself in a river out of that "love," and he wouldn't open his heart again—not like this.

She kept stroking his jaw, seemingly oblivious to his internal battle.

"Juliana, no," he groaned. "This is too much for me. Too soon . . ."

But her lips were already so close to his, already opening, covering his mouth. *No*, he thought again, even as his large arms folded her flush against his body. He was helpless, caught in her thrall as if she had spun a literal web about him. That pull of hers was palpable, and even his thoughts felt muddied and unsure in the wake of her actions, and his physical and emotional *reactions* to her return.

Her mouth brushed over his like a whisper, and he felt elegant fingers slide along his scalp, fanning his long hair away from his cheek. Time dissolved, and he was back in her drawing room, back to her settee and the very first time they'd kissed. His hair had been shorter then, but he'd dared to wear it a bit longer than current fashion, combing it back from his forehead. As they'd come together, wrapped in each others' arms, she'd playfully disheveled it as if *he* were the woman and she the man.

That delirious, head-swimming rush of kissing her was no longer a bittersweet memory, but an overwhelmingly current sensation. And, all at once, he was no longer a Victorian-era gentleman. He morphed into something much more dangerous, becoming simultaneously an ancient warrior and a modern man, possessing both impulses in one body.

"Juliana," he growled, low in the back of his throat, opening his eyes again so that he could see her clearly. He moved them against the wall of Leo's study. Pinning her there, framing her between his splayed palms, he stared at her for a long, breathless moment.

"Take me, Ari." She looked up at him, those pale eyes darker than he'd ever seen them. "I must feel you . . . inside of me. I need to know that I am truly alive, I need your touch, your body to confirm it."

"We *need* more privacy," he groaned, feeling a rush of pleasure race from his pounding chest, right to his hardened cock.

"I locked the door when the others left," she told him, a daring gleam in her eyes. "I knew what I wanted."

He swallowed hard, trailing a tentative finger along another tendril of auburn hair that had come loose, feeling it. "Like silk. And the color . . . like jewels. I always thought that."

She was no illusion; she was his. Real, strong, still pure . . . for now.

His black jeans grew uncomfortably tight as his cock pressed outward against the zipper. Without questioning, he found his fly, popping the button free, and she finished the job, very gently lowering the zipper. As she did so, her knuckles grazed his hard-on, causing him to gasp at the intimate contact. For one very brief moment, she stroked him through the opening in his jeans, brushing the soft cotton of his boxers against his heated flesh.

Panting heavily, he leaned into the wall. Keeping his eyes closed, he forced himself to forget the doubts, which proved shockingly easy as she pressed his pants all the way open, sliding one hand along his length.

"Oh . . . shit, Jules," he murmured. "That feels good."

Too damned good, a tiny voice reminded him as he moved his hips forward, thrusting slightly in reaction to her caress. *Dangerous to your heart, your sanity.*

"Yes, feels very good," she agreed on a sigh. "Your manhood is so warm. Even through this cotton, I can't believe how . . . alive it feels."

"It's . . . me. Part of me," he explained, dropping his head forward. He kept his eyes shut but felt the tickle of his long hair fall across his face. He caught her wrist with a groan, reaching for some remnant of self-control. "Jules . . . stop."

"Why?" Her voice was quiet, confused.

He forced his eyes open, panting roughly. Drawing in hot, ragged breaths. "Because you're a virgin," he replied softly. "I can't take advantage . . ."

She smiled at him, lovely eyes narrowing. "It's not taking advantage when I'm asking, Aristos."

With a toss of his head, he flung his hair out of his face. "I have to be honorable, no matter how bad we want to get right to it," he said at last.

She reached a shaky hand to his cheek, resting it there with steadfast reassurance. "I know what I want. What I always wanted. You were coming to me for this"—she paused, sliding her other hand low along his right hip— "that night. We've waited far too long."

"But are you sure?" he asked, searching her face. "About me . . . about . . . ?" Damn, it was the twenty-first century, but his once-adopted Victorian sensibilities had him blushing and stammering like a freak show. "Certain about making love?"

She stepped back and, reaching behind her neck, began unfastening the top buttons of her dress. The heat and invitation in her long stare as she did so were unmistakable. "I want to finish what never should have been taken from us."

Her body was burning. With the full return of physical sensation, and being so near Aristos, a driving need had overtaken Juliana. She'd never experienced anything so rough and sexual when she was alive. Alive the first time, she corrected herself, as she stared up at the large, gorgeous Greek man in front of her.

He had changed, his hair long to his shoulders, his body more muscular. He'd always been tremendous, larger than any other man she'd met, but now he seemed more gorgeously defined, in every part of his frame. Broader shoulders, thicker chest, stronger thighs.

And where she'd just touched him, well, she'd never been privy to that part before, but it certainly felt shockingly large. Were all men endowed thusly, with a member that she could not even accommodate with the full length of her palm? Surely the Adonis before her was unique in that way as well. She shivered, imagining how her own virginal body might accommodate such length and thickness, but kept on unfastening the buttons of her dress.

If she wavered, she might lose him, at least in this matter tonight. He'd been too hurt by her death, by his false assumption that she'd turned away from what he was. His heart was in a vulnerable place regarding her return, and the only way to convince him of her true feelings was by giving her body to him. Of that she was certain. And the hooded, ravenous look in his dark eyes—the flush upon his swarthy cheeks—they revealed his desire. And his own love for her.

His black eyes narrowed, and he pushed off the wall, growling low in the back of his throat. It was a threatening sound, a possessive one as he stalked closer. She shivered and then stood taller, dropping her hands to her sides. She couldn't reach the other buttons; Ari would have to unfasten them. Ari would undress her, unravel her, deflower her, she thought, swallowing hard in anticipation.

One look and she saw that he remained powerfully aroused, his thick erection having worked its way out of his undergarments, revealing its dark-skinned, very male reality. Flushing, he began arranging himself, fumbling with his zipper. "I want you, Juliana, same as ever, as much as ever. But I can't go this fast. I have too many questions, fears. I have a lot to figure out . . . and you deserve to be treated like a lady."

"I don't care about that!" she cried. "All I want is for

you to understand how much I love you. That I never stopped."

Ari looked away, such pain and remorse in his dark eyes that she had to stifle a cry. "I want to believe that."

She put her arms around him, holding tight. "Why would I have possibly left you willingly?"

He said nothing and slowly released her. "That's what I've gotta figure out."

Releasing a weary sigh, his big fingers moved to the collar of her dress, working at the buttons awkwardly. She felt the rough calluses on the pads of his fingers briefly, and ached for those hands to move beneath the dress's fabric, to find their way to her hips, to trace the length of her backbone. She sighed softly, swaying back into him, but he only gave her collar a tug, finishing the buttons. Instead of his embrace, or the heat of his breath against her exposed nape, there was only the tight, confining strictures of her gown, and the corset underneath.

"Come on," he said with a rueful smile. "Let's see if Emma can't find you a room around this place."

Chapter 14

Nikos had offered to drive Mason home since he didn't have his own car at the compound. They'd headed downtown first, grabbing a few beers at one of Savannah's oldest establishments, Pinkie Masters. The thick smoke and loud country music had provided good cover for Mason's introverted mood. Sometimes the man just needed to keep one foot in the normal realm, and Nik understood that.

In fact, he understood a lot about Mason Angel, including the memories that lived behind his pensive green eyes. Distraction was always the order of the day when Mason's past proved too much, even if it meant hanging together in silence. As a Spartan, Nik wasn't threatened by quiet; perhaps that was the reason Mason felt so comfortable around him.

They rode in silence now, Mason staring out the window, Nikos desperate for something—anything at all—to say or do to provide continued distraction. His mind grasped at the possibilities. Take Mace on a walk down his family's mile-long driveway; get him to put on the DVD of *Aliens* ... again. Hell, he'd do anything if it kept Mason from retreating into the dark place that had seized him earlier tonight, especially since that thousand-yard stare had finally vanished from his eyes after the past six months.

Mason had finally confessed the real source of that sad, distant expression in August, the admission changing the stakes between them permanently. Mason had let Nik behind the wire, admitting what even his own siblings didn't know: that he'd lost his lover while serving his final tour in Iraq. Not to an IED or sniper attack, but to the worse kind of insurgency—a supernatural one.

Sergeant Kelly O'Connell had been slain by a female Djinn, one who'd lusted after Mason during his deployment. When she realized that Mason wasn't attracted to females at all, particularly not those of the demonic variety, she revealed herself for what she truly was: a grotesque, devouring creature. Then she'd attacked Kelly as payback, leaving him to die in Mason's arms.

That had been the beginning of the pain—the charade that followed perhaps even worse. In the "Don't Ask, Don't Tell" military, Mason had pretended that Kelly was only his good buddy, another of their fellow marines lost to the war. That grief, Nikos knew, had been eating Mace apart for almost a year.

At least that demon had done her work on Kelly swiftly. Watching Mason struggle with his secrets and pain, still refusing to tell his siblings about that loss, or his sexual orientation, was excruciatingly slow torture. Sometimes Nik fantasized about carting Shay and Jamie off to the beach, confessing everything they didn't know about their beautiful, fierce brother. In fact, if he'd thought Mason's survival depended upon that kind of betrayal, he might actually have done it.

Except lately, the light had appeared in Mason's eyes again, for the first time since Nikos had known him. Shay had seen it, too, remarking that Nikos alone had been able to reach him. Such a bond was natural between fellow warriors, he'd tried telling her at the time—right after he'd saved Mason's leg, maybe his life, in a wicked demon battle.

She'd dismissed his denials, insisting that Nikos had a special way with the man; she'd seen it herself. That comment had returned to him in the past months, making him wonder whether Shay suspected just *how* attached he'd become to her big brother—or that he'd never wanted a woman in his entire life. He'd given Sparta a son out of duty and had lost his one true love at Thermopylae, just as Mason had lost Kelly in Iraq. There was a bond between them, all right, just not the kind he'd confess to anyone.

"Thanks for tonight," Mason said quietly, the sudden words causing Nik to jolt. They'd been riding in silence for miles. It was a good thirty minutes back to the Angel plantation from the city, and they were almost there.

"It was nothing," Nikos told him with a shrug. "Not a big deal, seriously."

"That's not true." Mason's husky-deep voice was as sultry as ever. "I needed you tonight, Nik. And you were right there for me. Thanks, man."

Nikos swallowed, eyes firmly fixed on the road. *I needed you.* He blinked, feeling his body tighten. *I needed you.*

Mason slung an arm over the back of Nikos's seat, a painful proximity. "You talked me down earlier," he continued. "I don't know how you always manage to neutralize my craziness, but you do."

"I've spent my time in the trenches. We speak the same language because of that. Have the same values."

"The marines worship the Spartans. You do know that, right?" Mason laughed. "They'd shit themselves if they knew how tight I hang with you now."

"Perhaps you should invite them for a day of training with Leonidas," Nik suggested with the straightest face he could manage.

Mason rolled his eyes. "Any idea how many of my buddies got lambda tattoos because they wanted to identify with your homeland? They chose the Lacedaemon symbol instead of wearing Spartan crimson into battle, I guess."

"Too bad," Nikos said. "Good for mopping up your enemy's blood."

"You'd make a perfect marine, Nikos. But sometimes I wonder how bad I'd have sucked as a Spartan. Leonidas would've probably booted me out of town."

Nik cast him a glance. "You were a captain in the corps. That didn't happen by accident, Mace. And you weren't even thirty? Isn't that quick advancement?"

Mason lolled his head against the seat, dropping his arm back down. "Somewhere along the way, I lost it. My mind, my ability to deal with shit. You saw me tonight. You saw how I reacted to that creature. And I'm telling you, she is a demon. You believe me, right, Nik? She's not human, and if Ari and everyone else tries to tell me she is, that's gonna be a big problem. I know demons. I've got the sight; I've had it most of my life, and the look in that thing's eyes was brutal. Vicious. Starved. I've seen it before . . ."

"In Iraq," Nik finished for him.

Mason glanced away, tracing a pattern on the window. "For only a moment, like a flash of lightning . . . but it was exactly the way that female Djinn looked at me back in the desert." Mason shivered slightly beside him. "Ari better be careful if they don't take her on out tonight, man. I'm serious. You should call him and check." Mason rooted around between them, producing his own Black-Berry, and then tried to hand it to Nik. "Call him now. Make sure they're gonna off the little bitch." He gave the phone a shake.

Mason was desperate, Nikos realized. And desperate, anxious Mason—the erratic bursts of energy and chatti-ness as opposed to his usual pensive quiet when upset—was more unsettling than any of those lost-eyed looks.

Nik made a turn onto the Isle of Hope, thankful they were almost to the plantation. There were probably only two or three minutes left; then he could put the car in park and give Mason his full attention.

Mace waved the phone again. "You gonna call Ari or what, man?"

"Let's get to your place first. Then we can talk."

"Shit, just the thought of being in that drafty old house is more than creepy after tonight." Then Mason brightened, lifting an eyebrow. "I should've offed that little demon my-self and then just crashed with you."

Nik's breath hitched. "You could certainly have stayed the night with me." As soon as the words were past his lips, he realized that he'd murmured them like an invitation straight into his bedroom.

Mason tensed slightly beside him. It took a soldier to notice that slight change in another's breathing rate, the subtle shift in the way a man held himself. "I could've stayed the night, sure," Mason agreed evenly.

"I . . . No, I didn't mean . . . *Skata*, not that, Angel."

"I know exactly what you meant," he replied in that lazy-accented Southern voice of his. The one that felt like warm cider sliding down your throat on a frigid morning.

Mason shifted in the seat, slinging his left arm along the back of Nik's seat again.

Nik was keenly aware of the curling hairs along that forearm, the sexy gleam of his masculine wristwatch. *No, that's just a relaxed gesture between good friends. Between fighting partners.*

That litany worked for a few seconds, until he caught a glimpse of Mason's eyes. The distant, haunted expression from earlier was almost entirely gone—replaced by a furnace blast's worth of heat.

Nikos felt the flames of that fire reach his own face and stared straight ahead. "I only meant that you could have used one of the ten million sofas in that house as a rack."

"Ten million? That many, you think?" Mason drawled.

"At least ten, so there'd be somewhere for you to make your bed, I'm sure," Nikos stammered. "Next time, keep it in mind."

"Nah," Mason told him languidly, leaning just a little closer. "I think I would have preferred your room. After executing the she-demon, of course. Crashing with you would be some sweet dreaming after a mercy kill like that one."

"On my floor."

"Now, I can't see that working out, can you?" Mason laughed bemusedly. "I've slept on the hoods of Humvees, in sand-filled tents, and in dug out snow caves. But your floor, Nikos? Not doing it."

"It is carpeted."

"That is beside the much larger point, my friend."

To that, Nikos could think of absolutely nothing to say, besides the fact that he wasn't sure whether Mason was simply joking around. Nik got his answer as he made the final turn onto the plantation's main drive.

"This heat between us," Mason murmured with a slow shake of his head. "It just never goes away, does it?"

Nik pulled the Mountaineer onto the side of the drive. He parked it and cut the engine, turning toward Mason. The world around them formed a cocoon of pure blackness, with the live oaks along the drive swaying in the stormy wind. The only illumination between them was the dashboard clock light, its pale green allowing him to see Mason's eyes and face. Myriad emotions were in that expression. Longing, a little bit of flirtation, and humor. But the never-ending sadness still lurked there, too. That lonely look was suddenly something Nik longed to kiss far, far away.

He reached, sliding a hand along Mason's nape, and moved closer, angling for that very kiss.

"Don't, Nikos." Mason broke the slow-motion spell by ducking sideways at the last moment.

Nik found himself cozying up to the leather of Mason's seat, feeling like an utter idiot. He shoved off of it, retreating to his corner of the car, face blazing hot. "Fuck that."

"I don't . . . I shouldn't have taken things so far," Mason said earnestly. "I'm sorry, man. Really sorry."

Nik launched into ancient Greek, furiously embarrassed, horny as a teenager, and outright frustrated. He railed at himself with a barrage of brutal self-talk: What an idiot he was for imagining that the tension between them signaled something deeper. That he was especially moronic if he thought kissing his close friend was a smart move.

Mason watched, looking increasingly uncomfortable, then finally told Nik to "be silent," using ancient Greek himself. Nikos was so agitated that he'd momentarily forgotten about Mason's proficiency with his own native language, a talent earned from years of studying religious texts on demonology and lore.

"A couple of things," Mason told him, leaning back in the seat with a sigh. "First, you're not a moron, and you know it. In case you failed to notice—and I'm guessing that you didn't—I was flirting my ass off with you a few moments ago. And second? That heat between us that I mentioned? I think somebody just turned it up a few more notches."

Nik drummed his fingers on the steering wheel and said the only clear thought that came to mind. "All it would take is a kiss, Angel. Just one kiss."

Mace looked at him, his green eyes filled with curiosity and confusion. "You saying I better start putting out or you'll dump me?"

"I don't have you," Nikos blurted. "But I want you."

Mason broke their locked gaze, staring into his lap. "Just one kiss is all it would take for *what*?" His Southern accent was a little thicker, the words raspy as he whispered them.

Nikos reached his thumb to Mason's mouth, daring to touch him more intimately than ever before. Slowly he brushed the full, sensual swell of the man's lower lip, making it a caress. A declaration.

"Just one kiss from you, Mason Angel, and I'd belong to you completely."

Mason's lips parted slightly, his eyes drifting closed. "I'm afraid," he confessed in a whisper, eyes still shut. "Afraid to feel again. To feel . . . where you're leading me, day by day.

I can't fight it. Already I'm just so caught up in you, falling despite myself. Hating it, but unable to stay away."

Nikos took hold of Mason's chin, forcing him to look into his eyes. "Angel, I would never hurt you. I would do anything, everything in my power to protect you. With my body, my sword, my shield, my wings. I would die saving you."

Mason blinked back at him, eyes suddenly watering. "That's exactly how Kelly felt. And precisely what he did. I'm sorry, Nik, but losing one good man was enough for me."

"I'm not Kelly. He wasn't immortal," Nikos argued, holding Mason's chin even more firmly.

"You can still die, and I won't let another man I care about do that much for me. Sure as hell not you, Nik, because you've already managed to wind your way all around in here." Mason drew a circular pattern over his heart. "Despite how fucking scared I am, I've let you in. Almost all the way. But I'm not giving over that last part of me—especially not so you can die in my arms like he did."

Now it was Nikos's vision that suddenly blurred. "When it comes to my own feelings," he admitted, "I'm afraid I don't possess your obvious talent for restraint." He stared out his window, discreetly rubbing a hand over his face.

Mason's strong, warm hand brushed over his nape, a tender, quick gesture that only had Nik's eyes welling anew. "I just wanted you to understand why that one kiss can't . . . won't ever happen," Mason said; then he opened the car door and stepped into the night without ever looking back.

It was a long time before Nikos turned the key in the ignition and pulled away.

Chapter 15

"There's a guest room downstairs, off the recreation room," Emma volunteered, standing up from the couch and stretching. "We can fix it up for you."

She looked tired, Juliana thought. "Thank you, Emma. For being so kind to me. It's been quite a long night for you, as well. I know that . . . well, the way you opened to me earlier . . . Channeling me was exhausting, I'm certain."

Emma smiled, rubbing her eyes. "I tire easily lately. It's no big deal, honest."

Juliana didn't miss the flash of concern in River's eyes. "I'm hauling you off to bed, Em," he said, sliding a protective arm around her. "And making sure you sleep in extra tomorrow."

"Thank God it's a Saturday," she agreed.

Aristos had brought her to Emma, bidding them all good night. But then he'd turned back toward Juliana, his eyes lit with undisguised fire. "I will see you tomorrow, Jules. Sleep well. Sleep and be rested."

Exactly what he wanted her rested for, well, the way his long-lashed eyes flared and his lips parted indicated something both passionate and threatening. Despite the fact that he'd been the one to hesitate earlier, perhaps they would become lovers soon enough after all.

Juliana stood, smoothing out the front of her dress. Only then did she realize how rumpled she'd become, hating how half-askew she must appear. Her disheveled appearance was a direct result of being in Ari's arms earlier, and she blushed intensely, wondering whether the others had surmised as much.

"The guest suite's really cozy," Emma said. "I can loan you some pajamas and tomorrow—" She stopped, noticing Juliana's gown. "Some clothes. Modern ones. Although you're definitely taller than me, so I'm not sure how much I've got that'll work."

Shay laughed. "Well, don't look at me. I'm shorter than *you*, Em, so my stuff definitely won't fit."

Sophie clapped her hands together, pale eyes sparkling with mischief. "Shopping! I am a prophetess." She pressed a dramatic hand against her forehead, closing her eyes. "Yes, yes, I foresee a fabulous trip to Broughton Street tomorrow."

"Oh, Broughton Street! How delightful." Juliana's heart surged. "Shall we have tea at the Marshall House, as well?"

The other women stared at her blankly, and then Sophie laughed. "I was thinking Banana Republic, the Gap, and then mocha lattes at Starbucks."

Juliana laughed, too, not recognizing any of the strange words. "Well, we have Broughton Street in common. You will kindly tutor me as to the other terms in the morning?"

Sophie bounded to her feet and slid a hand through Juliana's arm. "You, my friend, are going to love twenty-first-century fashion. Trust me, you've come to the right time, and nobody does shopping like I do."

"Brother, you need to just accept the Daughters' and Oracle's verdict," Ajax said.

"I have." Ari collapsed onto his bed. His body felt as ancient as it truly was, even with Sophie's healing. Like it had been drained dry of energy. He lay back on the feather pillows with a groan.

But his younger brother was as dogged as ever, seemingly oblivious to his exhaustion. "Then why are you still asking these questions?" Jax persisted. "Trying to dissect the facts?"

"Because what about Mason and his reaction to Juliana?" Ari asked, thinking of the tough marine and his own opinion on the matter. "He thinks she's the spawn of Satan, and that scares the shit out of me. What if he tries to harm her? What if he can't be convinced? I don't want to have to throw down with Mace."

Jax's expression grew somber. "He's my brother-in-law. Shay adores him, but we both know who would win if you had to go up against Mason. I don't want it to come to that, ever, but I just don't see him as the individual axis of evil here. He'll come around."

Ari wasn't nearly so convinced; he'd seen that stark, terrified expression that had come over Mason. It was almost as if something bigger had been going on, even beyond the supernatural nature of the moment.

"Mace is my friend, but Jules . . ." Ari's voice drifted off. "Brother, I never told you about her, but she was my heart. She was my soul." He touched his chest. "If I have to choose between them, there's not a contest."

Ajax rubbed his jaw thoughtfully. "I ever tell you how close Mason and Shay used to be? Not that anyone should have a favorite brother, of course." Jax caught his eye playfully.

Ari grinned back. "Never. That would be wrong."

"And not that she doesn't love Jamie just as much . . . but with Mace, they've always had a unique bond. Until his last tour in Iraq. Things changed significantly between them when he got back. Ever since, he's stayed withdrawn from her and everyone else in his life."

Ari shook his head in disagreement. "Not from Nikos. They're thick as thieves. And you know what? Nik's gotten a helluva a lot more pleasant lately. I'm even getting to be tight with the guy."

Jax took that in. "Well, not sure what that's about, but my point is that Mason's evidently been off-kilter for months. She says he's been improving lately, but I saw that look in his eyes when he met Juliana. Something got triggered for the guy."

"I know. That's precisely what I'm concerned about." Ari groaned.

"Mason will come around. I think you're avoiding bigger issues, to be honest. Emotional ones."

"Hell yeah," Ari said, fluffing the pillow beneath his head. "Like why Jules chose to kill herself as soon as she saw me winged. I came to her balcony in my hawk form, and she was horrified. She turned away, frightened."

"Are you sure that's what happened?"

"Yes," Ari said softly, his chest aching.

It was as if all the intervening years dissolved, and he was being informed of Juliana's death for the very first time. As if he were talking to her sister, there on the front porch of her brownstone, shaking so hard that his teeth chattered, his stomach seizing so much, he wanted to vomit.

Ari pressed his eyes shut and confessed the stark facts to his brother, things he'd been unwilling to speak about, with anyone, ever since Juliana drowned. "She walked to River Street during a hurricane, knowing the danger," he said, the words tumbling out in an anguished rush. "I was told that several people tried to warn her, to stop her, but she was unwavering. When they tried, she said . . . well, it doesn't matter what she said." Ari couldn't give utterance to those words; it hurt too damned much.

I must do this, because of what he is. That was what she had told those who sought to intervene. *Because of what he is . . .*

The words haunted and wounded him anew, raising even more questions. There was no one else she could possibly have been referring to that day—nothing else except Ari and his wings, which she'd seen the night before. The terror she'd experienced upon seeing him on the balcony had obviously caused her to end her life.

She claims that she found my wings beautiful. That she'd yearned to touch them.

Ari sighed. "Tonight she kept saying that she didn't do it because of me. That she doesn't remember much about what happened, but that she didn't want to leave me and that my wings were . . ." He couldn't admit the rest to his brother, how beautiful she claimed to have found his hawk-warrior state.

Jax obviously knew well enough not to push him, thank God, and just nodded. Then, almost as an afterthought, he added, "She loves you."

Ari rose onto his elbows. "You got no way of knowing that. You only just met her."

Jax swatted him on the top of the head. "It's obvious, you *pousti*. She found her way back to you, fighting eternity to do so."

Despite the tumult of thoughts and emotions in Ari's mind, he wanted to believe Jax was right. "Yeah," he conceded. "There is that."

"I waited more than a thousand years to find Shay. Your century or so isn't that long by comparison."

"Felt like ten thousand years to me. At least you knew

Shay was your prophesied love. All this time I only had one thing . . . my memories. Of loving Juliana, holding her, but as for any hope? It's been a pointless, heartbroken century, brother."

Ajax stood, folding both arms across his chest. The bastard even had the gall to look smug, like he'd figured out all the secrets of the universe now that he was a married guy.

Ari waved him on, rolling his eyes. "Yeah, yeah, just say it."

"I'd suggest this," Ajax said soberly. "That you give Juliana a chance to explain her actions that night. No judgment, no accusation. And no wiseass jokes. Listen to the woman."

"Are you implying I talk too much? I'm a veritable monk. Vow of silence is my code of operation."

"You're a monk, huh? Yeah, get thee to a wiseassery."

"*Kolos*," Ari muttered, hurling a pillow at his brother's head.

"*Pousti*," came the laughing reply, as Jax turned out the overhead light. "Get some sleep. I think you're going to need it. I have a feeling your life's just changed forever."

Ari wanted to share that enthusiasm. The problem, however, was that he just couldn't shake the eerie, unsettling feeling that Mason Angel was going to be a threat. To Juliana, her safety, her new life—and to the love Ari still shared with her. Mason might be troubled and suffering from posttraumatic stress disorder, but one fact remained. He was nothing if not deadly vigilant in his duties as a hunter.

Chapter 16

"Mace, it's damned near two in the morning." Jamie stood at the opening to the wine cellar that concealed the Deadly Nightshades' lore. The hidden room contained five generations of accumulated knowledge and expertise about demon fighting. A few key ancient texts were kept in special glass storage units with temperature and moisture control; the rest were on pine shelves that sagged in the middle, worn by time and familial usage.

"What are you doing exactly?" Jamie pressed, walking into the room.

"Trying to find some proof about that female," Mason said. "Something to show that she's a demon."

Jamie caught his arm. "Knock yourself out down here, but the Oracle herself signed on, and so did Emma and Sophie."

"Shit."

"And . . ." Jamie sighed heavily before adding, "I hate to break it to you, but so did your baby sis."

Mason looked up at that one. "Shay didn't believe me?"

"She accepts Juliana, but that's not really the same thing as not believing you."

"Of course it is."

Jamie shook his head. "No, but the Delphic word of four Daughters, Mace . . . that's pretty strong corroboration."

"When your own family won't stand with you . . ." He let the words trail off, realizing then that something had been changing between his siblings and himself. One of those minute, grain-of-sand-at-a-time-type subtleties that became obvious only in a crisis. Without his noticing, some essential faith or trust had begun ebbing away.

Jamie crouched down in front of him and made a great

show of neatening the stack of books. "Mace, it's just . . . you're the only one who's getting the red alert on this one."

Mason searched through the pile, agitated. His adrenaline was rushing so intensely, it was as if he were in a firefight with only moments to lead his marines to safety. If he couldn't make the cadre understand that this "Juliana" was related, somehow, to the female Djinn he'd encountered in Iraq, she might lash out at him again. By attacking, maybe even killing someone else he loved . . . like Jamie or Shay or Emma. Or, God forbid, Nikos.

His heart began thundering harder.

"Damn," he said, dusting off the stack with his palm. "This cellar's dirtier than some of those fleapits I had to sleep in over there."

Over there! Over there! The tune marched right up into his brain, catapulting him to a roadside. Up ahead in the convoy, an IED had exploded. The radio was going nuts, acrid smoke making his eyes and nostrils burn.

Mason blinked back the vivid images, struggling to stay in the moment. When he spoke, he heard his own voice from the end of a tunnel. "We both know that in warfare, all it takes is letting your guard down once," he explained distantly. "Relying too much on routine. Betraying that weakness to the enemy. One false move and a whole platoon dies. Or a civilian . . ."

"Well, Ari's friend isn't that kind of threat, Mace." Jamie actually laughed a little. Trying to make light of things. He'd always, always pulled that maneuver.

"Remember how we used to bring dad his dinner down here? When he worked late?" Mason asked. "Mom would make us do that, remember?"

Jamie nodded with an understanding grin. "Yeah, nobody wanted to come to the cellar at night."

"You used to laugh when it was my turn."

"Really? I don't recall that."

"I do. Know what else I remember?" Mason asked. "That you'd poke me in the ribs and take the plate down for me. You'd try to protect me, even though I wanted to scream at your back, tell you I wasn't afraid of the bogeyman . . . and it wasn't because my demon sight was awakening. It was all the stuff I couldn't see, all those unseen forces that scared me most."

Mason stared down at the book he'd opened, studying a reproduction of an ancient sketch. It depicted a warrior with thick, roping muscles. He was an epic creature, presumably intended to represent one of the Nephilim. In his arms, he held a winged female, stunningly beautiful, with hair that wound about her hips and the giant's. The image was erotic and sensual but also threatening, possibly lethal.

Mason looked up and met his brother's eyes without blinking. He felt the muscle in his right jaw begin ticking. "I *told you what I saw* in the desert, James. You *know* what I encountered there."

Jamie hit him with a gaze like high beams. "Whoa, now. You saying this has something to do with that female Djinn that spooked you so bad over in Iraq?"

"Everything to do with it." Mason sucked in a breath. "I lost someone over there, to that demon. Someone I really cared about, and it was ugly and violent and . . ." Mason rubbed at his temples, forcing himself to continue. "I can still see the look in that demon's eyes, the way they glowed, the smell coming off her skin. Rank, man. Death masquerading as life. I've only ever seen that same expression one other time . . . and it was tonight. The same hunger, same piercing, draining stare." Mason said, squaring his chin. "I'm gonna figure out the connection, and when I do . . ." He made a motion like he was cocking a semiautomatic. "I'm gonna get my payback."

Jamie shook his head warily. "Vengeance isn't a good motive, bro."

"This is protection. I can't let that Juliana hurt you or Shay or Emma or . . . Nikos. Not any of y'all."

"Nikos, huh?" Jamie's voice was odd, pitched higher than usual.

"Any of you," Mason rushed to explain, but Jamie didn't back down.

"Funny how you and Nik just get closer and closer, while you and I only drift further apart."

Mason blinked, his heart suddenly thundering. "That's not true," he denied after a moment. "I . . . Why would you say that?"

"If I asked Nikos about this person you lost, the one you cared about over in Iraq, would he know more—or less—than I do?"

Mason blushed, staring at his hands, only then realizing that they'd begun to shake. He could never confess the truth about Kelly or Nikos to his macho, totally hetero big brother. Jamie would never regard him the same way again, never consider him the strong, capable marine he'd once been, or the kick-ass demon hunter that he *still* was. Yet— and this fact galled him worst of all—he had no doubt that Nikos's masculinity would remain untarnished in Jamie's admiring eyes. He could practically hear Jamie excusing those ancient inclinations away with a "that was their training, how they bonded."

The heat in his face blazed even hotter as he struggled to explain away the relationship in question. "Nik is a decent guy; that's all," he mumbled awkwardly.

"Who probably knows all this secret crap you're hauling around like sixty pounds of fighting gear on your back, Mace. I'm your brother, not him, so tell me about this person you cared about and lost."

Mason scrubbed a palm over his bristling hair. "It's not that . . . Nikos doesn't make me talk. I can just be quiet around him, you know?" He looked up, hoping Jamie would understand. "It's not that I can't tell you shit. It's just he's cool with me *not* talking."

"I am, too, but that's not the question I asked."

Mason blinked back at his brother.

"Who did you lose in Iraq, Mace? Was it really a married woman or something? Is that why you've kept it so quiet? I mean, whatever it is, there's no shame. Were you in love with her? Is that it?"

Oh, I was in love, all right, he thought, his breath catching hard. But Jamie was waiting for some kind of answer, and he deserved at least part of the truth. Mason opened his mouth, then closed it, then stammered, "She . . . she . . ." He practically choked on the dishonest word, the betrayal that it represented to Kelly's memory. He tried again. "She . . . was . . ."

"She *was* married, wasn't she?" Jamie said, sitting back with a satisfied look—as if he'd solved the riddle. Then he leaned forward, a much kinder expression in his eyes. "That's got to be why you're keeping all of it a secret. Because she had a husband. Were there kids, too?" Jamie rambled on, as cocky as always that he'd nailed the facts like a bull's-eye at midnight.

"No, no, not married. A sergeant," Mason said awkwardly, forcing the words like pumping water from a rusty spigot. "Name was Kelly. Kelly O'Connell . . . ," he began, swerving around the pronoun problem. "*Kelly* was a sergeant, in my battalion. We were just, well, good friends from the start. A big group of us would go out, and Kelly was a killer pool player, and that became a thing with us. Whipped my ass most every time, too."

Jamie's eyes flared. "That's hot. A woman who can drop 'em in the pocket like that."

"There wasn't anything Kelly ever did that . . . *she*, you know, couldn't excel at. Challenged me that way. So we started dating stateside, and then I got transferred and we were in the same unit, and that was awkward. Things just got weird over there in Iraq, not like we could fraternize or date, not when you're fighting insurgents and eating sand twenty-four seven. And then . . ."

Mason buried his face in his hands. The thought of spewing these lies about Kelly and their relationship was almost more than he could bear. Especially to Jamie, who'd been his best friend for their whole lives, such a loyal brother, and who'd tried to understand how lost Mason had felt for the past months.

He felt his brother's reassuring hand on his shoulder. Looking up, he found Jamie squatting right beside him. "Go on," he said with a firm nod. "Tell the rest."

Mason sucked in a breath. "Kelly was killed by the demon. The one I told you I saw." He kept the words staccato, gender neutral. "That Djinn . . . caught me in Kelly's arms, and it set her off. She attacked me, and Kell got caught in the cross fire."

The truth flashed through his mind—an image of Kelly moving to protect him, absorbing the demon's assault with his own mortal body. A marine always watched his buddy's back; he'd give his very soul to protect the ones he loved.

He kept those words to himself. "Kelly died because that demon wanted me, Jamie," he continued. "Wanted me bad, had some kind of obsession . . . wanted to have sex with a hunter, she said. There was some kind of power she sought to gain by seducing me."

The words came tumbling out, the story of how she'd come to them in that clandestine doorway, appearing as a beautiful woman with hip-length flowing hair, packing hot curves. Then she'd revealed her true nature, claws and all, murdering Kelly in the process.

"Why didn't you tell me, Mace?" Jamie had settled right beside him, the two of them leaning against their father's old rolltop desk, the only light the antique green lamp above.

Mason clutched one of the dusty volumes against his chest. "I couldn't . . . just couldn't talk about it." He managed to squeeze the words out of his tight throat, feeling relieved at what he'd just confessed, but even more broken by all that he'd concealed. "My heart was just turned to stone inside me, man," he mumbled. "After losing . . . Kelly."

"So talk to me now."

"I am. I'm blabbing my ever-loving ass off."

"You're telling me more than you have before, sure."

Why was it his big brother sounded so totally dubious? Like some shrink poking around inside his head, hoping to expose all the dark secrets lurking there.

"I'm telling you the important shit, man!" he shouted suddenly, rubbing a shaking palm over his heart. "I don't talk about this, not to nobody."

"Except Nikos. You talk to him a lot," Jamie reminded him again.

"So the fuck what?" Mason barked, bounding to his feet. "Why the hell should you care who I spend my time with?"

"Look at you," Jamie said quietly. "You're sweating bullets right now. Your eyes are darting all around. That tells me you're hiding something."

Panicked, Mason began pacing the small wine cellar. "I gotta move. . . ." He should go upstairs, where he could breathe. Rivulets of sweat were running down his spine, making his polo shirt cling to his skin. He glanced toward the steps that led to the main floor, needing to break free.

But if he went upstairs, that would feel too open, exposed, where the enemy could strike. Vaguely, he understood he was in the middle of one of his attacks, but that didn't mean he was capable of stopping it. "I can't just sit here," he said, shaking out his hands, rolling his shoulders. Jamie watched him patiently without uttering a word.

He wandered into one of the aisles that housed the oldest part of the wine collection, trying to breathe, but got only nostrils filled with dust. He put his back to the shelf, scrubbing a palm back and forth over his hair. He still wore it marine regulation even now, ten months after his honorable discharge due to post-traumatic stress disorder. And the PTSD could still surface this viciously, too, even after almost a year.

Jamie followed him into the deeper part of the cellar. For a long moment they observed each other in silence. "You can tell me anything," Jamie said at last, his voice so quiet and earnest that Mason had to look away. "You know that, right? That there's nothing I can't handle," Jamie persisted. "Nothing I'd ever judge you for."

Mason snapped his gaze to Jamie. "What would you judge me for?"

"I mean, if you felt, I dunno." Jamie shrugged. "If there was something more to this thing with the demon and Kelly. Something even darker, maybe?" Jamie raised an eyebrow. "To what you saw or what that Djinn did to you?"

What did Jamie think? That the demon had violated him sexually? Molested him spiritually like a succubus could? His brother's circling questions were like wasps underneath Mason's skin. Any second and it seemed that Jamie would nail the real truth about Kelly having been a man.

Mason kept his mouth shut, and finally Jamie sighed. "There's nobody I know better'n you, Mace. That's all."

They were a family of mystics and demon hunters; it wasn't too far-fetched to imagine that his brother knew he was concealing something. But holy shit, he didn't want it to be the full truth about Kelly.

Mason waved the volume in his hand at Jamie. "I have to protect y'all," he insisted. "I have to make sure nobody else dies because of my mistakes."

Jamie took hold of his shoulder. "You didn't cause your girlfriend's death, Mace."

Mason smiled at all the wicked ironies in that statement and slowly lifted his eyes. "No, you're right about that."

Jamie winced at whatever he must've seen in his gaze. "Mason, bro, you need some sleep. In the morning, you'll see that there's no connection between this Juliana and your Djinn. You're the one who told me the males keep 'em locked up in the desert, anyway."

Until they need to let them out. Until they decide it's more useful to put them to work against their enemy.

"Yeah, okay; you go get some rest," Mason said, doing his best to appear composed and calmed, as he walked past his brother. "I'll be up in a few."

And then, to himself, he smiled.

Marines always loved a shot at some well-deserved payback.

Chapter 17

Juliana had spent a restless night in the guest room downstairs, tossing and turning every time a branch scratched at the panes, or thunder cracked outside the house. The storm had been relentless, battering the windows like an accusation against her past.

She'd cried at the height of the noise and rain, trying to recall why she'd chosen to walk into the heart of that long-ago hurricane. Ari had left her balcony that night—obviously believing that she'd rejected him. Everything after that, however, until the next day when she'd gone to the river, was as murky as that flowing water had been. And as threatening whenever she tried to delve into the memories.

One question, however, remained crystal clear. Why would she have left Ari by killing herself, or have hurt her family that way? Her gentle little brother, Edward, had been deaf, closer to her than anyone else in their family. He'd relied on her and Aristos, as well, who never hesitated to sprawl in front of the fireplace, playing a silent game of tin soldiers. She could not fathom having taken her own life, and that was the one sure thought that had come to her repeatedly all night long.

So she'd wrestled against those memories the entire previous night, tossing in the unfamiliar bed until at last the wind had died down; the sound of steady rain lulled her to sleep. Now the early-morning light had filled this unfamiliar room. Walking to the window, she pulled back the curtains, unsure of the world that might exist beyond the panes. A thicket of trees stood behind the house, a mixture of oaks and pines that marked the land as her native low country.

*　　*　　*

There were wicker chairs and rockers arranged on a slab of cement, with at least a dozen potted plants between them. Perhaps this was a paved garden of sorts? So many of the items were unfamiliar, including a shiny box that stood on a pedestal, a bag labeled CHARCOAL beside it. Surely this house had a more developed cooking space than this summer kitchen.

Pulling her thin robe about herself, she let the curtains fall back over the window. The morning was dreary, but at least those frightful winds had calmed. She shivered, recalling her final days, the way that hurricane had built strength offshore. None of them had truly understood the force that was approaching downtown Savannah, not until the winds had grown dangerously strong.

She'd left the town house that last morning as if in a trance, not even bothering with her parasol. That much she did remember, as well as her maid Natalie calling out to her, voice shrill with concern. She could recall certain physical sensations from that last morning. The rain slapping her cheeks, her hair plastered to her face, her promenade dress soaked. But, no matter how hard she tried, she never understood precisely *why* she'd walked into the heart of that deadly storm.

Maybe now that she was alive again, she could piece together that lost part of her past. And that would start with living in the here and now. With getting to know Aristos and learning his own secrets.

She wandered barefoot into the main area outside her bedroom, listening for any stirrings from the others, who apparently lived in this mansion. If they were awake, she should dress and join them, but the house seemed mostly silent, so she padded about the large room that Emma had explained was for recreation. There were many unfamiliar devices made of materials she'd never even seen before. A large, flat item sat at the center of the furniture grouping, an obvious focal point of activity. She touched its slick surface. Along the top portion was a raised band of silver labeled PANASONIC.

She'd have to ask Ari about the device's purpose, and why they held it in such high esteem. Did it offer guidance, like their Oracle?

A draft chilled her then, and she tightened the sash of

her borrowed robe. Such a skimpy item of lingerie: The cerulean silk clung to her body, revealing the lift of her breasts, the narrow curve of her hips. Staring down, she smoothed the fabric over her flat belly. Emma had loaned her the robe last night, explaining that it was for sleeping and lounging.

Emma had blushed. "River bought that set for me. It's from Victoria's Secret."

"What does the queen have to do with risqué undergarments?"

Emma's blush had intensified, and with a nervous gesture, she'd smoothed her own robe over her body. As she did so, the clinging fabric revealed a telling fact: There was a slight swell to Emma's belly.

"Emma! You're expecting a child," she declared. "Aren't you?"

Emma shushed her. "Nobody knows. Not yet. It's too early."

Juliana shook her head, confused. "But it's a time of joy for you and River. I don't understand."

"We don't know . . ." Emma sighed, rubbing her belly protectively. "It's because of what River is, you know? We just aren't sure how the baby's going to develop."

"What River *is*?" Juliana repeated in confusion.

Emma glanced away, looking nervous.

"What *is* he?" Juliana asked more urgently.

"A normal, mortal man, and our baby will be fine," she said as if trying to convince herself—and ignoring the much larger question.

"Does he not become winged?" Juliana prompted. "Like Aristos?"

Emma nodded slowly. "Yes, he can still transform."

"But he is mortal. You made a special point of saying that. Ari has lived a very long time—River is different."

"That changed for River recently." Again, Emma looked away. "I don't feel right telling you too much. Aristos needs to talk to you."

"I'm not an unwise woman, even if I've traveled an unusual path to arrive here tonight. I always knew that Aristos was not human."

"That's not true," Emma disagreed, touching her abdomen again, almost as if wanting to protect her child. As if the conversation itself touched on something dangerous. "Aristos and all of the . . . men are human."

"But they can become more than human?" Juliana asked, her thoughts whirling. She'd seen the broad, feathered appendages along Ari's back with her own eyes. "The wings . . . they're feathered. When these men transform?"

Emma began backing away. "Juliana, seriously, just let Ari—"

Juliana seized hold of Emma's hands with a desperate gesture. "I've never understood about Ari and how he's lived for so many years, and he never had a chance to tell me. So will you, please, explain about these gentlemen? Give me some indication as to their true nature? Is it that they are part bird? And if so, what sort? An eagle . . . a falcon? He's already insisted to me that he's not an angel."

"Ari, all of the men you've met, they're . . . amazing. Unlike anything you've ever heard about." Emma gave her hands a kind, sympathetic squeeze. "But the truth, well, it's Ari's secret to tell, Juliana."

"He does not trust me completely." Juliana frowned. "I fear he might never do so again."

"It's going to take time. Your coming back like this, it's pretty unusual," Emma said, walking toward the stairs. "Definitely different. But so is *he*, so he oughta have some patience about that."

Emma had left her alone after that, and Juliana had spent the night puzzling over Ari's nature—and her own murky past—ever since. Settling in a large leather chair, she gazed about the unfamiliar room. So many years had passed, yet Ari remained largely unchanged.

He does not die; that is obvious, she thought. *He's not aged a month or day since last I saw him.*

And even then she'd known he wasn't from her own time.

Glancing about the odd room, noting all the modern devices and foreign objects, she decided that perhaps she should explore her beloved's current era. The more she understood about who he was now, surely that would help her learn who he'd always been throughout the past.

Rising to her feet, she approached the PANASONIC frame. A button indicated POWER, and she held her breath and pressed it.

Visions of "Eat Me" and *Alice in Wonderland* danced through her head as a crackle of energy leaped to life before her eyes.

Ari took the steps downstairs two at a time, neatening his hair with a quick gesture. A thrill rushed through him at the thought of Day One in this new era with Juliana. He had questions, but as far as he could tell, there'd be plenty of time to ask them. Besides, he was finding it almost impossible to remain angry over her suicide. She didn't even remember what happened, she claimed, and, more than that, was so clearly determined to make him realize that she had always loved him. This was their second chance.

Yeah, and he could buy that one without much resistance at all. Besides, there'd be time for the *CSI* forensic analysis of her past soon enough.

And forgiveness seemed like an even better idea the minute he rounded the corner and found Juliana sitting on the floor. She was decked out in a slinky little azure number that made her skin seem even creamier than usual, if such a thing were actually possible. Just as that lingerie set made her appear even more voluptuous and alluring—again, if such a thing were even remotely possible.

But the most striking, breathtaking aspect of her appearance, one he'd never before seen, was how she wore her hair. It cascaded past her shoulders almost to the small of her back. How had he not realized how luscious those wild locks could be? The flame color contrasted with her gown beautifully; she was like the subject of one of those Pre-Raphaelite paintings she'd always admired so much.

He braced himself against the wall at the foot of the steps, watching her silently. So far, she hadn't heard his approach, and the reason for that was obvious. She sat in front of their flat screen—somehow she'd managed to turn the complicated thing on—and was watching the *Today* show with rapt attention.

It was one of those live broadcasts from the streets of New York, and she leaned forward, touching the people on the screen as if they might come alive beneath her hand. He smiled at the innocence and wonder in that gesture. Yes, this was Jules, he thought. She'd approached every aspect of her own world that way, whether marveling over a new gramophone or talking at length to her father about how they would eventually upgrade her townhome so it could rely on electricity.

Abruptly, the show cut away to a car commercial, which blasted much more loudly than the news program, and he couldn't help laughing at the way she startled, rearing backward.

"No cash down! No credit history necessary!" the salesman bellowed.

Slowly Juliana leaned forward again, reaching tentatively to touch a Chevy pickup truck.

"Horsepower?" she asked aloud.

He walked all the way into the room. "That's how people get around these days. Trucks, cars, SUVs."

She whipped around to look at him. "It's like a carriage, then? But I don't see any horses. How do they pull that machine?"

He extended a hand for the remote that she had clutched in her hand, and reluctantly she relinquished it. "One thing at a time, Juliana. You've got lots of catching up to do."

She pointed at the television. "What do you call this box? How does it broadcast pictures that move?"

"That's a TV. I'll explain it later." He hit the OFF button on the remote, and instantly the room was filled with silence.

She seemed to remember her scanty attire then, and wrapped both arms about herself, huddling on the floor. "You should not see me in such a state," she told him, her pale face growing flushed. "It is inappropriate."

He flopped down on the sofa, laughing. "Isn't it a little late to be worrying about what's appropriate? You were ready to hand over your virginity to me last night. Remember?"

She dropped her gaze. "I was a bit carried away in the moment."

"Oh, so that plan's a no-go, huh?" he teased, feeling his groin respond to the memory of how she'd unbuttoned her gown the night before. "All talk and no play, are we, now that you've convinced me that you really are *my* Jules?"

Her breathing became quick and heavy, and she gathered her hair in her hands, spreading it over her right shoulder. He swallowed, tracking the gesture visually, drinking in

her relaxed femininity. And wishing it were his hand drawing those thick waves within his own grasp. The color was
breathtakingly beautiful, a rare hue of deep auburn high-
lighted by shimmers of gold. He had the sensation that it
was almost a living part of her, an expression of her deepest, most hidden passions.

"Don't pull your hair back," he said. "All that wild
beauty of yours was concealed enough in the past. Not now,
sweetheart. And I'm eager to see all of you . . . every last
exposed bit of you."

She blushed even harder. He relaxed into the sofa,
satisfied—proud and cocksure as he watched her, loving
the way she reacted to his flirtations.

"I want to touch your hair," he told her, surprised by the
sultry sound of his own voice. "Let me brush it for you."

She grew wide-eyed. "I don't think . . . That's not appropriate, either, Aristos."

"It is in this time."

"Between lovers, I suppose."

"Aren't we going to be?" he drawled. "Because that's
the message you started sending the moment you landed in
my room last night."

She dropped her gaze, saying nothing with words, yet
promising *everything* with the slow, sensual smile that
spread across her face. "Well. If you insist, sir."

"I most definitely do."

"I've no idea where a brush might even be." She glanced
about the room, but he was already on his way to the bathroom. Emma had told him where to find all the toiletries
Juliana would need—brush, shampoo, toothpaste.

Having located the brush, he walked back to the main
recreation room. Juliana had positioned herself on the sofa,
right beside where he'd been.

With a shy, inviting look, she fanned her hair across her
shoulders, spreading it out. Never before had he seen her
quite like this, so unbound, not in the formal Victorian era—
but there had been plenty of nights when he'd burned in his
bed. Dreaming of a moment just like this one, of stripping
away all the corsets and petticoats and layers of clothing,
so that only Juliana Tiades lay waiting for him. Opening to
him and only him.

He turned the large brush in his hand, but then set it

down. Slowly, carefully, he began combing his fingers through the waving strands, savoring the silky feel beneath his touch. Leaning forward, he pressed his face to the top of her head. She smelled alive, fresh. Jasmine and gardens, so feminine.

He inhaled again and then turned his face, resting his cheek against her crown. "I always loved the scent of you," he admitted hoarsely. "I never knew you were this incredibly beautiful, though."

"You saw me often."

"Oh, no. Not like this. Never so . . . natural, with your hair loose and your body free. Without all that damned clothing hemming you in."

She giggled, her shoulders shaking lightly. "As I recall, Aristos, you were rather fond of a corset's effect."

"I was much fonder of imagining you without one." He slid one large hand to her waist, stroking the narrow curve. It was shocking, not to feel layers of clothing, to encounter almost no separation between his touch and her body.

She didn't move; in fact, she hardly breathed at all, and that felt like an invitation to him. He eased his hand upward along her ribs, then inward, until the delicate, full swell of her right breast filled his palm. Her nipple puckered beneath the silk in reaction, and he stroked a light circle, making his touch as gentle and tantalizing as possible.

She moaned, a quiet, low sound that was like a hallelujah right to his groin. His cock grew even thicker than it already was, and she turned in his arms. At once they were tangled together, all the hesitancy and shy exploration that they'd maintained when she'd been alive now gone—rushed away in the tide of each other's bodies and caresses, just as it had been the night before. Jules 2.0 definitely knew how to give him a head rush, just not the kind involving his brain.

He pulled her flush against him, seizing her mouth with his own. Their tongues began their dance again, only this time it was as if they meant to consume each other. He wrapped both arms about her back, urging her up against his chest. In reaction, she practically crawled into his lap, and suddenly he was falling backward, drawing her atop his much larger body. She followed him down, all the way, their shared kiss growing hotter and deeper. Desperately urgent.

Dimly, he was aware that his thighs had fallen partially open and that he was pressing her right up against his erection. And he also wondered whether feeling such raw maleness, a new experience for her, was shocking or intimidating.

She answered that concern by moving slightly against him, urging their hips even closer together.

With a gasp, he broke their kiss, cupping her face in his palms. Her disheveled hair fell like a waterfall across his face, and he blew out a breath, trying to see her eyes. She raked her thick locks out of the way, staring down at him. Her light blue eyes swam with lust and need, darker than he'd ever seen them, pupils enlarged with arousal.

She balanced herself atop him by splaying a palm atop his chest, and when a curl fell in front of her eyes again, she blew it out of the way. "Sir, surely you do not mean to stop now?" She watched him through narrowed, intense eyes, her breasts lifting with aroused pants.

"I think, Jules"—he barked a laugh—"that we can drop 'sir' from your vocabulary, at least when you're addressing me."

Or undressing me, for that matter, he thought wickedly.

She smiled, leaning down to kiss him. She tilted her head sideways, tentative, as if still trying to make sure they fit together after their years apart. He growled, slid a palm behind her nape, and dragged her mouth to his. He didn't make it dainty; he didn't worry about going slow—he wanted to get inside her, all into her, and since he couldn't do that with the rest of his body, not here in the main recreation room, not with his brothers and friends just one floor away . . . he made love to her with his mouth. With one of the hottest kisses he'd ever given a woman in his eternal life. He thrust his tongue against hers, lapping and twining, and he surged upward with his hips, riding that forceful kiss off the sofa beneath him.

She moaned, a low, purring sound that he'd never elicited from her before, and then she pressed her own hips downward, meeting his thrust. Her robe fell open, and for one suspended moment, he was aware of her bare skin . . . those feminine legs and rounded hips moving atop him. The frantic, feminine motion made one point very clear: She meant to take him inside herself. Not later, but now.

He swept his right palm down her back, the silk of her gown moving like flower petals beneath his hand; it was wicked, but he intended to drag the hem of her gown even higher. Squeeze her buttocks in his big hands, but first— and he'd be tender about it—he intended to peel her panties down her hips, letting the cool morning air kiss the bare skin of her bottom. She was riding high atop him, and his cock strained against his zipper as he pictured her. That pert, round little ass of hers, stripped bare . . . exposed and free as she moved her hips in rhythm with his own.

Their kiss grew hotter and much, much deeper— dangerously so, with Jules matching the swirling motion of her tongue with the swelling tempo of her hips, rocking them in a heated crescendo.

Ari moaned harshly, the sound lost in Jules's mouth and that out of control, wild-haired, tangled-limbed kiss. He slid his hand beneath the silk of her panties, and the warm skin of her left buttock filled his palm like a soft, ripe melon.

Oh, baby, I want to eat you up, he thought.

He tugged at her panties, rolling them down—but not nearly as gently as he'd promised himself. He was too worked up, almost overwhelmed with how badly he needed her, needed to get so much closer. Rubbing her rounded bottom in his palm, he pushed her against his groin, began working her into an even more aggressive rhythm. Each time he bucked upward off the sofa, he rode out their passion, following it through with his hips. It was like catching a kick-ass wave over on Tybee. Only the rush was a thousand times more intense, more thrilling to every part of his anatomy and soul.

He caressed her rounded bottom, loving that it was so shapely, savoring the way she reacted with slight shivers. No man had ever touched her, not like this, and he felt a swell of pride fill his chest as she whimpered her pleasure.

Her hair was all over his face, even in their mouths, but he couldn't stop what was mounting, the heat that was spiraling higher and higher between their bodies. He slid his palm from her sweet little ass and, very cautiously, moved his fingers lower, down to where he really wanted to be. Parting her legs, he felt slick wetness, and his mouth nearly watered with the need to taste it.

I want to take the tip of my tongue and lap at your sweetness.

He slid his fingers lower still, parting the delicate folds of skin between her legs. Her body tensed; she broke the kiss, pressing her mouth against his jaw. A low, raw groan dragged across her lips. It wasn't even elegant, just filled with honesty and need.

And then she cocked her hips off of him by several inches, still panting against his cheek, and began reaching between their lower bodies. Did she mean to stroke him as she'd done in Leonidas's study last night? She'd had his pants halfway to his personal equator when he'd finally put the brakes on.

His hard-on grew painfully tight as she ran firm strokes along his length. "I want ... I want you free, too." She gasped the words out, moving her head so as to get some of their hair out of the way—his was almost as much of a mess as hers, what with the sheen of sweat already forming on his brow and neck. "Help me unfasten your pants, Aristos."

She lifted slightly, pressing her forehead against his, moved her hand to his fly, and managed to unsnap it with one deft flick of her fingers.

"Sure you never done this before?" He laughed, his erection pushing hard against the front of his jeans in reaction. Every touch of hers seemed to make his cock strain and swell even more, although he doubted that was truly possible.

"Juliana," he groaned as she managed to lower his zipper an inch or so. He reached between them, taking hold of her wrist. "No, sweetheart. Can't. Can't do it. Not now." He could practically feel his balls changing hue. Maybe the Blue Man Group could use a new member, he thought, because these balls of his were going to be aching like they'd been given a shiner in just a few more minutes.

She planted both hands about his head, her full body still draped down the length of his own. "Why not?" she asked in a voice that mirrored his sentiments completely. "We must absolutely continue."

He shook his head, groaning back into the pillow. "Any second now? The Three Musketeers, aka Emma, Sophie, and Shay, are gonna come bounding down those steps, ready to bust our asses."

"Oh, to be discovered thusly would be most embarrassing," she agreed, brushing at her hair. "But surely they understand that we need more time." She glanced over her shoulder toward the open door to her new bedroom. "Private time, of course."

"Actually, I know for a fact," he said with a groan of sexual frustration, "that the girls want to take you shopping. That's the real issue. And they'll be humping around down here any second." He grunted at his ironic word choice. "So to speak."

"But I don't need any clothes. Not for *these* sorts of activities," Juliana whispered demurely. Then with a daring, come-hither look, she actually shrugged out of the robe, by way of making her point. All that remained between him and those inches of creamy, bare skin was a flimsy little spaghetti-strapped affair.

He got an eyeful of her breasts as she tossed the robe to the side, almost catching a glimpse of her right nipple. It beaded beneath the silk, too, revealing how aroused she was. His fingertips itched with the urge to stroke it through the silk, to make a little circular motion of that cool fabric against her heated breast.

On the steps, he heard laughter and female voices. "Here comes the ground assault," he muttered with a groan, easing her up off of him. "So, yeah, on the fashion thing? Maybe you should pick out something that's easy to take off."

"Like you and the others?" She gave his solid black T-shirt a tug. "Such simple design. No buttons, no fasteners."

"It's called a T-shirt." His mind flooded with a very vivid picture of her seizing his shirt's hem and dragging it over his head. He rubbed his tight abdomen, wondering whether she'd like what he had to offer her as a lover. He wasn't vain, but he knew he had a fine, developed physique; not because he thought he was special or anything. Because if the Spartans valued anything, strove for anything, it was always the perfection of their masculine forms. To become fighting weapons, yes, but to appreciate the beauty of their own maleness.

This had been the heart of their offerings to the god Eros, the reason they'd maintained a temple to him at their gymnasium: to seek his blessing on their masculine splendor.

Juliana quirked an auburn eyebrow. "Perhaps I should ask them to take me to Queen Victoria's secret store."

He had no idea what she meant, and she must've seen the blank look on his face. She pointed at her robe. "That's where this lingerie came from apparently."

"Oh . . . oh, no, no. You need something to wear in the daytime."

"Am I to dress like a man, then? Like Emma and Shay and Sophie?"

He laughed, thinking how he'd have never said any of those females dressed "like a man," even if their clothes were practical for demon hunting. And Sophie was always wearing those wispy sundresses and flowing peasant blouses. Not exactly guy clothes.

"No, you're all woman, sweetheart."

He heard Sophie and Emma laughing in the stairwell. Coming down, no doubt, to enlist his captive in their shopping expedition. He swung both feet to the floor, sitting upright, and tried to compose himself. He couldn't help it; he didn't like the idea of them thinking Juliana had gotten so down and dirty with him, at least not this fast. She was still a very proper woman, and he had to remember her feelings and sensitivity about all that.

He combed quick fingers through his hair, trying to neaten it up, but one quick look at his lap revealed the most damning evidence of their encounter. His faded denim jeans were tenting, with the pronounced bulge of his erection doing all the heavy lifting. He slid a hand to his groin, trying to adjust himself, but all he got was a palm full of intense sexual frustration and achy discomfort.

Juliana slid her own palm over his. "Aristos, I felt that . . . earlier. You are magnificent everywhere, aren't you?" she whispered, trying to pry his fingers away. She bent sideways, apparently wanting a closer look.

"Jules!" he hissed, right as Sophie and Emma bounced into the room.

She sat up and gave a gracious, innocent smile to the women. As if she'd not been attempting an eye-level inspection of his family jewels, nor just made her eagerness to become lovers more than abundantly clear.

As Emma came up behind the sofa, looping her arms about his neck, he squared a pillow in the center of his lap.

Em gave him a bear hug, squeezing her cheek against his. With a quick whisper in his ear she said, "I think it's a little late to hide *that* from Juliana, don't you?"

"Maybe if *your* timing were better, Lowery, you'd have caught a real glimpse of the goods," he said, prying her away from his shoulder. "You could've given River some dimensional pointers and all that."

"I think you're well aware that my husband's not lacking a thing." She swatted the top of his head.

"Did I miss seeing something?" Juliana asked, glancing between them innocently.

"Oh, Ari's just planning to take you on a tour of all his favorite sites around town, some definite special spots."

Emma smiled beatifically, and he wanted to leap over the back of that sofa and chase her around the house as if she were his kid sister or something. Maybe he would've except . . . she looked so radiant this morning, with a real glow to her skin, and he could tell a big part of that was because she was so damned happy for him.

For once, he thought smiling back at her, that restless, churning energy was quiet in his blood. Maybe Juliana's arrival had finally silenced it.

He almost believed, almost accepted the peaceful moment. Until he remembered that he had no idea how Juliana had brought herself back from beyond the grave, and a sudden chill chased over his skin at the thought.

Chapter 18

It was a sun-dappled, golden morning; Eros felt equally light and buoyant as he disrobed, gazing into his Pool of Romantic Enchantment. The water shimmered in slow, crimson-hued waves, and as always, the thought of submerging himself in the arousing water caused his whole body to flex and tense in anticipation.

Entering the pool, he brushed aside floating rose petals. They blanketed the water's surface, the perpetual flora a gift from his mother, Aphrodite—an appreciative offering for the romance and beauty he brought the world.

At least *she* loved him.

Ares will soon appreciate my talents, he reminded himself, feeling the pool's liquid energy seep into his body. Long ago—so many years past that he couldn't calculate the time elapsed—he'd created this pool as a repository for his special abilities. His Olympic powers were always renewed in these waters, as was his passionate desire to create love among mortals.

He dove beneath the flowery surface, feeling the eroticism of the water's energy wrap about his nude body. When he emerged again, raking wet hair away from his face, he smiled at the deep, sated feeling that overcame him. His groin reacted, too, tightening and then almost instantly releasing in pure pleasure. His own seed purified and enhanced the pool's enchantment, renewing him supernaturally every time he submerged in these magical depths.

He reached a hand between his legs, sighing in contentment. And was answered by harsh, barking laughter. He didn't have to look to the source; he instantly realized that his father had watched him orgasm.

"How long did that take?" Ares taunted, looming over

the water's edge. "All of twenty seconds for you to reach full ejaculation? And this from the famed god of love, no less." Ares covered his mouth, tittering. "Seems your *own* arrow is weak, the shaft wilting as soon as it strikes from the bow."

Eros bent his knees so that only his shoulders were above the water line. "I am gifted with bringing love and satisfaction to others. There is no need to prolong my own release. That is not the purpose of my body or its seed . . . or the focus of my desires. It is creating love between others that consumes me, always."

"Such a voyeur." Ares gave him a bemused look. "Surely you long for a female of your own to pleasure you? Or would that be a male? No matter; either way, Aphrodite informs me that you're incapable of coupling with anyone, mortal or otherwise."

"She did not," he denied, flushing. Could his mother have betrayed his most private secret?

Ares smiled. "You know that your mother must barter with me on occasion. I find that my son's private thoughts are a most profitable currency for such trade."

Eros stood upright, exposing his muscular, bare torso. The air about the palace had grown chilly upon his father's arrival, and he shivered. "I seek my pleasure . . . in pleasuring others," he explained, resenting his own words. "Love spelling is my Olympic gift, as is joining destined soul mates . . . choosing those who complement each other, who thrive together and love most deeply. That is my calling, whether you approve or not."

His father only shook his head in obvious disgust. "The flow of crimson," he said, staring at the ruby waters and floating rose petals, "should be a river of spilled fighting blood. Not used to represent egregious lovers' cards or cut-out hearts . . . or for this insipid pool of yours."

Eros rose to his father's bitter challenge. "Do not forget, Ares, that you've found recent need of my abilities."

His father arranged his face into a bored, bland expression. "And how goes your work with the Spartans?"

"I've secured my operative's position within their camp," Eros replied in a strong voice. "A veritable Trojan horse, no less. Even you would be impressed . . . were I inclined to reveal my soldier's identity."

A visible tremor coursed down his father's spine. "You have done this? You, my son?"

My son. How like Ares to offer such a paltry crumb of affection. If the war god needed something, all his cruelty burned away, an early frost beneath the rays of his sudden sunlight.

After too many years of experience, Eros had become immune. "You came to me with this alliance," he said. "You must have believed me capable."

Ares inclined his head demurely. "But of course. Now tell me of this 'operative.'"

"I don't think I shall reveal my full strategy or the name of my associate," Eros said, floating onto his back. "But know this, father: I have infiltrated the Spartan's inner sanctum, vaulted past Leonidas's wards—and placed one inside who possesses a vicious agenda of her own. It only remains for me to activate her, and that time is almost at hand."

Ares knelt beside the water's edge, greedy and desperate. "You said she was inside their camp."

Eros spread his hands at his side, relaxed, calm. "Patience, god. Time and my own amorous skill shall win your battle."

"I do not have the luxury of time!" Ares thundered, forming a fist against his chest. "That warrior Aristos carries my own power within his body. I demand its return now."

"Is nine more days too long to bear? After several millennia of toying with those valiant fighters, surely a few more hours are tolerable?"

A slow, wicked smile spread across his father's face. "I believe I can wait. And at the end of that span?"

"Their unity will be shattered. The mortals and Spartans at war with one another . . . and Aristos Petrakos a dead man. Or powerless, to say the very least."

Ares stood tall, beaming his approval. "You have done well, my son. Continue in this plan of yours."

Eros dove into the water, wishing that he shared in his father's joy at what he had unleashed.

"You want me to ride in this metallic carriage?" Juliana eyed the vehicle warily. They'd called it a Jeep, explaining that it belonged to Shay.

Women in this era truly carried more authority, which pleased Juliana immensely, even if the mode of transport intimidated her somewhat.

She stroked the machine's doors appreciatively. "How fast are you able to urge this conveyance?"

Shay cast her a wary glance. "I'll go slow. Promise."

Slow? If Juliana took this vehicular risk at all, she preferred the idea of going very, very fast, the wind from the open top rushing through her hair. She reached up and unfastened the clips that held her locks in place, smiling devilishly.

"No need for caution, ladies," she announced, summoning her confidence. "I love new experiences. In fact, I'm quite modern that way."

After some discussion, with the group trying to seat her in the back of the carriage, Juliana settled beside Shay, in the front. She couldn't help being amazed that a woman could drive herself—much less her friends—and in such a newfangled form of transportation.

"Buckle up," Shay advised, reaching to fasten the harness about Juliana's torso.

"Is the Jeep truly so swift that I must be confined?"

Emma leaned forward from the backseat, patting her shoulder reassuringly. "Maybe you should close your eyes."

Juliana faced forward. "Eyes open, ladies," she disagreed. "I am unafraid."

Those words were barely out of her mouth before she instantly regretted them. And began to panic, feeling for the door handle, hoping to escape the blasted thing. Shay swerved to a jerking stop; Juliana snapped forward against the buckled belt, hating the constraint.

Shay turned to her sharply. "You cannot ever, *ever* open the door while I'm driving," she warned, blue eyes blazing. "It's totally dangerous."

Juliana began shaking, and hated—absolutely despised— the fact that her eyes welled with tears. In fact, she didn't understand the reaction. She'd always been the first in her whole family to embrace anything new. Her sister, Ruth, had always been concerned with propriety and social standing—worried that anything she did might reflect poorly on their family. Their younger brother, Edward, had been even more reserved, in large part due to his deafness, therefore living in his own world most of the time.

Perhaps the cautious nature of her siblings was the reason Juliana felt so compelled to forge ahead, living boldly, loving freely. Hardly the opinions of a social conservative in the 1890s and certainly not appropriate for a woman.

Juliana had never cared about, or given heed to, the town gossips and the way they tittered, ridiculing her behavior and opinions. Her own path had been that of independence, whether in owning her town house at the age of twenty-two, or refusing to marry when many young suitors had been thrust in her path. And of course, she'd supported women's voting rights, even when several of her social peers had ostracized her for it. But her father had always doted on her, preventing her mother from reining in Juliana's freedoms. An immigrant from Greece, he'd made his own fortune in America and didn't believe in following social traditions like Mama had.

"Juliana, are you cool? Or do you need to sit here another minute?" Shay asked, drumming her fingers on the wheel, a musical sound. It was also an impatient gesture that no woman would ever have been "allowed" to display in Juliana's own time, not without seeming appallingly rude.

"Are women now able to vote?" she asked suddenly, curious about this newfound power the female gender seemed to wield. "Just as they can apparently drive themselves in 'Jeeps' like yours?"

Shay smiled. "Sweetie, we vote, we work . . ."

Sophie leaned forward from the backseat. "Girl, we can rule the US of A if we win enough support—and we can have hot, sultry sex without anybody stopping us."

Juliana felt her face flush. "I suppose . . . *he* would have to be willing. The man, I mean."

Sophie looped a thin arm about Juliana's shoulder. "We can also do whatever it takes to *get* a man willing, by, let's just say, inspiring him." Sophie waggled her eyebrows. "Know what I mean? With how we dress, what we say . . . And nobody's going to criticize us for that, for being strong and sexy. Or force us into ten pounds of clothing just to hide the truth of what we are."

Juliana faced forward, drawing in a breath. "Since all

of that is true, then I should certainly be able to ride in this modern carriage," she announced, lifting her chin resolutely. But then she had a much more calming thought. "However, might Aristos accompany us on this excursion as well?"

Shay glanced sideways at her. "Would that make it less scary for you?"

Juliana gaped back, aghast. "I am not frightened!"

"Of course you're not, *Auntie*." Shay giggled. It was a ridiculous title, even if true. Juliana was fairly certain that, despite the years between them, her renewed body was at least several years physically younger than Shay's.

"I'll call Ari," Emma said, flipping open a sleek apparatus. Juliana remembered Aristos shoving something much like it into her hand the night before, when Emma had still been channeling her spirit.

Emma lifted the device to her ear and then apparently began talking with Ari. "Okay, back in a sec," she said, then folded the unit in half.

"Is that like a telegraph? You can actually speak to him from here?"

Shay began driving—much more slowly—back up the long drive to the main house. Juliana did her level best to relax, grateful when she saw Ari. She smiled, realizing he'd been standing there watching ever since their departure. He'd never even gone back into the house, obviously waiting until her vehicle vanished from his sight.

Emma noticed, too. "Look, he's still on the steps." She sighed dreamily. "He really loves you, Juliana."

Juliana sank back against the seat, sighing, too. "He loves me."

Despite everything, how I hurt him, he is still able to love me.

"He still loves me," she repeated.

Emma leaned closer, looking her directly in the eye. "Sweetie, he never stopped loving you. Never."

Juliana studied Ari's broad-shouldered form, and tears suddenly prickled her eyes at an unexpected thought. With the overcast gloom, and the storm subsiding, she thought of what it must have been like for him the day after she died. How it must have been a morning much like this one.

"I will do anything in my power to take his pain away,"

she murmured. "I broke him, and I know it. But now . . . I'm going to put all those pieces back together again. I'm going to mend his heart by making him understand how much I love him."

Except, she fretted, some things never could be perfectly restored. Like when she'd torn her mother's strand of water pearls. Their jeweler spent many careful hours restringing them, but the necklace never fell quite the same way along her bodice again.

She prayed only that Ari's heart would prove more resilient.

Chapter 19

Sable followed Sophie from a distance as she darted out of Starbucks. No way would he get careless when other Daughters of Delphi might be roaming downtown Savannah. He concealed himself as thoroughly as possible, although even that would be no match for Sophie's spiritual sight if she focused it on him.

He followed her down Broughton Street, watching her swing her arms and whistle. Why did the freakish girl always seem so . . . happy? It was downright unnatural. He trotted lightly in her wake and then frowned when he noticed that Spartan Aristos coming out of the coffee shop. The warrior had his hand linked with that of a female, and not just any woman, either. He was with that obnoxious little society spirit, the one that he always saw lurking around Sophie's home. Interestingly enough, he noted, that female was completely material and corporeal now.

He halted, smiling at his cousin's fine handiwork. "So you did it, Layla," he muttered to himself admiringly. "You managed to fulfill your promise to that polite wench. Well done."

The triumph of evil was always worth cheering about— and watching its effect had always been his sporting pastime. So he should've been gloating in victory at his Djinn cousin's success; instead, a disconcerting twinge of concern shot through his chest. For if Layla had infiltrated the Spartans' midst, she might wish to harm Sophie or those she cared about.

No! he raged at himself. *Sophie deserves whatever suffering Layla can inflict. She's a mortal, born to suffer, bred to die, birthed for torture . . . by my kind.*

He stomped a back hoof furiously, switching his tail, but

still couldn't shake the sense of foreboding that overcame him about Sophie's potential endangerment.

"What are you doing here?"

He spun a turn, cursing himself a fool for having let Sophie out of his sights for even a moment.

"Sneaky little bitch, aren't you?" he growled back at her, working his face into a brutal, cruel mask.

She rolled her eyes, waving him off with a light, brazen laugh. "Oh, puh-lease, just stop with that stuff."

He palmed one of his horns, cocking his head. She confounded him, always. "You should be afraid of me," he cautioned.

"Yeah? Well just keep telling yourself that, Sable." She walked much closer, grazing a hand near several of the horned protrusions that still littered his side. "If you'd stop barking at me all the time, I could probably get rid of the rest of these suckers." She placed a fingertip on one of the sharp ends and said gently, "I know how bad they hurt, so just stay still."

He sidestepped out of her reach. "Don't do that," he snarled.

With every spike that she'd healed before, she'd literally absorbed his suffering into her own empath's body. Ever since that night, he'd been unable to forget that image—of her crying as she touched his hot, tortured form, literally feeling his pain.

She stood now, one hand still extended, as if half surprised that he'd stepped out of her reach. He trotted closer. "Just . . . don't touch the horns, Sophie," he said simply.

"What? You *like* to be in pain? That's just stupid and way too macho."

"I am not one of your Spartans! I have no need to prove my manhood at every turn."

"Then you do enjoying suffering." She nodded, sucking in her upper lip. "Yeah, makes sense. Demon. Check. Anguish as drug of choice. Got that, too."

"You are a very strange person, Sophie Lowery," he said honestly. "You confuse me greatly."

She beamed at his remark. "I'm so glad! That's a wonderful compliment."

He shook his head, mystified. "And you seem stranger by the day. Why would you want to help a creature like me?

I wish only to bring torment on you and your kind. Perhaps you'd do well to remember that the next time you try laying those healer's hands upon my body."

"And also like your kind, you trade in deceit and lies. Noted."

"Your point?" He stomped indignantly, folding both arms across his chest, which was smooth and free of horns because of how she'd touched him.

"You like me." She smiled up at him, her light blue eyes sparkling in pleasure. "A lot."

He shivered, rearing back. "And you call me the liar."

She shrugged, rooted to where she stood. "No, I just call it like I see it, Sable."

A movement in the distance caught his attention. It was the spirit—well, Layla and the spirit, joined in one physical body—walking down the sidewalk with Ari.

"What force does Aristos bargain with?" he asked absently. "Does he even understand?"

Sophie frowned, tracking with his gaze. "That's Juliana."

"Is it?" he returned evenly.

"Do you know her?" Sophie stared up at him, a flash of surprise, maybe even concern, in her expression.

Inside his chest, his heart began to thunder, hammering at an accelerated tempo. He should warn her, warn all of them, he thought. The Spartans shared a common cause with him. Two, really: the desire to keep Ares at bay, and to live according to their own rules, not the god's cruel will.

He gave his head a shake, trying to cling to his true nature, shoving aside the lying, half-human portion of his soul. Lately, that bastardized bloodline of his had become abominably irritating. He felt wave upon wave of malevolence rise inside of him like bile. *Yes*, he thought with satisfaction, *you are still wicked.*

He smiled, welcoming it, inviting the rush of depravity....

But not before grabbing Sophie's arm, shaking it harshly. "Be aware of the darkness you entertain in your midst," he hissed.

She stared up at him, her feathery black eyebrows lifting in confusion. Slowly she replied, "I walk in the light. You know that."

He shook his head. "Because of the light in you, Sophie Lowery, evil follows you everywhere you go."

Like me, he thought, galloping out of the square. *Like me, drawn to you and always unable to stay away.*

He turned back, his lips pulling into a twisted imitation of a smile as he gave one last warning. "Careful, Sophie. Something wicked this way comes."

They'd wandered in and out of several brand-name stores, but it wasn't until they left Broughton Street and started nosing around some indic designer boutiques on Oglethorpe that Axl got genuinely interested. Banana Republic had been an exercise in the sexually frustrated (himself) doing their level best to appear gentlemanly (occasionally himself).

While Em and Sophie had dragged Juliana back into the dressing room of that store to try things on, he'd been left with little else beyond his impatient imagination. It was rife with images of Juliana in that blue satin robe, hair tumbling all down her back. His hands working their way through those tresses and then skimming all over her body. Moving them over her breasts with long, careful strokes, then lower still, down between her legs, where he'd no doubt find a silky tuft of auburn that matched the hair atop her head.

Not exactly the sorta thing you were supposed to fantasize about while shopping in Banana Republic, but then again he wasn't exactly the sorta guy who usually frequented that store. Nor was Juliana their typical customer, for that matter. What was up with that chain's name, anyway? He'd done a few tours down in Central America, spent enough time to know that a banana republic was hardly a politically correct concept. And he'd never been particularly impressed by what anyone was wearing down in those regions, either.

While in the store, Sophie and Em had seemed determined to give him some sort of fashion makeover, with Soph muttering "*Project Runway* reject" at him under her breath every five minutes. That and "Slouchy black T-shirts don't emphasize your physique. At least get tight ones."

He'd plucked at the front of his tee, thinking that Jules had seemed to admire his look well enough earlier and she was the only one whose opinion really mattered. Still, a niggling bit of insecurity had gotten him trying on a few leather jackets, including a size XXL black duster that Sophie had discovered. She'd ogled him in it, saying, "Yeah, work it. Own it."

He'd given her a blank look until Emma had explained, "Ignore her. She's seen *Pretty Woman* way too many times."

Finally, the ladies had decided to move on, with a wide-eyed and somewhat dazed Juliana in tow.

"It's so . . . bright. All those electric lights and silver and mirrors . . . and that pounding music made my head hurt," she said, hesitating on the bustling sidewalk. Saturdays were big shopping and tourist days in downtown Savannah, even with the aftermath of Hurricane Eric still causing the occasional downpour. "And the smells are . . . not very pleasant here on the street." She rubbed her forehead, eyes fluttering.

"You all right, Jules?" He had his arm around her in an instant, afraid she might faint. It was a lot to process, more than a hundred years in the span of a few hours. For him, the past millennia had moved second by second, hour by hour, and although the years became a blur after a while, at least he had a human's timeframe for processing them.

"I'm fine," she said, smiling up at him, but he couldn't help thinking she looked a bit pale around the feminine edges. She wore a flowing sundress that Emma had loaned her, one that fell to just above her knee because Juliana was at least two inches taller than Em. But the fit had been close enough, and given the other alternative—that high-necked Victorian gown—the dress worked.

He reached for her hand, looping it through the crook of his arm. It felt strange to be out here on the same streets where they'd once walked, she in her promenade dresses, parasol in hand, he in his fine suits and gloves. To touch her openly, with his bare hands, took some getting used to on his part. No wonder she blushed and hesitated briefly before sliding her hand firmly through his arm.

"We gotta find something that'll work for you," he said, lower so Emma and Sophie wouldn't hear. They were forging ahead, leading the way. "Soon," he added more huskily, making it clear that he had important plans in mind.

Juliana glanced down at her borrowed dress, smoothing

it out. "I thought this was the fashion now." She chewed on her lip, dismayed.

"I'm not talking about you putting clothes *on*. I'm thinking about plans for later."

"Won't clothes be useful for any outings?" she asked, eyes mischievous. "Or perhaps they're no longer necessary in the twenty-first century." She glanced about, noticing a young girl wearing what he would've generously termed "denim underpants." The girl twitched her rear, the overall coverage scanty at best, lewd at level worst.

Juliana frowned at the outfit. "Although some young women display far more skin in public than we ever thought proper." She shook her head in wide-eyed shock. "Strange bloomers, indeed."

"Don't worry; diapers aren't really the rage in current feminine fashion."

"Perhaps you should try a pair of those pantaloons," Juliana teased, turning her full attention back on him. "They would undoubtedly accentuate those masculine portions I noticed earlier this morning."

Darling, you should see me in my leather Spartan garb, he almost blurted, wondering what she'd think about that tight loincloth—including how it emphasized said male endowments, and most spectacularly.

But that would mean confessing his full history, and the thought of making himself that vulnerable was like throwing cold water on the lusty flirtation.

They walked into an indie designer boutique run by one of Emma and Sophie's friends, and one of Shay's closest, he realized. The trio greeted the owner with happy trills of "Angelina Ballerina!" Then Emma introduced the coquettishly dressed woman as Angela O'Sullivan. Sophie immediately piped in, "A brilliant, brilliant designer! She'll dress Juliana up right! She's a total fashion muse."

Angela whisked Juliana off to the back area for a private fitting, her assistant Gregg flitting about like an agitated firefly. "Such a divine figure!" he proclaimed, already whipping fabrics and designs off the shelves as he scuttled after the women.

Emma translated the flurry of activity: Angela O'Sullivan was Savannah's most sought-after couturier. He could see for himself just by looking around the place that her creations, with their individuality and Victorian-influenced Goth style, were nothing like the processed Banana Republic outfits they'd been looking at.

These dresses, like the ones Jules had worn back in her era, were made of silk and lace and ruffles.

"Steam-punk rocks!" Sophie declared, then looking around, added, "But geez, I can't afford any of this."

"Knock yourself out," Ari said numbly, waving Sophie toward a flouncy wine-colored miniskirt. "I'm paying."

"For real?" Sophie gaped up at him in astonishment, her impish, almond-shaped eyes growing wide, and he just gave her a light shove toward the racks.

Seriously, he had bigger thoughts on his ancient brain than the cost of clothes. Like . . . by all the gods of Olympus, were those petticoats he was staring at? On open display, as if they weren't risqué at all? He moved closer, stroking the folds of a black satin one that made him swallow hard. These bustles weren't remotely like what Jules had worn. Instead, they flounced at a much higher and provocative length over flirty little short skirts.

His imagination took off like a thoroughbred running for Kentucky roses. Then it became most courtly, supplying an image of him trailing one of those victor's buds up Jules's thigh, stroking it beneath the layers of the petticoat's fabric.

Skata. He had to get a serious postmodern grip. It wasn't like twenty-first-century women waltzed around in this kind of stuff—did they? His gaze shot about the cramped boutique, taking in several women wearing punked-out versions of dresses that Juliana had worn more than a hundred years ago. Maybe they did.

The Trio of Feminine Influence, aka Sophie, Emma, and Shay, had vanished with Juliana into the dressing room at the back of the shop. A convenient fact since he'd been getting increasingly aroused by the designs on display, which meant that his erratic energy was gyrating like the storm-battered barometric pressure they were currently enduring. He loped about the shop, shaking out both his hands, trying to bring his body back in line. As he did so, his gaze landed on the front window display.

He'd missed those dresses when they walked in, but now he grew as hard as stone as he noticed a magenta-colored velvet affair, one with sexy, provocative black ribbons that crisscrossed over the bodice. The entire design was clearly intended to tease, to hint at a Victorian modesty that it had no intention of delivering. It was a fashionable lie, a come-on wrapped in velvet, lace, and bows.

He walked a little closer, trying to adjust his pants so that the bulge under his zipper wouldn't be obvious, and only then did he realize that the titillating ribbons revealed the most arousing secret of all: The dress was undergirded by a semi-exposed black corset.

Damn, this little hothouse was like landing on Park Place in the Bordello version of Monopoly. He wanted to toss his head back and bellow, "Lemme pass go and give me my two hundred bucks, okay? And give me my woman back . . . so long as she's wearing that dress right over there!"

"What do you think, Aristos?" Juliana asked from behind him, and he froze. He didn't dare pivot and face her, not with how aroused he'd already become.

Not with the husky, wine-rich timbre of her voice. As if she knew exactly how high his hormones were already raging and that whatever she was wearing now—whatever he was about to see on her body—would be his final undoing.

He drew in a slow, steady breath and braced himself.

"Ari?" Jules pressed. "Don't you want to see the outfit?"

Cursing inwardly, feeling fire burn beneath his skin, he turned.

The dress fell in flouncing layers of ruffles that flared outward just above her knee, making her look like some dainty, sexed-up little teacup. The kind he'd like to sip from slowly, lapping his tongue all around the edge while never taking his eyes off of her.

The neckline was as high as fashion had dictated back in her day, and her collar was accented by a proper cameo pin. But apart from the jewelry and the lace and ruffles, this dress shouted naughty sensuality. It was as if all the mores and limitations of Victoriana had been inverted, creating a very sensual version of the same promenade gowns Jules had once worn for their walks through Forsyth Park.

Sophie beamed with a stylist's pride; she brushed a hand along Juliana's hip, emphasizing the ripe curves. "And there's even a bustle," Sophie exclaimed with wide, suggestive eyes. She lifted the dress hem, exposing the undergirding lingerie made of wicked crimson. "See?"

Jules blushed, swatting at Sophie's hand. "Stop that, Sophie. Please."

Sophie ignored her, running fingertips along Juliana's waist. "And a corset, Ari."

"Oh, but there's another outfit, too," Emma piped in, and slung an arm around Ari's neck, hugging him. "You're gonna really love that one."

He'd already promised to buy as many outfits as Juliana wanted; wasn't that enough? He had the Spartan Holding Company AmEx. She could shop to her seducing little heart was content.

Especially because at that very moment, a burning sensation chased down his spine like a trail of electricity, and he felt the tightening of his skin there—a full-on threat that his wings were beginning to emerge. They became aroused, sometimes, just like the rest of him, all the more because they were a highly erogenous part of his immortal body. His hawk nature could become very aggressive about mating and lovemaking.

His hands began trembling, and he shoved them against his belly, suppressing a groan. It was the blasted power, hitting him like a tsunami of energy when he least expected it. A high-pitched buzzing kicked on inside his brain right then, and he was aware of Emma coming to his side.

He pulled at the collar of his T-shirt, trying to breathe. "Em," he ground out, feeling several feathers pierce his skin. "Emma . . . help me outta here."

She began shoving him forward toward the door, calling back to Juliana.

"No," he warned, seizing Emma's arm. "Keep Jules away from me. I'm . . . it's not safe. For her or me."

Emma hesitated, looking back once more, and he hauled himself onto the sidewalk, doubling over; his muscles were cramping and bulking, his hawk form determined to overpower his human one.

"Ari, tell me what to do," Emma said, placing a soothing hand on his back. Then she quickly withdrew it, undoubtedly feeling the change in his body. "I'll go get Juliana; just . . ."

"No," he snarled, standing tall again. Every direction he

looked, the world had washed out in hues of silver. He was becoming the warrior, the changeling . . . and, he now knew, a berserker. Just as River had always been.

"No," he repeated, panting, still feeling the heat and lust that had consumed his body in the shop. Why it had been different from at the compound, he didn't know, but something about the combination of his desire for Juliana and being back here downtown, where they'd been together in the past, had his power off the rails.

"I can't be near her," he moaned. "She's the one . . . causing my change."

Chapter 20

There were so many people, and in every direction that she tried to move, the crowd barricaded her. Juliana attempted to make her way down the sidewalk but found herself pressed up against a very obese man wearing a shirt that said, THE SOUTH WILL RISE AGAIN.

Had it fallen *again* during recent years? From what she could see, Savannah thrived with industry and commerce.

The man snickered and didn't move from her path, but instead stared down at the top of her tight bodice.

"Excuse me," she announced tartly, sidestepping around the man. Pushing forward, she frantically searched the sidewalk for any sign of Aristos. He'd fled the boutique moments earlier, mumbling something about needing air and not feeling well. Emma had been glued to his side, and when Juliana tried to follow, Emma told her it wasn't a good idea.

She'd flushed at the warning, hating herself for being jealous of her own relative—a pregnant, married woman no less—but Ari's obvious and very close bond with her felt threatening in that moment. Because Emma Lowery knew his secrets, understood why he had to flee the dress shop with barely a backward glance.

Goodness, Emma even understood how that flat, hard rectangle would purchase the clothing Juliana had selected. Emma had pressed the calling card labeled AMERICAN EXPRESS into her palm, saying, "Use this to buy whatever clothes you want. I'll call you guys in a little bit."

Juliana had watched them leave, turning the card in her hand. She was convinced that something was terribly wrong after watching the physical reaction Ari had experienced right before leaving the boutique. Sweat had broken out across his brow, and he'd turned from her, beginning to tremble. He'd behaved the same way last night, and then River had spoken in those low tones, managing to calm him.

Since she'd known him years before, Aristos had obviously changed in some very fundamental, critical way. A way that she'd begun to worry threatened his most basic well-being; she hated the agony she'd just seen in his gorgeous dark eyes, the way his lashes fluttered erratically, his hands shaking as he pressed them to his brow.

Shay had walked over to her just as Ari and Emma had left the shop. "What's going on? Why're they taking off?"

"I'm not sure," Juliana replied, handing the American Express rectangle to Shay. "Emma says this may be used to purchase the clothing? Is it a type of currency?"

Shay had explained it could be used to purchase the outfit Juliana still wore, that she wouldn't need to change before exiting the shop.

Now, darting among the throngs of shoppers on Broughton Street, she couldn't find any sign of Ari or Emma. Frustrated and worried about Ari, she stopped in the entryway of another store and tried to come up with a plan. There had to be a way to find Aristos and be sure he was all right. And then she had an idea.

It had been years since she'd attempted to exercise her gifts as a Daughter of Delphi, but surely she still possessed them. They were simply rusty from disuse, weren't they?

When she'd been alive before, she'd had several special gifts—that of being a medium who heard spiritual voices, the gift of discernment and knowledge, and one more talent that, as far as she'd always known, was unique among those who shared her lineage. By focusing her gifts, she could trail those she cared about, literally, as if they left footprints between her and themselves. If she had an emotional link or connection, she could locate that person or, at the very least, see the path left in his or her wake. For each person, the color was different. Ari's glowing link had always been silver, appearing for the first time the night she'd met him. She'd known then and there that an intense connection would form between them, as it was the quickest linking she'd ever experienced with anyone, male or female.

Surely such a powerful connection could be utilized now, even if her gift hadn't been used in more than a century. She concentrated, determined to discern Ari's location, and at once, a silver trail unfurled before her eyes, sparkling with a power unlike any she'd ever seen before. That had to lead to Ari! It was *his* color, the unique one that had always led a trail directly to him. She'd once followed this same glowing hue to find him in crowded society parties and winding garden paths.

She began slowly at first, following the gleaming silver thread down the sidewalk, working hard to maintain her concentration lest it vanish before her eyes. Deep in her heart, she couldn't shake a dark sense of foreboding about Ari's well-being. This couldn't be normal for him, to be overcome by these attacks. She'd never witnessed him experience anything like it when they'd been together in the past. So what had changed for him in the intervening years?

Even worse, what if she herself was the cause? Perhaps the bargain she'd made in order to come back to him had created a fissure—one that allowed the forces of darkness to attack him? She pressed a hand against her chest at the thought, terrified that she might be the cause of any further harm to him. She had so little understanding about what he truly was, after all . . . or the nature of the woman who had helped her back to the physical world.

Her heart pounded even harder, fear choking breath from her lungs.

I should have told him everything about the arrangement, she thought, following more people across the street. The vehicles had stopped, allowing the pedestrians passage to the other side.

I must tell him once he's calmed down, she resolved, walking faster. *Even if it means he becomes angry, he should know.*

As she came upon Madison Square, she turned her ankle on an uneven bit of pavement but barely noticed the jolt of pain. Her focus was acutely trained on the trail that seemed to end somewhere beyond the large bushes and foliage.

Then, on one of the corner benches, she spotted him. He sat beside Emma, slumped forward, holding his head in both hands.

"Emma!" she called out, nearing them.

Ari glanced up sharply, his expression panicked and his

eyes glowing as bright as the silver thread that had led her to him.

"Stay away," he warned sternly, but she pressed forward resolutely. When she was only a few feet away, his voice grew much louder and more agitated. "Jules, seriously. Back. Off."

"But you're not well," she contended, taking slow steps toward him.

Emma slid a hand along his back, searching his face. "Ari, what do you want me to do?" she asked, and Juliana realized that Emma was prepared to come between them physically if he so desired. "Should I ask Shay to take her home?"

Juliana stomped a booted foot adamantly. "No. I will not leave you, Aristos. Not like this."

He seemed poised upon some very dangerous precipice, that blaze in his eyes flashing and increasing every time he glanced at her. Perhaps that was why he turned away, putting his back to her. "Jules, I'm begging you. . . . I don't want you seeing me like this. I . . . have no control."

She rounded the edge of the bench and, kneeling, stared up into his eyes. "My love, please tell me what's wrong. How can I help you . . . make this pain subside? I'll do anything. But please do not ask me to leave you. Not when you suffer so."

He touched her cheek with a trembling hand, his eyes sliding shut at the contact. "You're in danger; don't you see?"

She shook her head firmly. "I do not, sir. You would never hurt me."

"Thought we agreed no more 'sir' between us," he grumbled, eyes still shut.

She covered his hand against her cheek, willing him to be soothed. "Ari, please tell me what's wrong. What happened in the shop to unsettle you?"

"You! You happened," he groaned, staring down into her eyes. His own pupils were pinpricks of blackness amid gleaming pools of silver—they actually seemed to swirl and change, slight ribbons of gold flowing through, as well. "You did this to me, Juliana," he added quietly. Not in accusation, but out of utter despair.

But his declaration hit her with a jarring, physical sensation that instantly had her shaking, too.

"I . . . I caused this?" She swallowed hard, hating the idea that something about her was causing him to suffer. Was it her return? Or something about her newly returned human body?

"Not you . . . my desire for you." He gave her a helpless glance. "You're so gorgeous in that outfit, I just . . . overheated."

If she'd caused such an unsettled reaction, then it should reason that she could soothe him, as well. "Come here, Aristos." She wound her arms around his neck and held him, murmuring soothing words in his ear. The tremors in his body were still dramatic, but she felt him settle slightly the longer she held him. From the corner of her eye, she saw Emma leave them, walking into the square's center.

Stroking his upper back, Juliana held him even closer. "Does this happen . . . often? Or only since I arrived?"

"It's a recent development," he said after a moment, the words tight and unrevealing.

"How recent, Aristos?"

He pulled back, placing strong hands on her shoulders. His eyes were black again as he stared at her for a long, intense moment. "You need to know what I am. Everything that I am. But not here. I can't predict what might . . . how I'll react when I tell you."

She bobbed her head. "Where would you like to go?"

"Someplace private, somewhere all my own."

"Then let's get that Jeep—"

"No," he blurted, shaking his head dramatically. "I'm still too . . . on the edge. Imagine if I transformed inside that thing." He laughed darkly. "Oh, crap, baby, you really have no idea how big I get . . . the rest of me does, too."

She leaned closer, whispering, "Your wings?"

He studied her, his expression growing mournful. "They're massive, sweetheart," he replied. "Don't you recall? They span almost six feet. Nah, I don't think that much of me's gonna cram inside the Jeep, at least not safely."

She thought about the vehicle's interior dimensions and could see his point. With a resolute nod of agreement, she glanced about the square, grasping for any idea of where they might find the kind of privacy he needed.

"There's an inn over there," she suggested, seeing a sign. It was a building that she recognized, one that had housed a bank in her own time. "Shall we seek a room so you can recuperate? And so we might speak privately without concern about any ... changes you might undergo?"

He tracked with her gaze. "A room together, huh? Isn't that a bit risqué, you an unmarried woman sharing a suite with a scoundrel like me?" When he looked back at her, he was smiling; the tortured aspect had vanished from his expression, replaced by an unmistakable flare of desire. "Then again," he continued languidly, rubbing his jaw, "I think we discarded propriety this morning ... and last night."

"You need rest, Aristos," she cautioned, concerned that he might lose control again before they even obtained the room in question. "You have a method for paying for this room? As you did for my dress—thank you, incidentally. I love it." She glanced down, brushing a smoothing hand across the bodice.

"Dangerous fashion," he muttered, then, rising to his feet, extended a hand to her. She took it, standing tall at his side. "And yeah, I can pay. We're all rich as the devil. Comes from living so long."

How long have you lived, precisely? she could barely restrain herself from asking. But there would be time for questions—and confessions—once they were inside their room.

He moved closer to her, and for a disconcerting moment, she could have sworn that his eyes grew narrower and that his cheekbones became more pronounced and stark. But as if a shadow had simply flickered across his moody features, that impression passed as he gripped her upper arm.

"I want that room with you, Jules," he said huskily. "And I want you—the rest of you that I've never held or touched." He slid a fingertip along the top of her bodice, outlining the exposed satin of her corset in a slow, tempting motion. "I want to have my hands all over this damned thing, beneath your dress." He bent his mouth to her ear, warm breath sending contrasting shivers across her skin. "I want to take all your ribbons, Jules, and unwrap you. Like you said you wanted me to on our last night."

She leaned into him, swallowing hard, and nodded once. He slid a palm behind her head, forcing her to look up into his eyes. "I want you to unwrap all of me, too," he said and extended his arm. "But we'd best leave this square and get to the proverbial higher ground, or I may just swoop down upon you here in public."

She shivered, slipping her hand through the crook of his arm. She was painfully aware of his bare skin brushing against hers, the tickling of the masculine hair upon his arms, the firm sinew of his muscular forearm.

"Take a last look," Ari said to her, waving toward the square.

"Why? We'll see it again . . . won't we?" Her heartbeat quickened instantly.

"I think you know what I mean, Juliana." His eyes flashed silver again, for only a moment. "You'll leave that room a changed woman, altered forever by what we're going to do."

She shivered again, trying to settle the fevered anticipation that built inside her body. He was right; deep inside, she knew that nothing—absolutely nothing—would ever be the same between them again after they entered that hotel.

Chapter 21

Really, he had no idea how he would explain himself. That one thought kept whittling away at his mind, and no matter how long Ari paced about their hotel room—or how often he turned and stared into Juliana Tiades' accepting, vibrant eyes—he couldn't figure out the best way to share the details of his immortal life. Of his onetime death in battle, his subsequent Olympian resurrection.

He leaned against the dresser and stared at the floor between them, trying to summon the words.

Hey, Jules, baby! Remember those history books of yours? How you loved Plutarch and Herodotus? Yeah, well, I'm a Spartan! Wanna see my crimson cloak?

With a low, perturbed growl, he started walking the floor again.

Juliana sighed. "Aristos," she said softly. "I always realized that you were not from my time. From the very beginning, if you will recall." She sat on the edge of the bed, hands folded neatly in her lap, her posture as refined and poised as ever. "In fact, I rather remember you stuttering in shock when I followed you out of that party." A little dimple appeared at the right corner of her mouth; it wasn't visible very often, quirking into view only when she grew devilishly amused.

"Your house blazed with golden candlelight," he said, practically smelling the sweet perfume of gardenias and expensive champagne that had floated on the night air. "I can still hear Chopin coming from inside your place."

"My cousin Harold played for hours," she agreed, "and I stood and listened and chattered with the guests. But all night long I waited for you, Aristos. I watched you from the corner of my eye, every one of my movements choreographed to capture your attention. But then you left!" She fanned herself with her hand, eyes growing wide. "I was flustered and frustrated, and so I did the improper thing. I followed you out to the street."

He gave her a sheepish look now. "I had a job to do. I didn't notice you until we were outside." He gave a courtly bow. "Until milady corrected that most grievous oversight."

Jules rose, a proud tilt to her chin as she walked toward him. It was a near-perfect re-creation of the tall, regal way she'd carried herself the first time he met her.

"I remember every syllable that passed between us. Every breath and touch and gesture." Her eyes fluttered closed, and when next she spoke, it was on a quiet, intense sigh. "I just want to know how it is that someone like you, sir, moves so easily in the physical realm." She laughed. "Do you recall me asking that?"

He swallowed, dipping his head low to capture her mouth with a slow, burning kiss. She caught his upper lip, sucking it, then kissed him again, angling for a much deeper connection. She coiled both arms about his neck, and he caught her narrow waist in his big hands. She gasped, ducking her head sideways when he moved to kiss her again.

"And I remember your reply, Aristos."

He laughed and repeated the long-ago words against her cheek. "You, ma'am, are clearly a bedeviled spiritualist."

"Now you know that I'm a Daughter of Delphi, and you understand my prophetic abilities."

He nodded, sliding his palms down to her hips. Although she was tall, her frame had always been slender and willowy, and she felt delicate in his firm grasp. Her heart was beating so strongly that the bodice of her dress vibrated with the rhythm.

She leaned up close to stare into his eyes. "Tell me," she urged, gaze never wavering.

That was all she said, those two simple words. *Tell me what you are, what you've become . . . what you've done over the past twenty-five hundred years.*

"I should've come clean with you back then." He flexed his thick forearms, feeling the hum of otherworldly power bristle through his body. "It's . . . gotten a lot more complicated lately."

She stroked his arms, watching the way the muscles rippled beneath her touch. "Complicated in what way?"

He pressed his face against the top of her head, dragging her scent into his lungs. White-hot need moved through his core in reaction, causing his groin to tighten like a fist. He ached to have her but focused only on Juliana and this confession.

"You coming back to me," he said, rocking his hips slightly forward. "For one thing."

"When you get aroused, do you . . ." She gave her head a slight shake, blushing as she grasped for the right words. "Are you . . ., well, do you become . . . uncontrolled? Is that it, Aristos?"

"Trust me; it's easy enough to lose control around you, sweetheart." He gave her his most dazzling, seductive smile, hoping it conveyed how deeply she had always affected him. "Any man would lose his cool if he tasted what I have of you."

"But . . . you touched me when we courted, and I never glimpsed such a strong reaction," she insisted. "Something about you has changed over the years; I'm certain. Something that's causing you pain."

He stared past her shoulder, feeling bitter despite himself. It was too much, the power that Ares had shouldered them all with, the burden of their calling. And to what purpose? So that the god might indulge his endless bloodlust. Finally Ari whispered, "Nothing about what I've become is familiar ground."

He wasn't ready to tell her everything, not the part about River's power—how it was altering him, bit by bit. So he asked a question, one that seemed incredibly relevant. "What was it like, while you were dead?" He flashed on the moment of his own death, how he'd felt the warmth of his blood before he'd realized the extent of his own injury. *The bright light enveloping him, warm, soothing; unlike the soggy, bloody muck of the battlefield.*

"And what was it like when you came back?" he pressed when she looked away. "What did it feel like?"

"I thought you were the one who wished to finally share your secrets," she told him, still staring off to the side.

"I died over twenty-five hundred years ago, Jules. I died a violent, brutal, warrior's death."

She snapped her gaze to his, blinking back at him. He continued. "See, you never quite had it right. I haven't lived forever. I know the stench of death, same as you."

"Did you make . . . a bargain? To return?" she asked hesitantly.

"Did *you*?" he countered.

"We're not talking about me, Aristos. We're discussing your life . . . Twenty-five hundred years." She shook her head in wonder. "Who were you then?" She glanced upward, her mind making quick calculations. He did the math for her.

"I was—I am—a Spartan warrior. Raised on the banks of the Eurotas River, one of King Leonidas's three hundred personal guard. I died . . ."

"At Thermopylae," she finished, a look of wonder and admiration filling her face. "My beautiful Aristos, you are a Greek god!"

He flinched as if struck. "No. No, Jules, don't ever say that." He stepped backward, but she'd already bounded to her feet.

She rushed at him, burrowing her face against his chest. "I always knew you were the bravest, boldest man I'd ever known. Our people . . . I am Greek, do not forget. You are the pride of us all. My darling Ari."

Gingerly, he folded his arms about her, feeling off-kilter in the face of such admiration. Somehow, always, it had been the last thing he'd expected from her, perhaps because he knew he'd attained immortality by bargaining with the devil himself.

"We were promised protection for Sparta . . . salvation for Greece and our families," he explained numbly. "In exchange, we were required but one sacrifice. To protect mankind throughout eternity, to battle every form of darkness that would seek their destruction. And that's what I'm still doing, today. Here. Now."

She shivered. "That's what brought you into a partnership with the Angels." She searched his face, clearly trying to understand. "They fight demons and so do you?"

"Yes."

She glanced away. "Do you believe there are ever good demons? In-between creatures of some sort?"

He captured her chin in his hand, forcing her to look back at him. "What do you mean?"

She leaned her cheek against his chest. "I saw so many

things during my years of wandering," she admitted, her voice filled with grief. "I . . . did not always understand the other world. *I* was in an in-between place."

"You were not a demon, sweetheart. You were born a human, with a spirit, with goodness in you. You believed in God and followed his commandments. You did not become a demon when you died."

"You said I killed myself," she answered in a small voice. "That is a great sin. Against God, against myself . . . and against all those who loved me."

He held her closer, aching for the torment he heard in her words. "But it did not make you evil."

"It made me . . . lost. Very, very lost."

They were silent for a long moment, with only the quiet sounds of their breathing, of the elevator door opening outside their room. Laughter and then a child's happy cries. Followed by silence again.

"Why did you do it?" he asked, and braced himself, wishing he'd been able to hold back his curiosity, his desperation to know why she'd abandoned him.

She clung to him, trembling. "Aristos, I was not lying when I said I do not remember. I . . . I would do anything to know, to understand what brought about my fate."

He stroked her hair, thinking, and then a perfect plan began to form in his mind.

"Trust me, okay?" Ari asked, leading her toward the bed.

"I always trusted you. That has not changed." She watched as he moved to the large windows, pulling back the drapes. A balcony was attached to their suite, and he opened the French doors that led to it. Dread speared her, hard. "What . . . what do you intend?" she asked, although she feared she already knew his intentions.

He turned to face her. "I want you to undress. I won't watch. Strip down to your undergarments, then climb into the bed."

Although he commanded her with authority, intent on his plan, his face flushed when she reached and began unfastening her bodice. "You may watch," she said, looking down shyly. "In fact, I wish for you to."

"Can't . . . not a good idea," he said, then added, "Yet.

We have to re-create that night's events just like they happened. It's the only way your memories might come back. We weren't lovers when I came to you then."

He moved to the dresser and turned off the lamp, and the room was instantly much darker. Although the rains had stopped, the day remained heavily overcast and gloomy.

"It's daytime," she reminded him. "Perhaps we should wait until midnight."

She unfastened another button, daring to glance at him. He'd already walked toward the balcony and braced a large hand on the open door. "No, I'm not that strong. I've never been the disciplined one in our ranks." He laughed. "And my will for resisting you, Jules? Pretty much nonexistent."

"You came with your wings unfurled," she murmured. "You stood outside my room, in the darkness."

"I can conceal myself from the mortal realm," he explained, and with a movement of his hands, he gave a nod. "Only you can see me now."

"Why do you have wings? Were you made . . . an angel? When you were given immortality?"

He sighed, staring out at the city. "I was reborn in the River Styx. Ares, god of war, did the deed himself. He made us hawk protectors, as he felt that suited our warrior nature. Lethality, grace, power . . ." He stopped talking, his back still to her, then continued somberly, "Ares said the raptor's nature, melded with our Spartan, human one, would make us the greatest warriors ever born." Raking a hand through his hair, he added, "Some consider our changed forms beautiful."

"I did. . . . I do. And I know that I still shall." She pulled her unfastened dress off and, for a moment, stared down at her corseted body, noticing how it vibrated with every pounding beat of her heart. "You'll touch me this time, won't you? You won't turn away . . . like before."

He said nothing but pulled his own shirt off, standing resolutely in that doorway. She noticed a few light scars upon his back, ones she'd not seen last night and, without even meaning to, reached a hand in his direction. He was at least five feet away from her, but she moved her fingertips in the air, outlining the marks. Frowning at the knowledge that he'd been injured and suffered . . . and that he'd died in battle. "I need you," she murmured, voice growing insistent. "I want you badly, Ari."

Still he said nothing, and she could see that he was breathing very heavily, one large hand braced against the door again. His grip tightened until his knuckles whitened. What was he warring against?

"Ari, are you all right? Are you ... in turmoil again, like earlier in the square?"

Slowly he shook his head, sighing, but maintained his silence. She began to panic, fumbling with the fastenings of her corset. "Please don't leave me in silence."

With an agonized sound, he whispered, "You worry that *I'll* turn away?"

Only then did she understand. She started toward him, but he extended a hand. "I shouldn't see you, can't touch you. Not until we've re-created that night's events." Then more softly, he added, "Not until I know that you won't be revolted by me."

"I never was! You must believe me."

"I'll know when I come to this window. The look in your eyes when you see the real me ... will tell me the truth," he said.

And without so much as a reassuring or backward glance, he walked onto the balcony, closing the doors behind him.

Chapter 22

H is mammoth appendages filled with air, and he caught a gust, circling the roofline of their inn. As he beat his wings, then glided lower, he knew he should land on the balcony and face the truth—confront Juliana with his transformed body. Yeah, it wasn't fair to her, dragging this out, but he couldn't seem to bring his emotions under control. Apart from the daylight—and the modern sounds of the city below—he'd perfectly re-created the night when she'd destroyed him. He hoped the experience would help her regain her memories and explain the circumstances of her death.

And so he beat his wings again, feeling the uneasy power in his body gain momentum. He was different, too, more powerful, he reminded himself. The city, the weather, Juliana herself . . . they weren't the only changes since 1893.

He'd not told her all of it, the harsh truth about the newly acquired power pulsing in his body. And what if they did come together in that bed, making love as he burned to do? What if he couldn't be restrained or, even worse, lost control? He'd seen River in the throes of his sexual berserker state, knew how dangerous it could be. He never wanted Juliana be on the receiving end of that violent energy.

But that was because River could also shift into weapon form, wasn't it? Still, Ari wondered whether he would suffer under the same compulsions, whether that part of the curse had blighted him, as well.

The wind rushed so intensely about his face that Ari's eyes watered. He narrowed his gaze on the balcony, feeling his features shift and his body become more hawklike. It was a mix of pleasure and pain, the transformation, and he shrieked his raptor's cry in reaction.

Turning, he approached the balcony, landing gracefully

on both feet. For a long moment he stood there, blinking back the moisture from his eyes, savoring the feel of his wings settling along his back.

He kept himself to the edge, away from the French doors, as he composed himself, readied for the moment he'd thought never to relive—and thrilling at the thought of Juliana, half-undressed, waiting for him. But dreading the possibility that she might reject him a second time.

Rubbing a hand across his chest, he furled his wings tight and neat along his back and took three steps forward. With a trembling hand, he opened the doors and stepped inside.

Juliana lay on the bed, hair cascading wildly over her chest. Her corset was half-undone, revealing creamy, full breasts that seemed on the verge of popping free of the lingerie's confines at any moment. The ties across the front strained, her breasts swelling upward and outward, and as he stared at the silk bindings, he yearned to tear into them. For a moment, his fingers nearly curled into talons; he was that eager to strip her bare. But he managed to restrain his hands from transforming and remained fully a man, save the wings across his back.

She blinked at him, her pale eyes widening, her lips parting. With a slight gasp, she assessed his massive, altered body. He became larger in every way while in hawk form, his chest bulking to provide the necessary strength for flight, his lower back thickening with bands of roping muscle. Even his manhood expanded when he turned to his hawk form.

Oh, what a shocking, horrifying, grotesque image he must make, he realized, reaching internally for the power he needed to become human again. To become the man she knew.

His eyes drifted shut. "I am revolting," he groaned. "I can't blame you for thinking so."

"Ari," came her throaty reply. "Look at me. Now."

He kept his head bowed, terrified of meeting her gaze: It was painful enough to remember glimpsing rejection in her expression years ago.

"Aristos," she commanded, and he heard the rustling of her satin and crinolines as she approached.

"Stay back," he warned without looking up, his raptor's voice rasping and rough.

She laughed lightly. "Why on earth would I ever do that?"

She just kept coming closer. Then closer still, until she planted her pale bare feet in front of his booted ones. Still he kept his blazing, silver gaze fixed on the carpet.

Man up or pussy out, he thought, recalling River's words from the night before.

With a resigned sigh, he tilted his head upward, bracing for imminent rejection. He was an unnatural creature, formed in an *unnatural* way, whereas she was everything soft and lovely that had ever existed in his universe. How could she possibly want him, a silver-eyed devil?

But when he met her gaze at last, what he glimpsed leveled him completely. There was such fiery longing in her blue-eyed stare that he nearly fell to his knees and wept. All these years, he'd felt the bitter sting of her rejection, but those eyes revealed nothing so much as . . . genuine love.

He swallowed, blinking back at her, already reaching to unfasten his ever-tightening pants . . . because now he understood that he had always been wrong about her reaction to him on that long-ago midnight. The heat infusing her stare, her face, her body, revealed the truth: She wanted him. She had never found him repulsive.

"You, sir," she said in a low, purring voice, "are the most beautiful, magnificent man I've ever beheld."

Thank Olympus their suite was roomy, because at those words, his wings assumed a life all their own and began beating with every pumping surge of his heart. He was still fully a man, even as his feathered appendages unfurled dramatically in reaction to her.

"Will he let me touch them?" Juliana whispered. "That's what I thought, the very first time I saw them, so long ago."

Only this time, there was no mistaking the raw need in her expression for rejection.

"Touch them?" he practically moaned back at her.

"I've never wanted anything so much in my life." She extended her right hand tentatively, and he noticed that it trembled. "Let me touch all of you, Ari. From your wings to your . . . other endowments." She lowered her eyes, staring at the pronounced bulge in the front of his pants. She shivered slightly, appearing daunted. She was a virgin, after all. But then she tilted her chin upward, meeting his burning stare with conviction. "I *need* to touch all of you. Every part."

"I won't hurt you," he tried warning her, but the words escaped as more of a hawk's cry. She jerked backward in reaction, withdrawing her hand, and he panicked—until she began giggling uncontrollably.

"Ari . . . your voice," she said, pressing a hand to her flushing cheek. Then she laughed more, beaming at him. "The rough sound of it . . . tires me physically. I know that's forward of me to admit, but . . ." She blushed more deeply, toying with the ribbons that fastened her corset. "Will you say my name? Let me hear the sound of it now that you've transformed? That would . . . *stir me* greatly, indeed."

He was on her before she could even blink, nuzzling her neck, murmuring his hawk sounds all across her skin. Her pulse skittered beneath his lips, and he licked and suckled that sensitive spot.

Along his back, his wings reacted in a display of deepest pleasure, fanning wide behind him. When he was this deeply aroused, they craved sensual touch as much as he did. The wings were one of the most erogenous areas of his body, too, another masculine, powerful extension of his form. His mouth found Juliana's, his urge to consume her, to take her, almost more than he could bear.

And that was when he felt it: the first, lightest caress of a fingertip along the feathers of his right wing.

Juliana began her exploration cautiously at first, not knowing what the feathers would feel like or how he would respond to her touch; as soon as she brushed her fingertips along the prickling edge, she shivered.

He was a Spartan. A hawk warrior whose eternal life had been spent in protecting humans from darkness and danger. A thrill sang through her own veins, a rush of love and need so intense that her eyes filled with tears.

"I need more of you," she cried, pressing her face against his chest, loving the way his light hairs tickled her face. She inhaled his earthy scent, savoring it.

Leaning into him, eyes closed, she trailed her fingertips all along first one wing, then the other. A hushed, hypnotic silence spun between them as if time itself had stopped for this one, shared moment.

As she became more aggressive with those strokes, he moaned, a low, rumbling sound that vibrated through her. Arching, he pressed his chest outward. Inviting, she was sure, more intimacy ... and letting her know how her touch pleasured him.

She moved her hands farther down, to his waist. Stroking the small of his back, she did something very daring: slid her fingers beneath the band of his pants. She could feel the firm shape and muscle of his buttocks, and the muscles flexed at her touch. Ever since he'd landed on the balcony and she'd gotten her first glimpse of his beautiful, unusual body, she'd been growing damp between her legs. Now, feeling the sculpted strength of his form, that wetness intensified, as did that aching, burning sensation that she knew only he could satisfy ... by entering her.

But there was something she needed first, desperately. "Please, Aristos," she asked. "Turn around so I can see your wings."

He hesitated a moment, then slowly complied, pivoting so that all she could see was the broad, unusual expanse of the appendages. Her gaze roved over first one wing, then the other, and she studied every feather. Then, spreading her hands wide, she reached out, feeling them with long, indulgent strokes.

He released a piercing cry, a hawk's reaction, and she pressed her face into the feathers, breathing him in. They tickled her nose, her cheek, but she didn't stop. Very gently, she began pressing kisses along his right wing, rubbing her lips along that prickly length. The wing jerked, and flapped a moment, then settled again. Gently, she moved her attentions to the other one, showering it with slow, velvet kisses.

"I love you. All of you," she murmured, closing her eyes and wrapping her arms about his thick waist. She was lost in his otherworldly body, tantalized by his strangeness, his beauty. "You're gorgeous. I want more of you."

In a flurry of feathers and motion, he turned, pulling her against his chest. The wings pressed forward, wrapping her close, and she could feel his thick arousal. It jutted into her belly, more threatening than his wings could ever be—and equally exciting.

He thrust his hips forward, groaning as he murmured

her name. The sound was foreign, changed because he was transformed, she realized. With a wildly beating heart, she dared to slide her hand between them, stroking the pronounced bulge in the front of his pants. His wings shuddered and unfurled wide at his sides.

She withdrew her hand and took a backward step. For long moments, they simply regarded each other. Then, never breaking that soul-binding stare, she reached to the top of her corset and began opening it.

He wasn't about to let her do his job, he thought, and took her hand in his much bigger one. He felt ham-fisted and awkward because of his size; she was a delicate, fine-boned china sculpture, and he was the proverbial bull in the shop, but such facts hardly mattered. Not with the way she watched him through hooded eyes, the tip of her tongue darting across her lips, her pupils dilated to pure black. Everything in her expression shouted need and desire— and an unwillingness to wait a moment longer to have her longing fulfilled.

As gently as he could, he led her toward the king-sized bed. His wings fell heavily across his back, tickling the bare skin. He flashed on an image right then, of Jules writhing and naked beneath him, those same wings brushing the bare legs she wrapped about his torso.

In a flurry of fevered motion, they were on the bed, tangling together in a graceless, surging motion.

"Gotta get these clothes . . . off," he cursed, but she was already beating him to it. She had her fingers working at his zipper, struggling to lower it. The task was made much more difficult by the way his cock punched against the thing. As if his hard-on could find its own way out of his pants and into her beautiful hands.

After a moment, she sighed, reclining against the pillows. "I think you'd better take over this job, my love."

He knelt beside her and cautiously unzipped his pants, pushing them down about his thighs. He'd worn boxers, and immediately his erection jutted out through the opening, the air cool against his heated flesh.

With a slow, catlike smile, she studied his erection. "I suppose, long as you've lived, that you knew Michelangelo."

He grinned like a fool, beaming at the praise.

"For surely," she added, drawing in a breath, "you represent his ideal of masculine beauty."

His wings spread behind him, dragging across the bedspread. That wouldn't do. This moment, this joining of their bodies, should be graceful, easy. He swallowed, and absorbed the feathered appendages again.

She leaned up on her elbow. "Later? You'll . . . have them again? For me?"

"Anything Juliana Tiades wants, milady shall have," he promised, wondering what she'd make of the soft down that covered his pubic area when in hawk form.

She collapsed onto the pillow with a delighted grin. "I want to be naked, wrapped all in your feathers," she said, and he blinked in shock, afraid he might come just from thinking about that idea.

With a heady, intoxicated groan, he followed her down onto the pillows. She parted her thighs, welcoming him much closer, and he began working at her layered bustle. Lifting it up about her hips, so he could settle between her legs, he was overcome by the image of her as a birthday present, one intended only for him.

"You said you wanted me to unfasten you," he reminded her with a growl. "That night when you'd ordered the French lingerie."

"I want you to open me. Completely, Aristos, because everything I am is for you . . . so I should belong to you completely, too," she encouraged, staring up into his eyes. He must have hesitated, because she nodded, dragging his right hand to the front of her corset. "Unbind me, Aristos. We've waited so long for each other. Make me yours for all time."

As if by some unspoken agreement, they began peeling away the layers together. Ari's pants went flying across the room in a balled-up heap; her lingerie vanished beneath his deft fingers. And then they were bare, totally, with no separation between their bodies at all.

"Take me," she urged, pulling him down atop her own body. "We should never have been denied this moment. . . . Please, make me yours now."

She twisted her hands through his hair, tongue mirroring that motion inside his mouth. They were all motion and heat, hands caressing each other. Rocking together, hip to hip, a crazy tempo already going between them . . . and he wasn't even inside of her yet.

Angling his hips, he pressed the tip of his erection against her slick opening. He wasn't sure any woman had ever been so wet for him. It was important to be gentle, but he almost wondered whether he was capable of restraint, what with the way she lifted her hips, urging him inside of her.

He shifted his weight, pushing more firmly, and she gave a light yelp. He lifted his body, but she instantly seized his hips, urging him back to her.

"You . . . surprised me; that's all." She panted slightly, burying her face in his long hair. "Do it, Ari. I'm ready; it's okay."

"I'm a big guy," he warned her, narrowing his eyes as he studied her much smaller body beneath his own. "It's gonna hurt a little, but I'll be good to you, baby. I'll make it as painless as possible . . . and as sweet as you deserve. Then the really fantastic part comes right after. I promise."

He leaned on his elbows, needing to look right into her eyes, but his sweaty hair waved across his face. She brushed it back, keeping that palm against his cheek. His late-afternoon beard shadowed his face, and she rubbed her fingers across it, frowning slightly.

"Juliana," he said slowly. "Don't look away from me. I don't want to hurt you; you know that. So let's move through it together. You and me, sweetheart."

After a moment, she gave a resolute nod. He started to apologize for the impending pain, for his monumental size—that he was bigger than a mortal man. But she cut the words off with a kiss, cupping his face between both her palms. She moaned and said, "Ari, do it. Now."

And so he did.

Having learned as a child that pain was best endured swiftly and without hesitation, he gave a single, jolting thrust, sheathing himself fully inside her. She tensed, a sharp little cry passing her lips, and he held his entire body still, even though he all he wanted was to start moving deeper within her.

Better for the pain to have its way, and then the sensation would be done. Forgotten, too, because he planned to obliterate it from her mind and body—to replace it with a series of pleasures so heavenly, there'd be no way she would recall this momentary unpleasantness.

She sucked in a breath and clung to him, her fingers digging into his broad shoulders. He waited, his forehead pressed against hers. At last, she relaxed, sighing beneath him.

She smiled up at him. "You're inside me," she whispered in amazement, stroking his face. "It feels . . . odd. But beautiful."

"It gets better," he murmured, giving a hesitant thrust.

Her eyes widened in surprise, and she gasped. He stilled again. Then, she wrapped her arms about his neck, nodding decisively. "I'm ready."

She'd spent enough time imagining this moment, Juliana thought, and yet she'd never come near its real power. As Ari began to move and push inside her, the waves of pleasure were more than she'd ever thought possible. But it was so much more than that, so profound, this realization that he was literally inside of her, the two of them separated by nothing at all. She clung harder, pressing her eyes shut at the wonder of it.

You are one with me. . . .

She couldn't stop shivering and thrilling at the knowledge that, after their years of physical separation by death and eternity, they were now totally joined; nothing could ever separate them again. Ari moaned loudly, almost seeming to sense her thoughts; he arched his long back. They made sounds of pleasure, free-falling into each other. He was hesitant and gentle at times, demanding and aggressive at others, but all of his motions seemed calibrated to heighten her pleasure and satisfaction.

Ari was every bit the romantic, tender partner she'd always known he would be. He had proven determined to pleasure her, driven by the same crashing need that was compelling her onward—that had her wrapping her legs tighter about his waist. Already she was discovering that doing so would draw him deeper within her, create a sparking jolt of pleasure in her deepest places—while eliciting a leonine purr from his full lips.

Yet no matter how deep he surged or how overwhelmed she felt with the lust and heat of it all, she couldn't seem to get enough. So she clasped his hips, speeding his rhythm, matching it with her own frantic motions.

This, he clearly liked very, very much. For he growled, shifting her slightly so that he pushed even deeper.

She moved her arms up to caress his back, holding him close, rising with every one of his movements. But it wasn't enough—she needed even more, a part of him that he was holding back.

As her pleasure spiraled upward, stealing her breath, she moaned, "Wings. I want you, Ari. All . . . of you!"

They came alive beneath her fingertips immediately, prickling the skin of her palms as they lengthened and expanded across his back. At that instant, pleasure trembled like a quake through her own body, her slickness gripping about him. Ari increased the friction and pace, hammering into her with murmured cries of wonder, pleasure. He whispered tender Greek words that she couldn't understand, and then he arched upward, wings beating with tremendous, rushing motions that mirrored the way his erection jerked inside of her.

Rolling waves of intense pleasure spun through her body, between the two of them; they clung and moved, riding the sensations to completion. Until, utterly spent, they simply held each other.

Trembling, awed, they pressed their faces together—she began to sob in response to the wild sweep of emotions, hot tears rolling down her face. She couldn't have stopped them, not if she'd wanted to. Especially once she realized that she tasted more than her own tears.

Face burrowed against her shoulder, massive shoulders trembling against hers . . . Ari wept silently, too.

Chapter 23

"Well, that's one mystery solved," Ari drawled. He was lying on his belly with one large wing curling her right up against him. "You're a wing chick. And you like me. You really, really like me."

"I love you!" she blurted in dismay. Didn't he understand the depth of her feelings by now?

He only nestled her closer, wedging her flush against his hip. "I love you more."

"So it's a contest?"

"Spartans are competitive about everything, Jules."

She frowned, a niggling thought edging at her mind. "I know my history, don't forget."

He grinned, propping his chin on both forearms. "Yeah, you know we were glorious."

"I know you were *married*. That you were required to have at least one son; that it was the only way any Spartan was allowed to fight at Thermopylae."

His smile vanished. "I had three."

"Wives?" she gasped, and he cut his eyes at her.

"Woman, I thought you just said you knew your history! We weren't polygamists," he snarled, and then more quietly added, "I had three sons. Amazing little men . . ." He rested his cheek on the pillow again, facing her. "I miss them every day. That's not something I ever admit to anyone, by the way."

"But River? Emma? You seem so close to them."

He sighed. "River's my best friend, has been for a long time. But I never told him about you, either. Some things . . ." He scrubbed a hand over his eyes, then looked at her. "Some stuff's just too painful to talk about, you know? So you lock it away, hide it inside. Like losing you. Loving you and then losing you."

"They had no idea I ever existed," she finished, already knowing that was true. "I wondered why you'd never mentioned me."

"Didn't talk about you; didn't chat about my boys. All of it"—he tapped his chest—"I kept in here."

"What happened to them after . . . well, once you stepped into eternity, so to speak?"

"I never found out." He flinched at the admission, his eyes drifting shut as if to escape the pain.

"Didn't you wonder how they fared?" she asked, surprised that such a deep-feeling man could have ever rested without knowing.

"Others among us, they watched their loved ones and families from the shadows. I just couldn't." He stroked her nose, letting his fingertip linger on the end of it. "You know, I'm a pretty simple man, always was, and that part of me . . ." His expression grew troubled. "Some parts of me never did change."

"I waited at the town house for you."

He said nothing, frowning. "Did you suffer?"

"Did you worry that I did?"

He shook his head. "I thought you were in Elysium. I had to believe that because the alternative hurt too fucking much." He gave her an apologetic look. "I don't know how it worked for you, living on all these years like you did, but I found avoidance a pretty handy tactic. I'm sorry. If I'd known, or understood that you needed me . . . still wanted me . . ."

She touched his cheek. "There are many things I don't recall about my death, Aristos, but I know that I had a choice. I remember a warm light, the way it beckoned to me. I was supposed to go on, but somehow I couldn't leave. I chose to linger . . . to wait for you."

"I should've come back to Savannah sooner," he whispered intently. "I never should have left."

"My choice wasn't your fault."

"Yeah, but I always figured your *death* was—my fault, I mean," he admitted. "That's the main reason I was so angry all these years. Not just your dying or . . . that it was because of me."

"Aristos!" she cried, but he waved her off.

"I should've revealed my nature more carefully, not

shown up so winged and eager. I mean, we were going to make love. That was scary enough, I'm sure."

"I did not kill myself. Know that."

After a long moment, he nodded. "I believe you now. Totally."

She ran her fingers through his long hair in appreciation. "And I thought you beautiful, my love."

He smiled languidly. "Yeah, pretty much got that one figured out, too."

She settled her cheek against the pillow, their faces only a few inches apart. Neither spoke for several minutes; they just lay there, drinking the other in. She studied every line and scar and mark upon his face, lifted a fingertip to a mole she'd never noticed, close to his left ear.

Oddly, she wondered whether his wife had ever done the same, reached out and touched that one detail of his stunning body. "Did your sons have any moles?"

He didn't answer at first, and she wondered whether perhaps she'd pushed him too hard about his past. Then with a laugh, he said, "They all had a birthmark. Same one as me." He lifted the long hair from his nape, turning so she could see a small red blotch. "Family gift. Kalias has it, too; Ajax doesn't."

But then he grew more thoughtful. "You know, if I'd seen my sons again—even once—my heart would have died inside me. I was aware of it from the beginning, that my life had ended, or at least my normal, human one, and so I never turned back. Let them mourn me however they saw fit, and just . . . lived my duty. My bargain was to save them, and I'd done that. But it didn't mean I could watch from the hidden places—not when I couldn't approach them, or talk to them, or . . ." He blew out a breath. "Love them."

"What of your wife?" It was impossible not to voice the question. "You loved her, as well?"

"I cared for her, but it was nothing like I felt for you from the first," he answered with a sideways glance. "We were childhood friends, given to each other at birth by arrangement between our fathers. I don't think she found me very handsome, nor did she care for my humor." He smiled then. "You, on the other hand, understood me from the get-go. You were the woman I'd longed for, the one I'd kept hoping to find in the back alley of some century, the dusty corner of a random decade. Little did I know that you'd be waiting for me, all flouncy and proper in good ole 1893."

She played her fingertips across several feathers, pretending they were ivory piano keys, a Chopin piece tinkling through her mind. "I wanted to be a spinster, you know. It was my grand plan. Until I met you."

"So independent," he said with a throaty growl. "Turned me flat on, woman. Still does."

"I do adore your wings," she admitted with a shy smile. "They're the most beautiful thing I've ever seen."

"Wish I'd known that years ago."

She rubbed her hand across his right wing, the one he had tucked across her bare body. "I do not understand why you ever thought otherwise." She scowled, thinking back. "Which means that several mysteries remain *unsolved*."

"You said someone else was in your room."

She fought against the hazy shroud of memory, reaching with all her strength and will to recall who that person had been. A shadowy figure emerged.

Clinging to Ari, she pressed harder, determined to learn the being's identity.

Ari was at the window, beautiful, waiting, but then someone called her name.

She turned; his deep voice was commanding. "Don't open that door," she heard him warn.

She tried to walk toward Ari, but the man moved closer, threatening. Some warning was issued, but she couldn't hear it now, couldn't recall.

The image grew dark and vanished once again.

"It was a man!" she cried. "Yes . . . but . . . no." She shook her head again. "Not a man. A *male*."

He leaned up onto his elbows. "You're saying there's a difference."

She closed her eyes, struggling to visualize details from that long-ago night. "It was a male presence. I'm not sure if he was truly a man, though. Do you understand?"

He studied her with interest. "He might not have been human?"

"I was a medium, Aristos. Perhaps he was a spirit of sorts."

"Or a demon," he added, eyes alert and bright. "I was in Savannah with my . . . uh . . . job. Trailing a nasty demon trader. A badass entity that had figured out how to convert mortal souls into demonic ones. Not just possession . . . I'm talking turning humans to the darkest side, the vilest kind of transmutation, and against their human wills."

"Did you ever find that man?" she asked, wondering whether maybe there was a connection between the fuzzy memories she had of a male entity in her room, and his work at the time.

He paled visibly. "Never. He left town, eluding me. We didn't hear of him again." Ari took her hand in his. "Jules, darling. Are you telling me you think that Caesar Vaella—that was his name—are you saying he might have been the one who came into your room that night?"

She reached into her recollections, but no matter how hard she tried to penetrate the veil, she could not clarify the male's identity. "I don't know, but I am certain," she said, growing fully convinced, "that whoever or whatever came into my room that night was unknown to me—and was male."

"If it was him," Ari said, still appearing highly unsettled. "Then it was my work and nature that caused your death. Jules, God. I'm so sorry."

She wrapped her arms about him, pressing her cheek against his heart, relishing the vital sound of its beating. "We do not know that. And even if that's true, that wouldn't be your fault."

"It might have been an act of retribution against me. Meant to scare me off his trail . . . or worse."

"Worse?"

"He might have intended to capture your own soul, and . . ."

She understood the direction of his reasoning. "Maybe my own gifts proved too strong for that, but somehow he lured me toward the river?"

"Or used some of his demon horde, all in an effort to strike at me."

"Again, you cannot blame yourself! What you do—I can't even fathom the kinds of evil you battle, the importance of it."

"But if I'd told you more about what I was—"

"I distinctly recall, Aristos, that you did not tell me sooner out of a desire to protect me. I would never blame you or fault you for that. You are not guilty, and my fate should not be on your conscience. I've returned; now we are together. Those are the only things that matter."

"What of the years when you waited here in Savannah for me? Searching for me?" he asked.

She cupped his cheek, looking deep into his eyes. "Darling, love has many costs. It is our greatest joy as humans, but also our gravest pain. I knew this when I fell in love with you. Knew that you were not human. It was a risk I gladly undertook."

He said nothing, stroking her hair for many long moments, and then whispered, "And if it's true that a demon trader targeted you, it means I spent a century blaming *you* for my own deeds."

Juliana dozed, lost in a dreamy half place where all that mattered was Ari, his body next to her, the rushing tide of love and pleasure that hummed through her. And the fact that he slept beside her, snoring lightly and fully at peace.

The moment was rare and precious.

Still, a disturbing sensation seemed to be edging closer, circling up against her thoughts like some vulture wanting to attack Ari and their newly reestablished love. The dream moved in on her, more threatening, seizing hold of her. She tried clutching at Ari's side, but she was lost in the water.

It was so deep, the waves so high, that she kept sucking down gulps of it. She worked her arms to try to stay afloat, but her dress was soaked, pulling her lower and lower.

Aristos! I do not want to die! She tried screaming the words, feeling the suction of the river. It meant to claim her. She began to feel tendrils wrap about her ankles and kicked at them, but the thick folds of her dress and bustle made the fight impossible.

The creatures hissed and moved up around her thighs, then caught her about the waist.

Even submerged, she could hear their laughter. "Daughter! Daughter is ours," they taunted. "Into the water; here you belong." They kept repeating those words like a wicked, deathly chant.

She tried to breathe, but her mouth filled with more water.

Aristos! I do not leave you willingly! she screamed inside the prison of her mind ... as everything went black.

But then, just as quickly, light encircled her, the water was gone—and she stood on West Jones Street. It was still stormy, yes, but ... different. There were fast-moving carriages, and she'd held Ari tonight, hadn't she?

Suddenly a woman approached her, and unlike so many of those always around her, this beautiful person could see her; in fact, she was walking right toward her.

Yes! This was the one who'd allowed her to come back, Juliana thought, and smiled joyously. It was her angel!

"I thought you'd rather not have that awful dream," the glorious being told her. "Nasty business that, and no real need for you to confront those memories."

"Was that how I died?" Perhaps this woman would know and could answer some of her many questions. Juliana glanced down the street. "This looks like the moment when we made our arrangement, but I'm alive again."

"Oh, you're alive again, and I'm communicating with you in your dreams. It's the only way I can surface. For now."

"Surface?"

"Poor choice of words for a woman who drowned herself, I suppose. I have a great love of irony—one reason I was so enthusiastic about offering you our special bargain."

Juliana fought a sense of confusion at the angel's words and tone, which seemed cruel and taunting.

"You told me you could help me live again, be with my Aristos."

"And you are alive. I fulfilled my portion of the agreement."

The entity's face, which had seemed so kind and lovely before, suddenly transformed, becoming threatening and harsh. Her eyes assumed a rapacious gleam that caused Juliana to shiver. "This is only a dream, *friend*. I had to speak with you in this quiet place, while you slept."

Juliana nodded, trying to understand. "There is something required from me? In repayment for your wonderful gift of life?" she inquired of the woman. "I ... I don't recall any such part to our arrangement."

"Of course not. I wanted it that way. And it was better for our purposes." She smiled sympathetically at Juliana, but that expression was chilling, not an encouragement. All that beauty seemed to be an overstatement, a garish attempt to hide an uglier aspect lying underneath.

The angel had thick mahogany hair that waved all the way down her back to her hips, utterly unlike the conservative style she'd displayed before. Now instead of being intricately braided atop her head, it fell like an exotic covering, the only garment that concealed her breasts. Upon her hips, she wore a low-slung skirt, a sheer wrap that gleamed with pearls and jewels. They sparkled in a suggestive pinnacle at the front, emphasizing her intimate area. Not concealing, but highlighting the tufts of dark hair that gleamed beneath the fabric. Before, she'd been in a golden robe, clad as Juliana had always imagined an angel would be.

"I am grateful," Juliana said, remembering her manners. "Very thankful for what you've allowed me."

The woman gave a flourish of her hand, smiling again. "But of course, *Juliana*."

"Forgive me. I do not seem to recall your name," she replied, suddenly alarmed.

"I never gave it," the other woman told her, eyes flashing as red as coals. "But I did give my word that I'd need something from you. When the time was right."

Juliana startled. "I have no recollection of that."

"You wouldn't. I erased the memory from your mind," she said easily. "But now I require payment for my . . ." She stared up at the night sky. "Well, for my services, to put it bluntly."

"I have no money, although I'm sure I could—"

"It's not money that I'm after, Juliana," she trilled, her blazing eyes turning from red to violet. "But rather something far more valuable."

Juliana felt as if she were drowning again, as if tendrils were wrapping about her chest, choking the air from her lungs.

"I want to use *you*," the woman said.

She gaped at the stranger, who extended a hand in introduction. "I am Layla." Juliana refused to accept the politely offered handshake, and slowly the woman frowned, dropping her arm back to her side. "Not so grateful anymore, are you?"

"What do you want to use me for?" Juliana insisted, wavering unsteadily. Her hands found the rough bark of the tree behind her, but that only reminded her of how desperate she'd been when this Layla had come to her. How pitifully insubstantial and tangled she'd been in this oak's branches.

"Ah, Juliana, don't trouble yourself," Layla chided. "I will help you remember everything." She placed a palm against Juliana's forehead, and a rushing tide of memories filled Juliana's mind. "I needed to conceal the details from you at first," she explained with an apologetic smile. "You had to convince them of your goodness . . . your true intentions, before I set you against him."

Oh, God, no, not Ari, she thought in a panic. "Don't hurt him," she beseeched. "Anything, any deed you require of me, I'll do it, so long as Aristos does not suffer."

Layla's eyes grew beady and intense. "Perhaps you should've thought to plead on his behalf at the outset."

And she hadn't; she'd been so overwhelmed with the possibility of being alive again, of returning to him, Juliana realized, that she'd forged ahead blindly. "What do you plan to do to him?" she asked.

Layla tossed her mane of hair and laughed uproariously. "*You* are the one who will destroy him. Not me."

Juliana felt much stronger suddenly. "I would never harm him, never hurt him in any way. Plus, he lives forever."

"Oh, no, no, no!" Layla extended a corrective finger. "Immortality does not mean that he can't be killed or die if the weapon or force used is strong enough. It only grants him a long lease upon this world." She stood taller, becoming officious. "Our terms, precious girl, were for ten days—you resurrected again, returned to Aristos. We did not, however, barter for any longer span, nor did we discuss me sparing your lover." She waved a bejeweled hand. "Do you remember now? Apparently just one day with Aristos was better than none."

"I will tell him what you've done. He'll know of your dangerous threat," Juliana seethed, lunging forward. But Layla caught both of her hands, bending her wrists at an awkward angle until Juliana cried out.

"You will tell the Spartans nothing," she threatened. "If you speak of me at all? I will overrun you and take Aristos's life by my own hand—and I will make him suffer a long, painful death as he spills his immortal's blood. No, you will not betray our pact or my plans."

"Overrun me . . . how?" Juliana asked in a panic.

Layla released her and smiled lazily. "Your body. I'm inside it, too, now. I have been from the moment I resurrected you. Cohabitation was always the objective, which is why we gave you physical form again. So I could inhabit it, along with your own spirit."

Juliana grew horrified.

"You're . . . a demon? You've possessed me?"

Layla inclined her head. "Aren't you a quick study, my darling."

"Who is we? Who helped you give me physical form again?"

"Now, I can't share everything, can I? Where's the fun in that!" Layla trilled.

Juliana's mind whirled. All that time she'd spent swearing and promising to Aristos that she wasn't a demon, she'd been telling the truth—but she'd also been dangerously wrong. She wasn't a demon, no, but she concealed one.

"You're inside my own body? Right now, while I'm dreaming—when I'm with Aristos?" Juliana asked quickly, determined to learn as much as she could. For knowledge, she well knew, represented power and strength and would be her only chance of fighting back. "Explain to me how this relationship works." She kept her voice as steady as she could. "For certainly this is most unusual indeed."

Layla leaned closer, confiding, "You're a real-life Trojan horse. Riveting, isn't it?"

Juliana swallowed, nodding. "Quite. But surely I can help you gain whatever you seek without Ari having to suffer."

Layla's eyes flashed beadily. "Do not seek to appease me or barter on your lover's behalf!"

"Don't hurt him," Juliana begged. "Please, please let him live. . . . I will do anything for you."

"But that's just it! You've already done the deed I required by gaining his trust. So, you see, you've destroyed him already. The rest," she said, stroking her nipples lazily and purring, "is up to me. And it's only a matter of time until my work will be completed."

"Why tell me this now?" Juliana asked, desperately wondering how this demon could be stopped. There had to be a way, some manner in which she herself could battle the creature. "Why reveal your plans at all?"

"Despair will weaken your resistance to me—and allow me more strength. I'm feeding off of your soul, you see." Layla moaned softly in pleasure. "It's intoxicating, really. And the greater your distress becomes? The stronger I am."

"I will find a way to drive you out of my body!" Juliana shouted, reaching to slap the demon's wicked face. Again, Layla caught her hand, twisting it painfully.

"Pitiful human weakness, your belief in your own strength and independence," Layla hissed. "Don't deceive yourself! You and I are joined like a pair of lovers now. Your body, your soul, inhabited by my own demonic spirit. I cannot be cast out, nor overcome. And, my lovely," Layla purred, moving up to Juliana and reaching to stroke her hair, "I'm going to consume you completely before we are done."

"I will fight back!" Juliana insisted, but then Layla took hold of her head.

Leaning close, she blew across Juliana's face, an acrid smell, and whispered two words—*fear* and *submission*—and at once a fog overcame Jules, rendering her mute and weakened.

Then the female drew Jules's hand to her own lips, pressing a perversely lingering kiss against the flesh. "I own you now, beautiful," Layla promised sweetly. "And, in time, I'll own your body, too."

Chapter 24

Ari stretched his legs and nestled Jules closer. A late-afternoon nap, the woman you loved beside you—your body all sated and happy from making love. Really, nothing could be sweeter, he decided. Turning his cheek on the pillow, he smiled because Jules was asleep right beside him. She lay on her back, secure beneath his arm.

His groin tightened at that physical awareness. Whoa, boy, maybe not so satisfied after all, he thought, shifting his hips. Later, once she'd grown more accustomed to love-making, he wanted to take her beneath his transformed body. He could even imagine her naked and in his arms, the two of them flying over the city, her legs wrapped about him. . . .

Well, there were certain things that even he'd never tried while winged, but he wasn't above admitting to his own virginal aspects. He grinned at that one, his imagination running wild—or flying wild was more like it—as he imagined them having mythic sex in midflight. Discreetly, he moved his palm along Jules's inner thigh, loving the warmth and softness against his calloused hand. He smiled, wondering whether even in her sleep, she was pleasured by his touch.

Suddenly, though, she cried out, and at first he thought he'd startled her. But she twisted beneath his caress, murmuring something frantically, over and over.

He gave her a light shake. "Jules. Sweetheart, wake up," he said, and she whimpered, flailing a hand.

He rose onto his knees and leaned over her. "Juliana," he said loudly. Stroking her hair, he gave her another shake. "Sweetheart, wake up. You're having a bad dream."

Her eyes fluttered open, and at first she just looked all around, as if maybe she wasn't even sure how she'd gotten there. "Aristos?" She stared at the open balcony uncertainly, then glanced all about the room. "What year is it?"

"You're with me, here in the twenty-first century," he reassured her.

As that fact really sunk in, she hurled herself into his arms, digging her fingers into his shoulders, clinging to him as if to life itself—or as if she feared he might just up and fly away on her.

"I'm here, baby. We're both here, in Savannah, at the hotel," he murmured, drawing her up onto his lap.

"Oh, oh," she said, burrowing against his chest. Her whole body trembled. "Ari, tell me this is real. Tell me I'm alive," she pleaded. "That this moment, here with you, isn't the dream."

He held her close, shushing her fears away. Or at least he tried, but no matter what he said, she continued to shake as she clung to him.

And then he was the one who began to tremor, maybe even harder, when she looked up at him. Raw terror filled her expression. "Tell me that no matter what, you'll always love me," she begged. "Tell me that nothing can ever change that."

He tucked a lock of hair behind her ear, making her look up into his eyes, to feel his reassurance deep in her heart. "You know that I never stopped loving you, and I never will." He stroked her back, needing her to know that he wasn't ever going to abandon her or stop loving her. He might as well have tried to halt the oceans' tides or grab the moon from the sky. "I will love you for all my immortal days," he pledged.

Finally she calmed, relaxing against him. "I'll love you for my immortal days, too," she said.

Immortal days? He'd never even stopped to consider whether she'd age or not, die a natural death or live forever like him.

But when he opened his mouth to voice the question, his shoulder began to burn and ache. He rubbed it, and slowly the twinge subsided, although there'd been something he wanted to ask Jules—needed to ask, he was certain. But now he had no recollection of what that thought might have been.

The blasted shoulder had done the same thing in Leo's

study last night, he remembered, suddenly struck by a marvelous idea. "I know exactly what will make you feel better," he told Juliana.

"What do you have in mind?" She still bore a slightly troubled expression, which only convinced him that his plan was the perfect way to woo her and eliminate the nightmare from her thoughts.

He rose from the bed, searching for his pants. "Put your dress on," he instructed, handing the garment to her. She took it from him and sat up.

"Do you see my bustle?" she asked.

"No, just the dress. You don't need anything else. In fact," he said, giving her his most devilish, charming smile, "you'd better not wear any undergarments. But first, I'm going to take a shower and freshen up. When I get out? Be prepared. Or actually, come to think of it . . . ," he said. "Maybe I should haul you in there with me."

She yawned, rolling onto her side. "I think I need a little more rest before we engage in any further . . . exploits."

He bent down and kissed her hungrily, tucking the sheet over her bare body. "A little rest, but I have other plans for later."

They had only a few days left, apparently. She struggled to process that fact, desperately searching for a way around the limitations of the bargain she'd made. Her heart ached at the thought of being separated from Aristos again, and how that fact would destroy his tremendous, kind heart. But that wasn't the most painful realization. It was knowing that the demon inside of her intended to end his life.

Tears stung her eyes; she lay in the bed, naked and aching for him. He'd traipsed off to the shower, looking happier than she'd ever seen him, which only made her cry even harder.

He'd feel betrayed, abandoned all over again once he learned of the deal she'd made. And he'd never be able to forgive her for having concealed it, from the first moments of her arrival. Except . . . she hadn't remembered the details; they'd been obscured, especially the time limit. But that was only a paltry excuse, and she knew it.

Eight days remained after this one, she thought, staring at the dark Savannah skyline visible through the opened

French doors. A breeze wafted the curtains, and it should have been pleasant, but the night air only felt like the cruelest of reminders of how briefly she would be here.

She turned in the bed, hugging her arms about her naked body. At least they would have this time. Perhaps he could forgive her for the brevity of their reunion; he would always know, now, that she loved him—and she had convinced him that she'd never intended to kill herself. Hopefully that would give him some peace.

That thought brought back the first part of her dream, and she began to cry, hot tears streaking down her cheeks. Would those horrid creatures drag her down again, at the end of the ten days? Drown her in the river's depths?

She sat up in a rush, brushing back her tangled curls. Perhaps she should broach the topic with Ari, confess what she now recalled about her death. He'd said that he was pursuing a demon trader while in town—were those slimy, choking creatures in the river also demons? Had she been killed by that fiendish lot?

The bathroom door opened, steam filling the room. Ari grinned at her, a thick towel draped about his hips. "Just wait. You're gonna love twenty-first-century bathing, Jules." He combed fingers through his dripping hair, brushing it back. She yearned to have her own hands upon him, feeling all those damp, beautiful locks beneath her palms.

There is time to tell him everything, she thought as he neared, his black eyes flaring with sultry promise. *Time to find a way to stay with him for good.*

He leaned against the dresser, looking proud of himself. The muscles across his chest and in his bulky upper arms flexed and rippled.

"You're doing that on purpose," she declared, feeling heat move to her most sensitive place.

He lifted first one eyebrow and then the other. "Why, whatever do you mean, Miss Tiades?" he asked in a high-pitched, Southern accent.

"Do not make fun of me, sir!"

"Jules." He let the towel fall open at his hips. "I keep telling you—we are way, way past you calling me 'sir.'"

She dropped her gaze to his groin, eager for what he revealed of his body, but then a strange, tinny noise began from the other side of the room. She turned toward it, jarred, confused.

"Oh, crap." Ari lumbered across the floor. "Probably River, checking up on my ass."

"It's one of those small telegraphs?" she asked. "I didn't realize it could make such a musical sound."

"Got a Rolling Stones ringtone. You'll love their stuff eventually. Although 'Sympathy for the Devil' might not be my best choice even."

She watched as he picked up his trousers, digging in first one pocket, then another. "One thing you'll learn about this era, though," he said, still rooting around, "is that you're never really alone."

Finally he retrieved that telegraph what she now knew was a phone—and placed the device against his ear. "For whom the cell tolls," he muttered into it. " 'Sup, River man?"

"So nobody's seen Ari since this afternoon?" Mason asked Emma, holding the door open so she could step ahead of him onto the sagging veranda of his family's home.

River followed in their wake, tapping a number into his cell phone. "I'm sure I'll reach him this time," he announced, pressing the receiver to his ear, but he didn't appear convinced. "I hope I will," he added less certainly, walking out to the balcony's edge.

They'd been talking about how Ari had gone off the rails while downtown, his power overloading to a dangerous extent—a common reaction these days, they'd explained with obvious concern.

Yeah, well, the guy would likely get a whole lot more unstable now that he'd aligned with a demon, Mace almost revealed, but he held his tongue. He was a lone operator on this one, which meant he had to prove the Djinn's identity by working the situation like a good recon marine—gathering intel first, then waging a campaign of subtle, aggressive violence based on that data.

"Hey, man! Been trying to reach you," River announced into the phone exuberantly. Covering the receiver, he whispered, "Got him," clearly relieved to have located his AWOL friend. He nodded, listening to whatever the Spartan was saying, and moved down to the farthest end of the veranda, where he could talk privately.

"I'm so glad he found him," Emma said, watching her husband for a long moment, as if she still needed reassurance that Ari was fine and stable, not in danger.

Yeah, Mace got that one. He was worried, too, and could barely restrain the urge to eavesdrop, although that had little to do with Ari's power problem and everything to do with the female company he was keeping.

Mason turned to face Emma once they were alone. "So," he ventured, keeping his voice as casual as he could, "what's Ari's deal, anyway? Why's he having these outbursts? Oh, and keep him off *my* Wii, thank you very much," he added. "Nik finally made me get Rock Band the other day." He played air guitar, singing "Mississippi Queen." "Southern rock, dude. I'm there."

Emma cut her eyes at him. "Don't let Nik on the drums. It's like an obsession once he gets going."

"Oh, trust me, Nikos and Nirvana? Didn't see that one coming, not from ten clicks away."

They laughed together, and then he brought the conversation back around. "So, seriously, what's going on with Ari? He having a cosmic meltdown or what?"

Emma sighed, wrapping her arms about her abdomen in a protective gesture that didn't quite make sense to him. "He's really struggling lately," she explained, her kind face appearing troubled. "Working to internalize the power exchange, learning to live with it . . ." She shook her head, still frowning. "It's been a lot for him." Again, she glanced toward River, who was still on the phone. Much lower she said, "There's been a huge cost. That Ari's so . . . boisterous? I think that's made the process harder."

"Boisterous?" He snorted, unable to help himself. "Yeah, that's one way to put it."

"Exuberant?" she tried with a bigger smile.

He only laughed harder, sidling against the veranda railing, thinking of all the many ways he'd describe Aristos Petrakos. "Let's see. Wisecracking smart-ass, loudmouthed bastard, irreverent SOB . . ."

She poked him in the chest. "He's one of my best friends—watch it."

He directed her finger away, still grinning despite the

gravity of the situation. "Are you kidding? He's a madman, but who doesn't love that guy?" They all did, with his easy acceptance, no matter who you were, or what you'd done. That was why he had to protect Ari from the Djinn—or at least it was one very compelling reason.

Her eyes grew sad, and she released a heavy sigh. "The thing is," she continued, "River had *millennia* to grow accustomed to the power. For all we know, it might even have built and increased inside him over time. But when Ari stepped up for us, for River . . . that monumental energy was plopped down inside of Ari's body in the space of a heartbeat. That was a lot to internalize without any preparation."

Mason nodded appreciatively. "That's one helluva big payload delivery; you're right."

"River blames himself. He loves Ari like a brother and feels guilty, even though Ari never hesitated. It was such a huge gesture of friendship, and he's never looked back, but . . . we're worried for him."

Mason flashed on Kelly then, the way he'd moved right between him and that demon, eager to offer his own life as protection. Lover, friend, brother—the label didn't matter. The real people in your life, the ones who would lay themselves in the road for you, never hesitated or debated potential consequences; they just stepped up.

"He's strong," Mason reassured her. And he meant it. "Ari's a Spartan; don't forget that. He's disciplined and tough as an oak. He'll be all right. Just give him some time to, you know, process things."

But Ari didn't have that luxury, not with that Djinn having targeted him. This time Mace was the one who had to lay down in the road—do the sacrificing and figure out how to watch everyone's back. Because one thing was obvious: Ari was just too much in love to see the truth about the female demon's identity. Mason would protect his friend and get him to understand the facts—and kill the creature before she harmed Aristos.

Quietly he said, "Ari's good people. That'll see him through, in the end."

She lowered her voice confessionally, not quite meeting his eyes. "We think he might even be experiencing some of River's old berserker issues. Intense stuff, you know?"

She got an embarrassed look right then, and no wonder. He'd heard the stories. There'd only been one way River had ever calmed *those* problems, and it had always involved sex.

Mace lifted an eyebrow significantly but didn't offer any commentary.

Emma blushed at his unspoken observation, abruptly changing the subject. "Look," she said. "It's not just Ari I'm worried about. Are you okay, Mason? How are you doing . . . really doing?"

"Oh, Jesus," he cursed, shifting away from her slightly. "You're not gonna start in on me, too, are you?"

She gazed up at him with quiet, caring intensity. "I know things have been hard since your last deployment. I should've reached out to you when you got home, and I'm so sorry that I didn't, but I had my own . . . Well, I had issues. I'm here now, though, and I miss you and I want to know you're all right. I want to be close again."

"Yeah, Em, me, too," he agreed softly, staring at the warped planks of the veranda, way easier than looking into her open eyes. "And for God's sake, of course I'm okay. Why wouldn't I be?"

"I don't know what happened over there—"

He cut her off at the pass. "I'm good to go; always have been. Totally frosty."

Fucking liar, he thought, assuming an even more obstinate expression as Emma searched his face. He hadn't slept in more than thirty-six hours, studying demon lore and texts until his eyeballs nearly bled. Plus, it was longer than two days since he'd had a decent night's rest; the nightmares he'd brought home had been tormenting him every night. But sure, he was dandier than a Georgia peach, righter than a summer rain. Roger that.

Emma was talking again, he suddenly realized, but he'd missed her words, drifted off to his zoned-out place.

". . . Nikos was concerned about you," she continued, capturing his attention completely. "I know that you didn't click with Juliana last night, but she's awesome, Mason. Really sweet, no matter what our initial concerns might have been."

Our concerns? No, those doubts had belonged only to him, but his dear cousin was sensitive enough not to draw attention to his lone-wolf status.

He didn't have a comeback, not one that wouldn't open a giant can of worms, a shitload worth of them. So finally she added, "That's why I told Nikos we'd check on you . . . stop by on the way back from downtown. Just to be sure you're all right. Nikos was worried," she reiterated.

Something in the way she said Nik's name—like it was *the* special calling card, the one that would make him open up completely, had Mason blushing like a fool. He looked away, but Emma caught his arm. "Mason, talk to me," she encouraged gently. "Please, just tell me what you're thinking. Right now, this moment."

They'd been so close at one time, but in the past years, everything between them had been hard work, and he hated that.

He touched her face briefly. "Nikos . . . just overthinks things sometimes." He forced a laugh. "Get him going on Rock Band later. He'll stop worrying about me."

"He doesn't strike me as much of a worrier," she said uneasily, stroking her sleek ponytail as she studied him.

He gave her one of his most charming, winning smiles. The kind that had convinced his shrinks at the VA that his depression was gone—when it wasn't. And that the PTSD attacks had stopped—when they hadn't. "Darlin'. Please. Y'all gotta stop treating me like I've got ten screws loose just 'cause I did a few tours over in that big sandbox from hell."

She laughed. "Fair enough, cuz."

"Superkeen, jelly bean," he said, using one of their childhood expressions.

River seemed to be wrapping up his phone conversation, walking back toward the middle of the porch as he asked, "So where are you staying tonight?" Mason's ears pricked right up, and he grew alert at River's next question. "Yeah, dinner *where* on Tybee?"

How utterly romantic; Ari was taking his woman out to the beach. The guy was clearly in so deep, he couldn't see the spiritual truth of the situation, or the reality of the demon he was currently wooing.

Mason swore under his breath, but in a very friendly tone he called out, "Tell him the Crab Shack rocks."

River repeated the recommendation and then turned back to Mason. "Ari says marines must *rock* a lobster bib if that's your favorite dining establishment."

Mason smiled despite himself, grabbing his balls with a crude, requisite USMC gesture. "Tell him he can rock these."

They both laughed, but Mason's mind was already in overdrive. So was his truck, even though he'd not started the vehicle's engine yet. He didn't relish the knowledge that he was going to have to face down Aristos; in fact, it filled him with a heavy sense of dread, right in the center of his belly. But as a marine, one thing he'd always understood was commitment to duty, and in this case that involved protecting Ari from his greatest enemy in this skirmish: his own heart.

Chapter 25

Ari leaped onto the railing, standing there like a mighty angel overlooking the city of Savannah. A light breeze caught his long hair, blowing it away from his face, and his profile struck her as nothing less than magnificent. His agile strength, his immense stature as he surveyed the evening sky, all of it was breathtaking. In the distance, the sun burst through the clouds, a streaking explosion of red and orange that glowed across his proud face and wings, painting him in shades of flame. He was epic, mythic, the most beautiful man she'd ever looked upon.

His chest was bare, and he wore only his pants and boots, although he'd tied the long-sleeved T-shirt about his waist in preparation for their impending flight. She swallowed hard, trying to imagine dining at a public restaurant, fully aware that she would not be wearing any undergarments. She flushed at the impropriety of it, thinking about the thoughts Aristos might have on his mind as they shared the meal.

Turning along the edge of the rail, Ari extended a hand down toward her. "Now or never, Miss Tiades," he said gallantly. He unfurled his wings with a flare, which made a kind of rustling noise that shocked her. It was so . . . dangerous, so primal.

She gulped, frozen. Suddenly the Jeep seemed downright tame, and yet the thought of flying in Ari's arms was far more thrilling. She took a step forward and raised her left hand.

With a firm grasp, he pulled her upward, swinging her lightly into the cradle of his arms . . . right as he stepped into the air.

Immediately she screamed, hiding her face against his chest; she felt his laughter rumble against her cheek.

"I would never endanger you, sweetheart. You know that logically."

"Yes, but I still refuse to look."

The quiet rush of wind blew across her skin and filled her skirt, causing coolness to waft against the heat in her most intimate area. It was a sensual feeling, one Ari had undoubtedly planned when he'd told her to leave off her lingerie. She was keenly aware of every physical sensation. His muscled chest, the play of its strength with every motion of his wings. She also noticed something surprising as she nuzzled against him: light feathers tickled her cheek.

Curious, she splayed a palm against his chest, rubbing it over his heart. Yes! That area was covered in light down, a much softer variety of feathers than those along his wings. She kept stroking, loving the velvet feel of it brushing beneath her fingertips. Apparently, the down feathers had replaced his usual curling chest hair.

"That feels so . . . lovely," she murmured, closing her eyes. Everything about Aristos was beautiful, exotic. And a constant surprise, a new discovery every time she touched him or explored some new aspect of his unique warrior's body.

"When I fly," he explained, his voice vibrating with hawklike timbre. "My body changes even more. The feathers on my chest . . ." His voice drifted off, and she wondered what he'd been about to say.

He adjusted her slightly, clearing his throat. "I have down feathers along my male parts," he admitted shyly. "When I'm flying and more . . . hawkish. Still a man—"

"Quite obviously," she agreed with a firm nod.

"But, uh . . ." He soared suddenly, the air catching her loose curls about her cheek. "Well, I thought you should know about the additional transformation. With the . . . well, like I said, the down feathers along my groin."

She began giggling and pressed a hand to her mouth. "I bet that tickles!"

"Nah, I don't feel it at all," he countered, holding her tighter. "Well, that's not totally true. I do feel it, but because they're so soft and light, it heightens my sensitivity in my masculine . . . uh . . . regions."

She nuzzled against his neck and murmured wickedly, "I want to feel your down feathers tickle me. Inside."

He groaned in her ear. "You're tempting me most devilishly, Miss Tiades," he said, thrusting his wings against the air with more force.

"Well, *Mr. Petrakos*, I must find some way to occupy myself during this terrifying experience," she said, closing her eyes. "I cannot believe that you have me in your arms soaring through the sky. I only rode in my first Jeep this morning!"

"Yeah, time for you to engage here, baby. You're right." Hooking one arm more securely beneath her legs, he turned her slightly forward. "You really should look at the city below, sweetheart. You're missing a breathtaking view."

She burrowed her face against his feathered chest, hiding her eyes. "I'm terrified. I've never even been on one of those Ferris wheels my brother, Edward, loved so much. Remember how I made you take him on it?"

"Yes, and now you know why I wasn't afraid of heights." Cupping her cheek, he urged her to look at him. All she could see was his face, right up against hers; his eyes blazed with that rare silver hue; his hair tickled at her cheek. "I want to show you my world, Juliana. That's why this is important . . . for you to see the universe the way I have for the past twenty-five hundred years."

He gazed down at her, searching her face, and there was a flash of insecurity in his otherworldly eyes. She swallowed and made her decision.

She wanted all of him; that's what she'd promised—and this flight was a significant part of that commitment. With a hand clinging to his shoulder, she slowly turned her head and, for one free-falling, heart-stopping moment, screamed. Screamed and screamed . . . and then began laughing deliriously at the tiny buildings down below. The cars and vehicles were like ants, busy conveying crumbs and dirt to and fro.

The river shone with what seemed a dozen colors of sunset; and there were so many ships! The world didn't just appear different from this supernatural view—at that moment she knew it had changed more than she'd been able to grasp.

"I'm taking you out over the water in a minute," he told her in that harsh voice of his. "But first . . . want to see your old street? Or Forsyth Park, for memory's sake?"

She shook her head, eyes wide. "No one can see us? None at all should they look up? You're sure?" She dared another look at the ground below, eyes watering from the whipping wind.

"We are in the mid-dimensions, the place where my kind live and fight . . . and love," he murmured, sliding a strong hand between her thighs. "Hawks mate midair, you know. Quite a fracas they make, as well."

She looked up into his eyes, surprised, a little jealous. "You've taken women sexually while winged before?" She didn't like the idea of anyone else sharing in this special part of him, this almost-sacred change.

He flushed, deep crimson coloring his cheeks. "Milady, no woman has ever glimpsed my wings . . . besides you." He blushed more deeply, and she instantly understood the significance behind those words—and how overcome he'd been with his power around her, so shy yet eager about revealing himself. It was because his winged nature was tied to his masculinity on some very elemental level.

"You awe me," she murmured, stroking the down feathers that dusted across his muscular, human chest. "How would any woman ever resist you . . . all of you? I feel humbled that you chose me, that you love me."

He smiled slowly, then spread his wings wide and began beating them to fly much higher into the sky. *You're showing off for me*, she thought with a grin of her own. He'd always been so proud and handsome; now she knew why. He'd had to compensate for hiding these gorgeous, rare wings. She imagined him waltzing into her town house, Harold at the piano, her mother in the parlor, and everyone staring up at these same midnight black feathers.

Savannah never would have been the same. In fact, it never had been, not for her, once Aristos Petrakos had set foot in town.

She smiled, wondering what her family would have thought about a winged immortal Spartan stealing her heart and whisking her off into the evening sky like this. That was the moment when she felt his warm hand slide between her thighs—and understood why he'd asked her to leave off the lingerie.

He wasn't entirely sure how to accomplish what he wanted, but his body burned with need; he was inflamed from the crown of his head to the length of his hardened cock.

Feeling that slick dampness along Juliana's tight little curls, the way she parted slightly the moment he touched her, it had him eager and urgent despite their midair position. His body trembled with lust and hunger for her, and his wings only pushed harder at the air in reaction.

"I want inside of you," he told her, the words vibrating over his tight vocal cords. "Here . . . now."

She wrapped both arms about his neck, holding tight, and then nodded her wordless assent.

"You trust me, I know you do," he said, easing her dress up about her hips. "Let me shift you in my arms."

She licked her lips and then gave another, determined nod; he turned her gently, opening her legs and then hitching them up around his waist. She now faced him, those shapely thighs tight about his hard abdomen and lower back. He felt her toes brush against his wings every time he beat them. Closing his eyes, he bent forward, capturing her mouth with a rough, demanding kiss. His hands were all over her back, stroking, rubbing, feeling, and the hum of power came even more alive inside of him. That kick of supernatural heat triggered a deeper level of transformation, the lines between arousal and shape-shifting blurring. His changeling body felt the surge of adrenaline and need, and delivered the goods— more of his hawk nature.

The bones of his hands began altering, and he tried to prevent his talons from emerging, but it proved an impossible task. Couldn't be done—not here, while flying. Not now, when he was so desperately aroused. So he pressed his forearms against her back, keeping the sharp claws away from her sensitive skin. Next, his cheekbones shifted slightly, his face becoming more sharply angled, hawkish, but he never broke their kiss.

Alarmed, he wondered what she'd think, but when her hands dug into his scalp and she urged him to kiss her more deeply, he let go of any hesitation. He yielded to her invitation, drawing her closer against his chest.

She slid a hand along his low back, stroking his buttocks, squeezing and fondling him. Then . . . most daring of all, she pushed that dainty little hand down between his thighs, squeezing his balls. Through the tight fabric of his pants, she brushed and outlined him, caressed and demanded.

How the hell was he supposed to get out of these pants?

he thought, working a hand between them. He couldn't get a good angle on his fly, but she eased her hips backward and, with a flirtatious smile up at him, popped the damned thing open. Then, never blinking or looking away—didn't she notice his modified features? how harsh they'd become?—without seeming to care at all, she lowered his zipper.

And then his pants were dangling open, and he shoved at them gracelessly, needing to be inside of her, and now. He spread his wings open their full span, taking them on a long, graceful glide—right as he positioned his hips against hers and began another low, graceful glide . . . into Juliana's eager body.

Ari leaned against the tall spire of the cathedral, looking most satisfied with himself. He folded his arms across his chest after fastening his pants; meanwhile, she was a rumpled mess, splayed flat against the spire, unwilling to take a single step lest she fall.

"If you toppled, I'd dive for you," he drawled. "I think we both saw how extremely capable I am at maneuvering midflight."

She flushed, neatening her dress. "You mean to take me dining looking this . . . this . . ."

"Postcoital?" he volunteered with a devilish grin. "Yes, sweetheart, I mean to take you out in public and promenade you like my brand-new bride. I want to show you off."

Her heart leaped at his casual mention of the word *bride* but she kept her expression nonplussed.

"Surely the other patrons will know what we've been up to," she said, attempting to fix her unruly hair.

"Flying? Making love—with only the setting sun as our chaperone?" He released a low, sultry laugh. "No, Jules, I don't think those mere mortals will have a clue."

She pressed an explanatory hand against her bodice. "My breasts are . . . unrestrained, Aristos." With a downward glance, she was dismayed to see that her nipples budded through the fabric.

"It's gonna be dark, anyway. We're eating outside. Folks are gonna be more interested in trying to break their crab claws open than in noticing your state of undress."

"You said you were going to fly me over the river," she

reminded him, growing chilled. "This restaurant, it's out on Tybee?"

"Yeah, out on the island."

"So we will definitely be crossing the river," she said, drawing in an anxious breath. "I suppose I must face it sometime."

He stepped gracefully around the spire, leaning up next to her. They watched the street below in thoughtful silence, the traffic and city noise drifting up to them. "It might help you remember," he said after a moment.

She pressed her eyes shut, the earlier nightmare returning in vivid, horrible detail. "I think I already do," she admitted, glancing sideways to gauge his reaction.

He said nothing, just waited for her to continue, but his eyes were filled with eager interest.

Blowing out a breath, she confessed, "I had a dream this afternoon. There were . . . creatures. Terrible, choking beings in that water. They dragged me below the surface—and kept pulling me farther into the river's depths."

He scowled. "That sounds like water demons."

"I don't know what they were, but they kept taunting me, communicating to me somehow even though they were yanking me deeper and deeper." She stared down at the street with a shudder. "I couldn't breathe or cry out, and all I wanted was . . . you. To tell you I loved you, would always stay with you."

She felt dampness on her cheek, and only then did she realize that she'd begun to cry. "I did not want to leave you, Aristos." She turned to search his face. "On the contrary, I most desperately wanted to remain with you; even in my very last moments, you were my only thought."

Only a few days left, she thought in a panic. *And when the end comes, he'll believe I wanted to leave this time, too.*

She opened her mouth to confess the rest, the bargain that she'd remembered, but a pain staked through her chest. "I . . . You should . . ."

Get far away from me, as far as you can, she wanted to warn him, but the words would not come forth.

"I love you," she said instead, crying even harder.

He drew her into his reassuring embrace. "You're here now, Jules. We're together. No need to cry anymore. The memory scared you; that's all."

"I need to tell you something. . . ."

A voice screamed inside her mind, a shrill, piercing warning that was not from her own thoughts. She recognized it as Layla instantly.

Don't warn him! If you do, I will make sure he dies.

That horrifying voice spoke inside of Juliana—making it clear that Layla's dream threats had been true, that she shared a place deep inside Juliana's own physical body.

If you warn him, the demon threatened, *I will clip his wings with my claws and shove him off the spire so that he plummets . . . without any way to save himself.*

"You don't have enough power yet," Juliana argued aloud, clinging to Ari.

Naturally, Ari thought she was talking to *him*. "Sweetheart, right now I've got enough power to light up this whole city," he said with an easy laugh. "What do you want to tell me?"

I'm growing stronger with every second. I will devour him as I send him tumbling to that street far below! Layla taunted, and Juliana tried to blot out the image, to resist the powerful terror it elicited.

Juliana wrapped both arms about Ari, holding him closer as her breath caught. "It doesn't matter," she blurted. "Nothing matters except you knowing, truly believing, how much I love you."

Chapter 26

Ari's broad wings fanned out, at least six feet in span, as he did a slow glide into a sandy lot lined with various vehicles. A sign near the paved road said, THE CRAB SHACK, and she was grateful they'd reached the restaurant. Her stomach had been growling for the past half hour, despite the sandwiches they'd eaten at the inn.

"You're absolutely certain that those patrons can't see us?" Juliana pointed to the people dining on the large exterior deck as Aristos brought them earthward, running a few paces upon landing. That motion jostled her slightly against him, so she held on tighter, feeling the strong bands of muscle across his shoulders.

"No," he told her, halting and swinging her onto her feet. He bent double, hands on his knees, breathing heavily for a few moments. "Not as easy as I made that look." He laughed, finally standing tall again. "Whew. That's some heavy lifting, flying you and me both."

"Well, excuse me, sir! Are you implying that I am not delicate?" She popped an indignant hand to her hip, playing at being insulted.

He gave her a leveling look. "Now, Jules. You are the lightest, most perfectly shaped female I've ever hied away in my arms." He smiled slowly. "In point of fact, you are the only one, as I already told you."

She lifted an eyebrow. "Well, I'd certainly hoped you didn't make a habit of deflowering virgins, then whisking them off into the sunset."

"You always were the subject of my most"—he paused, placing a hand over his heart—"courtly attentions. And I pegged you for a wing girl, so there you have it."

He took her hand and began slowly strolling across the sandy lot. "Let's walk a minute. Let me cool down, and then

I can dress and will remove the protections that are making us invisible to normal humans."

He swerved, sidestepping out of the path of a couple who, indeed, seemed entirely unaware of her and Ari's presence. "And inaudible, in case you were worried about that, too. We're totally concealed."

Several moments later, his breathing remained labored, and Juliana became concerned. "You should have told me that the flight was too strenuous for you. We could have acquired a Jeep for this journey or chosen someplace closer for dining." She touched his tight abdomen, brushing away a rivulet of sweat.

"Darling, are you suggesting I can't fly you anywhere your heart so much as contemplates?"

"I'm suggesting," she answered, widening her eyes, "that perhaps you overtaxed yourself by hauling me so far and by making love to me in the midst of the whole process. I'm suggesting that . . . you're human."

He thrust his chest out defiantly. "Superhuman, thank you very much."

"Superhumans don't have limitations? Oh, but I forgot— you're actually an Olympian god!" She giggled, trying to think of how best to tease him. "Ah, but which god would that be? This is the tricky point. I could name you Prometheus, and then we could bind and unbind you, a rather naughty thought, no? But since I'm the one you adore unwrapping, I'd rather that not be our little scene. So . . ."

She had an idea and turned to him abruptly. "But of course! You are Eros, the god of love, wrapped in feathery wings, and I am Psyche. Although, you won't become invisible to me, I hope." She gave a little pirouette; she'd always felt this way when Ari courted her, a little intoxicated and giddy. As she came to a stop in front of him, she realized that, unlike her, he wasn't laughing or smiling at all. In fact, he seemed quite somber as he pulled his long-sleeved shirt over his head.

"You don't want to be Eros to my Psyche?" she asked softly, not understanding what had darkened his mood so suddenly.

"He's the son of Ares," he told her bluntly.

Now she understood and grew equally somber. "The god you bargained with."

"The one who controls my destiny," he said in a grim voice. "They're real, the Olympians. You need to understand that. Demons, angels, gods and monsters, Djinn and Titans." He waved his arm about them, as if the unseen world lurked in every direction. "Anything you ever dismissed as myth . . . anything you imagined was nothing more than folktales from ancient times, sweetheart?" His voice got louder, more intense. "It's all real, and most of it's dangerous as hell!"

She averted her face, staring at the pebbled sand. Demons were real. Of course they were—a fact she now understood all too well. But how could she confess everything about Layla? And he had worried about revolting her? A ridiculous notion all along, but especially now that one of the entities he battled dwelled inside her own soul.

He stepped sideways until he stood just in front of her. "Look at me, Jules."

She kicked at a palm frond; it was broken on the sand, probably a victim of last night's storm.

"Juliana, sweetheart," he coaxed, tilting her chin. When at last she met his gaze, he said, "You didn't do anything wrong. I . . . I'm not in control lately. You've seen it yourself, and it needs to be explained."

"I was thoughtless and unkind to make those jokes when you bear so much on your shoulders."

A devilish gleam filled his eyes. "I love the idea of pretending to be Eros, while you are Psyche, my fair maiden who can only *feel* my feathers in the dark, but never see me."

She closed her eyes, losing herself in the image of him as Eros. "Sling your quiver across your shoulder, release your wings, and . . . capture me," she said, releasing a slow, aroused breath. "When I least expect it, seize me and fly me to some high peak, where you will ravage me in mountain grasses warmed by the sun . . . and your body."

He blinked at that scenario and touched his groin, adjusting himself. Only then did she see the way his manhood jutted prominently against the front of his pants, his arousal undisguised. She reached forward, stroking fingertips over the heated, thick flesh, their bodies separated only by thin fabric. He sucked in a breath, tilting his hips forward ever so slightly.

"Eros is quite the role for you, I believe," she teased, voice all throaty. "Let's enact that scene very soon."

Fire chased down his spine at the seductive promise. His body, as ever, remained poised on the verge of reactions that he couldn't seem to control. But then he caught her hand, halting her caress. "I have things to tell you," he said, his words quiet.

Oblivious to his turmoil, she smiled at him, sliding her arms about his neck. "I want to hear everything over dinner. About your life, about your friends—"

"This is about my power. And not just about me being a protector or immortal."

He planted his palms on both her shoulders, and when her expression convinced him that he had her full attention, that she clearly perceived the gravity of the moment, he blurted out the truth.

"I am a demigod," he confessed. "I carry the power of Olympus itself in my veins."

Juliana braced herself against the wooden railing of the exterior deck, studying him. To her credit, she didn't look like she was about to bolt, but she didn't exactly seem pleased with him, either. "How, precisely, does one *become* a demigod?" she asked after a moment. "I thought they were born, not made."

"Not always."

"Not always," she repeated, and he looked away.

"That's all you wish to say on the matter?" she said tartly. "You have no further explanation to help me understand what you, my beloved, are in your most core nature?"

He sighed. "Look, Jules, it's a really long story, but no, I haven't always been like this." He extended his forearms, and they rippled with silver, his hidden power flaunting itself against his will. "I was changed into a demigod, not born one."

She placed a hand on her hip. "Oh! Well, when did that happen, Aristos? This afternoon? Were you transformed as we made love? Such small details, I suppose, in the balance of coupling and sex and union."

"You're mad *now*? This is when you finally freak? Wings were okay, immortality a snap!" He popped his fingers together. "Not even a bump in the road for you, baby. But *this* puts you over the edge?"

"I'm not upset about what you are," she assured him, becoming much gentler. "Rather that you didn't tell me about this part of yourself. That you don't seem to fully trust my love for you. Or realize that nothing could ever make my feelings for you waver." She shook her head sadly, pain visible in her blue eyes. "Not even learning that you're a god."

"For the love of Olympus, I'm not a god! I'm *half* of one!" He screamed so loud, it made his throat hurt. Then, centering his hands on her shoulders, he bent down until they were eye level. "I shouldn't have yelled. I'm sorry. But please, just tell me you're not about to bolt on me now."

"Aristos, look at me. I'm standing right here," she reassured him.

He released his hold on her. "But you've got leaving in your eyes," he said, and put his back to her. His own eyes had started to water, and he wasn't about to let her see him turn into a complete and total pussy when she took off on her own.

She followed him, and his whole body tensed as she leaned into him, nuzzling her cheek against his back. Now, *that* didn't seem like the action of a woman about to break up with you. It was a whole lot more like an "I'm here for keeps, thick or thin, Olympus or Savannah"-type gesture. And it only made the tears in his eyes come faster. She wasn't leaving, wasn't running. Wasn't dying on him. She was pressing a warm, solid, and very human body right up against his own.

"I'm assuming that we are still in our own private place?" she asked softly.

"Sorry, but I haven't lifted my Herculean arms to reveal us just yet," he answered in a restrained tone.

She ran her palm up his chest, and his body burned anew. His nipples reacted as she brushed her fingertips back and forth. She wrapped her arms about his torso, squeezing him close. "Oh, my beautiful man. My feelings have not changed! Aristos, I was only a bit upset that . . . that you told me everything else this afternoon. And in turn, I accepted every part of you." She took hold of his hips, forcing him to grudgingly turn and face her. He swiped the back of his hand over his damp eyes.

She leaned up onto her booted toes, brushing at the wetness herself. "Can you tell me why you would ever imagine that I'd not accept this last thing, the one which seems to be the most important part of you?"

His shoulders sagged. "It's eating me alive, Jules. This power—it really, truly is. That's why I lost control at the boutique; it's why I was shaking and my eyes were silver. It wasn't because of being an immortal or a hawk changeling or even a Spartan. It's this godsdamned"—he held out both forearms, flexing them—"Olympian strength burning along inside of me, like acid, like lava, and I can't ever rest or just settle down. I hate this stuff." He patted the veins on his wrist. "But I didn't have any other choice but to ingest it." He held his arms out, watching silver chase all through his veins and arteries; it reminded him of flying over a city at night, the network of twinkling lights. It was like Ares' fingerprint all over his body.

"Why did he have to be so cruel? Wasn't it enough that we were willing to dance to his battle songs? Follow his war drums for eternity? No. He had to do this." Ari formed furious fists, watching the silver pool within his hands, then seep out like a waterfall.

"How did he do it? When?"

"He seeded this power into River, at the moment of his transformation. His idea of a big rollicking joke to give our slave a secret overdose of his own god's strength. He planned to activate it, harness it . . . whatever; I don't even know for sure. But he created River as his secret weapon in our midst."

Juliana rubbed her forehead. "I am most confused. River is not a slave."

"No, you're right about that, although he once was," he said in an anguished voice. "I took on River's curse so he could live a mortal life with Emma. . . . This was the power he endured for thousands of years. I'm enslaved now . . . to this power."

She drew him into her arms and held him; she gave no words, no easy solutions. Just her warm, comforting, human body wrapped around his epic one. Something about that, well, it made him believe that maybe freedom could still be within his grasp.

Chapter 27

Nikos plopped down a big loaf of bread and jar of peanut butter in the middle of the kitchen table and sat down to make himself at least three sandwiches. He really was that hungry. All day until this moment? No appetite at all. He'd been too worried about Mason, about his state of mind, yet not comfortable with the idea of calling and checking on him. Not after the things they'd said last night.

But with River and Emma's report that he was all right, not having some cosmic meltdown, he felt like he could breathe again. He stacked six slices of bread on the plate, dipped the knife in the jar, and started spreading.

"Six sandwiches, Nikos?" River asked with a grin, dropping into the chair beside him. "That hungry, huh?"

Nikos lifted an eyebrow. "Mathematics never has been your strong suit, brother. This will be three sandwiches when I'm done."

"Not if I swipe one of them from you first." River laughed, reaching toward the sandwich Nikos was almost done making.

He elbowed the guy away. "Emma?" he called out across the kitchen. "Can you bring another plate over? Apparently I've got to feed your husband."

"See? Amazing," River said, kicking back in the chair. "You can actually be nice to me when you put some effort into it."

It was meant as a joke, but Nik's own smile faded, and try as he might, he couldn't find one damn thing to say in return. He just quietly made his sandwich, studying the pattern the knife's serrated edge made in the smooth peanut butter, looking anywhere but into his brother's green eyes.

"Nikos," River said after a minute, "I was just kidding around, okay?"

Nik nodded, wishing as he always did that he could find a way to be closer to River. There was always a distance between them, the gulf that Nikos couldn't find the courage to bridge by just telling River the truth about the secret connection they shared. He'd almost done it two months ago, right after that battle in Hades when he'd thought River was going to die. But he'd lost his nerve and backed down and hadn't summoned it again since.

Nikos decided the best thing, really, was to just change the subject. "Tell me more about Mason. You said he seemed settled, but . . . did he talk about Juliana anymore?"

Emma joined them at the table, setting down two more plates. "He really was okay about it all," she said right as Jamie came into the kitchen.

"Hey, you guys seen Mason?" Jamie asked, then, seeing the sandwich spread, laughed. "Oh, fine dining tonight, is it? Regular filet mignon special."

Nik looked up, gesturing with his knife. "Hey. I happen to like peanut butter sandwiches. Way better than blood soup, let me tell you."

"We should've gone to the Crab Shack, too," Emma said with a sigh, going to work on her own sandwich.

"That's where Ari and Juliana are," River explained to the group of them. "They were heading out to Tybee, and Mason suggested it."

Jamie stopped in the middle of the kitchen, his expression deadly serious. "Wait; are you saying you told Mason where Ari and Juliana were going to be?"

"Well, not exactly. Mason suggested that restaurant, though. Why?" Emma repeated, confusion in her eyes. "He was fine about everything."

Jamie sighed, shoulders slumping. "No. My brother ain't fine, not even close. That's why I came over here just now. 'Cause he isn't answering his cell. This morning I got the total impression he'd never even gone to bed. Just sat there, studying the lore, trying to find some way to explain his theory about Juliana being a Djinn. But it's more than that. Some of our weapons were gone. . . . He obviously took 'em, but normally we have a checkout procedure for all the Shades. He bypassed that altogether."

Nikos's heart began hammering. "What kinds of weapons? His usual or something more . . . intense?" he asked, keeping his voice as calm and unrevealing as possible. Because he knew Jamie was dead right about Mace's mental state; that was why he himself had worried about the man all day, after seeing firsthand how unhinged he'd been last night.

"His Desert Eagle . . . his Glock. But, like I said, we have a policy among us, just to make sure we know where the weapons are at all times. He didn't follow that . . . like maybe he hoped I wouldn't notice? Only, I was specifically watching his ass, so yeah, I know he's armed to the teeth."

Emma reached for Jamie's hand, squeezing it. "Jamie, I promise you, Mason seemed all right. He didn't say a word about Juliana or any of that." Emma looked toward River with a searching expression. "Didn't you think he seemed fine?"

River thought a moment. "I didn't really talk to him. I was on the phone with Ari most of that time, but yeah, I think he seemed like himself."

Jamie sank into the other open chair, raking both hands across his short hair. "That, my friends, is for one very good reason. My brother is a consummate actor. He's had to be, after everything in Iraq . . . with his PTSD and the pain he's been lugging around. He's learned exactly what to tell us. How to behave to convince us all that he's A-flipping-OK." Suddenly Jamie looked at Nik—really looked at him. "Well, most of us, that is. Because I'm guessing that *one* of us," he continued, his eyes laser locked with Nik's, "has known the truth all along. That my brother's in a shitload of pain." Jamie kept on looking at Nikos, his eyes practically begging for help, or insight, and softly added, "Nik, please help my brother."

"I . . . I'm not sure I can," he replied just as quietly, remembering how firmly Mason had shut him out. "I doubt he wants to hear from me right now."

"No, you're wrong, Nik," Jamie insisted, clasping Nikos's shoulder. "He's in trouble, and he needs you. Please . . . go after him. Before he hurts Ari or Juliana . . . or, most of all, himself."

Juliana now faced a most difficult quandary. It seemed that Layla should not, at all costs, learn about Ari's power. Had the demon heard everything Juliana herself just had? Was she biding her time, waiting until the end of the nine days—almost eight, really—when she would have permanent, full control over Juliana's body, and she could fulfill her terrible plan?

Layla had threatened Ari's life and well-being, but surely the demon didn't understand his true power. Would she present a danger to a demigod? Could he be killed, or was it a different sort of immortality, one where any injury would instantly heal and death could never make a claim? Perhaps he would not be at risk from Layla's efforts at all.

Jules kept asking herself these questions, drumming her fingers on the table, feeling edgy and overly warm, which only reminded her of Layla's existence inside her. She had no idea how to warn Ari, not with the threats Layla had issued—she couldn't turn to him for assistance. She couldn't think of a single way to confess all that she'd learned about the "angel" with whom she'd actually bargained without bringing danger upon him.

Meanwhile, Ari studied the menu, oblivious—so light-hearted since their discussion. He was wearing that dopey, sweet smile of his that she loved so much, hunching over the table as he read, and seeing him so happy made Juliana want to weep. She refused to let any harm come to him, no matter what, and would find a way to overcome the demon inside of her. Perhaps a priest could be consulted, she thought hopefully. Yes, that was what she needed to do, discreetly locate a spiritual adviser, someone who could help exorcise Layla. The problem, however, was that she had no way of operating one of the Jeeps. But then she recalled that Googling phone that Shay had shown her.

"Aristos," she inquired casually. "What is Google . . . exactly?"

He looked at her in surprise. "You've been back, what, a day, and you already picked up on that?"

She smiled despite herself. "I've always been most modern. You know that."

"Then Google it." He tapped something into his phone, then handed it to her.

"Pardon?" she asked in confusion, taking his cell phone in hand. Looking down she saw the Google search feature was open.

"You can type anything—and I do mean anything—into Google, and it will tell you what it is. Including the term *Google*."

She stared down at the phone, wondering how she might clandestinely search for a priest without Ari noticing, although he was probably too giddy to notice. He studied the menu some more, then released a slow whistle.

His smile widened impishly. "Hey, they got seventy-eight live alligators. Says so right here. They're over in the gator lagoon."

He handed her what appeared to be a large napkin. "Here," he said, "you're gonna need a bib for the crabs."

She felt completely numb; all she could do was keep trying to smile back at him. Her stomach churned, and meanwhile Aristos seemed unaware that anything could be wrong. He didn't know that their happiness was under threat. He'd relaxed into his seat, sipping a beer. That smile never vanished from his face, not for a single moment.

Looking at one of the servers dressed as a pirate, his face got even brighter. "Oh, and we should totally go to Pirate Fest next year."

"Next year?" Her heart skipped several beats; she'd have sworn it.

"You'll still be with me, right?" His sweet smile broke her heart, and she had to stare down at the menu to conceal the tears that welled in her eyes.

"I would never leave you willingly."

"Okay, then! We could get River and Emma, and all dress up. I mean, we work our asses off all the time, right? So long as the world isn't meeting some epic end that weekend, we gotta do it."

"Ari, I . . ." She discreetly blotted her eyes, searching the restaurant for a private area.

"You need the ladies'?" he volunteered cheerily, then pointed the way. "Just follow the signs."

She kept her gaze away from him, feeling the intense nausea and heat inside her body grow stronger. And praying that Ari wouldn't glimpse the tears gleaming in her eyes . . . or notice that she had discreetly hidden his cell phone beneath the folds of her skirt ruffles.

*   *   *

Mason stared at the marsh, the golden blond grasses glowing with the last light of the day. The drive out to Tybee was always damned gorgeous at this time of day, and he particularly loved the sight of the returning shrimp boats, the gulls following them.

Normally, that was. Normally, he'd have driven slowly, opened the windows on the truck, and inhaled the briny smell of his native low country. Of course, normal didn't exist for him anymore, and hadn't in almost a year. Maybe it would soon, however, now that he was going to take down the demon who'd caused his spiraling descent into hell.

Keeping his eyes on the road, he leaned across the seat and opened the glove compartment, making sure that he'd fully secured his semiautomatic in there. The pistols were in the side compartment, but depending on what went down at the restaurant, he might need the heavy shit.

As he closed the compartment, his cell phone rang; he'd been ignoring the thing all damned day, especially because Jamie was hovering over his ass like a mother hen. With a downward glance, he saw that it was Nikos this time. Now, that guy had been utterly conspicuous with his lack of calls and texts, considering they usually pinged each other half a dozen times a day. But he'd seen the quiet pain in Nik's big brown eyes last night, even though the guy had tried to look away. No wonder he'd sent Emma and River to check on him, not done the proverbial drive by himself.

Yeah, because you fucked up yet again, Captain Brilliance, he thought, staring down at Nik's name on the caller-ID display. What must it have taken for the reserved, quiet Spartan to call after the way things had gone between them last night?

Simple: Nikos Dounias wouldn't call, not after that, not after the rejection Mace had seen in his eyes. He knew that because he knew Nik—really knew him—and he wouldn't call, not without a very compelling reason.

Like he suspected that Mace was up to something and wanted to stop him; unless someone else had put him up to making the call.

Mason hit IGNORE on the phone, turned it off, and sped faster toward the Crab Shack.

Chapter 28

A ri watched Jules leave for the bathroom, loving the way those sexy-as-hell boots accentuated her shapely legs— as did the short skirt. He got a sudden image of taking all that ruffled fabric and peeling it away to reveal her bare bottom. Oh yeah, that would be fantastic, even right here in the restaurant; he could use his power to make them invisible. He imagined lifting her up onto the table and spreading her legs about him, and instantly the front of his jeans bulged outward.

He shifted around in the seat, grateful that it was nighttime and that the restaurant patrons were too busy with their corn on the cob to worry about the megastiff cob in his pants. He actually snorted aloud as he recalled Jules's love of fresh corn.

And he was still laughing, leaning back in his chair for a sip of frothy draft beer, when Mason Angel slid right into Juliana's vacant seat.

Ari grinned, greeting his friend with a rousing, "Oorah, dude! What're you doing out here?"

Mace wiped at his sweaty brow, setting down a half-consumed cup of beer. "Aristos, look, we gotta talk," he said, scooting much closer and seeming out of breath, like he'd sprinted all the way here, even though that couldn't be true—not with that beer in his hand.

"You having dinner?" Ari looked all around the deck curiously. "Who else is here? Scooby members or just your lonely ole jarhead?"

Mason gave him a forbidding look. "Just me."

Then things started to come together, and fast, as Ari recalled that Mason himself had suggested this restaurant to begin with. "You followed us out here." It wasn't a question.

"Had to, man," was all Mason said in reply.

And then Ari figured out the rest of the drill. Mace had shown up for only one reason—he still believed that Jules was actually a demon. He hunted her kind by both profession and calling, and he wasn't going to let this go.

Ari leaned forward, planting both palms on the table, and growled protectively. "You're not going to touch her, Angel."

Mason mirrored his gesture, stabbing a finger at Ari. "I'm here to tell you that she's a stone-cold killer, man. Not who you think at all. She is the darkest kind of demon."

"You're basing that on what?" Ari hissed, subtly surveying Mason's golf shirt and jeans, searching for a concealed weapon. He appeared unarmed, but Ari didn't relax for a moment, because he knew Mason was trained to be dangerous in much less obvious ways.

Ari's whole body was poised for attack, to protect the woman he loved—and at whatever cost might be required. He would hate it, but he knew he'd go so far as killing Mason, if necessary. Anything to guard Juliana against the demon hunter's lethal aim.

"Have you looked into her eyes?" Mason asked. "I mean, really gazed into 'em?"

Ari thought of Juliana's luminous, adoring gaze, the way she'd stared up into his eyes as they made love at the inn— and the abandon in those same blue depths as they came together midflight. There'd been nothing reflected there except her inherent goodness, the truth of who she was— and her unabashed, genuine love for Ari.

"Hundreds of times today alone," Ari answered firmly. "My girl's not what you think, Mace. Not even close. Jules is . . ." Ari pictured her naked body beneath his, luscious auburn hair fanned out on the hotel pillow. "Well, here's the thing, buddy. You want to get at her? You'll have to come through me."

Mason stared at him and then barked out a laugh. Leaning back in his chair, the guy just kept on laughing, too. "You've had sex with that demon already. Haven't you?"

Ari tore into a packet of saltines, ignoring the question.

Mace shook his head with narrowed eyes. "Motherfucker," he said, whistling low. "Geez, even I didn't think that you were that much of a dumb-ass. But I guess the rumors on that count are true after all."

"What I have or haven't done with Juliana is none of your godsdamned business."

Mason's expression grew deadly. "Actually it is. It goes against everything in my nature to let something like that creature live."

At that, Ari was up out of his chair and on Mason Angel before the other guy had time to set that beer down. It sloshed all down the front of his shirt as Ari seized his collar with one hand and his throat with the other. Several diners around them noticed the disruption, an older woman swatting Ari with her umbrella in an attempt to break up their skirmish.

Her irate little gesture finally knocked some sense back into Ari, reminding him that they were in public. Slowly he released his grip on Mason. "You come with me," he commanded, ripping off his bib and tossing it on the table indignantly.

There were some things, he decided, that you just didn't do with a bright red lobster pinned to your chest.

Ari kept Mason cuffed around the back of his neck, forcing him off the patio and down onto the palm-lined drive of the restaurant. They reached Mason's pickup, and Ari gave him a big shove, sending him sprawling against the vehicle's door. But then some redneck dumb-ass gunned his truck on the way out of the lot, spraying them both with gravel and sand.

"Get a designated driver, asshole," Ari cursed at the departing tailpipe, wiping the sand from his eyes.

Mason seized that moment to jump Ari, riding on his back as Ari staggered forward, spinning to the right, then the left, trying to shake him off like just another swamp mosquito. Knocking Mason up against the truck cab finally dislodged him, and Ari shoved him there.

"You want a fucking rumble, you got it," Ari seethed. "You little prick, what do you mean showing up and threatening Juliana like that? Then you try the takedown on me? You're just gunning for it, aren't you?"

"Fucking A I wanna fight, Petrakos," the man fired back,

and suddenly Ari was the one backed up against the truck. Ari kneed the hunter in the groin, though, and then they were down on the gravel, going to town. He managed to get the human in a wrestling lock, arm around his throat, and there was no way for him to break loose.

"I'm a Spartan, Mace," he reminded him, feeling bad for the dude as he clawed and worked at Ari's forearm. It had to be an ego blow for a marine, being knocked on his ass like a baby mouse by a housecat; and it wasn't fun to have your windpipe a few millimeters away from being flattened, either. He knew that one from personal experience.

"You gonna be nice about my girl, or not?" Ari asked gently, but not releasing his firm grip.

Mason sagged into him, and Ari worried that the guy was blacking out, so he lessened the pressure on Mason's throat.

"Come on, give it on up," Ari continued. "You're my buddy. I don't wanna make it hurt like this."

Mace just coughed and cursed, then elbowed Ari nastily in the gut before scuttling away. Ari let him go, knowing that if he had to, he could do the takedown all over again.

Mason glared up at him from where he sprawled on the pebbled drive. "She's dangerous, dude. I don't want you . . ." Mason began coughing all over again, rubbing at his windpipe. "Damn, I wrestled at the Citadel. What kind of maneuver was *that*?"

Ari gave him a proud, sideways grin. "Pure Spartan, that's what."

"Show me sometime . . . when we're on the same side."

"We are now."

Mason frowned, overcome by another coughing fit. Finally, he managed to squeeze out, "I gotta make sure you don't get hurt . . . nobody does."

"Why's that all on you, huh?"

Mason was loyal to a fault; more than once the hunter had stepped into a vicious demon battle and covered Ari's back, all of theirs, without any thought for his own safety. It was obvious that the only reason he was being so dogged about Juliana was because he truly perceived her as a threat.

"Listen, I thought Jules was a threat at first, too. I understand this theory of yours, but she's not a demon. Trust me on that."

"She's a Djinn," Mason corrected, still rubbing his windpipe. "It's not a theory, either. And much as I hate you at
the moment, you're still my friend, Aristos, and I gotta be
sure you don't get killed. That my family stays safe. So,
yeah, it is all on me because I'm the best protection y'all
got right now."

Ari thought of flying Jules over Savannah, of the way
she had stilled for a moment, hands clutching his shoulders,
eyes filled in wonder. She was the very essence of beauty
and light and love. She could not—not in any world or universe that Ari knew of—be a demon. Mason Angel was just
flat wrong, and it was obviously up to Ari to make the man
see the error of his assumptions.

"You just need to spend more time with her to see that
she's who she says she is," Ari insisted.

Mace shook his head. "It's in her eyes. You'll see it . . .
eventually. Like I did from the first."

"In her eyes," Ari repeated.

Mason pointed to his own face, opening his green eyes
wide. "The hunger. You'll catch it eventually; she'll lower
her guard at some point, and you'll see her for the demon
that she is," he explained, and the words sent an eerie chill
down Ari's back.

Mason stared into the distance, and his next words
sounded almost mechanical, memorized, as if he were at
a great remove from the scene. "She reveals her true self
because it can't be helped. The greed and ugliness are part
of her core nature." Mason frowned, still gazing at some
imaginary or unseen point in the distance. "That's why she
always exposes herself in the end."

Ari shivered again, not liking the tone Mason used. It
was like listening to Shay or Emma when they got rolling,
speaking words from the Highest God. Truth that couldn't
be denied.

"You sound like you're prophesying," Ari said warily.

Mason turned his magnetic gaze back on him. "Maybe
I am."

"Then why is your prophecy at odds with those I got
from all the Daughters?"

"I . . . don't know."

"It's 'cause, Devil Dog, you're wrong this time. You're
just too much of a stubborn freak to admit it."

Mace looked back at him, a light sheen of perspiration forming on his forehead. "I have history with that demon."

"You have history with lots of demons. But you ain't got shit with my woman," Ari joked, aiming for their usual banter. If he could get Mason laughing, maybe the guy would let go of his vendetta.

Ari stood, brushing off his hands. "Look, buddy, let's go have a beer. Spend some time with Juliana, and you'll see that first impressions, well, sometimes, they're just flat wrong." Ari reached for Mason's hand to help him up. "I'm betting they have a nice cold Bud in there, one with your name on it."

Ari pulled Mason into a big bear hug. "Still friends?" he asked.

Mason groaned. "Oh, for fuck's sake. Are you actually patting me down, Petrakos?"

Ari didn't answer but did finish the job of frisking Mason for any weapons.

As they stepped apart, Mason looked at him in surprise. "My weapons are in the truck. You honestly think I'd play O.K. Corral in the middle of the Crab Shack when a bunch of civilians are likely to get caught in the cross fire? Do you really think I'm that reckless?"

"I love her, Angel," he said with a shrug. "Someday, you're gonna love someone, too, and then you'll understand what it was like when she died on me. How long I grieved, only to get her back again."

"The dead don't generally come back to life," Mason said in a distant, disembodied voice.

Ari just pointed to himself. "No, sometimes they do."

"Not when I fall in love."

Ari had some guesses as to where Mason's affections lay these days, so he didn't totally understand the man's reaction, the way his gaze stayed long and far, far away.

"Come on, let's go get you another beer, and you can ask my girl how cool it was when Savannah smelled like horseshit 'cause of the carriages, and your great-granddad got his rocks off by trying to marry her."

But Mason didn't laugh; in fact, his gaze grew even longer and farther away. Ari hated how unnerved the man seemed, and that it was because of his theories about Jules.

"You're gonna see, dude." Ari clapped a hand on Mason's

shoulder, walking him back toward the deck. "The Oracle vouched for her; your sister did; Emma and Sophie."

Mason shook his head. "They're wrong."

"I'm not wrong. I know she's the woman I loved. The goodness in her, the light in her eyes ... Yeah, man, you just need to look deep into her eyes, like you said. That, a few Budweisers, and you'll see the light."

"Or the darkness," Mace said somberly. "And how am I supposed to protect your ass then? Unarmed and rogue as I am?"

Ari shivered despite himself but tried to make a joke of it. "Well, if it comes to that, I'll go full-on hawk and fly you to higher ground. Just don't go getting a crush on me or saying 'my hero' in a swoony voice." Then he popped his forehead with his palm. "Oh, but that's right! Nikos already has that gig covered."

Mace turned to him, face instantly red. "Excuse me?"

Ari slapped him on the back of the head playfully. "Don't get your macho panties in a wad. I'm just calling it like I see it. You got a big-ass thing for my Spartan brother? Knock yourself out with the guy!"

"Fuck you, Petrakos," Mason swore, but Ari didn't miss that the guy blushed a whole lot more. Which was fine, because if Mace was busy being embarrassed over Nik, then he wouldn't be working his obsessive theory about Juliana. Distraction, a perfect military tactic when dealing with friends suffering from well-meant but potentially lethal intentions. Now, if Ari could just keep Mace on this even keel, he knew the guy would come to see the truth about Juliana's goodness.

Thankfully, Juliana was the only one in the ladies' room. She leaned closer to the mirror, staring at the reflection, practically expecting to see Layla gazing back at her. She stared for a long moment, shivering slightly—but saw nothing beyond her own familiar blue gaze.

Blotting a hand towel to her cheeks, she tried to work some of the flush out of her face. Her lips were swollen, her pale skin abraded from Ari's rough beard. Surely the entire restaurant knew that they'd been having tumbling sex earlier in the day. The evidence was written all over her face.

She pressed the wet cloth against her mouth and throat,

wishing some of the heat in her body would cool. It seemed unnatural—it was late October, she was barely wearing any clothing whatsoever, yet her skin burned as if touched by hot coals.

She frowned at that realization. Fiery heat inside her body? It had to be Layla, beginning to take firmer possession of their shared body.

"This is still my body," she hissed at the mirror. "It's mine—not yours."

Then she noticed that the blush in her cheeks was growing much stronger, sweeping down her neck like a rolling wave. Panicked, Juliana opened her dress and watched as her entire body reddened. Her breathing became quick and unsteady, and she had to lean her weight into the counter to keep from falling to the floor.

Oh, God, help me! She prayed, feeling the air rush from her lungs. *Save me from this demon . . . and protect Aristos!*

Sliding to the floor, she crumpled there, and the cell phone went clattering out of her grasp. "No! I won't allow you to take control over my body!" she cried out, and with a weak hand she tried to reach the phone.

She could feel Layla's strength mounting inside her, the sensation manifesting as a twisting, horrific pain in Jules's belly. "I . . . am . . . a fighter. Like my Aristos." She panted the words, still grasping for the phone, and finally managed to lay hold of it.

She barely managed to sit up against the counter, and stared down at Ari's cell again. It was called a BlackBerry, and although she had no idea how to operate the sleek, black device, she was certain she needed the help of a priest.

She'd kept the Google open, and with shaking hands she began working the phone's buttons, typing in the word *Savannah*.

Would the BlackBerry speak aloud to her? Call the priest directly on her behalf? She wasn't sure how it worked at all, but she had to act quickly, lest Layla have the chance to lash out against Aristos.

She began typing the word *priest*, but before she'd finished fumbling with the buttons, she heard the sound of Layla's wailing shrieks inside her mind. Her body instantly burned more fiercely.

You will not seek help! Layla screamed, and Juliana's head felt as if it would split open.

At that precise moment, the BlackBerry began vibrating and playing that song from earlier. The one Ari had called the Rolling Stones. Her hands shook uncontrollably, but she tried to keep hold of the cell. Could this be the priest, calling her?

Looking down, she saw the name "Nikos Doumas." He was one of the Spartans; she'd met him last night.

She hit a button and heard a man. "Ari? Where are you?" the accented voice asked.

Her head hurt even more, as she tried to bring the cell to her ear. "Nikos," she barely managed to rasp "Help . . . me."

A choking hold seized her throat, stifling speech, and the cell went clattering onto the floor. Again she heard Nikos; this time he was calling out her own name, but his words were instantly drowned out by Layla's tormenting screeches. She clapped hands over both ears, which was fruitless since the sounds were coming from inside her own body and soul.

"No!" she screamed as her skin flamed even hotter and trickles of sweat began forming rivulets between her breasts and thighs.

Reaching with all her will and strength, she battled against the demon. Opening her medium's gift, she attempted something that she'd not done in years—she worked a barricade around her own private thoughts, but she had no idea whether it would be effective. She'd never had access to her supernatural gifts as a spirit, and although she knew her talents had been resurrected along with her body, at least based on the way she'd been able to trail Ari downtown earlier, she wasn't sure about this protective barrier.

Another knifing pain erupted behind her eyes, and she heard Layla shriek again. *That is no shield against me! You are weak. You were always weak; that's why you died*, the demon taunted. *It's why you believed my bargain. Weak, pitiful human.*

"I belong to God. To Jesus Christ . . . you can't have me," Jules protested, doubling over. Her belly spasmed, and she began writhing on the floor, unable to control her body's reaction to the demon's surging power inside of her. She began panting then, overwhelmed by a scorching heat that burned right inside her abdomen and chest. She felt her vision grow dim and bleak, everything a single grayish color—washed out and ugly in its sameness. It was different from when she'd been dead; something about the landscape, the way she saw it, was filled with despair.

Layla's vision, she realized. *Layla* was taking control, and no matter how hard Juliana battled, the demon couldn't be stopped. Her chest rose and fell frantically, and she knew she was about to be overrun. Knew that she could not prevent Layla from seizing control of her body, not by her human will or even by physical action, not now. Then, her physicality actually began to transform, and she felt her skin tingle as it changed to a duskier hue. Layla wasn't just taking control; she was . . . altering Jules physically. But the demon had said that it inhabited Juliana's own form, so what was this?

Oh, precious one, I can force your body into assuming any appearance I choose. But perhaps it will be more interesting to go to your Aristos as . . . you, Layla trilled inside Juliana's mind.

"The Lord is my shepherd," she began reciting, barely managing to get the words out. "I shall not want. . . ."

The words stopped then, sizzling on her tongue, trapped in her throat. Her world became fully dark, like the deepest bottomless well.

"Oh, but I want very, *very* much!" Layla said, her voice a distant echo. "And I'm in charge of this body now."

Chapter 29

Nikos was already in the driveway, stripping out of his shirt and about to take flight. There wasn't time to stick around, have a group meeting, and try to vote by committee, which was how he knew things would go if he told the others about his call with Juliana.

Jamie was right. Mace really was in some kind of trouble; he had to be, if he wasn't answering his cell. Particularly since he never screened calls, at least not ones from Nik, but it was obvious that he'd hit IGNORE from the way the phone had instantly rolled to voice mail.

So, Nik wasn't having a hard time putting facts together—Mace was working on his own, planning to take down Juliana. And, given the way she had sounded on the phone? Mace might actually be at least halfway right about her true identity. Except what kind of demon begged for help? It was a bizarre, threatening situation, from top to bottom.

Which meant Mason might be in danger, Ari right along with him. Tying his long-sleeved tee around his waist, Nik considered going back into the main house and making sure he had backup. But he knew how the cadre operated, and every minute spent deliberating might put Mace and Ari in even greater danger.

But as much as he cared for his Spartan brother, it was the thought of Mace landing in a demon's crosshairs that sent a frisson chasing across his bare arms and chest. Because he'd meant what he'd told the man last night: He would die saving him, would use his wings, his sword, and his body to protect him rather than see him hurt in any way.

Reaching into his jeans pocket, he retrieved his cell phone. Maybe he was overreacting, he thought. Except then he recalled how worried Jamie had been earlier, the fear Nik had seen spark in the man's eyes—fear that his brother was in true danger because of his PTSD. Because of how upended he currently was. Even Mace's own brother considered him to be at risk right now, and he didn't even know that Mason might be right about Juliana.

The way she'd cried out for help, the strangled sound of her voice, couldn't be good. He dialed Ari's number again, his hands shaking slightly as he held the cell phone up to his ear.

"Well, hello there," a female voice purred. The timbre sounded like Juliana; the tone and attitude definitely did not.

"Uh . . . Juliana?"

"Indeed it is. And you are Nikos Dounias," the female trilled, startling him until he recalled that she'd have seen it on the caller ID. "What a beautiful name. A mighty warrior, are you?"

"Is Mason with you? Is Ari there?" he rushed on, shifting his feet on the sandy drive impatiently.

"Don't you want to talk to me?" she purred into the phone, sounding very much like a coquette—and not at all like the woman he'd met the night before.

"I'm worried about Mason," Nik insisted. "Put him on right now."

"Is that because you *like* Mason? You know, in the way Mason likes men?" she asked with an easy laugh.

"Give the phone to Mason!" he shouted, realizing that something had to be very, very wrong. And that Mace had obviously been very, very right about Juliana's identity.

"Oh!" she cried out in a delighted voice. "I understand now. You're the new Kelly!"

Nikos slammed the phone shut and, with a running leap, took to the sky. The Djinn's words revealed the truth: Mason was in terrible, deadly danger. That demon had obviously found a way to track him all the way from Iraq, and right into the center of their ranks. That kind of targeting could only mean one thing: She intended to destroy Mason completely this time—and Ari, his beloved Spartan brother, was right in the cross fire.

Fifteen minutes later, Jules still hadn't come back to the table. Had she wandered over to the gator pit and fallen in? Ari wondered. A simple trip to the bathroom shouldn't have taken nearly so long.

Across the table from him, Mason maintained a death grip on his beer, and Ari was starting to get restless himself. He'd wanted her to make a good impression on Mace, not vanish like the mists blowing across the deck.

Thankfully, she waltzed out on the deck right then. Well, maybe sashayed was more like it, swinging her hips in what could only be described as a very un-Victorian manner. If she'd tried that during one of their long-ago strolls through Forsyth Park, someone would have sent her off to a sanatorium strictly on the basis of being indelicate.

She looked different to him suddenly. While in the bathroom, she'd unbuttoned the top of her bodice so that it fell open and revealed the swell of exposed breasts. Her cheeks were flushed, and she carried herself with a feline, sensual gait that he'd never seen her use before.

She arrived at their table with a flirtatious flourish, handing over his BlackBerry with a coy smile. Why had she taken his phone without telling him? He didn't have time to ask, because she turned and stroked a hand along Mason's shoulder with downright proprietary sensuality, eyes ablaze as she touched him. "Well, how do *you* do, Mr. Angel?" Jules asked in a coquettish voice, sliding an arm around him like he was a hot target. "Your arrival is a very nice surprise, indeed. Have you missed me? It's been a long time, after all."

Ari clenched a fist against the table, cutting his eyes at her as a warning. This little outburst was totally the wrong move—whatever her intentions were. She was what? Coming on to Mason like some tawdry whorehouse seductress? That wasn't the way to win that demon hunter to their side of things, and it sure as Hades made him jealous. They'd bared everything to each other earlier today, and here she was bestowing those lustful caresses along Mason Angel's nape. And was she seriously running her fingers through his hair?

Ari leaned forward, gaping in silent fury. "I've never seen Jules behave remotely like . . . like this. I have no idea what's gotten into her."

"Ironic choice of words."

Ari kicked the guy's chair with his foot. "I told you she's not possessed."

Mason gave him a long, skull-drilling stare for at least five seconds. "This isn't Juliana. Already told you that."

"Trust me, gentlemen; I'm a lot more fun." She laughed and exchanged a long look with Mason, but Ari couldn't see her face clearly because of the angle. Couldn't get a read on her mood or why she was acting so oddly with Mace.

But whatever Mason glimpsed had him ready to pounce out of his chair. Ari jabbed his finger in unmistakable warning. "You stay; you play nice. That was our arrangement," he cautioned. "You gonna follow those ground rules?"

"Your 'girl' gonna stop manifesting?" Mason shot back, settling down. "Maybe you should keep her on a leash, like the unruly hellhound she obviously is."

Ari turned back to Juliana, his mind riddled with so many conflicted thoughts, he could hardly make sense of them. He stared at her in hurt disbelief, not sure whether he should demand to know why she'd suddenly been all over Mace— or look into her eyes and try to glimpse her soul.

Just then she ran the tip of her tongue over her lips, giving Ari a coy, sultry-eyed examination—as if she'd never gotten a good look at him before. "My, my! You *are* nice. No wonder."

"No wonder what?" he asked carefully.

She only smiled at him through half-lowered lashes, a very naughty expression on her face. "Not going to tell right now," was all she said before turning her scorching gaze back on Mason once again.

Ari tugged on her arm. "Sweetheart, have a seat," he insisted, trying to divert her bizarre attention from Mason. "You're not acting like yourself."

"Forgive my appalling manners, in that case. I did not mean to be rude, Aristos, nor behave in a way ill-suited to polite company. My deepest apologies, good sirs," she pronounced, fluttering a hand against her breastbone. As if she were back to being her usual self, she spread the layers of her dress out, making a great show of settling herself primly in the seat between them.

And then the game switched all over again. She swiveled her body in that chair, focusing wholly on Mason, putting her back to Ari as she did so. "However, this marine and *hunter*"—she lingered on the word significantly—"is, as always, so very, very fine, it's no wonder I can't resist him."

Mason motioned his head toward her, giving Ari an expression that said, "*Now* do you understand what I'm talking about?"

Ari gaped at her as if she'd sprouted horns and a forked tongue, because he honestly had no idea how to process these abrupt behavior changes. In fact, he was too busy feeling insanely, brutally jealous to see anything but the brightest shades of red . . .

And then silver. His whole damned vision washed with it, his hands clenching along the table's edge. Mason glanced all around the restaurant, obviously wondering whether Ari's transformation was being observed by the dozens of patrons all around.

Ari dropped his gaze, determined to regain control, but couldn't hold back his furious question. "Juliana," he demanded hoarsely. "What . . . what exactly are you trying to do with Mason? He's my friend, and it's like . . . like you *want* him."

"Aristos," she purred, "don't feel jealous. I'm simply remarking on Mason Angel's alluring appearance. He's my own . . . Well, what is he, precisely? My great-great-nephew? Why should you feel threatened by him? He's family.

"Besides, Mason doesn't even like women. Isn't that right?" she trilled. "I found that out the hard way. Who is Nikos, anyway?" she asked in an innocent tone.

"*I'm* Nikos," came the deep-voiced reply from behind Ari. Nik stepped around the table, folding strong arms across his chest. "The more important question is, who the bloody hell are you?"

"Nik, why are you here?" Mason asked in a tight voice, never taking his eyes off the demon. He'd be damned if he gave her any opportunity to lunge at Nik or strike at him. Mace didn't even blink, just kept his total attention focused on the Djinn.

"I called Ari," Nik answered, his thick accent betraying his heightened emotions. "And *she* answered." He pointed at the Djinn significantly. "Hauled ass here after that."

Nik dropped into an open chair, and the female preened, unbuttoning more of her blouse. "Nikos was so very concerned about you, Mason," she said sweetly. "It was touching how much he cares for you."

Mason's heart began to hammer, adrenaline rushing into his system. "He . . . he doesn't mean anything to me. Nothing." Mace shook his head in denial, hating the flash of pain he saw in Nikos's brown eyes. But he wouldn't have Nikos wind up like Kelly had at this demon's hands.

"Leave everyone else out of this," Mason told the Djinn firmly. "It's you and me, period."

She leaned much closer, surreal eyes riveted on him. "Are you admitting this is all about the two of us?" She stroked her fingertips along the back of his hand; he'd begun clutching the edge of the table like a vise the moment Nik showed up. "That this is our dance, Mason?"

"Yes," he said, swallowing. "This is all about you and me."

She beamed, triumphant. "Good. You do know how jealous I can get," she said with a quick glance toward Nik.

Every instinct demanded that Mason begin using his *spiritual* weapons of warfare against the demon, especially since he didn't have his physical ones within easy reach.

Mason rubbed at his temples, struggling to clear his mind enough that he could start praying for some serious heavenly backup. He glanced around the restaurant, hoping he might spot an angel. He didn't see just demons; sometimes he glimpsed the good guys, especially in the thick of a bad fight. But not tonight, he realized as thick dread filled his belly.

Turning back to Aristos, he confirmed that the huge Spartan was too lathered up to see straight, not in full control at all. In fact, Ari's whole face seemed on the verge of glowing, and Mason shifted in his chair uncomfortably. No wonder Emma and River had been concerned about his stability, or obvious lack thereof.

"Aristos, could you tone down those Vegas Strip lights? Otherwise known as your eyes? Cause they're looking very, very bright, my friend. You're gonna blind somebody with those things."

The immortal's shoulders rolled forward as he released a low, feral growl.

"Fine." Mace tossed his napkin onto the table. "Go on and expose your berserker side to all of the low country. I'll even video it with my cell phone and post it on YouTube if that'll make you happy."

Ari's blazing eyes narrowed and his growl grew lower, deeper, but he seemed to be regaining at least slight control, no longer in the full thrall of his power surge.

"Uh, Nik, do me a favor? Take on off, okay?" Mason tried casually. "Got this under control."

"Not going anywhere," Nikos growled back at him.

Then Nikos slid his chair back, putting more physical distance between him and the demon. "I'll take action if you need me," Nik said, his voice calmer, his expression fierce. He was one hell of an amazing fighting partner, had been from the beginning, and even with Mace's concerns for his well-being, he felt stronger with Nik at his side.

More confident, Mason turned back to the Djinn, who was the true threat at their table. "Whatcha doing over there?" Mason asked her in a chatty, relaxed tone that he didn't remotely feel. He tried to shut down the background chatter in his brain, which kept reminding him that he was in the presence of Kelly's killer.

He barely summoned the discipline to remain in his seat, as the demon stroked his arm with a long, sensual caress. "Oh, Mason Angel, you are even more beautiful than the last time I saw you." She sighed appreciatively.

As if it had been a tryst, as if that night hadn't practically destroyed him. "I was covered in blood and guts and sand the last time you saw me," he seethed.

"Well." She pouted a little. "I know how you loved him, but ..." She leaned into his physical space, smiling wickedly. "But perhaps you could find *some* women alluring? I mean, with the right inducement."

Ari groaned at those words, a sound of soul-wounded despair. "Aristos, it's gonna be okay," Mason tried promising under his breath.

But Ari didn't even seem to hear. He had a glazed look to his eyes and just kept rubbing a large palm over his heart, back and forth, like maybe the damned thing was breaking that hard.

And Mason felt bad; honest to God, he felt terrible about this moment of vindication. Ari obviously loved Juliana, truly, or he never would have bought into the demon's lies.

The Djinn moved her attention back to Mason, brushing through his hair with a lover's adoration. "Such interesting thoughts in here," she murmured, pressing a hand to his forehead. She frowned down at him, and Mace went into a fire-alarm panic. She'd invaded his thoughts, probably seen exactly what Nik meant to him.

He shoved her hands away. "We both know the nasty history we share. So cut it out—now. Aristos," Mason said carefully. "You catching on to what I been saying? Are you tracking with me now?"

The Spartan stared down. Mason could see how badly he shook; in fact, the harder he gripped the table, the more it started rocking, too. He wasn't sure Ari was really clued in to the unfolding events, not with the way his own body seemed poised on the verge of a violent change.

That was the moment when the demon swiveled her attention away from Mason . . . and fully onto Nikos. "So tell me about Nikos," she said. "How does he fit into this scenario?"

She stroked a fingertip along Nik's jaw, licking her lips voraciously; he never even blinked beneath her inspection.

"He looks delicious," she purred, eyes narrowing hungrily.

Mason became desperate then, the sounds of the restaurant roaring at him like a freight train, every clinking glass or eruption of laughter like the distant popping of an enemy's AK-47.

And then he had an idea; two, really, and both were ideal strategies for fighting this crafty Djinn. Reaching into his pocket, he pulled out his BlackBerry. "Let me take your picture," he said, employing the same sultry tone she'd been working on him. "You know, to commemorate our little reunion."

Her eyes turned bright red. Only for a second, but he knew she didn't want to be photographed. Too damn bad. He lifted the camera and took the shot, knowing already what he'd see.

"Tell me your name," he added. "Come on, sweetheart; give me that at least. For ole time's sake."

To have a demon's name was to command that demon. A demon could be controlled when someone with spiritual authority invoked the demon's name—along with that of Jesus Christ. If Mason could get this little demon to slip up and reveal her private, intimate name, he could destroy

her. They both knew it, which was why she gave him only
a bland smile in response. But he wasn't about to give up
that easily.

He took another photo, the flash electrifying the night.
Setting her off-kilter.

"Come on, pretty darling; just give me your name," Mason cajoled. Then, dropping his own voice into a husky, tantalizing timbre, he added, "Don't you want to hear me say
it? I know you do. So give me just that little bit of you."

"Which bit do you want?" she asked, her blue eyes turning a brilliant mixture of red and violet. "Surely something
can be arranged so long as I keep Juliana at bay."

Mason's mind whirled. She made it sound as if she'd
possessed the woman Ari knew, meaning there were two
distinct entities, linked together in a single body.

The female covered Mason's hand, "You're not still mad
about that other little thing—are you?"

Mason yanked his hand free, and thank God above, Ari
suddenly focused again, his eyes returning to their usual
shade of almost black. "What other *little thing*?" Aristos
barked.

The Djinn brushed a lock of hair back from her eyes,
and with an otherworldly vibration, auburn turned much
darker, but only for a split second. "I have a feeling Mason would rather I didn't say anything"—she laughed
musically—"about our special past in Iraq."

It took everything in his power to remain composed, but
Mason didn't lunge at her. He just prayed that Ari could
see the truth here—even as he himself was beginning to
sort out facts.

Leaning much closer to the woman, he lowered his voice.
"Where is she right now? Juliana?"

The Djinn scowled back at him. "She's not in charge."

"You are." Mason nodded.

She shrugged. "For the moment. But I'll be in control
soon enough. I feed off her fear and despair. And I'm getting stronger by the second because she's so *very* afraid for
you, Aristos." She flashed a cruel smile in his direction. "So,
yes, I am in control."

Ari's face crumpled, and Mason wished he could feel
more vindicated. But with the facts becoming as clear as his
nana's Waterford crystal, he felt only angry and vigilant and

ready to get down to the real work this mission required. Juliana—dead, gone, lost Juliana Tiades—had somehow managed to bind herself to the most vicious demon Mason had ever encountered.

Which made her not the enemy, as he'd come into this scenario thinking, but a vulnerable human soul. A victim of a demonic attack who desperately needed his spiritual-warfare capabilities, probably those of all the Shades combined.

Mason knew that Juliana's only hope for survival was if he figured out the most complicated of answers: how to free a dead woman from a demon's lethal grasp.

"We need your name," Mason insisted bluntly. "Give it over."

"I'm not that naive, Mason," she trilled, the violet brightening in her eyes like a backlight. "To have a demon's name is to command it," she recited, as if quoting from *Demon Fighting for Dummies.*

"Let Juliana go," Ari urged, his own eyes growing bright. "She's innocent. She didn't want you. . . . She didn't invite you. Are you inside her body? Is that it?"

"I resurrected her, yes," she said easily. "For now, we're sharing this body and all its many pleasures."

"No!" Ari roared at her. "Let Juliana go!"

The demon snapped back in her seat, startled, and then began coughing. "Her prayers are working! The bitch doesn't even have a voice now, but she's . . ."

Suddenly, the tone of her voice, even its timbre, became familiar. Like Juliana's voice, with its refined and gentile inflections. "Aristos? Aristos . . . help me." Juliana was back, gasping and choking. "Oh, God. Oh . . ." She started pulling at the collar of her dress. "I can't . . . breathe."

Her eyes became wide and frightened, and she turned to Ari with a horrified cry. "I'm so sorry," she said, and then went limp in the chair.

Chapter 30

Somehow, Mason had gotten them out of the restaurant, and they were on their way to the Spartans' compound. One minute, Ari had been battling the tide of surging power in his own veins, all the while trying to process the truth about Juliana and the demon that had possessed her. The next, the cocktail bill had been handled and Mason was wrangling them all out the door.

Mason drove his truck in silence, eyes focused on the dark road, and Nik rode shotgun, equally serious. They were like Grim and Grimmer. He could only imagine what his own face might look like.

Jules stirred, her head in his lap. "I'm so sorry," she said, apologizing yet again.

Ari didn't know what to do, so he stroked her hair as reassuringly as he could.

"I'm not sure what happened," she continued, her voice filled with anguish. "I'm . . . not feeling myself." She tried to sit up, reaching a shaky hand toward Mason. "I'm sorry, sir, for behaving horribly toward you. Please, will you accept my deepest apologies? Both of you, truly."

"You're not sure what happened, yet you're apologizing for it?" Mason asked, casting a glance in the rearview.

Jules glanced down at her half-opened bodice and yanked it shut. "At the very least, I am not properly dressed. As for the rest, I remember enough to be deeply regretful."

Nikos turned in the seat, as reticent as he always was, but seeming like he felt the need to say something to her. Finally he settled on, "No problem," and faced the road again.

"Goddamn problem for me," Mace muttered under his breath, handing his BlackBerry over his shoulder. "Take a look," he instructed Ari. "That might bring some memories back for your girlfriend there."

Ari stared down at the saved image—damn, but did Mason have to make it his screen saver? It was a picture of Juliana, lips parted, a seriously depraved come-hither expression on her face.

But that wasn't the worst of it; she seemed to have a kind of aura about her, like a second skin. An afterimage, maybe? Some result of the flash at night? No, Ari knew better—now. Juliana hadn't come back from the grave by herself; oh, no, she'd done something even more spectacular. She'd brought along a hitchhiker, a truly vile Djinn. He stared down at the picture and wanted to be sick. He thrust the phone back at Mason. "Your point?"

Mason met his eyes in the rearview mirror. "Something's fishy in Denmark, Petrakos; that's what."

"I think I realized that over the Budweisers, dude," Ari fired back. "So, your grand plan, other than showing me that picture? And you better not say . . ." *Offing her*, he finished mentally, pointing his finger like a gun at Mace in the rearview.

Mason rolled his eyes impatiently. "Jesus, I wasn't gonna say that."

Ari shoved him in the shoulder. "You showed up saying it."

"Saying *what*?" Juliana lurched forward, intercepting the BlackBerry. She scooted sideways against the window, studying it. Then, pressing it against her breast, she began shaking her head but said nothing more.

"Jules," Ari ventured. "You passed out cold, but do you even remember all that went on at the restaurant?" He had to figure out if she was aware about the genie inside her personal bottle, so to speak.

Juliana blanched. "No."

"That's all you gotta say for yourself—just no?" he roared, seizing hold of the phone and forcing her to look at the image. "You were . . . Damn, woman, you were wanton! A . . . a . . . hoyden," he sputtered.

She turned to him, genuinely affronted. "And this from a man who believes that the sex act should be completed against a church spire," she said low enough that Mace and Nikos wouldn't hear, thank God. "One who claims to have loved me, yet never once questioned the doubtful circumstances of my death! Instead, sir, you made assumptions that painted me in the worst possible light!"

He stared out the window, not wanting her to know how deeply that accusation hurt. But she knew, anyway; she knew everything about him, heart and soul. She moved across the seat, burrowing her head against his shoulder.

"I guess it was the hoyden bit that really got ya, huh?" He tried to laugh.

"I am not feeling myself at all." She slid a hand beneath his shirt, and her palm was surprisingly clammy. "I'm over-heated and chilled at the same time."

Ari stroked her hair again and bit back a sarcastic comment about swine flu symptoms mimicking demon possession; even *he* knew it wasn't the right moment to be a smart-ass, and especially not when Jules didn't understand her predicament.

Mason cleared his throat. "Uh, Aristos?" he said, changing lanes on the expressway. "We should talk, probably. After a while?"

"About me," Jules finished. "I'm quite aware that you don't believe I'm to be trusted."

To his credit, Mason gave her a kind look over his shoulder. "No, but I do think you're in trouble."

She sank into her seat. Then, straightening to a dignified posture, she addressed Mason. "Sir, unfortunately, you are correct. I believe that I'm in a very great deal of trouble."

Mason nodded after a moment. "Yeah, well," he said, meeting Ari's gaze in the rearview, "maybe I can help."

Eros paced the length of the Spartans' drive, overwrought that he'd lost contact with Layla for the past hour. Everything had changed the moment he'd observed Aristos and Juliana in the parking lot of the restaurant. From that moment, the gaming table had tilted, the stakes entirely altered.

Because their love was one of the purest forms he'd ever encountered between any coupled pair of young lovers. They'd even invoked his name, playing at the idea of being "Eros" and . . . and *her*. He pressed his eyes shut, as always refusing to even think her name. To allow its musical sound into his head. But that love, what he'd shared with her once, so long ago—he saw it reflected in Juliana and Aristos's passion.

His chest swelled at the exchange he'd witnessed, a pure example of the love Eros brought to the world, and yet . . . he was meant to bring about that couple's destruction. It was only by *his* hand that Layla had joined with Juliana; by *his* power that she'd been resurrected at all.

But not to create the rare, enthralling love he'd seen displayed so exquisitely between Aristos and Juliana.

No, he had used his power to create destruction. To sow heartbreak and suffering.

His stomach gave a terrible spasm, and he grasped the rail, struggling not to lose his evening meal. His actions, his participation in Ares' plan, all were an act against his own divine purpose. He was literally, perhaps by his father's intended will, destroying himself. That realization had been confirmed when he'd watched Aristos and Mason in that same lot, the discord between them.

This was the mission he'd agreed to, certainly, when he'd made the alliance with his father. But now, watching events unfold, he reconsidered whether his actions weren't too much at odds with his own gift.

And then there was the matter of Layla herself. . . .

He'd found her in the desert, the place where all female Djinn were locked—unless someone was given authority to free them, or possessed it by virtue of his or her god's power.

One glance into the reflective waters of his pool and he'd instantly perceived her to be the most effective, cruelest form of destruction against the Spartans and the Shades. He'd seen everything in that brief glimpse, the truth of what she would be capable of, the profound division she could create among them. And once a team was split apart, it lacked real power.

"I can give you Mason Angel," he'd told her simply, and those violet-red eyes had glowed, illuminating the desert night.

Then she'd calmed a bit, had become focused with ferocious intensity. "Can you make him want me?"

Eros had known that, perhaps with the right aim of his arrow, yes, he could bring about that unlikely outcome. "I can cause anyone to love or lust for another. That is my gift," he'd answered, knowing then that he would wait to see the unfolding of events. He was thankful that he had.

Layla had seemed most aroused by his offer. "May I kill? Destroy as I see fit?"

"You are to use your own erotic abilities," he'd answered evenly. "That is the way you will infiltrate their cadre."

The way she'd stared, that craven lust in her eyes, continued to unnerve him even now.

And yet there was little Finn could do to stop the unfolding plan. Juliana and Layla were already bound as tightly as any lover's knot. Even if he'd wanted to extricate them, it would mean final, lasting death for Juliana, not that she wasn't headed toward that fate, anyway, and most expeditiously.

But then he had a thought. There was one who could help, one who had always loved and cared for him, even in the face of his father's neglectful disdain. And she, too, had her reasons for supporting the Spartans. In fact, it was only a matter of time until she returned to this compound once again.

Chapter 31

Jules wandered about the guest bedroom, trying to sort through her myriad, disturbing thoughts. What should she tell Aristos about Layla? He deserved an explanation, but would he be harmed if she shared any of the facts she'd learned? So many years apart, all that time spent searching for him, waiting, hoping—she refused to let Layla take him from her. She'd die again before she allowed him to be harmed at all.

As for Ari, he was much quieter than usual. He'd sprawled on the bed, his long legs stretched out, leaning against the headboard.

"I think you should sit down," he said, patting the spot beside him. His expression was dour, but he didn't seem furious. More . . . troubled. A feeling she certainly understood at the moment.

She sat on the edge of the mattress and removed first one boot, then the other. "I thought maybe you were still angry with me."

"I'm upset because . . . ." He looked away. "We've got a problem, Juliana. A big one. I'm just not sure how much *you* know. You remember anything from the restaurant?"

The memories were murky, muddled, but she was certain of one thing. She had a demon inside of her, one that apparently planned to kill Ari if she revealed details about its presence.

She buried her face in both hands, fighting tears. "I don't want anything to happen to you," she gasped.

He sat up a little taller, reaching for her. "Baby, I don't think it's *me* we need to worry about."

"I think," she said slowly, "what we need . . . is a priest."

His black eyebrows cranked down over his eyes. "So you know about the demon."

As if in answer to his statement, her stomach seized tight, the muscles rippling with wrenching spasms of pain. "She doesn't . . . I can't tell you. Can't admit . . ." The pain stabbed even harder; her breath left her lungs.

Ari sprang to her side, trying to hold her, but she shook him off. "Don't! Get away from me. . . . Don't you see? She'll . . ." *Hurt you.* The words were there, on her tongue, but no matter how hard she worked her mouth, they wouldn't come out.

She pointed at her throat, gasping for air, but only a rasping sound came forth. Ari struggled to hold her, and she sagged against him, still rendered mute.

"Just breathe," Ari instructed. "In and out, one breath at a time. That demon's not in charge. You are."

She nodded, rubbing the column of her throat, desperately wanting to communicate with Ari—to explain why she feared revealing anything more about Layla.

"Now," Ari murmured after a moment, apparently believing her soothed, "tell me what you know about the demon."

She'll hurt you! She screamed the thought in her mind, still clinging to Ari. And then she recalled one very wonderful fact.

She'd once taught Ari sign language so he could communicate with her young brother, Edward. The two of them had been so close, and Ari had worked diligently to become proficient with his signing skills, even though the method had been unpopular at the time.

Working her fingers quickly, she signed, "She will hurt you. If I tell more." She gave him a hopeless, pleading glance. "I did not know what she was. I believed her an angel."

Ari's eyes grew wide as he watched her fingers fly, and then a furious, protective expression filled his face. He cursed in Greek and then signed back to her. "Demons are angels, love. Fallen, dark ones. I eat them for lunch."

A knock came on the door, and Emma called out from the other side. "Can we come in?"

Ari slung an arm around Juliana, propping them both against the headboard. Using a friendly, upbeat tone that he surely didn't feel, he called out, "Okay, Witches of Eastwick, get your butts on in here."

"They're not *witches*," Jules scolded, cutting a look at him as the door opened slowly. "They're Daughters."

Sophie, Emma, and Shay entered the room, and Ari grinned at them. "We heard Juliana wasn't feeling so hot," Sophie said, then, getting a look at Jules's flushed face, added, "Or, yeah, I guess *too* hot is more like it."

"The Crab Shack was a bust, huh?" Shay asked, her blue eyes riveted on Juliana.

"Geez Louise, girl!" Sophie said, bounding onto the end of the bed with a little hop. The whole mattress shook from the impact. "Your head isn't fixin' to do a three-sixty or anything, is it? I might be a healer, but I'm not sure even I could help with that."

Emma waved dismissively. "Ignore her," she said, flopping down beside Sophie on the end of the bed.

Shay strode to Ari's side. "Mace is waiting on you. He and Nik are in the great room looking at some more of the Shades' lore. Something that Mace brought with him from the house."

Ari shifted against the headboard. "Leonidas back yet?"

"Nope," Emma said. "Nikos made some calls to gather the troops, but it's going to be a little while still. The others are all out in the field still."

"Here, baby," Ari said, gently dislodging her from his arms. "The girls will hang with you for a bit. I gotta go pow-wow with Mason and Nik."

She searched his face. "You know I'm not evil, Aristos. Please . . . tell me that you understand I'm not bad."

He kissed her forehead, holding her close. "Darling, I know who you are. And what you are."

She pulled back and used sign language. "But do you know what's *inside* of me?"

He gave her a bittersweet smile and answered, "I'm still working on that one. I just need a little time."

The only problem, Juliana knew, was that time was one luxury they couldn't afford. Ari clearly saw the anxiety in her eyes. He bent down, pressing his lips against her forehead. "I'm going to protect you, sweetheart. I promise. Nothing's going to keep us apart ever again."

"I'll keep fighting, too," she whispered in his ear.

"Actually," Shay volunteered as soon as Ari left the

room. "I had an idea earlier. Something we Daughters can do to help. It's one reason we came down here."

Emma added, "We're all ready to fight for you, Juliana."

"Go on, absolutely," Juliana said, bobbing her head. "Tell me what you have in mind, please."

Shay deposited a drawing pad in the center of the bed, tapping a charcoal pencil against the blank page. "So," she told Juliana, "we all have our unique gifts as Daughters, right? Several, sometimes. Mine is that I draw prophetically."

"How does that ability work?" Juliana asked, as Shay began to move her pencil across the page.

"I get visions, scenes that I am compelled to draw—sometimes a trancelike state overtakes me. I'm sensing that there's something related to your situation," she said, the first lines of a balcony emerging on the page. "Something crucial."

Jules watched as Shay quickly sketched in more details; a set of French doors emerged, then a very recognizable pair of wings. Jules held her breath, knowing what might be coming next.

Shay tightened her hold on the charcoal pencil, releasing a slow, pained groan as she hesitated.

Emma reached for her cousin. "What is it? What's wrong, Shayanna?"

Shay trembled slightly and then resumed drawing, her eyes assuming a glazed expression. Her hands flew across the page, nimbly outlining more details from that pivotal night . . . and roughing in the shadowy figure of a male. The male who'd been in the room!

In a distant voice Shay said, "He's talking. This man in the room. He's saying something. Don't recognize the language . . . strange, foreign." Shay closed her eyes and began chanting, repeating whatever she heard in an eerie monotone.

"What does this mean?" Sophie whispered, glancing among the rest of them with saucer-sized eyes. "Geez Louise . . . redux."

Shay's whole body swayed, back and forth, more of those alien words passing over her lips.

Juliana's body began to vibrate, a kind of humming sensation starting in the middle of her belly. It was a demon language; she knew it based on how Layla was apparently reacting from within her own body.

This might be her only chance to find out what had happened the night of her death—and how it was possibly linked to the current situation with Layla.

Jules closed her own eyes, reaching deep inside to try to activate her own prophetic ability. Perhaps, just as she'd been able to track Ari that afternoon—the ability still alive in her—she might also be able to see the events Shay was conjuring.

She reached out her hands to Emma and Sophie. "We need to link," she said. "Join our powers as Daughters. All of us tied together, to try to get additional information about what Shay's channeling and seeing."

The other women nodded, and they immediately formed a four-way circle, their hands clasped. As they did so, a powerful jolt of electricity rang through Juliana's veins. Her vision changed, the room around her vanishing, time itself dissolving.

She was standing in her own bedroom in 1893.

All time had folded back, like tissue paper in a gift box, revealing that past moment as something real and alive. Vivid. Exactly as it had been.

Ari stood at those French doors, the midnight dark shadowing his form; the outline of his wings gleamed, illuminated by the gaslights below. She took a step, mesmerized, and a deep male voice came from behind her, chilling her. "I will destroy him."

She spun and found herself staring into the coldest, most lifeless eyes she'd ever seen. "Who . . ." Then she reached back, toward Aristos, in a panic. He stepped closer to the door, shielding his eyes and looking through the glass.

"Turn away from him now. Or he dies," the stranger threatened.

Horrified, she put her back to Aristos, even though he stood on that balcony waiting for her. Expecting her. "What do you want? . . . Who are you?"

She pulled her robe about her lingerie-clad body, needing to place whatever barrier she could between this menacing stranger and herself. The man sneered in response, tugging on the satin pink ribbon that fastened the lingerie. "He'll never touch you, not now."

She slapped his hand aside. "I insist, sir, that you reveal your identity!"

His answer was to plant a cold palm atop the crown of her head. "*By this* curse that I place upon thee, you shall die . . . that *his* soul may die with you."

"No, no, you're wrong," she tried denying, but his hand tightened about her skull, a sensation like fire flowing out of his hand and into her scalp.

"This curse will live—and live beyond your grave," he proclaimed. "It shall live through every woman of your heritage. Death to the voice of life!"

Juliana cried out, trying to get Aristos to hear, even through the closed doors. Over and over she kept calling his name, but the man would not release her. In fact, hands were all about her, grasping at her, pulling.

Help me! she thought.

"Juliana!" That voice—it belonged to someone who cared, a female. "Juliana, snap out of it!"

She blinked, the scene fading, replaced by the guest bedroom. "Oh, dear God. Oh, thank you, Shay," she said, realizing that the huntress had been shaking her. That because of her physical intervention, the horrifying vision of the past had been broken.

Emma pulled Juliana into a sisterly embrace. "What were you seeing? What happened? You were shaking all over, sweetie."

Jules rested her cheek on Em's shoulder. Closing her eyes, drinking in the reassuring comfort of Emma's arms, she finally whispered, "I saw the man who killed me."

Nikos kept rolling his shoulder, rubbing the obviously knotted muscle. Ari knew, from years of experience, that Nik did that only when he was in a tremendous amount of pain. It was an old injury, one he'd earned at Marathon, and when the warrior got tense or distressed, the discomfort kicked in triple time. "Man, you should get Straton to look at that shoulder," Ari suggested.

"He's not back yet," Nikos said.

"Call him. Last thing we need during this shit storm is for you to wind up sidelined. Get him to rub you down."

Mason's gaze flicked sideways, the first time he'd looked

up from the leather-bound book he held in his lap since they'd gotten back from the Crab Shack.

"Why don't you spend a few minutes in the hot tub?" Mason suggested.

Nikos shook his head. "I want to help you. I can soak later." He rotated his shoulder once again, wincing. "Although, ah . . . yes, it is definitely tight."

That was about as close as ole Nikos would ever get to admitting, "This hurts like ever-living bloody hell."

"Dude. For real," Ari insisted, motioning him toward the doorway. "Go take a plunge right now. Leonidas will be back in forty-five minutes. I'm gonna need you in on that meeting—and feeling tip-top. Need you both for that."

Thank the Highest that Mason had been won over, a significant victory. He'd said something in the truck that gave Ari particular hope that Juliana could be saved.

He'd clasped Ari's shoulder after they pulled into the compound. "It's my job to protect the innocent and defenseless against creatures like that Djinn," he'd promised. "I'll do whatever I can to help your Juliana. You can count on that."

"Taking it to the bank," Ari had answered. "The fucking bank."

Mason Angel was nothing if not a man of honor and integrity. His loyalty, his commitment to those he cared about—his service as a marine—all of those qualities emanated from his core nature. The man didn't make a pledge, not of any kind, unless he intended to fulfill it, even if he died doing so.

"Shit," Mace muttered now, flipping several pages of the book he had in his lap. "Can't find what I'm looking for." He sighed, rubbing a hand over his hair in agitation. "I know it's in here, and it might help your girl out. Might help all of us out, actually—and in a much bigger way than I'd imagined."

Mason held up the volume; the cover was tooled, stained leather, the abstract design like something from an old monastery. "I spent all last night, most of today, studying our lore, determined to find an explanation for Juliana's arrival. But for some reason, I only looked at *The Final Crossing* briefly." He pressed the book against his chest protectively. "Should've thought more about its discussion on the nature of Djinn. And Nephilim . . . and even all of you. You gotta read deep and sorta between the lines, but there's information in this book that I'm sure Ares wouldn't want any of us getting hold of. I mean, do you know anything about Djinn, really?"

Ari scowled. "I know they fueled the Persians' battle lust at Thermopylae. Sable—bless his happy little soul he's one of them."

Mason nodded, drumming fingers against the book he cradled. "And he's obviously made his choice."

Ari leaned forward. "What do you mean, his choice?"

"Djinn aren't born dark or light. They decide whether to follow darkness . . , or something more holy. More true. By joining your ranks recently, Sable staked a claim to . . . well, let's call it the better side of his nature. But they're mostly dark, yeah."

"Any of them I've ever met up with have been miserable, evil creatures, eager to create destruction and suffering." Ari scowled, remembering the masses of them that he'd seen flying over the cliffs of Thermopylae after Ares brought him back to life. They'd swarmed the sky, their arrows flying, wings beating at the wind. "You really think Sable's turned light? He was one nasty bastard at the Hot Gates—and after."

"Well, turning *lighter* is probably more accurate. It's a process, but Sable exercised his free will when he joined your cause in Hades a few months ago. They were created that way, with a built-in choice. That makes them, you know, a little better model than your average demon. But it also means they're more dangerous, because you can't predict which way they will choose. Oh, and when they do switch from dark to light—or vice versa? It's excruciatingly painful for them. The transformation isn't immediate, and it's an agony to their souls as they walk the line."

"Johnny Cash allusion noted." Ari hummed a riff. "Noted and appreciated. Good ole Man in Black."

Mason laughed, smiling a little, which for some reason made Ari really happy. He hated to see any warrior, especially such a noble one, live in torment.

"So here's the thing," Mason continued. "Your Juliana? She's back; you're right. The problem is that nobody—and really, why is that—nobody's wondering *how* she got here. Resurrection's a pretty nifty trick, when it comes down to it, don't you think? Besides you guys and Jesus, who do you know who's managed it? Don't you think that should've raised questions from the very beginning?"

"She told us that an angel helped her. We all believed her."

"A little too easily," Mason answered and handed over the book. "Take a look at this."

Ari stared at the page, squinting to decipher the ancient text. It was rendered in his native Greek, thank goodness, but his immortal eyes still strained with the small lettering. Scanning the page, he stopped on one key passage. He read it, several times, trying to absorb the stark reality of what it contained.

"You see it, too." Mason leaned forward, gripping the sofa's thick arm until his damn knuckles went white. "You see what caught my attention."

Ari squinted harder, read the words again, then really looked at the sketch. "Gods of Olympus, that's Ares," he told Mason, who'd never actually seen the god.

Mace got a satisfied look. "Exactly what I thought."

"And you're telling me that the female is a Djinn? Ares is—what—getting it on with a demon?"

"Not just any demon—one who just so happens to look an awful lot like our vicious little Djinn in residence. This is how she came to me over in Iraq, that hip-length hair, dripping in sensuality."

Ari rose slightly in the chair. "Whoa! You saying this is *her*? The same demon that's possessed Juliana?"

"No, but I *am* saying this. If this book is right—and we have every reason to believe it is—then it reveals that Ares has a connection with the Djinn outside his relationship with Sable. It means that he has a special relationship with them, an alignment. A greater reach of sorts."

"He's always had Sable doing his dirty work," Ari pointed out. "That's nothing new, but you're right—we've never known of Ares being connected to any other Djinn. Ever."

Mace rubbed his jaw, thinking for a moment, then asked, "But Sable was *forced* into that relationship, wasn't he? By Ahriman, after Thermopylae?"

"Yeah, that was his punishment because the Persians got their asses kicked—by us." Ari grinned, pride surging in his chest as it always did when he recalled how valiantly he and his fellow Spartans had fought. "Sable was supposed to motivate bloodlust and violence among the Persians, and he did his best; I'll hand him that. But Ahriman was shamed and gave him to Ares."

"As a slave?" Mason asked him staring down at the open page of the book.

"No, the control's more subtle than that. Ares enforces Sable's submission psychologically, physically. Look how he's used that centaur curse to tether him—that's just one of about a dozen methods. Our jolly ole war god gets his rocks off by controlling and torturing everyone around him."

"So I'm right," Mason said. "This drawing proves that Ares has had more than one Djinn in his life—and apparently been pretty fucking passionate toward at least one of their females."

"But I don't get how this helps us. Explain it to me like I'm a nitwit," Ari urged.

Mason nailed him with a sarcastic look. "When you actually set yourself *up* for an insult, Petrakos . . ."

Ari responded with his middle finger. "Insult this. But tell me what theory you've got brewing—and fast."

"Two things. First, this image tells us there's a chance that Ares himself is the one who sent Juliana back to you. He used the female Djinn to somehow . . . I don't know. Bind with her spirit? Give her physical form? And second, the Shades' guiding principle has always been to know our enemy as best we can. To get their true name to command them, to understand their identity . . . to determine if they are a demon of fear, despair, whatever they are. The more knowledge we gain, the better it enables us to destroy and defeat them, one by one."

Ari saw where the hunter's logic was leading. "So you're saying Ares might've put her up to this, so to speak?"

"He might've known about my past with her—and your past with Juliana. So he sets up the scenario. Your Juliana walks right into our midst, my greatest demon enemy hidden inside of her. Perfect plan to create chaos while waging war against us all—from the inside of the ranks."

Shay walked into the room but stopped in her tracks when she saw the ancient volume open on the coffee table. "That's *The Final Crossing*, isn't it?"

"You say it like it's a bad thing," Ari observed.

"No, but it's a very powerful book," she answered, looking down at the sketch. "I mean, duh, brother-in-law, it's the only written record of you seven immortals, least that we know of."

"Just testing you," he grumbled.

She sat down on the other side of the table, and Mace slid the book toward her. "I've got a theory going. Something that just might help Juliana get free. Take a look at this drawing."

She stared at her brother and then at the picture of Ares and the Djinn. "Okay, that's just way weird. Way, way weird, Mace."

"What do you mean?" he asked.

"Because the reason I was coming in here, right now?" Her eyes grew very wide. "Was to tell you that I sketched something a few minutes ago. I got a prophetic vision. . . . Something I think might explain what's going on."

Ari stood, ready to go get Jules, but Shay caught his arm. "Ari, wait," she said. "I need to talk to you first. Juliana . . . She got a vision, too. A really vivid one."

The gravity of her tone made the hair on his nape bristle. "A vision of *what*, precisely?"

Shay steeled herself visibly. "The man who . . . killed her, Ari." She drew in a sharp breath. "Juliana saw the man who caused her death."

She'd seen the male presence, the one she'd recalled when they were at the inn.

Mason was already moving. "I'll get her now! Y'all hang tight; this might be just the break we need."

"How you get that?" Ari asked, rubbing his eyes.

Mace paused in the doorway. "Her death, if it was foul play, might have been what opened the proverbial door— the one that allowed the demon control over her. If she really was murdered . . . her soul suffered. That's a spiritual opening. A way for a Djinn to gain a foothold."

Chapter 32

Nik walked into the recreation room toweling off his hair and face, grateful that the throbbing pain in his shoulder had let up at least a bit after his soak in the hot tub. Tightening his terry cloth robe, he listened to the sounds of voices upstairs, wondering whether Mason might come to check on him. He'd seemed concerned enough, but Nikos was no longer willing to pin his hopes on such flimsy encouragement.

He means nothing to me. That was what Mason had said to that demon earlier. Now those words stabbed Nik in the heart anew, even as he tried to remind himself that Mason had been talking to Kelly's murderer at the time.

He paused, blotting a rivulet of water from his neck. Perhaps Mason had been lying, he thought brightly. Trying to protect Nikos from the demon's violent jealousy.

But then those hopes crashed and burned as he remembered Mace's words from the night before. They would never be more than friends; the man had made that much abundantly clear.

No, they were fighting partners, nothing more. He couldn't allow himself to think otherwise. They were fellow warriors, linked by those tethers that bound all men who fought together in the trenches.

Nik groaned, rubbing the towel back and forth across his eyes. "We are friends. That is all," he muttered aloud, wishing he could convince his heart of that truth.

"God, you look good with wet hair. Fucking gorgeous."

Nik froze, towel at his face. Mason had come downstairs after all. And maybe . . . shit, maybe he wanted to make things right between them.

Slowly Nik lowered the towel and found Mason propped against the bar, watching him through hooded eyes. The man was sinfully handsome, always had been, but something in his gaze felt more dangerous than usual.

No way was Nik playing this game again, not after last night, not after the humiliation of that failed kiss. He made for the steps. "I better get dressed," was all he said, but Mason was behind him with almost preternatural swiftness.

He placed a warm, strong hand on Nik's arm, turning him. "Don't go. I want to be with you," he said, and Nik's heart began beating like a war drum. "And by the look in your eyes, I'd say you want me, too."

Nik blinked, surprised, but with hope stirring anew. Mason smiled up at him flirtatiously, lowering his thick lashes with an almost feminine flare. "Oh, come on," Mace teased, planting a hand on the wall beside Nikos, framing him. "I'm not that shocking."

Something felt off, even as Nik's emotions soared like the winged warrior he was. "I . . . this . . ." *This is all I've wanted for months, all I need.* "This . . . is a significant change in outlook, Mason," he finally managed to say.

Mason moved closer, backing Nikos against the wall. "Please. Just one kiss?"

Mason braced a steadying hand against the stair railing, feeling like his shaking legs were about to give out. Mortar attacks, roadside bombings, holding Kelly as he died—he'd endured them all and never passed out. But the scene he was watching now? It felt like someone had just aimed an AK-47 dead at his heart and fired the fucking thing.

How could Nikos do it? That was all Mason could think as he gaped at the scene unfolding before him.

He'd come downstairs to get Juliana. But the last thing, the most insane thing he'd have ever imagined, was waltzing in and finding Nikos kissing that demon—with her looking exactly as she had that nightmarish night in Iraq. He recognized how powerful she was, working those seductions and caresses, but Nikos? *His* Nikos? How could he fall prey to the female Djinn's damned wiles?

Mason's throat constricted painfully; he couldn't even find his voice. Nik was sprawled on the sofa, the female demon wrapped up in his arms like a beauty queen—and he was kissing her with an obvious enthusiasm that made Mason feel ill.

Nikos released a quiet moan, and Mace went from being paralyzed to going straight up ballistic. With a roar, he hurled himself across the room, eating the distance with long strides.

Nikos jerked upward, staring at him in shock. "Who ... ?" he asked, then stared in horror at the woman in his arms. She just smiled up into Nik's eyes, beaming at him.

Nikos gave her a light shove, trying to shake her off him, but she clung to his strong torso like a lover. She even had the gall to tremble, leaning into his very masculine protection.

Mason vaulted over the back of the sofa, landing gracelessly atop the pair. "Fucker!" he cried, seizing hold of Nik's robe with shaking hands. "You motherfucker!" He dragged Nikos from beneath the demon, hauling him against the far wall with a loud thwack.

"Mason, gods," Nikos tried to say, looking over at the demon as if he were seeing her for the first time.

"Her, Nik? That demon?" Mason said in a low, dangerous voice. "How could you? Anyone but her. Anything else." Mason released the thick folds of terry cloth that he'd been twisting in his hands. "Guess I was right, though, when I asked if you wanted me to start putting out." He shoved Nikos in the chest, hard. "Well, you got your one kiss, didn't you? Just not from me."

Nikos flinched at those words, paling visibly. He sagged against the wall as if Mason had just struck him. "But I thought ... I believed it was ..." Nikos sighed, a truly heartbroken sound. "It *was* my one kiss."

Some demons could give humans visions, make them see shit that wasn't there at all.

The reality of the situation washed over Mason with a sudden, appalling clarity. "Oh, God. She made herself look like me?"

Nik swallowed and gave a single nod of affirmation, his large brown eyes filled with anguish. "The whole time I ... I was holding *you* in my arms. Never her."

She'd made Nik believe he was getting the one thing the Spartan wanted—the kiss Mason had denied him last night.

The demon, so typically cruel, had used Nikos's own feelings as a weapon against him. And she'd manipulated the situation in an effort to divide them . . . to put them at each other's throats.

"If we're fighting each other," Mason said softly, "then we're not fighting her."

Nikos answered in a low voice, eyeing the demon menacingly. "I wouldn't have kissed that . . . thing . . . willingly."

"He was certainly passionate about it," the demon volunteered, staring at her fingernails absently.

Something broke inside of Mason right then, all the rage and hurt he'd felt morphing into cold, lethal confidence.

He stalked toward the demon. "Not this time, you don't," he pronounced icily. "You do not so much as *touch* the ones I love." Mason seized hold of the demon, shaking her by the shoulders. "Not a hair on their heads."

She worked her face into an expression of mock innocence. "Love? Hmm, such passion for this big Spartan. I wonder what Kelly would think." Then she waved her hand dismissively, giving him a slow, burning smile. "Of course, some things really are better left dead and buried, right?"

That was it. Mason slid his hand about her throat with choking force. "Reveal your true self. The one I saw the night you killed Kelly, the claws and scales and wings. Expose yourself, and let's fight. Come on, you little bitch—manifest!"

Ari came barreling into the room, undoubtedly having heard the commotion. The minute he saw Mason's death grip on the Djinn, he went bug-eyed. "Where's Jules?" he demanded, lunging toward Mason. "Tell me where Juliana is!"

The demon rasped out a taunting laugh. "She's right here. This is still her body, but I can make it appear . . . altered. Just as I brought her back to life."

Mason tightened his hold on the demon. "Tell. Me. Your. Name," he growled. "Yield to me, demon. Give me your true Djinn name."

"Let her go, man," Ari tried reasoning, pulling at Mason's hands, working to free the demon from his grasp. "I know she's a demon, but my Jules is still in there. Mace, come on. Don't kill her. Don't destroy the Djinn before we can free my girl."

The mortal was still inside, Mason reminded himself. Juliana was an innocent, one of those he'd sworn to protect. Beyond that, he'd promised Aristos to help her at all costs.

With a groan, he eased his hold on her. "It's okay," he reassured Ari. "I'm all right. . . . Don't worry."

Ari moved in on the demon. "Juliana!" he bellowed in anguish, as if searching for his lover somewhere inside that demon's body. "Where's my Jules?" he asked, eyes turning silver as several lights exploded over the bar.

"I have a piece of news for you, demon," Mason announced boldly, stepping in front of Nikos and body blocking Aristos. It was a subtle maneuver, but that demon would have to plow him under if she intended to harm either man. "It's not so much news as a number, really. Four hundred and twenty-eight."

She said nothing, her eyes drinking him in. The lust was obvious, despite everything that had happened between them.

"That's the number of your kind that I've killed so far as a demon hunter. Pretty healthy career, don't you think? But my real point is more of a message. For you. That you'd better start memorizing a different number," Mason said with a calm laugh. "Four hundred and twenty-nine. That's *your* number, Djinn, and it's coming up very soon."

"Mason Angel, how manly you are," she trilled in response. "Killer instinct, warrior code . . ."

Mason cut her off. "Four hundred and twenty-nine," he repeated. "And I'm coming for you."

"Well, Mason Angel, if you'd done that when we first met, things would've been much easier. Wouldn't they?" The Djinn tilted her chin upward, giving him a coy, sensual smile. But then she grew unexpectedly weaker; the intimidation he'd been wielding was a literal weapon, one that could level any demon if he inflicted his threats with enough force.

In horror, she began hissing. "Too soon," she said, spitting and shaking until her teeth rattled. "I am in charge! I rule this temple!"

"Shit!" Mason said, staring at the demon in shocked wonder. Right before all their eyes, her image began wavering and realigning—until Juliana stood before them all, appearing terrified and very confused.

*   *   *

"Tell me you're all right," Ari insisted, pulling Jules against his side. They sat on the sofa, she with a shaky, weakened demeanor that had him panicked. Mason and Nikos had cleared out, allowing them a few moments of privacy, a good thing considering how unsettled Jules was—even more than earlier, in the truck.

She leaned into him. "I was in the bedroom, and then suddenly . . . I was out here, and all of you were shouting and staring at me. Everyone was so angry and upset." She looked into his eyes. "I don't remember anything about what happened this time. Unlike the events at the restaurant, when I was able to recall a bit of what happened."

Ari held her close, stroking her hair and trying to soothe her. But he wasn't calm himself, not by a long shot.

Jules had quite an aggressive alter ego, it seemed, and as much as that angered and frustrated him with the cursed Djinn, his primary concern was for Juliana's well-being. She needed him strong and collected, not running roughshod with his emotions. And he needed to find out as much as possible about the demon they were dealing with.

"Jules, baby," he tried gently. "Do you remember anything about a woman? One with long dark hair, exotic skin? Is that what your . . . uh . . . angel looked like?"

Juliana's face distorted into a mask of suffering. She quickly signed, "If I tell you the truth about her, she'll hurt you."

He shook his head, then said aloud, "No. No, that's not true. I'm strong and alive. So are you. We can sort the rest out. You know that we can." He tugged her up against his chest. "Lies are the only thing that can keep us apart."

Juliana moved backward on the sofa, separating their bodies. She planted both hands on the cushions, giving him a determined, resolute stare. "I have not deceived you, not intentionally. Aristos, you must believe me."

But *did* he? For a crazy moment, he honestly wasn't sure what he thought at all. Especially after decades of mourning her death, blaming himself for it, only to have her here— beside him—once again. To learn that she'd gotten here by bargaining with a demon was nearly too much.

He bowed his head. "I know you love me." That much was true, and he meant the words.

"But do you still love me?"

"Of course I do. I never stopped," he reassured her. "I never would, sweetheart."

"No matter what I've done?" she asked, searching his face.

And suddenly she wasn't the only one shaking. His heart began slamming like a mother inside his chest. "What do you mean? . . . What *have* you done?"

She leaped off the sofa, frantically moving about the room.

"Juliana," he asked more firmly. "Tell me what you mean. What you're talking about."

"I'm afraid that's the worst of it," she admitted, turning to him with a hopeless expression. "I really don't know. Just promise you will forgive me."

He seized her by the shoulders, forcing her to stand still. Every question that he should've asked, about how and why she'd managed to come to him from beyond the grave—all of it came crashing down on him in an instant. Mason had been right about that; none of them had asked nearly enough questions.

"Juliana, what have you been hiding from me?" he roared, and she burst into tears.

"Won't you promise that you'll still love me? I thought you believed in me . . . in our love." She swiped at her tears.

"Jules," he said, feeling his own eyes burn. "You've hooked up with a demon. Of course I love you, but . . . you've lied to me about it?"

She hesitated, and then her hands moved quickly as she began signing. "In my dream this afternoon, there was a woman. The one who came to me and helped me regain physical form." She sank down onto the edge of the sofa. "Apparently, when she made the offer, I agreed to a payment of sorts in exchange for her help."

"Oh, fuck," was all he could think to say. Visions of Ares and his chariot and trident danced in his head like a scene from a schlocky Ed Wood movie.

"She could return me to my physical body; that's what she told me," she signed, then added, "That much I *do* remember. Now."

Ari's signing skills were too rusty for this detailed conversation, and it frustrated him. "Do you feel her now? Do you think we can talk aloud?" he signed slowly.

Juliana frowned for a moment, then looked up at him. "I don't think she's strong enough to manifest again. I think we're okay to talk ... for now."

Okay, so he'd cover current events quickly—and quietly—before they were interrupted by the seductresses from hell.

"Why didn't you tell me about the demon as soon as you woke from the dream?" he asked in a sharp voice. "That's all you'd had to have done—say, 'I made a teensy little arrangement to get here. I remember now.'"

"Because she told me she'd hurt you, like I said," she whispered, reaching a hand tentatively to her throat, as if waiting for the demon to choke her again. After a moment, when the Djinn clearly didn't manifest, she continued. "Besides, you'd been so busy storming around, claiming I was a demon or a devil when I first arrived. How could I possibly have hoped you would listen to me or believe my heart if I told you how I'd returned?"

She leaned forward, trying to reach for his hands, but he kept them out of range. He wasn't ready for cuddling, or even forgiving—not yet.

"Fear kept me silent. Fear for your life ... fear that you'd reject me. Abandon me and our love. I planned to tell you, but first I had to make sure you understood that I was not a demon."

"Sure sounds like you bargained with one!"

Jules shook her head. "No, no, she was very kind and lovely. Beautiful, in fact."

He groaned and reached for her shoulders, fighting the urge to throttle her. "Aren't they always? They're deceivers and liars by nature. I can't believe you weren't able to see that?"

"While a ghost?" she snapped back. "Thank you, sir, for being so fair and open-minded on this matter."

He sighed. "What did she say when she came to you?"

Juliana began talking very fast, rushing to explain. "She seemed trustworthy, and I wanted to return to you so badly. She was eager to offer assistance that I was more than ready to accept. Nothing seemed wrong or evil about her kindness, not then. She said she knew firsthand what it was to want a man, to need him so terribly, that nothing else—nothing in the universe—mattered. I believed she was sincere, and she gained my trust with those words."

Yeah, well, leave it to a Djinn to come wrapped in layers upon layers of good-seeming intent, Ari thought.

"I had no other avenue for returning to you, so I chose to trust her. Foolishness, obviously. I didn't realize that ... Oh, holiest God, what have I done?" She clung to him, seeking comfort from his presence. "I didn't know I'd put you in such grave peril. I'd have died again ... many times over ... if I'd realized how brief a time we'd be together."

He grew utterly still, the words echoing all through his mind. *How brief a time we'd be together.*

He swallowed hard. "Wh what do you mean? There's some kind of time limit?"

"The bargain," she said and began to sob. "It's short; she didn't tell me in the beginning."

"How short?" he managed to ask, chest painfully tight.

She pressed her face against his, crying even harder. "We only have another eight days."

A popping noise went off in Ari's brain, releasing a whirlwind of fury and reaction. *Only eight days*, he thought, feeling like his chest was tearing open—like his skull was expanding. His body clicked into a terrible, reactive overdrive as the words drilled into him like the cadence of a battle march. *Eight days ... eight days.*

He'd lose her again—he was definitely going to lose Juliana, and it was going to hurt a thousand times more this time. He knew it already, same as he'd recognized his moment of death at Thermopylae, felt the slice of that Persian's sword as it took off his arm.

Juliana was like that Persian, wielding a scimitar into his chest, cutting out his heart.

"It's nine days from tonight, eight as of tomorrow morning," Jules rushed to explain, holding him tighter. "Her name is Layla; that's what she told me."

Ari shook his head vigorously. "Wouldn't give her real name," he said tightly. "Gives you too much ... power." No Djinn ever willingly gave its spiritual name. They'd learned Sable's true name of Elblas only because Ares allowed it.

"She made me the offer, to return to you, while I was lingering by the town house. But I didn't know, didn't understand what she was or the bargain's short duration. Nor that she'd endanger you. I truly believed that she was an angel, come to help me."

His body was in a full-scale nuclear buildup, one unlike any he'd experienced to date. The emotional distress he felt was so intense, the power was swamping him, overwhelming him faster than he could even process the changes. Vaguely he was aware that the lights all around the room were exploding. The acrid smell of smoke filled his nose, and he heard raised voices from upstairs. But he couldn't rein himself or his body back in; all he could do was submit to the rapid escalation, reeling first in one direction, then the other, as it overtook him.

"When?" He barely managed to squeeze the question out.

"When did I know?" she asked.

He tried to force the words out but finally gave one firm nod.

She wrapped her arms about his neck, and he shook like a storm-battered barn in her arms. "Shh, my love. I'm here; it's okay."

He clutched at her, trying to get her even closer, wanting nothing more than to hold her for eternity.

"I only found out after we made love this afternoon. She came to me in my dreams while I slept next to you. That's why I was so upset when I woke."

Still, his voice failed him. He wanted to beg her to cheat her bargain, throttle her for having made it at all. But he pressed his face against hers, feeling their tears mingle against his own cheek.

There was a disastrous explosion from the entertainment center, and Ari didn't have to look to realize it wasn't just the Wii this time, but the Xbox, the DVD player, and every other piece of electronics housed inside it. The whole room was dark now except for a dim light over the bar of the kitchenette.

Nikos came down the stairs, and taking one look at him, declared, "You're not all right. I suspected as much when I smelled the smoke. Let me help you to your room, brother. Come now, ease up."

Ari shrugged him off and didn't even look up. "Mason. Now." He kept Jules close against his chest, trying to ignore the humming in his skull and the silver in his eyes. "Need Mason . . . help."

Ari heard his retreating footsteps on the stairs and clung to Jules even harder. If he could just focus, will himself to feel her—smell her—he could stave off the waves of painful power. He knew it; he'd seen River regain control numerous times.

By using sex, some part of him thought. But that was after River's shape-shifting. This? The overdose of pain and power and transformation being rammed down his throat right now? There was no fighting it; he was almost sure.

"Ariston, look at me," Jules said, pulling back to touch his face. She placed a soothing, warm palm against his cheek. "You're shaking all over, like earlier today. Are you all right? I know this is upsetting. . . ."

Ari blinked at her, suddenly unable to see anything *except* silver—rivers of it, floods. He'd gone blind with it, and his ears rang so sharply, he could barely hear anything at all. He struggled to his feet, dragging frantic breaths into his tight lungs.

He stumbled back toward Juliana blindly. Clearing his throat, and determined to ask the most important question in his heart, he regained control of his vocal cords. "Tell me you believe we can free you," he demanded slowly. "Tell me you'll fight to stay with me. . . . I can't survive losing you again."

But he couldn't hear her answer, just the storming tide that filled his ears. He sank to the edge of the sofa and, groping with his hands, he felt her face, her neck, her hair. Needed to be connected to her even though he couldn't see her at all. She pulled his head against her breast, holding him and rocking him—trying everything in her power, he could tell, to soothe him.

It did nothing to stop the tide of change. His muscles bunched and bulked across his shoulders and back; his spine began burning with sharp fire. Staggering out of her grasp and to his feet, he felt his wings emerge, cutting through his T-shirt, shredding it.

He was uncontrolled, rabid . . . utterly berserk. The force in him, the demigod's pressure . . . was overtaking him.

Which meant there was only one option left, and he'd die taking it—die loving the only woman who could help him.

"Jules," he cried in a voice that barely sounded human. "Juliana." *A shriek; a shrill hawk's song.*

He reached for her, trying to protect her from his talons, and hauled her toward the guest room. The only way to stop this tide was by taking her sexually. River's old cure; it had to work—or he'd never survive, he was certain.

Chapter 33

"Aristos, tell me how to help you," Juliana begged, as he pulled her toward the bed. He'd become much larger in the past few moments, his wings broader than she'd seen them yet, gleaming a pure shade of midnight. And yet, silver seemed to move across the feather tips, just as she could see it move through the bulky muscles of his forearms.

He blinked down at her but couldn't seem to see her; even the pinpoints of his pupils had vanished. She reached for his hand—and pulled back instantly. Talons replaced his fingers, just as his voice had morphed into something truly raptorial.

"This is my fault. It's the things I told you," she said.

He said nothing, already struggling to unfasten his pants.

"Shh," she murmured gently, covering his twisted, hawk's hand with her own. She kept her palm there for several seconds, willing him to feel soothed, loved. "I'll unfasten your pants for you. Is this what you need to help you right now?"

His head fell forward heavily, and he pressed his face against hers. "So . . . sorry," he told her in that scraping voice. "Berserk."

Working with gentle urgency, she tugged his zipper, peeling his pants down. He breathed in quick, huffing pants, the heat of it blowing against her cheek as he obviously tried to still himself, to settle down a bit—but at the same time he'd begun a powerful, needy motion with his hips. They were still separated by clothing, and his pants weren't all the way off, but he'd started a wild kind of thrusting.

Reaching between them, she yanked the folds of her dress upward—thank goodness she wore no undergarments this time—and then worked his pants all the way down his hips.

With a sharp intake of breath and another eerie cry, he sheathed himself inside her, full hilt, without even pausing. She flinched, still tender from earlier, and yet she needed all of him. Craved having him full inside her this way; that need overcame any physical pain.

She angled her much smaller hips, taking him as deep as she could, knowing instinctively that her body was his cure; that releasing his seed, spending himself inside of her, could possibly remedy the wild heat raging all through him.

"Yes," she urged as he began rocking inside of her, raising his hips, them crashing into her again. "Take all of me, Aristos. I'm yours, yes. Lose yourself inside of me."

She tightened around him, a kind of ecstasy that she'd never known, not even in their previous joinings. Not until this moment. Perhaps because what they were sharing now was so raw and wild and dangerous. Suddenly she felt a clutching spasm of pleasure deep inside, a rapturous sensation that had her crying out his name with no care that anyone else might hear. He mimicked the sound with a beautiful hawk's song, pitched low in her ear, even as his hips' tempo became frenzied.

So quickly this time, she felt his seed pulse inside of her, that shudder of release, as suddenly his fingers were stroking all through her hair. The talons were gone, and as he brushed her hair back from her eyes, she saw that his gaze wasn't silver anymore. And he was smiling, downright beaming at her, with the sweetest, giddiest look she'd ever seen on his face.

"Oh, dear God above," he whispered in his own, normal voice, still breathing heavily atop her. "You're *magic*, Jules darling. Sweeter than Elysium, better than love itself."

She wound her fingers through his damp hair, equally satisfied. "You're sure you're better now? That the . . . berserker"—she said the word carefully—"is gone?"

He captured her mouth with a kiss, answering her with a gentle, tender pressure that was thoroughly unlike the aggression he'd just displayed. As he did so, she felt for his wings, wanting to stroke them, only to realize he'd absorbed them, as well.

Aristos Petrakos was thoroughly human again. She relaxed slightly, sinking back against the pillow, only then realizing how his stormy, threatened state had worried her.

Not out of concern for her well-being, of course, but for his.

She sighed, breaking the kiss, and forced him to look into her eyes. "You promise me that you're well now, Aristos? That you're not suffering or hurting or—"

"We're going to work this all out," he told her, cupping her chin. "I am fine, and you're going to be, too. I get like that because the power in me—it goes thermal when I'm upset. If I'm on edge or emotional, it amps up. I just haven't learned how to keep it contained, but I will. I swear that I will, cause I don't want you having to put up with that every time we have a fight or, gods forbid, hot sex."

She blushed. "It's all right, Ari, so long as you're safe. But you seemed to be in a most terrible amount of pain out in the other room."

"Not once we got in this bedroom," he growled, rolling her onto her side. They nestled close, facing each other, but she missed the fullness of him inside her. A trickle of what he'd left behind coursed down the interior of her thigh, and it was an odd thought, but she wondered whether they'd conceived a child, some permanent gift from that moment of breathtaking communion.

Sliding his fingers along her leg, he traced his finger along the rivulet of his own seed. "It's miraculous, isn't it? What happens when a man and a woman join? That I leave my stuff behind like this, then maybe, eventually, it does another very miraculous thing," he said softly, as if reading her thoughts.

"Do you know my mind?" she asked, and he trailed that slickness up into her pubic hair, spreading it around.

"Nah." He gave her a lopsided grin. "I'm just proud to be your man. I'd love to have lots of redheaded babies with you some day."

She thought of his three sons, the ones he'd never seen again, and how he'd grieved that separation. Perhaps she could make him another beautiful son, one he could love in this lifetime.

He slid a large hand along her bare hip. "So, I'm okay— but how do you feel?" Slowly he lifted his gaze, and his lovely eyes seemed very vulnerable. "Do you sense . . . well . . . *her*?" He whispered the last.

She hated the reminder of the limit to their time to-

gether, realizing that all their dreamy thoughts about babies and a family would be only that—dreams—if Layla
had her way. She had to fight tears back but refused to let
Ari see her pain, not when he needed her strength.

"I don't feel her inside of me right now, but she's proving difficult to anticipate or predict."

He grunted. "Probably likes it that way. Her strategy, ya
know?"

"Do you believe Mason has the power and ability to
free me from her? I want to hope, and I'm praying so very
hard, but . . ." She stared at the ceiling of the dark room, the
only illumination the lights from the outside porch. "But I
am frightened, Aristos, and not of dying again or roaming
this earth, restless for eternity." She lowered her gaze, staring right at him. "But of being separated from you."

He cupped her face firmly. "Hear this, Juliana Tiades. We
haven't come this far, waited this long, only to be driven
apart now. I will not lose this battle. I will find a way to keep
you—and for as long as the Highest God will allow." Suddenly he seemed to remember something, his eyes growing
narrow. "The Oracle told me we'd face a great trial. She
said this was coming; she saw it—but she also prophesied
about defeating the evil within."

Juliana sat upright. "Yes!" She patted her chest. "She
must have been talking about me and . . . and *Layla*," she
whispered, with a quick glance around. She obviously
feared the demon's reprisal, the way she held her breath
for a moment after speaking.

Then slowly she exhaled. "She has less control right
now," Jules said very quietly. "I think our lovemaking . . .
the intensity or something, forced her into submission."

He opened his mouth to comment on that idea. That
they could use sex to battle demons was, after all, a really
appealing idea. But he was interrupted by a loud knock on
the door. "Ari, it's River," his friend called out. "I just got
back—are you all right? The house is in chaos."

Ari was already searching for his pants, moving toward
the door. "Oh, crap," he muttered, glancing at Juliana. "I do
this little thing with the lights when I'm like that."

She smiled at his obvious embarrassment. "I think it was
perhaps a bit more than the lights this time."

He froze, looking back at her. "How *much* more?"

"Some of your odd inventions—the Panasonic, the other items? I think you destroyed them."

"Oh, damn it," he cursed, stepping into his pants.

River knocked on the door again. "Buddy, come on, need to know you're all right."

"Look, Dr. Feelgood, I'm coming. Hold on a sec. I had to, you know, employ the 'River cure.' Know what I mean?"

Silence came from the other side, then a muffled laugh. "So, in other words, I should mind my own business and come back later?"

"We're done, dude, and I want to assess the damage to the house," Ari said, opening the door at the same moment he zipped up his pants.

Jules dove beneath the linens, barely peeking out so much as her nose lest River see her in a state of undress.

She heard River laugh again. "Just so you know," he announced. "I think some of the front windows blew out."

"Oh, crap. They're gonna break my balls over that for months, aren't they?"

"Actually, big guy, you'll probably get a pass ... all things considered." Then in an ominous tone, he added, "You should see the wards."

Ari bounded up the stairs, unable to believe what River had just told him—needing to see the proof with his own eyes. River chased in his wake. "Calm down; look, just take it easy," his friend tried telling him. "Don't get worked up; it's not helpful to you right now."

Ari hadn't even put on a shirt, nor had he fastened the snap on his pants. Damn, he'd barely bothered zipping them at all, but that hardly mattered. He moved ahead with a freight train's urgency, barreling out the front door and onto the front steps. Every Spartan was gathered; Emma, Shay, and Sophie were there, too.

Jamie was the only one still missing, but there wasn't exactly anyone taking roll call; everyone's attention was focused on the field itself. He'd figured River was just being melodramatic, but his best friend hadn't overstated the situation at all.

The wards were on fire, burning in leaping, crimson flames like some neatly contained blazing strand of fuel. They were popping and sizzling with so much heat, Ari's face burned—and he was a good dozen yards from the edge. It was an eerie, unsettling sight, running the length of the pasture as far as he could see.

Leonidas stood closest of all, rubbing his chin and appearing perplexed and deeply troubled. These were *his* wards; they all knew it. He felt almost fatherly toward them, not because they had a soul or spirit, but because his own energy fed their strength, fortified them, and in exchange, the wards kept them all safe from spiritual darkness.

Tidying up his appearance, Ari strode to his king's side, wishing like hell that he'd brought a shirt. "Sir," he announced, clearing his throat.

Leonidas's crimson cloak billowed behind him regally as he studied the scene with a concerned, almost mournful expression. He wore a simple linen shirt and leather loin covering; of all of them, he still dressed traditionally most often, perhaps as an expression of leadership. Seeing his king dressed in the old garb, with the fires burning in every direction, Ari shivered, feeling as if they were staring at the battlefield toward the end of fighting at Thermopylae. "Sir, what happened?" Ari asked, flanking his king's side.

"They're destroyed. The wards are . . . they're clearly ruined. All of you, unprotected." Turning, Leo lifted his chin and addressed them all with a commanding air. "I have no idea what could have done this, but we don't want to wait around to find out. We evacuate tonight and move everyone to safer ground, Spartan and human alike. We must fortify our position."

There was only one place their king could have in mind. "To the Angel plantation?" Ari asked.

Leonidas nodded. "Those wards there are much older, going back generations. So they're naturally stronger. Also, Jamie and I have worked on the perimeter since the attack two months ago. We'll camp there until we can reestablish firm base operations at our own compound." There was genuine sadness in the king's eyes as he stared at the disintegrating protections.

Ari touched the man's arm. "I know you put a lot of your heart into them, sir, and I'm sorry. But we'll re-create them. You will."

Leo studied the blaze, golden-red light dancing across his rugged face. "I find them beautiful," he explained quietly. "It's difficult to explain, but they're . . . alive. In some way that I don't even understand, I know that to be true." He seemed to think a moment, and then added more softly, "Watching them die pains me."

"Die, my lord?" Ari asked, surprised at such a dramatic phrase.

"Their life is fading away, Aristos. Is there a better way to term it? Not that I can think of." Their king's spirit had seemed so troubled lately, and Ari had the idea that there was a greater import behind his words. "All living things and creatures must die eventually," Leo said. "No matter how strong or resilient."

Now, what did that comment mean? Ari turned to him, about to ask, but was cut off. There was an explosion along the barrier. It ripped open a whole section of the protective links, causing sparks to rise high into the night sky.

Ari watched the destruction, his eyes watering against the blast of heat. Leonidas turned, about to walk away, but he caught the Old Man by the arm. "Commander, do you think I caused this? When my power went haywire a while ago? That could be what brought them down, sir."

Leo planted a gentle hand on his shoulder. Although only a few years older than Ari, his king had always been paternal with every one of them. All the responsibility and leadership he carried on his shoulders seemed only to add more maturity as well. Lately, it was strange, but Leo really had started to seem . . . older.

"Aristos, this began before the windows on the front of the house exploded, and before I observed many of the interior lights extinguish." There was kind reassurance in the man's eyes. "Even if you had caused this trouble, you only assumed River's power to help your friend and Spartan brother, not out of any desire for your own gain. I would not blame you."

For the space of a moment, Ari was relieved, but then a much more sinister thought nailed him, hard. Oh, by the gods, he knew he was right, too.

He cleared his throat. "Uh, my lord? I think maybe I know why the wards are reacting so violently." Ari drew in a breath. "They were trying to protect us, sir, because . . ." He sucked in a deeper breath, steeling himself, and pointed back at the mansion. "Because there's a demon in our house."

Leo's eyes narrowed. "Explain how that is possible."

Ari sighed. "It is such a long, long story, sir; I'm not sure where to begin."

Ari hadn't felt so exhausted, so eager to just *stop* talking, in longer than he could recall. But he inclined his head to their commander and said, "Forgive me, my lord, but I believe that ultimately—if not directly—I created the whole stupid mess."

Chapter 34

Daphne walked the beach, the cool sand squishing between her bare toes. Delphi Island had become her temporary home, the brightly colored beach cottage a refuge far from her brother's band—and yet near enough to Leonidas and her beloved Spartans that she could reach them quickly, as needed. Teleporting from England wasn't quite as fast or easy.

The surf roared because of the offshore hurricane, high waves raging, and the weather seemed to reflect her inner turmoil.

She was sure now that Ares had revoked Leonidas's immortality. Her brother had hinted at it enough times, but after glimpsing the gray in his beard last night, she was convinced that was Ares' punishment. On her, on Leonidas ... on all of them. He would age now, and eventually die.

With a pained cry, she plopped down on the sand, watching the silver fingers of light that played over the roaring surf. There had to be a way to save him, she was certain, but she couldn't seem to arrive at a plan. Her father, Zeus, had outright refused to intervene, but she was a demigoddess, possessing some power, even if it was limited in scope. She also had alliances on Olympus, those who cared for her and felt at least an iota of loyalty toward her. Like her nephew Eros, for instance; he'd always been kind to her—grateful for the respect and affection she offered even in the face of his own father's cruelty.

Yes! she thought, sitting up taller. Eros could surely be of assistance. He lacked Ares' brutal strength and her own father's authority, but he carried more sway on the great mountain than she did, without a doubt. Beyond that, wouldn't he be naturally sympathetic to her lover's plight? She felt much lighter, until an odd shiver coursed down her spine. Her connection with Leonidas ran so strong, she always sensed when he was troubled—or *in* trouble of any sort. And something was definitely very wrong.

Leaping to her feet, she was already raising her arms as she began hurtling through the dimensions, flinging herself to his side.

In response to Leonidas's orders to roll out, the past hour had seen a flurry of activity, organizing supplies, packing up vehicles. It was like the old time in Sparta, but instead of mules and horses, they had Mountaineers and Jeeps.

Ari had stayed out in the pasture, talking quietly to Leonidas about everything he'd learned about Juliana—and how it didn't contradict the truth of their Oracle's prophecy.

"Even our lady admitted that we had a very challenging road ahead," Ari reminded Leo, half-afraid that he'd want to do the very thing Mason had threatened at first. Just kill Jules and be done with her.

"I remember what she said." Leo grew quiet, drawing his cloak about his shoulders. "I noticed it at the time, actually. There is always more to what Daphne says or even intimates than meets the eye." Leo smiled to himself, his affection for the woman obvious, and he kept on smiling that way.

"You love her," Ari blurted like an idiot, wishing he could reel those three words back in the moment they were out of his mouth. But, well, he'd done the math lately, and he knew he was right, so there you had it. When something true came to his mind, he couldn't seem to hold back.

He braced, waiting for censure, some gentle rebuke, but Leonidas kept his eyes on the dying wards. Silent at first, he began to smile more broadly after a moment. "I suppose I am not nearly as mysterious as I would like to believe." He tucked his cloak even closer about himself, facing the fires again. "But please tell no one, Aristos. As you might imagine, this is an . . . ah, need-to-know type situation."

"Well, well, *boy* talk? I wonder if it's anywhere nearly as thrilling as girl talk," Daphne asked, waltzing right up to Leo. The king stood taller, more handsome somehow, and his joy at her unexpected arrival sparkled in his eyes.

She squared herself in front of the commander, smiling

up at him. Her hair was different—again. Long past her shoulders, the trademark cobalt blue strands were there, but this time she'd added crimson, too.

Crimson for Spartan kings, Ari thought, smiling despite all the struggles that lay ahead.

"You knew I needed you," Leo said, and although his hand moved slightly, reaching, he did not touch her.

But she solved that problem, looping an arm through his. "Come," she said soothingly. "Let's inspect your wards, good king."

With a quick glance around, Leonidas pulled her off to the side. Ari heard them murmuring low, and although he didn't eavesdrop—he would never do anything as obnoxious or rude as that—he couldn't help catching a few passing words between the couple.

"I thought you would not be with me," Leo said in a low voice.

"I'm starting to think I cannot be anywhere else," came her reply.

"But your brother?" He searched her face, and Ari didn't like the genuine concern he saw in their king's eyes.

She chewed on her lip, but then River was approaching them, calling out.

"We'll talk later," she said in a rush.

With a bright voice and even brighter expression, Daphne turned to greet River. Nikos was lumbering behind him, looking unhappy.

"I told him to stay back from the fires," Nik complained, walking faster because River had broken out in a run. "I told him that it's dangerous for a *mortal* to go near something so *powerful*," Nikos continued. "And you are mortal now, River. Don't forget that."

River ignored him completely, making a beeline for the rest of them. "I just realized something, Leonidas. Ari, come closer." He was waving his hands, all dramatic like he did sometimes when he was worked up. "We all know that this power I once carried caused me plenty of issues over time. The violence, the . . . other things." River blushed slightly, avoiding the Oracle's eyes.

"Physical urges," Ari volunteered, all helpful like.

River nodded, still flushing. "Ari, I more than anyone realize how much you've had to adapt to. So I started thinking. There's no way that the demon caused this breakdown. She was here last night, again all this morning, and the wards were fine. It has to be something to do with your new power. And yet . . ." River stared at the wards, puzzling over something else that had occurred. "And yet you've been here for months, too, ever since accepting our exchange. So you can't be the cause, or it would've happened before tonight."

"What are you saying, River man?" Ari asked, not sure what his friend was trying to explain.

"That there's a way to destroy the demon inside Juliana." River's expression became intent. "Come on inside and I'll explain."

River started walking toward the house, but Ari caught his arm. "I need to know now. . . . If it means Jules is gonna die, I need to know right now." He couldn't keep the desperation out of his voice or the tears from stinging his eyes.

But his friend clasped his shoulder, embracing him. "Friend, you've always had my back. This time? Let me cover yours . . . and Juliana's. For once, let all of us step up for *you*."

Leo had ushered Ari and River into his study, closing the door with a heavy click. They now sat in front of the king's desk, and Leo settled across from them.

"Okay, so my theory." River pressed his palms together, glancing between Ari and Leonidas. "It's certainly radical, but it would explain the reaction we're seeing with the wards, all around the property."

River leaned forward, placing his palms on the edge of Leonidas's desk. "Sir, I believe the demon inside of Juliana is reacting to Ari's power. He and Juliana are . . . well, they're obviously close, and we know that a demon wouldn't exactly enjoy cohabitating with a demigod. Or enduring the experience of love, either."

"You think Layla's aware when Jules and I are . . . well, you know?" Ari asked, mortified. He wasn't gonna go there and picture that kind of uninvited sharing, not with the vixen he'd met tonight at the Crab Shack.

"I think you have a god's power—and that could mean, especially given your closeness to Juliana herself—well, that you could free Juliana from the demon's hold. Because of your gifts."

Ari whistled despite himself. "You're saying I've got the power to destroy this mean Little Djinni Who Could? That I could help root her out of Jules's body?"

"Maybe. It seems that you two are certainly creating a seismic reaction, no?" River asked.

Ari leaned his head back, remembering the conversation he'd had with Mason until all hell literally broke loose.

"Mason Angel," he said.

"He thought she was a demon," Leonidas pointed out. "Is that why you mention him?"

Aristos shook his head. "No, he's got a book, *The Final Crossing*, and it talks about the gods and their relationship with Djinn. There's a special connection with Ares, something beyond his alliance with Sable. And that means River is right, about the power inside of me being able to combat the demon."

Ari locked his fingers behind his head, leaning back in satisfaction. He knew they were going to be impressed with his deductive analysis.

Unfortunately, no dice. River spoke first. "I don't get it."

"I have some of Ares' power inside of me—that Olympian . . ." Ari reached for the right word, actually grasping his hand at the air. "Creativity. And that really ought to mean—"

Leonidas stood regally. "That you have the power to destroy her as well."

"Bingo!" Ari cried, his heart soaring as he realized he could free Juliana. "Newton said it, right? Balance. The equal and opposite action to the creative god's power inside of me is destruction, or some such shit." Then, remembering to show a little bit of respect, he muttered an apology.

Leo was unfazed, rubbing his beard thoughtfully. "But we need Mason Angel's help, since he's the one who understands the book. Otherwise, Aristos . . . you might well destroy the one you love as you attempt to strike down her demon. Mason's knowledge of the text will be crucial, so it's good that we are relocating to the Angel plantation, where we'll have access to their full library of lore."

Chapter 35

Juliana folded the last of her new clothes into one of Emma's valises, and then reached to add Shay's sketch to the bag's contents.

"You've already been here long enough to have a suitcase full of clothes?" Mason asked.

Jules looked up, startled to find him standing inside the open doorway to her room. Although he had a friendly expression on his face, his unexpected arrival caused her stomach to knot. He was a hunter, after all. True, he had promised to help her, but she hadn't yet been alone with him—and he despised Layla.

Perhaps he doesn't mean to protect me, after all, she thought, panicking.

"There's something I need to do, Juliana," he told her, taking several steps toward her.

Her heart pounded, and she backed up several steps of her own.

"Juliana," he said, advancing even closer—and much faster.

She scuttled toward the window, but he tracked with the move, his expression intently focused on her. "Juliana, stop," he said firmly.

"Please . . . don't," she managed to say, her hand tightening around the sketch she still held in her hand.

"Don't what?" he asked with a confused expression. Then his eyes grew much wider. "I'm not here to hurt you! Good Lord, I promised to protect you, and I meant it."

She released a long sigh. "I assumed . . ."

"The 'something' I gotta do is this," he said, gesturing toward the sketch in her hands. "I need to see what my sis drew earlier."

She handed him the picture, watching his face to see

how he reacted. His green eyes swept over the page, taking in the details; then he looked up. "This is from your perspective. I mean, you aren't in the picture, so it's a depiction of what you saw. The view through your eyes."

She nodded. "I couldn't remember much about the night, not until Shay drew that. After, I went into a trance state and I traveled back to the moment—as if it were literally happening, I mean. That man? He did something evil to me, Mason."

He looked up in surprise. "Evil how?"

"He put his hands on me and, it's hard to describe, but I believe he . . . well, he willed my death. He compelled me to die. I believe he forced me—somehow—to drown myself in the river."

"But how could he take away your free will? Make you kill yourself?"

"He mentioned a curse."

Mason ran a hand over his face, releasing a long, heavy breath. "Not. Good," he said. "Can you tell me exactly what he said?"

She tried to recall the precise words, but the trance state had been unnatural and frightening. "He used the word *curse*. Said the curse he placed on me would live, and live beyond the grave. That it would kill me . . . to kill Ari's soul."

"Losing you sure did a number on him," Mason agreed. "And you didn't go to heaven after your death. . . . You wandered in torment, didn't you?"

She shook her head. "I chose to stay. I told Aristos that there was a moment when . . . I stayed to find him. I don't remember much about it, but I know that I stayed to search for Ari."

"Still, that curse—I do think it lived beyond the grave, Juliana. And I'm sorry, but I also think it's why you've got this problem with the demon. There was an opening for her to do her work, to fool you . . . a spiritual mark on you, so to speak."

Then Jules remembered another part of the vision. "Oh, and he said something else. About death to the voice of life, to every woman of my . . . heritage. That was the word he used."

"Are you sure?" Mason asked. His voice was tense, his expression alarmed.

She nodded her head. "Absolutely."

"Then we've got an even bigger problem," he said. "Cause that means Shay, Emma, Sophie? They're all under the curse, too."

Ari came into the room. "What curse are you talking about?"

Mason handed him the sketch, and Juliana explained, "Shay drew that earlier, darling. It's the moment when you came to my balcony. Look, that man is in the picture, too."

Ari cursed in Greek, eyes wide and filled with fury. "The bastard!"

"You know the guy?" Mace asked, but Juliana's suspicions were now confirmed.

Ari waved the sketch at them. "Caesar Vaella. This is him. The man I was pursuing here in Savannah when I first met Juliana. He got away from me back then, just seemed to vanish around the same time Jules died. Now I know why—because he'd targeted her. And he did *that* to drive me away from Savannah."

"He used her," Mason agreed, "to get to you."

"Exactly." Ari pressed his face against the top of her head. "I'm sorry, Jules. So sorry that I put you in that kind of danger. That you suffered and died because of my efforts to stop that freak."

"I told you earlier—you cannot blame yourself, Ari. I loved you—I still love you. That was worth any price."

Mace cut in. "The price is still being paid, y'all," he said. "That curse he put on her? It's still on her head, and that's giving the demon a foothold. We gotta break that thing if there's any hope of routing the Djinn."

"Uh, Mace," Ari said, still holding Jules close in his arms. "We know her name now."

"What?" he roared. "If you do, then we can command her, hopefully exorcise her."

Ari shook his head. "Yeah, but I'm not sure *Layla* would give us her true name."

"Layla," Mason repeated with a dark laugh. "Was somebody an Eric Clapton fan over in demonville?"

"Think you got your order wrong there, bud. The Djinn are ancient."

"I was kidding," Mace said. "I know Layla's Persian, too. Any chance she'd have given us her true name?"

"Only one way to find out," Ari said. "That's by trying to use it."

"Yeah, but we gotta work on that curse first, or she ain't going nowhere. Trust me on that one."

"So I've been doing a lot of thinking," Daphne said, walking to the bookshelf in Leo's study, thumbing over the various volumes. *Such a brilliant, smart man,* she thought, overwhelmed with melancholy. All his knowledge would die with him. His memories of important, heroic battles, his philosophy of leadership, all of that would vanish from the earth.

But when would that be? Next month? Another hundred years from now? She couldn't bear the thought of revealing what she now saw written plainly on his handsome, weathered face, the visible proof that her brother was fulfilling his threat.

"Yes, my beautiful king," she continued, retrieving his beloved volume of Herodotus. "A lot of thinking, and although sometimes that's dangerous, in this case, no."

He was behind her then, hands snaking down to grasp her hips. "Whenever you think too much, you always decide to stay away, and that's very dangerous," he rumbled against her ear, trailing kisses down onto her nape. "Think with this body, my body. Let's join those thoughts together and reach a brand new conclusion," he told her hungrily. "One that includes more of this."

He pressed up behind her, and she could feel his full-on arousal, that he was hard and thick for her and not trying to hide it this time. In fact, he seemed eager for her to feel his manhood completely. "I'm done with being polite and kingly, for I am no boy. Not even a young man," he added. "I must have you, Daphne. This man's body has need of you, burning, aching need, and it must be slaked. Tell me you want me, too." He nibbled on her ear and pressed his groin flush against her backside. "You feel how badly I want you."

His calloused hands slid up under her T-shirt, stroking the smooth skin as he moved upward until he cupped her breasts. That tender, soft flesh thrilled at his contrasting roughness. His hands were those of a warrior, a man who had handled weapons and shields, and something about that—about his life's experience—made her crave him even more. Just as he'd said, he was a genuine, real man, not a boy, which was one reason she always felt so feminine whenever she was around him. But now that he was holding her, from behind like this? Now that he seemed even more driven to take her than ever before? Her love and need for him spiraled to a dizzying level.

And then he lifted her miniskirt out of the way, and her reaction was so intense, her legs began shaking. He slid one palm between her thighs, stroking her languidly.

"You like this," he said, voice husky, filled with desire. "And I like the leather . . . the skirt, the boots. You're the sexiest woman I've ever met."

She relaxed into him right as he started unzipping her skirt, but then she caught his hand. "Leo, much as I crave this, your men need your guidance for the move. They're expecting orders and instruction, aren't they?"

"Ajax is in charge," he growled in her ear. "I gave him command as soon as you arrived. I'd already told myself that if you ever came back, I would no longer accept your reluctance or hesitation. I mean to make you mine this time, Daphne."

He moved even closer, bracing one large hand against the shelf, so she was framed against it—and against his body. "Tell me you're here to stay. No more fleeing me, or leaving me for Olympus or Delphi, England or wherever it is you go. Tell me, here and now, that you'll stay with me from now on."

She closed her eyes. "I can't stay always, but I'm here with you now. Because of my powers and . . . other things, I can't promise that I won't leave sometimes."

"No, that's not what I mean." He panted in her ear, suddenly trailing his fingers between her thighs. He stroked them much higher and closer to her intimate place, and she gasped. Leo had never touched her there, not yet.

He paused, rubbing his thumb along her inner thigh in a slow, sensual caress. "You won't fight me, not anymore? Not about being together?" He groaned, parting her legs wider, and worked his fingertips beneath the silk of her panties. She felt his rough fingertips brush against her intimately, and he parted her slick folds. "Yes," he moaned as he made that contact. "I need to be inside of you, Daphne."

She squeezed her eyes shut, body tensing at his daring tenderness. "No resistance from me," she whispered, feeling his beard scrape her cheek while he kissed her nape and her jaw, leaning over her from behind. "I won't fight you, not anymore. I am yours, my sweet king."

"I hate to interrupt, especially such erotic, delicious interplay," came a male voice from behind them, one she recognized. "But, Aunt Daphne? I need to speak with you a moment."

Leo froze, his hand still pressed into her most intimate spot, his fingers slick with her wetness.

"Tell me who that is," Leo said slowly.

"My nephew," she said, yanking her skirt back down from around her waist.

"I gathered as much," Leo drawled, shielding her with his big body as she reassembled her outfit. "I'm merely trying to think how many nephews you might have. And how many of them might be, shall we say, *well-known*."

"It's exactly who you're thinking of," she murmured under her breath, turning.

"Which only makes this position more awkward "

"Trust me," she said, arranging her face into a bright, welcoming expression. "He's seen it before."

With a flourish, she spun in Leo's arms. "Eros! Darling of mine, what brings you to my part of the world?"

Eros appeared deeply troubled, Daphne thought, leaning up against the shelf and studying his demeanor. The way his blond eyebrows furrowed together—something in his gaze was unsettling. He kept pacing the room, bow and quiver across his back, long blond hair drawn back at the nape, not yet telling her anything about why he'd shown up.

She wasn't exactly delighted that he'd witnessed her with Leonidas, not with her pressed against the bookshelf with her black leather mini hiked up, and Leo's hands touching her down low. It was a little bit mortifying that the god of love had popped in on their heavy-petting session.

Nope, she couldn't stop blushing. This was her nephew, after all, and he was so oddly innocent, despite his work and trade in all things erotic. In his own life, she knew him to be . . . well, if not a virgin, very inexperienced. Rumors suggested that he kept himself celibate so that he'd be more imaginative in striking others with passion and love. And there were those occasional whisperings about Psyche. Apparently the mortals hadn't gotten that tale even close to right.

"You seem upset, Eros," she said, and he cut his eyes at her with a "You noticed that?" sort of look.

"O-kay, you are upset. I'm definitely picking up on some unhappy vibes from you."

Eros turned suddenly as if remembering himself. "I've been rude. Please introduce me to your king." He flourished a bow toward Leonidas. "Such an admirable warrior you are, my lord."

Leonidas touched Eros's shoulder, urging him to an upright posture. "Please, no bowing. Not from the god of love," he said, with a light tone. "And certainly not to me."

"He's not keen on bowing," Daphne stage-whispered. "Too modest."

"I am pleased to make your acquaintance, Leonidas." Eros rose to his full stature, lifted his chin, and said to them both, "But I am not here on a social visit. I have created some turmoil in your midst, and truly, I regret that now. I've come to change alliances, to try to mend my mistakes."

She shook her head. "Eros, I'm not following you."

He sighed, withdrawing an arrow. He held it in his palm, turning it for a moment. "My purpose, the very gift birthed in my loins, was to bring love and passion between mortals and immortals." His face grew darker, his gaze angry. "My father's only purpose is to turn the bow against humanity; all he craves is war. My arrows bring love; his only cause destruction." Eros looked at her, that flash of anger intensifying.

"Uh-oh, Eros, tell me that you didn't . . ."

"Ares conscripted me into his own battle—against all of you," he said. "I am sorry, but he came to me and wanted an alliance. He also made it sound as if love spelling would be involved." He extended the arrow that he held in his grasp. "This is Eris. She brings confusion. That's how the demon managed to infiltrate your camp. It's why none of you asked about how Juliana came to be here, because I wielded Eris against all of you."

Leonidas formed his hands into a temple beneath his

chin, seeming to gather his next words. "Eros—is that what I should call you? Is that appropriate?"

Eros beamed, a strange warmth filling his brown eyes. "Yes, good king." His smile became even larger. "I'm honored to have you use my familiar name. And may I call you Leonidas?"

Leo nodded. "Those closest to me sometimes call me Leo."

"I couldn't," Eros said, and actually fanned himself for a moment with his hand, as if overheated.

He was blushing, and Daphne couldn't quite figure it out, until she saw the admiration gleaming in Eros's eyes. He'd never been treated with respect by his own father, and yet here was Leonidas, who by his very nature was a paternal presence, showing him kindness and deference—even in the face of Eros's admissions about what he'd done.

"Eros," Leonidas ventured again, "your father despises me a great deal. I think you probably know that. So if you align with me, with all of us, is that a risk for you? Will he retaliate? I want you to understand the stakes going in."

Eros pressed his arrow against his heart. "I wish, truthfully, to strike back at my father. So if he decides to make a move against me, so be it. Or, as humans sometimes say in this era? I believe it is . . ." He searched about for the words he wanted.

Daphne blurted, "Bring it on!"

Eros bobbed his head. "Yes. My father may bring it on. I have weapons of mass seduction at my fingertips," he declared, retrieving one beautifully feathered arrow. "I can use these arrows for love, for confusion, for brotherhood. Many arrows, many effects." He stepped closer, lowering his voice with a glance around the room, as if Ares might somehow be just in the wings, ready to strike them all. "But I have another weapon at my disposal, one that's far more significant. It can save Juliana."

"You know about her?" Daphne asked. "About Ari, all of it?"

"I have dossiers on every romantic relationship and attachment within your ranks," he announced proudly, and then his eyes grew sad. "Things have been going so well, for many of you. I refuse to allow my father a victory over love itself."

Leonidas spoke, his mind clearly working through the revelations. "What sort of weapon can you use to free Juliana Tiades?"

Eros's face grew less bright. "I cannot help with that. I can save her, not free her."

Daphne chewed on her lip. "I'm not getting that distinction; sorry."

"I can't help destroy the Djinn," Eros explained. "That must happen first, for otherwise Juliana cannot go where my greatest power lies, my greatest weapon, and that is her only hope to live a full and immortal life."

Daphne asked, "What is this weapon, Eros? I don't know what you mean."

He smiled, a warm, genuine expression. "I have an enchanted pool at my palace on Olympus. I believe that Juliana, if we lead her into that pool, will live because of the love she shares with Ari. That the two of them, they must bathe together, and allow that power to join them for eternity."

"Why can't we take them there now?" Daphne asked, already imagining how easy it would be to convey them. "Why can't she go with Layla inside of her? Might that not destroy the Djinn within her?"

Eros bowed his head. "It cannot be done. The demon would poison the pool, make its waters toxic, and that, in turn, would obliterate love from the world. Drastic, vile consequences."

"All right," Leonidas said resolutely. "We will do our work. I presume that your, uh . . . your aunt knows how to reach you?"

Daphne leaned up onto her toes and kissed Leo's cheek with a giggle. "You funny man, we don't need a cell phone to reach Olympus." She held up her pinky. "You've got me and all the stardust in this little finger."

Leo grinned back. "Of course, my lady. How could I ever forget your ability to toss any and all of us through the heavens." He held her close, brushing a kiss against her own cheek. "As always, your power enchants me thoroughly."

Warm, masculine laughter rang out, then a hearty, "I approve."

They both looked at Eros, who was still smiling when he vanished from the room.

Chapter 36

Juliana stared up at the sixteen-foot-high ceiling of the main entry to the Angel plantation, smiling in amazement. "It looks nearly the same," she declared, reaching out to touch the gleaming, polished stair rail. The sweeping steps led up to a landing where a tall portrait hung of Demitri Angel himself. She laughed, pointing, "And there's Demitri!"

Ari growled low in his throat, taking her arm. "Come on, darling. Shay's got us a room upstairs on the third floor."

He guided her up the stairs as Straton and Kalias came in the main entryway, carrying supplies across their shoulders. River followed, bearing Spartan weaponry—what looked to be a pair of bronze shields. Emma was right beside him, toting several long spears, a sight that made Jules grin as she paused on the steps to watch the crew in action. Perhaps she, too, would be given the opportunity to handle such epic weaponry.

Ari brushed his lips against her ear. "Like what you see there?"

She glanced at him. "Do you use such shields, as well? Fighting as you did in the old days?"

He slipped an arm around her, walking her up the stairs. "Leonidas is old school. Our spears bear fire from the River Styx; the arrows carry elixirs that are particularly lethal to demons. Sure, we'll handle a Kalashnikov or an M16 now and then, but mostly we do it the commander's way. Which has always been the best."

"Of course," she agreed, taking another few steps; then she paused. "Aristos, would such weapons work against Caesar Vaella? If we can find him?"

"I'd planned to use them when I was tailing him before. Problem is, we haven't seen or heard from him since your death. . . ." Ari caught himself, coughing. "Since, you know, back in the day."

"But you believe the curse can still be broken. Even if we can't locate him?"

Ari stroked her hair. "I don't know," he said honestly. "But Mace and the Shades? These guys understand this stuff even better than we do, which is saying a lot. If there's an answer, it's got to be down in their library."

"Can we go there now? Is that where Mason is?"

"Might be," he said. "But I'm worried about you. I think you need rest."

She shook her head firmly. "No, Aristos. I want to fight. Take me to Mason and this cellar, please. Tonight, not later."

Mason would be damned if Layla won this time. Then again, that was a pretty bad way to put it, he thought, kicking his father's antique desk in frustration. To learn that there was a curse on his sister, his cousins—Juliana herself—that had given Layla the opportunity to come after those he loved? Again?

It was like the moment in the movies, the proverbial "now it's personal" one. Kinda like Ripley when Newt gets taken by the alien queen. On behalf of all his family and friends he felt like shouting, "Get away from her, you bitch!"

Reaching into one of the tall bookcases, he retrieved their best volumes on family curses. It had critical info about generational curses—which this really wasn't, since Caesar Vaella hadn't invoked the thing on Juliana's descendants. Oh, no, the fuckball had marked all of her female relatives.

It was a problem that prophetesses came by naturally because they spoke life. Their very words were life—they came from God himself. That meant that spirits of darkness waged death against them, tried to strangle and smother them so that they couldn't speak that life.

Flipping through the book, he sat down in his father's creaky old chair—and he would always think of it as Daddy's desk and chair, no matter how many years passed.

"Thought I'd find you here," Nikos said, his deep voice filled with concern. "I think you need rest. Jamie told me you never slept last night, that you—"

Mace cut him off. "I'm not kicking back, not now." He held the book up. "There's a curse on all the women in my family; Juliana's only got a few days left before that demon has full control. . . ." Mason stood, striding toward Nikos. "And you are in danger because of her. She saw how I feel about you, Nik. She wouldn't have masqueraded as me, not if she hadn't glimpsed my thoughts . . . and feelings."

Nik stared down at him. "Your feelings?" he asked, and before Mace could move, the guy reached out and touched his jaw. Just a quick gesture, but one that contained vast amounts of tenderness. Mace's face burned, even as Nikos withdrew that hand. "Are you saying that you care for me?"

"Nikos, you know I have feelings for you," Mace said, unsure why Nik could possibly think otherwise.

"Of friendship."

Mason's face burned as he admitted, "A lot, lot deeper than that, Nik."

"But you said I mean nothing to you."

Mason gaped at the guy. "Where'd you get that dumbass idea?" he blurted. "If you're talking about last night in the car—"

Nik shook his head. "The restaurant. You told the demon, 'He means nothing to me.' Those were your words."

Mace blinked back at him in surprise. "Because you mean so much."

Nik smiled very slowly. "I misunderstood."

"Damn straight, you did."

"Then . . . you've changed your mind?" Nikos asked uncertainly. "Since last night? Because you did not want . . ."

"I never said I didn't want you," Mace corrected, and was about to blurt a whole lot more. Truly dangerous stuff, from an emotional standpoint, but Jamie came barging in. Mace snapped away from Nikos, putting plenty of physical distance between them.

"Uh, bro, what's up?" Mace said lamely, avoiding Nikos's presence on the other side of the cellar.

"Gonna help you work on the curse sitch," Jamie said, then with a quick glance toward Nikos added, "Hey, man." He gave Nik a friendly swat on the back of his head, and for some reason Mace had the idea he was . . . what? Trying to reach out a little more? Maybe Jamie had heard their conversation, he thought, barely suppressing a groan.

And then Juliana popped in the door, followed by Ari. It was a town hall meeting, the way things usually went with their group. Nobody could so much as take a crap without three or four others commenting on how the stuff smelled.

"So, it's gonna be a group op, huh?" he joked, flopping down in the desk chair.

"I can't simply go to sleep, Mason. I want to help in some way," Juliana explained, looking about the room. "Although, admittedly, I don't know how I might do that."

Mace handed her the volume about curses. "I do," he said. "Find the section that talks about bloodlines and curses. Then tomorrow? We get to work on breaking the curse . . . and exorcising Layla."

"Holy-freaking-moly!" Sophie shouted, bounding up from the kitchen table. The sudden noise caused Jules to startle, especially because of how tired she was. They all were, after the hours they'd spent in the dining room, poring over the various books and Bibles and compendiums. Jamie had actually leaned back in his own chair and started snoring a few minutes earlier, until Mason gave him a light nudge.

Aristos had read quietly, but she could see circles beneath his eyes. Shay and Ajax had called it a night about an hour before, as had Nikos and River. Emma, however, had insisted on staying, along with Sophie.

"Seriously," Sophie exclaimed. "I can't freaking believe this!"

"Sis, not quite so loud," Emma said gently. "It's after three in the morning."

Sophie pointed at the book she'd been studying. "I know, but I just figured something out. How did we all overlook it?"

"Overlook what, Sophie?" Juliana asked, trying to see what she'd discovered. But Sophie clutched the volume close against her chest.

With her eyes as wide as moons, she swept her gaze among them all. "Get this. The text here talks about curses being of 'like kind.' As in, if they extend across a bloodline, the curse is the same. And that got me thinking. . . . Juliana, you drowned, we know that."

"Yes, in the Savannah River," she said, noting how Ari's expression grew briefly pained.

Sophie turned to Emma. "Leah. I'm thinking about Leah."

Emma's eyes instantly filled with tears. "Oh . . ." She covered her mouth with a pained sound. "You're right, Sophie. You have to be."

"I don't understand," Juliana said, hoping someone would explain.

Emma stood and walked to the other side of the room, discreetly wiping at tears. Sophie explained in a low voice, "Em had an identical twin. Leah. And she drowned."

"And I almost drowned in the River Styx . . . and out on Tybee," Emma added, turning back to them.

"Then what do we do? How do we fight it?" Juliana asked.

Mason stood, actually smiling. "You know, I just love it when the forces of evil make it easy on me," he said, walking toward the breakfront. He opened the doors, retrieving a sealed silver container. "Holy water," he explained, indicating the vessel, "You ladies are under a water curse? We anoint you with this, and that curse is broken. Easy as pie." Then he frowned. "Of course, it doesn't change things for any of our descendants or relatives, but we can work on that after we get rid of Layla."

Mason walked to Jules. "You first. But a word of advice? Layla ain't gonna like this. Not one little bit."

Jules look at Ari, afraid that if she answered Mason vocally, Layla might lash out. He caught her eye, and she quickly signed, "Tell him she's been quiet. Ever since we made love. Well, don't say that." She laughed, and so did Ari. "He should know I haven't felt her in hours."

Ari nodded, explaining the situation to Mason, who answered, "Then this is the right time to anoint you. Actually"—he waved Aristos over—"given what we know about the power inside of you, Ari, you should do this."

Mason pressed the pitcher into Ari's hands, and very gently her lover began to pour the holy water onto her head. She closed her eyes, recalling the sensation of drowning, the hopelessness of it. But this moment? It was the antithesis to that day; she began to feel warm inside, more alive, joyous. It was God's love, washing over her, healing.

"I'm free," she said as Ari finished. "God just set me free from the curse. I know it! I feel it," she said, only then realizing she'd begun to cry. They were tears of release.

After so many years of wandering and searching, feeling separated from God's love—from Aristos's love, too—she'd come home.

"Thank you," she whispered prayerfully.

"And now we're gonna get ready for tomorrow," Ari said.

Mason laughed. "Yep, tomorrow's game day!" Then he pointed at Emma. "Get over here, Em. Time for a little bit of God's water. All you ladies, line up."

Chapter 37

Jules was restless and unsettled, desperately eager to be free of Layla—but terrified that their attempt to exorcise her would fail. It would be early evening before they began because the Oracle had advised that they spend the day in spiritual preparation. Some were praying and meditating, others training physically.

At the moment, the "girls," as Ari kept calling them, were attempting to distract her. Anything would be better than the endless, timeless wait she was currently enduring. She walked around the upper-floor library, a truly beautiful room with high ceilings and ornate moldings. Unlike the Spartans' compound, it possessed all the ornate beauty that she'd known in her own time.

"Juliana." Emma beckoned her back toward the group. "Come on back. We need to stay together."

Juliana paused, wrapping both arms about her torso as she looked out the window. The storm had mostly passed, but the sky remained a slate, dull gray that reflected all their moods.

Sophie cleared her throat loudly. "Uh, *so*," she declared.

"Ah so?" Shay replied. "We've gone samurai now?"

Sophie's eyes narrowed. "So," she said, "nobody's asked me what my big idea is."

"Which big idea?" Emma laughed. "You're a veritable buffet of suggestions so far—"

"I'm going to talk to Sable!" Sophie blurted, cutting her sister off.

"What?" Emma shrieked right as Shay cried, "No way!"

Juliana settled back beside Sophie, who gave her a dazzling, kind smile, then resumed crocheting. She'd been working on a scarf for the past half hour as they talked. Sophie worked the hook, in and out of the yarn, never taking a break. "Well, point is, dudes, we know one Djinn and pretty well. I just think Sable might give me the 411 on how to battle her or whatever."

Emma gaped at her younger sister in alarm. "Soph, you need to avoid that guy. He's a *demon*, don't forget."

Sophie finally set down the crochet, placing it beside her. "Demon, schmemon. He's got a total soft spot for me since I healed him. I know he'll help me if I ask."

Juliana found that information most curious. "You healed a demon? Of what sort of illness? A malady of the soul?" Perhaps Sophie was right, that there was valuable information to be gleaned here. "Could you heal Layla, as well, thereby driving her out of me?"

Jules felt an instant choking sensation, as if an icy, firm hand were slipping around her throat and squeezing. She coughed, rubbing it, and understood the warning.

Emma moved right to her side. "Layla?"

Juliana nodded once, touching her windpipe, coughing again.

Emma put an arm around her shoulder, cradling her close, as a sister would. "Shay, get over here. We're gonna sing together," Em explained to Juliana. "We've learned that hymns can work as a sort of weapon against demons. Because the Bible explains that praise and worship is a kind of warfare against evil—that the Lord inhabits the praises of his people."

Shay drew Juliana against her and gently murmured a very old, sweet hymn in her ear. It was soothing, comforting, and she could feel Layla growing docile inside of her.

As soon as the piece was finished, Sophie sucked in an exaggerated breath and simply resumed her talking. "Besides, Sable's not all bad, not by any stretch of the imagination. You know, it's the whole *Return of the Jedi* thing: 'I sense good in you, father.' Only it really is true in this case. Did you know that sometimes his eyes are blue? Honest to Pete, they turn blue when he's around me." She shook her head, getting a faraway look in her eyes. "Yeah, weird, I know. But pretty. Really pretty when it happens."

Shay tossed down the drumsticks she'd been tapping on

her knee while singing. "You are talking about a very evil being, Sophie. Just don't forget that. He's brought Ajax a lot of pain—he caused some of the mayhem and death at Thermopylae, too."

"For which Ajax punished him, right?" Sophie asked, her eyes growing really big. "Because I'm pretty sure someone around here"—Sophie eyeballed Emma—"told me that Jax staked him to a mountain by his wings. That Sable, in turn, had to burn those wings off just to survive, and that's why he's so scarred. Because he consumed himself in his own demon fire just to get free. So, yeah, cousin, I'm thinking Jax got his revenge there."

Juliana followed the entire discourse, eyes moving back and forth as if she were watching a game of lawn tennis.

Shay's face grew flushed. "He tried to kill me, too. *Cousin.*"

Sophie talked much more loudly. "But he *didn't.* Because, again, I think someone told me"—she swung her head back in her big sister's direction—"that when he realized you were a Daughter of Delphi, he didn't want you harmed."

"He's dangerous, that's all," Emma pointed out, folding her arms across her chest and settling back into the sofa.

Sophie slapped her forehead with the heel of her hand. "Oh, wait, I'm sorry! Didn't he jump into that fight with y'all? That little fiery hoedown with Ares in Hades? I thought, and of course, maybe I'm totally wrong here, but I seem to recall hearing that he fought with y'all. That he kicked some Olympian butt, no? And I also thought—again maybe my memory's flawed here—that he put Emma on his back and rode her out of the River Styx and away from danger."

Emma smiled at her. "We forget about your gift of compassion, Sophie."

"He deserves a chance with y'all—with us. That's what I'm saying."

Emma pulled her little sister into an embrace. "I'm sorry, and you're right. He could be an important ally."

"Then you won't mind my saying that he's kind of a friend of mine now. And I am going to see him, because you know what else? He might be able to help." Sophie leaned into Emma, hugging her closer. "Is your *stomach* poking out?" she asked suddenly, and Juliana choked back a giggle. "Or did you just eat too much barbecue at lunch?"

Sophie stared down at Em's belly, then touched it gently. "Sissy, what's going on down there?"

Emma stared down, too, touching her stomach. Juliana had to admit, it seemed to have gotten surprisingly bigger in the past few days.

"Oh, crap," Emma blurted, suddenly running from the sofa and into the hall bathroom. Even though she slammed the door, they could all hear her retching.

"I didn't realize a woman's body could change that quickly," Juliana observed, trying to tune out the sounds of Emma's morning sickness.

Sophie and Shay stared at each other a long moment, eyes growing wider. Sophie picked up her crochet and began working her hook feverishly. "I can't believe she didn't tell me."

"That's one big baby," Shay replied.

"Or maybe two smaller ones," Sophie said, then popped a hand over her mouth as if she'd just blurted something she'd seen but knew she shouldn't reveal just yet.

Chapter 38

Sable stared down at the woolen piece that Sophie had just handed him. "What is this?" he snarled, turning her gift in his scarred palms. She'd returned home and discovered him lurking at the end of her street.

"It's a scarf, silly." She beamed up at him innocently.

Right then he noticed the little tag that she'd sewn on the edge: HANDMADE FOR YOU BY SOPHIE!

She rushed onward, ignoring his silence. "It's just that this is supposed to be one of the coldest winters we've had in years." She made her eyes as big as saucers. "*Hello?* Global warming, anyone? You go around shirtless constantly, and even here in Savannah it's gonna be really chilly, so I thought I'd make you a scarf to keep you warm until spring."

"I go around shirtless," he muttered, parroting her words. "You thought you'd keep me warm until spring."

"Well, not *me*, duh. The scarf. Although you should think about getting a coat or turtleneck." She assessed him and then waved off the idea. "Maybe a leather vest, though?"

"Would you please shut up?" he roared.

She startled visibly, reminding him of one of her fostered cats that always lurked around her front steps. They way they'd arch their backs, ready to bolt if anyone became too noisy or cross with them.

"I guess I annoy centaurs and demons just like I do my own family sometimes."

Those words, for some reason, stabbed him hard. A ringing, hollow pain filled his chest. Surely she didn't believe her loved ones felt that way toward her? And if she did . . . he'd just reinforced the thought.

"I am not annoyed, Sophie. My question is simple." He kept his voice even, not screaming in her face, not railing at her harshly. No, he spoke, at least for him, very gently. "I'm unclear why you crocheted this scarf for me, a creature of heat and darkness. My body burns by its very nature." He patted his bare chest. "I am fire. I've no need to guard myself against the winter winds."

"But even you must get cold sometimes?" She peered up at him, genuinely concerned. She reached a soft hand and touched his withers. "I don't want you freezing to death this winter; honest I don't."

"You are . . ." He was going to say *considerate, kind. Thoughtful.*

But then all those words burned up on his tongue.

Wait one blasted moment, he thought. What was he doing, being so reasonable and pleasant with the obnoxiously nice girl?

As if coming back to himself, he hurled the scarf at her violently. She was caught off guard by the throw, and the scarf slapped her in the face, tumbling into a small puddle by her feet. Without a word, she squatted down and retrieved it, ringing it out.

"You know," she said, "I picked the color black because of your coat . . . and your hair."

"I don't have any hair," he growled, touching his bare scalp self-consciously.

"You used to."

He made his face a mask, gave her no reaction at all. How could she know what he'd looked like twenty-five hundred years ago? She'd not even been alive when he'd still been glorious and handsome and winged, not yet cursed to this work beast's ungainly body.

She touched the scarf, staring at it thoughtfully. "And I chose the cobalt blue edging for your eyes." She lifted the scarf, showing him the vivid blue. "See?"

"My eyes are crimson!" he thundered, and conveniently enough, his vision suddenly washed out in that furious hue. How dare she insinuate that she knew about his other heritage?

She shook her head. "Not all the time. Every now and then they're a very pretty blue." She sighed, damn her, a bit dreamily. "You probably have no idea how handsome that is, that flash of lightness against your darkish skin. It always amazes me when it happens."

He looked away, despising the way his cheeks grew warm at the compliment.

"Why don't you grow your hair back out? Is it because of your horns or something?" She stood, clutching the scarf against her chest. "Although, come to think of it, I guess you always had those, even when your hair was so long and shiny."

"How do you know about that?"

"I've seen the way you used to look . . . before."

He dared a glance at her. "When you healed me?"

She nodded. "It was the color of rich ebony, all the way to your hips, and I *so* wanted to brush it." She sighed, eyes drifting almost shut. "And maybe even run my fingers through it, too. Yeah that would've been amazing. . . ."

His face burned; his scalp burned; every part of him grew overheated and tense—all because of her quiet admission. She wanted to touch him. Who, in all these years, had done more than gape at his ugliness in abject horror?

He stared at his hooves, still flushing. "The scars . . . all over my scalp. I can't . . . I don't grow hair, not on my head, not since . . . ever since . . ." He cleared his throat and said finally, "I am hairless now."

"They're burns?"

Frowning, he nodded and touched the top of his bare head, feeling the nubs of his horns beneath his palm. They lengthened and retracted, depending on his frame of mind or whether or not he was in battle; right now they were almost all the way inside his skull. "My skin here is ruined," he told her, patting his crown.

She only smiled and then crooked a finger. "Bend down, Sable. I want to see the scars."

He stood taller, indignant. "Oh, no you do not. I won't allow you to attempt another healing on me."

"Get over yourself!" She swatted his withers with the scarf. "I used to work at a salon, and maybe we could do something."

He kept rubbing his crown, imagining what she'd think of him with that long black hair cascading to his hips. He'd be almost . . . attractive again. Maybe he would let her brush it, just once. After a moment, he bent down to her level, quite a feat because she was a tiny woman compared to his gargantuan size.

"A little lower," she urged, and he caught her scent as she pressed soft fingertips against his burning scalp. "Yes, that's good. I just need to see . . ."

All at once, she had those palms open wide and spread across his head. He squirmed, knowing her intent, but she only held harder.

"No, I'm doing this," she said, as he pried at her fingers.

"Do . . . not . . . heal me!" he bellowed, remembering all too well the pain she'd experienced with the spikes.

"It's your hair, for crying out loud! You deserve to have that . . ." She squirmed as he yanked her up against him, knocking her with his right foreleg, and they were in an outright scuffle, she determined to keep her healer hands on his scalp—and he equally resolved to block the action.

But the pain, that heat that always radiated across his skull—it did the most miraculous thing.

It stopped. And then so did she, letting her hands fall to her sides.

"That wasn't so hard, now, was it?" she asked softly, then added, "Uh-oh."

And fainted right against his chest.

"What am I supposed to do with you now?" Sable asked, giving Sophie an awkward little shake. She'd collapsed against him like he was an upright bed or her favorite pillow, and passed out cold.

"Sophie!" he hissed, shaking her harder. She released a quiet moan, turning her cheek against his chest, and settled in.

He stomped first one hoof, then the other, staring up at the night sky as if a solution might come tumbling down. "Spartans!" he thundered, just in case one of them might be in the area and could retrieve the bizarre human. *The warm, good-smelling, incredibly soft human*, a tinkling voice whispered in his mind.

"Stop!" he cried, as much to himself as to her. With a start, she woke, squeezing his arms to steady herself.

"Oh, golly Pete. I hate it when I do that. How long was I out?" She rubbed her eyes, backing away from him, and he found that he sorely missed holding her, all that softness against his own body.

He swished his tail, trying to control his reactions. Getting away from Sophie was the best plan. He trotted down the street but then turned back. "Why did you come for me? Tonight you sought me out."

She held up the scarf and then tossed it right at him. "Catch!" she urged, and he did so on pure reflex. This time, he balled it in his fist, keeping it.

"I wondered what you could tell me about something important, actually." She moved closer; he trotted farther away. She followed again, he jittered sideways. Finally, rolling her eyes, she plopped down on a stone bench.

"What can you tell me about female Djinn?" she asked.

He grew very still. She knew about Layla; she'd ask for no other reason.

"What do you want to know?" he returned.

"Can they do a little trick, this thing where they can, I don't know, bind together with someone's soul? Someone who died?"

He barely breathed, but his mind warred with itself, torn between warning her about Layla's vicious strength and protecting his cousin so that evil might wax strong in the world.

If Layla were victorious, that would possibly mean that his traitorous thoughts toward this particular human would be snuffed out. Because Sophie would be gone, too. If Layla went far enough.

"Female Djinn will do anything for sex. They have very specific compulsions for men who don't want them. They're consumed by the need to capture unwinnable affections— this is because they were cursed by Ahriman that way after one of their kind tried seducing him. If you've encountered a Djinn, a female sort . . . she's probably after a particular male."

Sophie leaped to her feet, walking much closer. "But can they bring back a dead person?"

He glared at her. "I've said too much."

"I need to know. It's Aristos—you know him, right? He's a really sweet guy, and my cousin Mason's in some kind of trouble with this thing. . . ." She pressed both hands to her face. "It's just too much to even think through. But can a Djinn be separated out or whatever, if she's done something like this?"

"There is no hope for your world or your friends," he

said bitterly. "There is no life left if a creature like me has entered your midst."

"But you're *good*," she insisted, stomping her foot. And by the gods, the woman seemed to mean it.

He'd be damned if he offered her any further help after that insult.

Chapter 39

"Jules," she heard Aristos hiss. She was sitting in the library, having begun a small crochet project with Sophie's yarn, anything to pass the time until the exorcism. And that would be soon, perhaps within the hour.

Ari called to her again, but looking all around the room, she didn't see him. Emma and Shay had left to go make sandwiches, so she was alone.

Then he called her again, whispering her name urgently. "Jules!"

She followed his voice, walking toward the veranda door. All at once, he yanked her out onto the long porch, a conspiratorial gleam in his dark eyes. He pushed her up against the exterior wall, stroking her hips beneath his large palms as his mouth covered hers. It was desperate, the way he kissed her, and as arousing as it was, as much as she wanted it, his intensity worried her. Holding her palms against his chest, she braced him away from her slightly.

"What's wrong?" She searched his face.

He was breathing heavily. "I thought you were liking that." He propped an elbow against the wall, staring down at her with a lazy, sensual expression. "I missed you. That's it. It's been hours since I held you, and I couldn't go another minute without tasting you."

He played with her hair. "I needed this. You." His words were seductive, but his eyes told a different tale. He was deeply worried for her safety and their future.

She cupped his face. "It's going to work. I feel it, Aristos."

He looked away for a moment. "I don't want you to be hurt . . . not by my power, or by Layla."

"Where did Juliana go?" she heard Emma ask from inside the library.

"She might have gone to her room." Shay volunteered, her words carrying through that open door.

"Well, shoot," Emma said. "I made her a sandwich. I'll check her room."

Ari put a finger to his lips, motioning for her to keep silent. Taking her hand and tiptoeing, he led her around the far side of the veranda, the part that overlooked the river.

Again, he pressed that finger to his lips, guiding her toward a wicker settee that was filled with plump, soft cushions. Because of where it sat on the porch, no one inside could even see it, but it was luxurious and would definitely hold them both, while affording a lovely view of the river below.

"Let's watch the sun set over the water," he whispered, and he smiled as he looked up at her, but again, that fear and melancholy lurked in his expression.

He settled into it, opening his legs, and then pulled her down into an embrace. Snuggling her back against his chest, he held her close, one hand on her abdomen, the other along her inner thigh. "I like being sneaky," he whispered in her ear. "It's hot. And holding you, all up close, that's even hotter."

He stroked her belly, trailing his fingers lower, walking them teasingly. "Look where I'm going." He laughed. "This little man's gonna get some. Although, my man"—he patted the bulging erection that he now sported in his pants—"isn't all that little, is he?"

"You are very . . . hot," she said, using the modern expression a little uncertainly.

Ari beamed with pride at the praise, brushing a hand through his long hair. "You think so? That I'm a hot guy?"

"You make me very, very hot," she agreed enthusiastically.

Jules had no idea why or how it happened, but suddenly her body really did get hot. Literally. Like it had done in the bathroom of the Crab Shack. "Oh, no," she moaned, gripping her head. "No, I won't let you," she told Layla. Raw terror gripped her, and even though she knew that the emotion fueled Layla's power, gave the demon more strength and command, she couldn't fight the tide of fear that rushed over her.

"What's wrong?" Ari asked, trying to sit up, but Juliana's whole body went rigid, and she began to shake. As she started convulsing, sensing Layla's dominance emerging, she struggled to battle the demon back inside and away. Did everything in her power to tamp down her own fear so that the demon couldn't feed on it, growing stronger and in control as a result.

"Jules, sweetheart, don't let her do this. Don't give her the power. Stay calm," he urged, trying to still her writhing body within his arms. He fastened her back against his chest. "Fight her by focusing on me. Think about our love," he urged, but no matter how fiercely he worked to calm her, she couldn't settle down. The fear inside her heart was reaching a crescendo—feeding and strengthening Layla— and her awareness of that fact only birthed more fear. It was a terrible murderous cycle between them.

Ari pressed a strong forearm over her chest. "Juliana, I am here. Holding you. You have nothing to fear. She can't emerge if you don't give her the power to do it."

"I . . . I don't want her to hurt you," Jules whimpered.

"Then fight her!" Ari insisted. "Your love for me, your strength—focus on that."

She swallowed hard, nodding, and felt a surge of God's strength and goodness inside her spirit. "Layla, I command you to back down," she said. "This is my body. Not yours. I have nothing to fear!"

Inside her mind, she heard a screeching taunt. *Nothing to fear but fear itself!* The words cackled inside Jules's head. *And all the wicked things I'm going to do with Aristos while posing as you. Think he'll recognize the difference? I can be very convincing, as you well know. Ah, and he is quite the handsome man. Wonder what I could do with his wings?*

"No! You won't!" Jules screamed, seized again by a convulsion of panicked terror. "Stop toying with him! I insist that you leave my body at once."

"I'm not stopping anything," were the words Jules heard in reply, only this time they were coming out of her own mouth as she hovered on that precipice. The spiritual brink where she was losing control over her own body—and Layla was emerging, taking charge.

No! Free me! she cried out, unable to work her mouth any longer, feeling the demon grow dominant. She was being shoved inside, locked away, and even as she tried to scream no longer had a voice at all.

She went tumbling into the blind, dark, frozen place, and the last thing she heard was Layla laughing. "Be still in there, Juliana," Layla whispered to her, her emergence complete. "And don't worry about being gone. I'll keep Aristos quite busy. I'm only getting started with your man."

"Layla, get back," Ari said, trying to shove her out of his arms. Her whole physicality had morphed, and she wasn't even trying to masquerade as Jules. She sidled down between his legs, turning slightly, and the minion actually tried fondling him.

He flung her off at that, and leaped out of the chair, putting as much distance between them as possible. "What are you trying to prove?" he asked, edging toward the library door. He'd get backup, serious Shades and Daughters cover, and they'd deal with her. Now, not later.

"I'm only curious about the very sexy and powerful man who keeps having sex with me," she said lightly.

"I'm not doing shit with you, demon."

He remembered Jules saying that she'd not sensed Layla at all during their lovemaking. It was only another tactic. From inside the house, he heard Emma and Sophie, and, sprinting toward that open door, he roared, "Layla! Manifesting, and now!"

Then everything seemed to be happening in a hyperspeed blur. Shay was out of that room, running faster than he'd ever seen her move. His body went haywire, no warning at all about it. Power started flooding into him, such raw energy—it was more intense than any he'd ever known.

I have to keep control. Have to destroy Layla . . . but not Jules.

He spun, and the Djinn had moved right up onto his ass. "Aristos," she purred. "I love it when you get so lathered up over me. That is definitely *hot*." She stroked a hand over her half-exposed breasts. "Like my body. Touch it! Mason's not here right now, so why can't we play?" She pouted, looking up at him.

"Juliana's not here, either. She's who I want. Let her have control again—now."

"How boring would that be?" She waved him off and sauntered toward the library's door. "Mason? Where are you, baby?" she called out into the main hall.

"Leave him out of this," Ari seethed, forming fists against his thighs. The power ratcheted up, increasing by several large increments, and he could smell sudden smoke from down the hall.

Great; don't burn the Angels' home down, he thought, but he couldn't stop the overload. He moaned with it, feeling his stomach spasm and his spine burn.

"Show me those wings, won't you?" Layla teased, walking back toward him like Delilah herself. "I can think of lots of things to do with a feather."

That was it. Enraged and overrun with his own power, he seized Layla by the upper arms. "Give me Jules back!" he roared into her face. "Leave her body now, Layla. By the Highest God, you may not command this body."

Layla shrieked at the words, recoiling in horror, and he kept on. "By the name of the Highest God, you must leave her. By God's authority, you must go." She began coughing and sputtering, but still there was no sign of Juliana.

"Stop invoking his name. You have no right," she hissed, her eyes fully red. "You're not a hunter!"

"No," a surprisingly calm voice said, "But I am. And you're going down tonight, once and for all." Mason Angel moved right up to the demon and slapped his hand across her face.

The whole crew had moved into the library, setting about the work of the exorcism once the proverbial starting whistle had sounded. They'd prayed and warred and commanded—and Layla hadn't relented for a moment. Not by leaving Jules altogether, and definitely not by returning control to her.

Mason's frustration had started to show in the past few moments, and he finally forced her down onto the hardwood floor, pinning her there by sheer will, because she was strong.

"Come on, Ari!" Mason urged. "Get on over here and do your thing."

Her eyes rolled back in her head right then, and she began muttering something unintelligible in Persian.

"Why won't she let Jules come back out?" Ari demanded, kneeling beside her.

Mason shook his head. "Don't think about that. Just lay your hands on her."

Ari couldn't help hesitating. What if he couldn't control himself enough to keep from hurting Jules?

Mason's voice got more insistent. "Aristos, seriously. If you ever wanted to go nuclear, do it now. Unload your power on her. Do it now, buddy. Come on!" Mason coached him.

Jamie Angel moved to her other side, squatting beside Mason. "In the name of the Highest God of all, relinquish this body," Jamie said. "We claim the blood of Jesus Christ over her."

Wonderful, Ari thought, because right then Layla, in true demon fashion, began foaming at the mouth like a rabid dog.

"We might hurt Jules," Ari said, watching Layla's violent reaction. She began convulsing against the floor, eyes rolling even farther back in her head.

Mason saw his hesitation and, in a decisive move, forced Ari's hands down onto Layla's chest. "Come on, man. We might not get a shot like this one again. She's weakening. Lay it on her!"

Ari focused hard and let loose every bit of power inside his body. It just rolled out, so much easier than usual, a burning cauldron of intensity.

And for a moment, he saw Jules's auburn hair, a subtle realigning.

"No!" Jamie shouted. "We don't want Juliana right now. Keep her back," he commanded the demon. "I have spiritual authority over you. And, Layla, this is you and us, right here and now. Juliana stays out of it."

The Spartans had circled about them, and as Ari glanced up, blinking at the silver in his vision, it was reassuring to see his brothers. He dug in deeper, unleashed more of what roared in his bloodstream.

Layla howled, a low and rabid sound that made his hair stand on end—and, for just a moment, he eased up. Which was the precise moment she sprouted leather wings and claws, and her whole body became covered with nasty green scales.

"Fire in the hole!" Jamie shouted, and Ari lunged for her, but was too late. She flew out of his grasp, beating those hard, ugly wings right in his face as she moved.

Moved, in fact, right toward the circle of his brother warriors. "Watch out!" Ari shouted, leaping to his feet, chasing after her, but she had the advantage of flight.

River tried to intercept that movement, stepping right into her path.

"River!" Nikos's voice was filled with true panic. He windmilled his arms, trying to catch the demon's attentions. And it worked. Layla trained her full focus on Nikos, hissing and panting as she stared him down.

"Me," Nikos said calmly. "Bring it on. You and me, Layla."

"Nikos, don't," Ari tried cautioning.

But before Ari could fully object, she'd launched herself on Nikos. *Fuck, fuck*, he thought, lunging to block her; he wasn't fast enough.

There was an ensuing blur of wings and scales, and everyone was moving . . . most especially Layla. She swiped her long claws into Nik's chest, ripping and tearing at the warrior's flesh. She was literally unstoppable—as he did everything possible to shake her off, crying out in pain as they swung first in one direction, then another. No matter what that Spartan did, she only rode him harder; blood came pouring out of Nik's chest, pumping outward in a warm, crimson stream. The demon laughed, flying upward toward the ceiling. "Oh, my," she said. "I seem to have caused some trouble!"

Mason stood paralyzed, gaping at Nikos, then took one staggering step toward him. "Nik . . . Nik," he cried out, both hands reaching toward the man.

"Oh, Mason!" Layla trilled, suspending herself high above them all. She gave him a flirtatious little wave. "If I can't have you, darling," she said huskily. "Well . . . we've already learned that nobody else can."

Dangling her hand in the air, she held something that looked like a necklace, and it swung back and forth like a pendulum. "Been looking for these?"

Mason stared up, his face crumpling. "No . . . no," he cried out.

"I took these as a reminder of our special night. A souvenir, if you will. But you can have them back now."

Not a necklace; dog tags, Ari realized with a chill; they went sailing out of Layla's hands as she flew toward the open doors to the balcony. The tags soared downward, barely missing Mason's head and clattering on the floor.

Mace didn't even look at them, never watched the demon fly about the room. Didn't even seem to hear her taunting declaration, "It's always the men you want. Such a pity that you can't want me."

Mason didn't register her words at all. His eyes were locked on Nikos, whose shirt was now soaked in crimson blood, a growing stain covering his chest.

Nikos glanced downward, touching the gaping wound in surprise. As if he couldn't quite believe all the blood and guts that were pouring out of him were actually his.

And, oh, by the gods, Ari realized, it wasn't just his chest; Nik had a big, gaping hole in his abdomen that might even have been worse.

Nik just kept staring at Ari, clearly realizing he'd been mortally wounded—but neither of them moved or said a word. It was a silent, slow-motion moment, one Ari had experienced countless times on the battlefield. Then Nikos glanced down at his belly, pressing his hand against the horrific wound. Eyes widening, he released a distended "Ohhh" sound.

And then, that brave warrior, a man Ari had fought beside for most of his life, dropped to the ground like a felled, mighty oak.

She could regain control—Juliana knew it, sensed some fundamental weakening in Layla's hold over her right then. But were they . . . flying? Had Layla levitated, used her wings? Jules couldn't see a thing, not in the place of darkness where the demon had her locked away. But she could sense those shackles loosening very rapidly; Layla's strength, she'd learned, always had a time limit, and the demon was losing her hold.

Still, what if they were midflight when Juliana regained dominance over her own body? That could be deathly, truly disastrous—couldn't it?

Juliana pushed the hesitation aside. There was no time to worry about the consequences of forcing Layla into submission. True, Jules might fall, but if she were fortunate, Layla wasn't very high up.

I won't let you, Layla hissed inside her mind.

Actually, Juliana insisted, *I won't let you stay. Or hurt anyone else!*

Juliana reached with her spirit, how she couldn't say, but she propelled every bit of internal will and determination that she'd ever possessed, and then she was coughing. The room's lights were shockingly bright, so she blinked, still coughing.

That was the moment she realized she was tumbling down from the full height of that sixteen-foot ceiling. She screamed, flailing her arms, almost fooling Layla's absent wings upon her back, but knowing they were gone. That she was helpless.

Face-first, she hurtled downward, knowing she would die . . . again.

Except she didn't. All at once, she was cushioned securely by the most comforting, reassuring presence she could have hoped for. Aristos scooped her right up into his arms, his bold wings beating against the air. He held her suspended in his grasp, feeling over her with his hands, obviously needing to know that she was all right.

"You caught me," she said, beginning to cry. "I was going to fall." She sobbed, burrowing her face against his chest. "Oh, Aristos, your wings saved me."

"I've got you," he murmured into her ear, and then it was the oddest, strangest thing. He flew her right through the library. The action seemed more supernatural than anything else he'd done so far, she thought, staring at the others on the floor below, noticing the towering shelves of books as they soared past them, through the veranda doors and onward over the railing. Ari's wings worked at the air, his gaze fierce and protective. "You're in danger," he said, sailing out into the night. "Layla just did something very brutal. Cooler heads might not prevail right now, so until we sort everything out, I can't have you around all those hunters. Or around Mason."

"Wh-what did Layla do?" she asked, bracing for the truth.

He nestled her closer, making a turn over the tops of several live oaks, but said nothing.

She clutched at his shoulders. "Don't protect me from the results of my own actions, Aristos. *What* did Layla do? I have to know, please."

He closed his eyes. "I think she just killed Nikos."

*　　*　　*

Mason wrapped his arms about Nik's torso, trying to use them as a tourniquet against so much bleeding, but every time Nikos's heart pumped, Mace saw more and more blood gush out. He was blind with tears, cradling the Spartan as close between his legs as he could.

"Don't you dare die on me. Don't you do it," he murmured in Nik's ear, and the guy arched slightly, crying out in obvious agony as Sophie applied pressure to the brutal chest wound.

Sophie's hands were all in the mess, as blood soaked as Nik's body was, as drenched as Mason's clothes and hands were. She moved around Nik's side, angling for a better position, and Mason wondered whether she wanted him out of the way. "Sophie, I don't want . . . I need to be here," he said, hearing the anguish in his own voice.

"He needs you here, too. You're helping to stanch the flow," Soph agreed softly. "That's good."

Protectively, he tightened his hold across Nik's chest, pushing his forearm against the wound. But even beneath the pressure, the blood kept surging out of the center of his chest. "Nik, come on," he begged. "Heal on up. Respond to what Sophie's doing."

Nik groaned, his eyes fluttering briefly, but then he grew still again.

"I can do this!" Sophie said. "I know that I can fix this. I know it," she said, and kept repeating her determination, over and over.

But then suddenly she slumped against Nikos, becoming very pale.

"Sophie!" Mason shouted, trying to rouse her. "Hang in, okay? Please . . . he needs you. Keep going."

"I am," she said, sitting taller again.

Mace couldn't see a thing, just Sophie's face, so close to his. And Nik's big body wrapped tight in his own embrace. She kept moving her hands across Nik's massive chest, swaying slightly. Then she stilled, her shoulders drawing tight and her face twisting into a mask of vivid pain.

Mace held Nik even closer, wanting to protect him from whatever she seemed to sense or experience. "*What?* What is it, Soph?"

She said nothing, moaning briefly, and he raised his

voice. "Sophie! Tell me what he needs. What do *you* need? Talk to me," he rattled desperately.

"It's all right." She released a heavy breath and began working her hands around Nik's abdomen, and for the first time Mason realized there was a second, equally grave wound down there.

Oh, God, help him, he prayed, shaking deep down in his bones.

Sophie bent forward, all her focus on that lower injury, and whatever she did—however it changed her ministrations— Nikos jackknifed off the floor, coughing and screaming out the pain.

"Keep him down!" Sophie shouted, pushing on Nik's broad chest.

Mace pulled Nikos back into his arms, pinioning him between his legs and holding him fast. But the man had grown deathly still. Deathly. Mason stared down at his chest, where his heart had been pumping all that blood out. The tide had stopped; no blood surged forth at all.

Mace groped around over the wound, needing to feel that strong, steady beat of Nik's heart, but there wasn't any motion there. "His heart's stopped!" he cried out.

"I know, I know, I know," Sophie said, moving her hands right over the spot. "Come on, beat!" she urged, pressing down both hands, her eyes shut.

For one endless moment, Mason clung to Nikos, desperate to moor him to this world. Holding his breath, Mace silently prayed, watching Nik's torn-up chest for any sign of life.

And then, all at once, Nik's heart gave a powerful surge, blood covering Sophie's hands again.

"Oh, thank you, God!" Sophie cried out, her eyes welling with tears.

"You stay with me," Mace whispered in the man's ear, pleading with him to live. God, he wasn't above begging, not about this. "Promise me. Promise me that you won't die in my arms. . . . I need you. Don't die. Please, you can't do this to me, too," he just kept blabbering through his own sobs, trying to make Nik focus on the moment, on staying. "I am yours," he vowed fiercely. "You gotta stick around, okay? Because you've got me now. No more fighting about it. . . . I'm yours."

And it was as if Nik actually heard him—or came back around a little. He shifted slightly and looked up into Mace's eyes. All the color was gone from his face, and his eyes were slightly glazed, but there was fire still in them. "I wouldn't . . . do that . . . to you," he said, blinking up at Mason. "Not you . . . You're my angel."

And then with a sigh, Nikos passed out against Mason's chest again, relaxing into his embrace, his breathing easier and steadier.

"He's better," Sophie confirmed with a relieved grin. "Whatever you said, I think it helped. He got stronger."

Mason knew exactly what had gotten through to Nik: Mason's promise that he now belonged to the man.

In his mind and heart, he pledged the words again, willing the strength of them into Nik's ravaged body. *I am yours*, he promised, closing his eyes. *I am yours.*

Chapter 40

Mason staggered out into the drive, drenched in blood; it was on his shirt, his hands, in his hair. The metallic coppery tang rushed into his nostrils, making him sick. Running to the bushes, he heaved and heaved until there was nothing but dry coughs rattling out of his chest. He had to get away, go somewhere, breathe somehow. Stop smelling Nikos's warm blood all over him.

He scraped his palms along his pants legs and wandered out onto the mile-long drive that ran from their plantation house to the main road. He'd walk out to the street, just keep going, moving, he thought.

Nikos had died, hadn't he? He'd totally flatlined in Mason's arms for several seconds.

But then he'd come back, and with such simple words— ones that had Mason dropping to his knees in the drive. *I wouldn't do that to you. You're my angel.*

Nikos might die again. Tonight. He could so easily die. . . .

Mason pitched forward against the sandy ground, his whole body shaking and rattling with a year's worth of bottled up pain, grief that was so heart deep it hurt physically to release it. But he couldn't stop. He clutched Kelly's dog tags to his forehead, sobbing against the ground, praying that Nikos truly was all right.

Because if he wasn't? Mason knew he'd never live himself, not after that.

Behind him, he heard heavy footsteps, but he didn't even look up. Solid hands took hold of Mace's shoulders, but he shook them off, still bawling like a baby on that drive.

"He's *okay*. He's going to be all right, Mace." Jamie's voice. Jamie's reassuring hands trying to wrestle him off the ground. "You saw that. You know it."

"I loved Kelly so goddamned much," Mace cried.

And all at once, he was being pulled into his brother's safe arms, still shaking and crying.

"Shh, little brother, it's okay now. You're all right. Nikos is fine. . . . They healed him. You saw him stand up; he's okay. I'm right here, brother. Not leaving you, not for nothing."

His brother kept on murmuring and soothing until Mace finally calmed a little.

But then he remembered Layla.

He couldn't have that murderous demon see this moment! She'd realize how important Jamie was to him. She might not draw the line at lovers and boyfriends; maybe her deathly reach extended to brothers and sisters and friends, too. He shoved Jamie away with such force that his brother sprawled backward.

"Everyone I love . . . she tries to hurt them. Stay away from me!"

"We're gonna deal with her. Right now, this is about you."

Mason hurled the dog tags at him, and they pinged off Jamie's chest, but he still managed to catch them with a flip of his wrist. Staring down at the tags, he turned them in his palm.

He raised both eyebrows. "Catholic, huh? O'Connell. Guess that made you two like the great melting pot, his Irish to your Greek?" he said. "How hot did that get?"

"Pretty hot," Mason said dully. Then, "There's no gender on those tags."

"No, but last I checked, I'm not a moron, either. Dude. I'm a hunter; that's what I do. We ferret out the truth, and sure as shit listen when a demon runs off at the mouth."

Mason groaned, burying his face in both hands. "She outed me, didn't she? I couldn't even . . . I couldn't hear or think, not when she went after Nik."

"She pretty much told the gang that you're gay, yep." Jamie placed a palm atop his head, looking him hard in the eye. "But don't worry—she tossed that in while saying how generally hot you are, and that it's a doggone shame you can't get worked up over her."

Mace groaned. "That makes it so much better, doesn't it?"

Jamie pulled him into a big, brotherly hug, kissing him

on the forehead. "You really think a person in that room will judge you? That I'd ever love you less or think you're less for just being who you are?"

The tears came all over again, and Mace sagged into his brother's arms. All these months, almost a year, keeping it bottled in. The loss, the grief, the blame.

"I loved him so damned much," Mace blurted. "He was my first love, the only one until   Oh, just fuck. I loved him, and she killed him, and now she's done the same thing to Nikos, gone for his throat because of how I feel."

"Nik's okay." Jamie kept on holding him. "He's gonna be just fine."

"Not if he sticks around me."

"We're gonna deal with that Djinn. She won't get another shot at hurting anyone else you care about," Jamie pledged fiercely, and something about the promise unlocked the last of Mason's pain. His big brother pulled him even closer, rocking him like a baby.

"You just let it on out, Mace. Let it all out right here with me. I won't let go. I won't ever let you go."

Mason wasn't sure how long he stayed like that, but after a while, he heard more footsteps behind them, crunching lightly.

"Group hug?" Shay called out, squatting beside them both.

Mace pulled back, wiping at his eyes. He couldn't meet her expectant, loving gaze, nor face her questions. So he stared into his lap, saying nothing.

"I think your brother's got something to share with you," Jamie said, clasping him on the shoulder. "Tell him you're proud first."

"I've always been proud of both my brothers." She reached out and gently stroked his hair. "And I'm not sure I've ever been more proud of you than right now, Mason."

"You heard what Layla said?" he asked, daring to look at her.

She laughed softly. "That you're gay? Newsflash—I figured that one out months ago, when Nik came to see you in the hospital. Before then. I've been waiting for you to say something for a while," Shay said.

His siblings shared a look, each seeming to ask the other when, precisely, they'd figured out their brother's sexual orientation. Shay spoke first. "I'd say since, well, maybe June?"

Jamie smiled slowly. "I'd say since a few nights ago in the cellar."

Mason scowled. "You thought I was with a married woman!"

Jamie shrugged. "I also know that the USMC doesn't let females into combat positions." Jamie reached for Mason's hand and very carefully dropped Kelly's tags into his palm. "So, do you want my advice?"

"I don't recall asking for it," Mason answered, sitting back.

"When Nikos wakes up?" Jamie continued without pausing. "You be right by his side. They've got him cleaned up, but he's gonna need to rest for a good while. Oh, and I told them to stick him in your room, by the way."

"My room," Mason repeated.

Jamie grinned. "Where else would we've put him?"

"Someplace safe?" he volunteered, worrying anew. "What are we going to do about Layla? How can we stop her? My theory about Ari's power—it doesn't mean shit if it doesn't impact her."

Shay stroked his hair. "We are going to keep fighting. Nik's going to be fine because—oh, crap." Shay's eyes grew wide, and Mace whipped his head in her direction. "*Major* crap," she said.

Mason would have used stronger, harsher words himself, but Sable beat him to the punch.

"Fuck," the centaur swore, giving them each a harsh glare. "I shouldn't be here."

Mason opened his mouth, about to demand the demon explain his presence, but then Sable sucked in a deep breath and blurted, "But I came, anyway. And I'm here . . . because I think I can help."

"How you figure that one, Mr. Ed?" Jamie fired off.

Mace caught his brother's arm, silencing the sarcasm. After rising unsteadily to his feet, he approached the Djinn. "What do you have in mind? I'm open and willing to listen."

Sable's eyes went wide at the sight of the blood drenching Mason's shirt, and he seized hold of Mason's shirt in his gnarled hands. "I smell Sophie in that blood! What happened? Tell me what Layla did," the demon demanded with an urgency that was shocking. "Sophie . . . she is all right? Uninjured? Where is she?" He looked toward the house, frantic. "Tell me where she is!"

Mason wavered on his feet, afraid he might face-plant on that drive at any moment. "She's fine," he told the Djinn unsteadily.

"Her scent is in this blood," Sable snarled.

Mason shook his head. "Soph's not the one who was injured."

"But . . . but I thought . . ." Sable trotted backward, rubbing his scalp with both hands, appearing unnerved, "I can smell her, in that blood."

Mace wouldn't have believed it, but the goddamned Djinn was shaking—over Sophie's well-being. His hands were trembling as he pushed them against his chest with a desperation Mace fully recognized; he'd felt exactly the same way moments ago, holding Nikos.

"She did the healing; that's why," Jamie offered, now on his feet. Walking up to the centaur, hands in his pockets like it was a casual thing, his big brother asked, "So what's your idea, Sable?"

The Djinn glanced toward the house one more time, as if still trying to reassure himself that Sophie was all right. Mace didn't even have time to try to analyze what *that* was all about; he knew she'd healed the Djinn recently and that some sort of bond had been formed between the two of them. Maybe that was what motivated this highly protective streak?

Wait, Mason thought, remembering his own words about Sable having staked a claim on the light side of the things.

Ari showed up right then, flying over the drive and landing in front of Sable. He pointed an accusatory finger at the demon. "You got past the wards. They're secure, so how'd you pull that off?"

Shay grabbed Ari by the arm, stopping him. "He's here to *help*, Ari. Isn't that awesome, that he's offering to *help* us?" Her words were spoken carefully, meant to clue Ari into Sable's cooperative mode. "I mean, the assistance of a *Djinn*—right now—that's a really good *thing*."

"Elblas," Ari seethed, using the Djinn's true demon name, "tell me how you vaulted past the protections, or I'm going to instruct these guys—my friends—to take you out, and fast."

Sable shrugged. "I had no problem entering the property. I merely assumed that the wards had been dismantled."

Ari shook his head. "They're fully in place, and they're all intact."

Sable blinked back at him, clearly surprised, and then Ari started grinning like a bastard. "Oh, my, my, you have turned, dude," Ari declared, pointing at Sable. "I can't freaking believe it."

Then Ari swung around and faced Mason. "It's like what you told me, from the book." Then, doing an almost kind of victory dance around the Djinn, Ari shouted, "You have turned light, old friend! Congratulations, and so much better for us. You're one enemy that's off our backs."

"Stop that!" Sable growled, stomping an indignant hoof.

Mason moved between his friend and the demon, warning with his eyes to pipe down. When Ari clamped his mouth shut, Mace turned to face the centaur. "Sable, tell us how you can help with Layla."

Sable stared at the ground for one long moment, almost as if still warring with himself. "She's my cousin, Layla," he began slowly. He hesitated, still fighting an internal battle; Mace could see it in his eyes.

"We need your help, Sable," Mason urged, then whispered, "Sophie needs it, so she can stay safe."

His eyes flared at her name. "I have the key for battling Layla. The one sure way you can get her to release this Juliana."

Mason knew exactly what Sable meant. "You know her true name, don't you? The one that will enable us to bind her and force her out of Juliana's body."

Sable lifted his gaze and one more time looked at the house. "Llayais. She's called Llayais. Now use that name . . . and keep Sophie safe."

Chapter 41

Juliana began unbuttoning her torn bodice, staring at the flowing, dark river below the dock's edge. Somewhere along the way tonight, her pretty new dress had been ruined. Maybe by Ari's talons? Or perhaps as he'd swept her into his arms midfall. It hardly mattered, she thought, blinking back tears as she stared at the churning surface of the river, mind resolved.

If she didn't take her own life—and permanently this time—the demon inside of her would kill again, and her greatest fear was that Layla would lash out at Aristos. That was why the singing voices were right this time. They'd begun calling to her from the depths of the river.

"*Juliana!*" they wooed. "*Return to us . . . now, now. We want you. End it all.*"

She sighed. "I believe I should cooperate with your plan," she spoke to the voices. They were hypnotic, so familiar.

Her dress slid down, over her hips, pooling about her feet. She began unbuttoning her corset, stripping it away. It was stupid, pathetic, but she didn't want to go to her death in the beautiful clothes that Aristos had purchased for her. They were a reminder, a heartbreaking one, of the future they should have shared together.

Stop it, she told herself. *There's no time to regret or grieve, not if you truly love him.*

And she did, with so much intensity that she'd take this step in order to protect him—and to protect the others, friends and family whom he also loved.

She let the corset fall to the wooden dock and stripped away her silk panties until she stood perfectly nude on the platform. The time was now; she would not hesitate.

The sooner she acted, Aristos would be safe, as well as the others. They'd all been willing to fight for her life; the least she could do was offer her own now, before Layla tried to kill again.

She stood fully nude, staring up at the moon. She swallowed down the tears that ached to come out, and with one last look back up the incline at the distant lights of the plantation home, she stepped off the dock and plummeted into the water.

The current was powerful because of the recent storm, and Juliana felt it rip and pull about her body, but the tide's force was nothing like the slimy, slithering creatures that began twining about her feet, dragging her down.

Her lungs filled with air, briefly, as she flailed against the surface, even as she knew this was the only way to protect Ari. She had to save him, couldn't be the cause of his death.

Yes, the demons taunted. *Go down, down into the depths, Daughter of Delphi. Consumed by us, by the curse.*

Curse? They'd broken her curse! These demons had no hold over her.

And then it was as if she woke up, came back to herself and fought against them. What was she doing out here in the river? Why would she have given up on their efforts to exorcise Layla?

It's the only way to save him, the demons taunted, their words entering her mind. *Your Aristos . . . you must die to protect him.*

Ari had been in danger, yes, but . . .

No! she thought. *There is still hope!*

She began trying to swim to the surface.

Ari was practically skipping as he made his way to the dock where he'd left Juliana. That bastard Sable had really pulled off a miracle on their behalf—choosing a new path to follow! And at just this moment when they needed him? He hummed under his breath, barely able to wait to tell Juliana the news.

"Hey, baby!" he called out, walking onto the long wooden pier. It reached across the marsh grasses, traversing some twenty yards or so before ending in the middle of the river. "Darling!" It was dark, and he hadn't heightened his hawk's vision, but he began to grow concerned that she didn't answer back.

He scanned the length of the wooden structure, allowing his eyes to transform so he could see in the night, but Jules was gone.

"Damn it," he muttered, sprinting the length of those boards, feeling them sway beneath his heavy footfalls. "Juliana!" he bellowed, looking all around, even out in the water. But she wouldn't have gone there, would she?

Something gleamed at the farthest end of the dock, and he walked toward it, heart in his throat. "She wouldn't," he said to himself. "Darling, no. No."

He fell to his knees, fingering her delicate dress and lingerie; she'd left them in a neat pile. They crumpled there against the planks as if she herself had been vaporized, leaving them to cascade downward.

"I'm not going to let you do this," he said, staring at the water furiously. "I won't let you sacrifice yourself for all of us."

The only way she could have been persuaded to try to drown herself a second time was from the conviction that she'd be protecting him—all of them—from Layla's deadly presence.

Yanking off his shirt, he unfurled his wings and flew out over the water—listening, all the while, for the siren calls of water demons. Because he knew one thing, deep in his heart: Juliana would never leave him willingly, not unless she'd been hypnotized into it a second time.

Flying over the water, he kept screaming Jules's name, sniffing the air, ramping up every sensory ability he held in his fighting arsenal. In the distance, he swore he heard the high-pitched squeals of demons and swooped in, talons raised.

A scaly head popped up, then dove below with a splash. The little minion had spotted him; he shrieked his intent, diving down to the water, raking his talons through the bubbling waves. Jules had to be there, fighting those same demons. As he scraped his talons through the water, he latched onto one of the demons and put a quick and dirty end to it. He hurled the water demon to the shore like a gutted fish and then soared upward in the hopes that he could get a better view of the terrain below.

There, up ahead, rocks protruded from the flowing water, and he saw something gleam for a moment. He turned down into a furious plunge, heading right toward that quicksilver image, screeching his hawk's cries the whole way down. With an agile leap, he landed on that rock, scanning in every direction. Whatever gleaming thing he'd seen, it was gone.

He stood there, breathing heavily, trying to swallow the bile in his throat. He could not lose Jules again. He spread his wings, taking flight again, and then paused midair. He'd have sworn he heard his name!

"Aristos!" came Jules's weak voice, and he flew toward the sound, beating his wings faster than ever, expanding his chest to gain more strength. He wasn't in full hawk form, as that would prevent him from rescuing Jules, but rather in his hawk-warrior state—with the muscular, strong body he possessed as a man, and his powerful, mighty wings spread across his back. He beat those wings now, soaring downward as he dove just above the water.

There was her arm, flailing in the waves, and he could see the coppery flash of her hair. As he reached her, he grasped her arm, pulling, but never stopping the motion of his wings. The water demons would strike out, try to keep her, so he took hold of her arms and kept going. She dangled from his grasp, and it was awkward, but he used his knees to press her up into his arms.

Finally, after soaring back toward the dock, he could hold her against his feathered chest, soothing her. She kept coughing up water, and he rubbed her back. At last she settled against him, soaking wet, and blinking at the water. She was so cold, too, teeth chattering as he nestled her in his arms.

"I'm not done fighting to free you," he told her seriously. "And I don't believe you tried to kill yourself just now."

She shook her head. "I don't want to die," she said, pressing her cheek against his chest. She moved it back and forth against the downy feathers, closing her eyes. "I wanted to be with you. . . . I just didn't want Layla to hurt anyone else. Those water demons, they used that against me."

"Layla isn't going to harm anyone—never again," he promised as they touched down on the creaking wooden boards. "Most especially, not you."

Maintaining his hidden place in the shadows along the drive, Sable watched Sophie sink onto the top step of the

Angel family house. She seemed weary, truly exhausted, and that tangy smell of blood was still on her. With an ambling gait, he moved out of the shadows. "You are not well?" he inquired.

She dropped her hands away from her face, lighting up. "Sable! How did you get here? When?" There was relief in her eyes, as if his arrival gave her new strength. She bounded to her feet, walking down a step or two, and then sank back down weakly. "Oh, crud," she muttered, closing her eyes.

"You are injured?" He bolted forward, trying to climb a couple of the steps, but it was too awkward with his hooves. "Sophie, come to me," he insisted, reaching toward her.

She took his hands, and he pulled her to her feet, helping her down to the very bottom step. That brought her a little closer to eye level, although he still towered over her.

"I can see you better this way," she agreed, then wavered slightly on her feet. He caught her about the waist, steadying her, but snapped back his hands as if he'd just been burned.

Aristos was wrong. He was not light, not turned at all. He was just . . . drawn to this woman, for reasons he couldn't understand. "Are you a witch?" he blurted suddenly.

"Excuse me?"

He cursed under his breath, about to leave, but then she began sinking fast, and leaned into him for support. "Please, hold me," she said, tears suddenly in her eyes. He clasped her waist, steadying her. "Just like this. I'm so worn-out after tonight. Healing . . . all the spiritual warfare."

"Why did they involve you in this intervention?" he asked sharply.

She looked at him in surprise. "I'm a Daughter of Delphi. I had to be there! And Nikos almost died when Layla attacked him, so I healed him, no choice there," she chattered. "Same with Juliana, duh. You know that! You understand who I am."

He released her from his grasp. "*You* are impossible, female! Without a bit of self-preservation or self-concern in your body." He pointed at the few thorny protrusions that remained along his flank and sides. "Why don't you go ahead and touch me again as well? Add that additional pain and anguish to your own frail, pathetic little body!"

Wordlessly Sophie walked forward and pressed her face against a smooth portion of his withers, and began weeping. Her small shoulders heaved, and several soft sobs were muffled against his side. The damp tears instantly burned his body; they were pure. He was evil.

"Stop that!" he roared, swiveling his torso to get a better look at her. "Move off me, woman!"

Before he could stop himself, his hand shot out, reaching toward her, but then he froze midgesture. He began laughing cruelly, ignoring the way her tears seared his side. "You pitiful mortal. What help do you believe I can provide?"

"Sable, for once . . ." She didn't finish, just pressed her face harder against him, her left hand now rubbing across his withers. "For once just stop fighting it."

Staring at his own hand, still outstretched, still halfway extended toward her, he grew enraged by her existence— and that he cared for her, that he couldn't shake her or resolve the conflict inside his perverse soul.

With an infuriated growl, he felt his horns lengthen and sharpen, his vision washed pure crimson with rage. He was at war with himself. The horns twisted again, wrapping about his forehead. He was at his ugliest and most foul, and still, despite the transformation, in spite of the pure crimson that washed through his vision . . .

He did not hurt her. He did something that went against every ruined instinct humming in his mind. He drew Sophie Lowery closer against his side.

"Wh-what happened?" he stammered, aghast at his own need to be a source of strength. "Why these tears?" he asked more softly, his gnarled fingers catching and pulling in her unruly curls.

She released another sob. "Juliana . . . we might not be able to save her. I hope you're right, about Layla, but if not . . ." She cried harder. "Juliana will die. Aristos will lose her, again, and it's . . . heartbreaking. I feel that sadness inside of me. It seems so cruel."

His mouth watered at the word. She was treading dangerous territory; darkness roared inside his heart. "Cruel?" he forced the word past his lips, panting slightly with need. A need that only grew as he felt her warm, soft body fold closer against his own.

"Don't you think so?" she asked softly. "But at least their love lives forever."

"Don't talk of love," he warned her. "Not around me. The word does not inspire me to . . . behave."

She only clung to him harder, as if he represented her next breath of life, the only stability in a foundering landscape. As if, he thought with a painful gasp, he was her *beloved*.

"I knew you'd make it better," she said with innocent frankness. She rested her cheek in his fiery palm. "I knew . . . I needed you."

The words pierced his heart, made him feel alive, and at once the world was no longer red. He blinked at her, still cupping her cheek.

"Your eyes," she murmured wondrously. "They're blue again. . . . Why does that happen?"

Because some small part of my soul isn't craven, he almost shouted. *Because you are dangerous to my basest nature*.

As the hurricane of conflicting emotions rose even higher inside his chest, he gave a shake, bucking slightly so he could throw her off.

She cried out, and he flinched when she fell awkwardly against the base of a large oak tree.

"You are *such* a liar. You know what you feel," she accused, pointing a finger at him. "What happens inside of you whenever I'm around."

With a flick of his fingers, he'd summoned his fighting swords. Their hilts were encrusted with gleaming rubies and emeralds. "This is what I am, Sophie Lowery! A demon. A murderer." He sliced the weapons dramatically through the air, and when she didn't even blink, he drove first one, then the other into the tree where she leaned, framing her between the vibrating blades.

"Right now, Sophie, I could relish killing you. . . . I'd drag it out, get drunk on the pleasure." He leaned closer into her space and sniffed the side of her neck right at the jugular.

She didn't recoil. "You can't do it."

She wasn't shaking, damn the bitch. Wasn't trembling or crying out. That stillness in her was an accusation.

"I am death. Not your comforter or your . . ." *Beloved!* He couldn't even say the damned word.

She finished for him. "Or my friend?" She just looked up into his eyes, her expression sad but not intimidated. She'd never even glanced at the sharp blades beside her cheeks.

"We are not playmates!" He thrust a hand against his chest. "You seem blind when you look upon me. Unable to sense or understand my true nature no matter how plainly I reveal it to you."

She shocked him by suddenly smiling, and brightly, as she tilted her chin and met his gaze. "That's just it. I *do* see. Your truest nature. Not the one you wear now." She waved a hand up and down in front of him.

"Tell me this truth, Sophie Lowery," he seethed, leaning so close against her face that his hot breath undoubtedly burned her cheeks. "Tell me what *I*, with all my thousands of years of roaming this world, do not know about my own nature."

Reaching before he could stop her, she touched his cheek. "You're going to love me. Completely. And you'll do anything to make me love you in return. I've seen it. That is what is true." She shrugged easily. "It's the only truth, really, between you and me."

He tightened his grasp on the twin swords, ready to inflict deathly wounds, anything to end her babbling. "I am incapable of love!" he roared. "Incapable of caring."

"Or holding me close while I cry?" she reminded him on a gentle whisper.

His eyes slid closed, and somehow, all the roaring fury inside of him evaporated at the quiet words.

He *was* a liar; she was truth itself, so pure and lovely that he could not fight her tide. It was a losing, drowning effort to cling to his own fading darkness.

"I . . . hated that you hurt," he admitted, wincing at his own confession. "I had to stop it. Do anything to take it away."

She stroked his scarred cheek, so gently. "Yes, see? It's not so hard, after all. It's just that this change inside of you—it's painful, I know. But it's okay. It will be worth it."

Closing his eyes, he turned his face so that his lips grazed her palm, and with the faintest, lightest touch, kissed the center of her hand.

"You gave us Layla's true name. Why?"

He opened his eyes and stared down at her. "You, Sophie," he admitted hoarsely. "I did it for you."

Juliana brushed out her damp hair, fastening the white lace blouse she'd bought from the boutique. She wore it with a multiticred skirt, black taffeta cut above the knee. It was ridiculous, she supposed, but she wanted to present herself to the others appearing composed, especially if it was the last time she would ever see Aristos. For surely, she felt in her bones, if they could not defeat Layla by using this new information, then Layla would consume her.

Not entirely satisfied with her appearance, she set the silver-handled brush down and walked out of the room. Aristos leaned up against the wall outside her door, looking as sinfully handsome as ever, even though his eyes revealed fatigue and fear.

She walked right into his embrace. "I love you," she promised him, needing him to hear it, now more than at any other time. "No matter what happens next, always know that I love you."

He slid his arm about her, leading her down the hall. "I love you, too, but this isn't good-bye, baby. It's our beginning."

"I want to believe that, too," she said, leaning into him as they entered the library. She flinched when she saw the bloodstains on the floor. Someone had tried to clean up, but without much success, and soaked rags and a mop lay on the floor. She shivered, staring at the bloodshed.

Ari pulled her along. "Don't look at that. You didn't do it, remember. And Nikos is all right now."

"For now. But if Layla gets loose again?" She fought tears, still gawking at the scene.

But then another hand grabbed hold of her arm, touching her softly. "Juliana, hi." It was Mason, and he was looking at her with a surprisingly kind expression. "You ready for this?"

"Do you hate me now?" she asked bluntly. "Because, sir, I would not blame you at all if you did not care to assist me. Unfortunately, I still very much require your help." She glanced at Ari, who hadn't let her go for a moment. "We both do."

Mason rubbed an eye for a minute, then said, "Like Ari

said, you didn't do all this. You're a victim of Layla, sure
as anyone else. She's lethal, but it's my job—it's my calling, Juliana—to protect you from her. You're one of the
innocents that her kind prey upon, even, apparently from
beyond the grave."

They directed her to the sofa, and Shay took position
behind her, laying gentle hands on her shoulders. Ari settled beside her, and his strength and solidness reassured
her more than anything else, including the group that now
knotted all about her.

Ari leaned forward and gave her a sweet, long kiss.
"Here goes, sweetheart," he said.

Ari began praying much harder right then. Layla was *not*
going to do this again, he thought, as she transformed beneath his grasp, becoming slithery and clawed—even displaying gleaming fangs this time around.

"Take two, anyone?" Jamie barked, but Ari never even
looked up.

"Let's contain this thing," he said, forcing Layla onto
her back. Her leather wings beat against the sofa, bunching
beneath her shoulders. "Whatever you guys do, nobody let
her get free."

She writhed and fought him, scratching up at his face,
and he barely managed to duck out of her reach before
Mason pinned her wrist down with brutal strength. "Don't
even think about it," Mace growled at her.

"Kelly didn't have nearly the fight that you do," she said
to him.

"Ignore her, Mace!" his brother cautioned. "Don't let
her use his memory as a tripwire."

"I'm using his memory for fuel, brother," he said, pinioning her down. "Ari? Go! Now—do it."

Ari leaned right down over her and produced his own
genie from a bottle. "Llayias, you ready to rock and roll?"
he asked with a smug, satisfied smile. "Because we're about
to bind you and boot you back to where you came from."

Jules moaned, her body covered in cuts and welts, but as far
as Ari could tell, Layla was truly gone. She'd released her
hold on Juliana, flying with a murderous screech all about
the room, until Mason had dropped low, semiautomatic in

hand, and fired a single sniper's round. She'd fallen like a swatted bug to the floor, writhing there for half a second, then just vanished in a squealing puff of smoke.

Done. Gone. *Hasta la vista*, baby.

In that aftermath, though, Jules wasn't looking very good, or seeming to possess much strength at all.

Sophie stroked her hair, laying her healer's hands all over the marks and bruises. "Oh, poor thing," Soph said softly, murmuring against her cheek as she kept releasing her gift into Juliana's body. Ari had tried—and failed—to do the same; too much of his energy had already blown out during the demon battle.

Daphne approached, leaning against the sofa's arm. "Aristos?" she said very gently. "We have to get her to Olympus. She's not strong, but I worry that if we don't take her now, she may not survive. She needs to be in Eros's pool immediately."

He stared at Jules's wan expression and felt torn. If they teleported her, that required strength, and in her current state, would she survive it?

"She's so weak," he argued.

Sophie leaned closer, working more furiously. "She's getting a little better."

"We really need to go now," Daphne pressed.

Juliana was drowning again. This water was warm, light, though, not asphyxiating. She felt it seep into her body, restoring her and bringing life. She tried opening her eyes, but there was only the glowing crimson water in every direction. She kicked and used her arms, trying to figure out which way was up or down so as to know how to reach the surface. Was this some aftereffect of her original curse?

Strong arms seized hold of her shoulders, pulling her. She felt the cool breeze of air on her face and, blinking, sucked in a deep breath.

Ari knelt by the pool, pulling her toward the side. She reached for the edge, but he stopped her. "You have to stay in; that's what Eros told us."

"Actually," a warm, musical voice informed them, "you both need to avail yourself of the water's special properties. There is life there that you must absorb while you're together. Let's put it that way, shall we?"

She gaped at the tall man—god?—who loomed over the edge, right beside Ari. "In you go," the beautiful man instructed Ari, giving him a light, playful shove. Ari went tumbling into the pool with a huge splash, and then swam back toward her.

They were alone, thank all the gods who lived on this mountain, Ari thought, pulling Jules to him. Her soaked clothes bunched about her, and he began unbuttoning absolutely everything. Something in these waters aroused him beyond anything he'd ever known before. *Go figure*, he thought, barely swallowing a laugh. Eros would have the hot tub to end all hot tubs.

Jules had already become much stronger, her face and smile radiant as she clung to him at the pool's edge. Her small skirt came free from her hips, sinking. She stared down. "Wait! I like that design," she argued, fumbling for it, but he caught her hand.

"Darling, I'll take you shopping every day for the next year if it makes you happy."

"With that flat, plastic card?" She stared up at him joyously. "Truly?"

"Can I watch while they truss you up in all the finery?"

"That is not polite, sir." She swatted his arm, but he pulled her against his chest, swimming them toward what was obviously the shallow end of the enchanted pool.

"Once and for all . . . ," he started.

"I will always call you 'sir,'" she said. "I find that doing so is rather . . . sexy."

"Oh, how you adapt to the twenty-first century," he growled, nipping her ear. "I like it!"

Then they were in the shallow area of the bathing pool, and Ari stood, drawing her up against him. His own shirt dripped heavy rivulets, and she reached to pull it off, but he held out a hand, yanking it over his head and hurling it across the water's rose-petal surface.

Jules held to him, thinking that the flowers along his arms were only a lush reminder of his very masculine beauty.

Never taking his eyes off of her, he was out of his pants, too, so that all that remained was her white lace blouse. She began removing it quickly, needing to be naked and bare against Aristos.

Then, with a self-conscious glance, she searched all about them. "Are we truly alone?"

He captured her mouth, kissing her, and then whispered. "Eros himself told us to get it on."

"Get it on?" she repeated, then intuiting the meaning, made her eyes wide. "He did not! He said we were to spend time together in this pool."

"Together, baby. Subtext is king."

Hitching her legs about him, she felt how very aroused he was, the thick length of him pushing between her legs. "This pool has some wicked mojo in the water." He laughed, drawing her right up into his arms. "Not that I need any help when it comes to wanting you, darling."

He cupped her buttocks, sliding her up against him, and before she could hold her breath, he was pushing up inside of her. "Yes," he said, eyes sliding shut with pleasure. "That's what I want."

They rocked together, wordlessly, and a warm wind fanned across their semi-exposed bodies. They dipped in and out of the water, moving and thrusting, but always that magical quiet wove its way between them. To be alone like this, together on Olympus, at the very seat of Eros's power of love and magic, made the moment of joining breathtaking.

"I . . . geez, I can't hold back," Ari barked. "This . . . something here makes me want to really lose it, fast."

She could feel him releasing inside of her, the jerking motion as he filled her completely. He gripped her hard, right up against his chest, and her own body responded in kind, gripping and pulsing and needing.

When they were totally spent, he still kept her in his arms, so close and tight, she could hear the hammering of his heart. "Sweet Jules," he sighed against the top of her head. "Nobody does it better. Trust me on that one."

They kept clinging together, unwilling to let the other go, and Jules marveled at the strength she felt, like a bell ringing all through her body. "I'm going to live, Aristos," she whispered into his ear. "This pool has saved me. You have saved me."

A whispering sound came overhead then, and they both looked up with a start. It was Eros, flying right over the pool, an expression of absolute glee and joy on his handsome face. "Love has saved you!" he crooned. "And *I* have defeated my father . . . this time!"

Then, raising his bow, a flaming arrow—a crimson one—he fired right over their heads. "Live forever, my young ones!" he sang. "Both of you, eternal. Your love, immortal. Yes, live forever!"

Chapter 42

Nikos turned in the bed, blinking his bleary eyes. How long had he been sleeping? And why did his chest hurt so badly?

He rubbed his eyes, trying to recall how he'd gotten here in . . . Where was he? Another look, and he saw Mason's antique dresser and the framed Harley-Davidson posters on the wall. He sank down into the pillow.

He'd almost died, and they'd healed him—and apparently, someone had brought him here to Mace's room. Why here, of all the blasted places, he wondered miserably. That was when he noticed an empty chair beside the bed, and he felt his eyes burn. Mason wasn't in that chair, because undoubtedly he'd been too spooked by Nik practically dying in his arms.

He groaned slightly, rolling onto his back, knowing that he'd lost Mason Angel for good. There was no way around it.

"You're up, huh?" Mason asked softly. Nik hadn't realized he was sitting beside him on the bed. "About time, too, Dounias. Don't get soft and lazy on me in your old age." Mason brushed a hand through Nik's hair. "Might have to call you Sleeping Beauty if you keep this up."

Nik blinked up at him, confused, his body still hurting. Desperately wanting to believe that having Mace in bed beside him meant something.

Mason wore shorts and a faded Marine Corps T-shirt. A sudoku magazine was propped against his knees.

"How long have I been out?" Nik asked groggily.

Mace checked his watch. "Going on about seventy-two hours now. You were starting to worry me, but Ari and Soph kept saying you just had to sleep it off. So . . . I took up guard duty." Mace grinned down at him, his green eyes filled with undisguised tenderness and affection. "I was starting to miss you in a pretty big way, man."

"I didn't expect I'd have you here," Nik said honestly. He knew what Mason must have felt, holding him, injured and bleeding to death. All the man's worst fears and memories had surely been brought back—and every one of his reasons for avoiding a relationship fully confirmed by that horrible scene. "I . . . just figured you'd be scared off for good by now."

Mason's light eyes became teasing. "After that dying act? Look, you gotta stop going for the attention." Mace slid down on the bed and propped his head on one elbow. " 'Cause, for the record, you've had my attention all along. You copy?"

Nik nodded, feeling ridiculously shy, especially when Mason moved a little closer, and continued. "So, I've been doing a lot of thinking. About you. About us . . . And about me, my stupid issues, my past, Kelly. So here's the thing," he said, staring meaningfully into Nik's eyes. "You deserve a boyfriend who's got his shit together, you do." Mason drew in a breath and announced, "I'm gonna go back to the VA. Get some help to deal with my PTSD, all of it. Because you deserve a guy who's not gonna run scared every time you try to get close. You deserve . . ."

"You, Angel," Nik said, pulling Mason into his arms. "You are all that I want and deserve."

Mason began stroking his hair very slowly, such a gentle, sweet thing that Nik got sleepy. Really, really sleepy, and then he was floating into the dreamworld again. Until with a start, his eyes popped open. He turned to Mason, who had apparently just been lying there, watching him rest.

Nik stared into Mason's eyes. "Aristos often says I am too reserved, and I suspect he is correct, so I'm going to do something very, very risky right now." Nik cupped Mason's face, murmuring, "I'm not asking this time. I'm telling you what I want, what I need . . . my one kiss. *This* kiss. It's mine, Angel. You are mine. Make no mistake on that matter."

"Roger that." Mason began grinning like an idiot. "You're about to become one of the few, the proud . . ."

"*Mine*," Nik growled with Spartan brevity.

Mace began laughing as their lips brushed together and murmured, "Oorah!"

But then suddenly he heard someone clearing his throat, and Nik froze, Mace still in his arms. Shit, he wasn't ready for the cadre to really know the full truth about what they had going, not so early on.

"Sorry," River said sheepishly, hesitating at the threshold. "Didn't mean to interrupt."

"The door was open," Mason said, sitting upright and waving him on into the room.

River walked closer, hands in his pockets, seeming awkward and unsure.

"So, uh, how are you feeling, Nik?" River ventured, taking the empty seat beside the bed. "You've had us all worried."

Mason slid a hand onto Nik's shoulder and in a soft voice said, "River's been in here for most of the time you were sacked out."

"You didn't have to . . ."

"You moved to save me when Layla attacked." River's green-gold eyes weren't going to brook any argument, not this time. "Just like you tried to help me down in Hades during that recent battle. Like you searched for me while I was lost in the ocean, trapped in dagger form. Like, it seems, you've been doing for years."

Nik averted his eyes. "You would have done the same for me. We are brothers."

"Are we brothers?" River asked, his voice unusually vulnerable.

"Always. You know that." Nik closed his eyes. "I hope that you do."

"What about the krypteia? That memory I had recently?"

Nikos kept his eyes closed at that one. River had come out of his recent captivity remembering a moment in their shared past that Nikos had done his best to erase from the warrior's mind. He'd never wanted him to remember that confrontation.

"I never put the death squad on you," Nik said after a long moment. "You can't imagine that I'd do that, not to my . . . brother."

Mason shifted beside him, planting a reassuring hand on his arm. Solid; strong; unwavering. Nik opened his eyes and looked at River. "I would not have sent the krypteia to harm you, River. Know that. I would always protect you."

"My point," River said firmly, "precisely. We are warrior brothers, yet you've always shoved me away. Always kept me at a distance intentionally. Leonidas won't tell me why, but I've decided . . . three times you've put your life on the line for me. That's what brothers do. But I want to know what the secret is, the reason you won't be friends with me. Brothers, *yes*. Friends—never."

Beside him, Mason began to laugh. "Hmm," he said in a teasing voice, "I think I recognize that dance. And you didn't even learn it from me if it's been going on that long. Jesus, you got something going with River I should know about?" Mason nudged him in the ribs with his elbow. "I need to be jealous or what?"

Nikos groaned, his eyes sliding shut. All these years, and he'd kept the secret; he did care about River. Tremendously.

Without looking at either of the men beside him, he said simply, "We *are* brothers." He sank farther down in the bed, his body weak, his spirit tired. "I couldn't tell you."

"Shit, Nik!" It was Mason. "Are you saying . . . ?"

He dared to open his eyes, trying to focus on River. "My father . . . He lusted after your mother, wanted her despite her being married. She had no choice; as a slave, how could she resist a nobleman? She never had any choice, and I was ashamed of that. I hated you for it. . . . You were the living proof of what my father had done to her."

River gaped at him, sharp blotches of color hitting his cheeks. "You . . . you . . . We are . . ."

"I'm your half brother," Nikos said, battling deep exhaustion. But River needed him to finish this conversation, so he forced himself to stay awake. "That memory, the krypteia. They did come for you, but I gave myself instead. Had them beat me. You never knew."

"You protected me," River whispered, eyes wide, amazed. "You're my brother. My brother, for real . . . Why wouldn't you tell me? How could you keep this from me?"

"Well, brother." Nik sighed. "I should've told you many things. Long ago, but my father—our father—spent a lot of time comparing me to you, making sure I wouldn't want a relationship. That night? With the death squad?" Nikos hesitated, recalling the humiliation, the physical pain. "They extracted quite a price, and made sure it lasted most painfully. I didn't want . . . I was ashamed," he admitted. And he prayed that neither Mason nor River would ask exactly what was done to him in the dark field once the beatings were finished. "I didn't want anyone to know. Least of all you."

"I wouldn't have judged."

"I judged myself," Nikos said gruffly, daring to look into the other man's eyes. All he saw, the only emotion, the only reality, was true acceptance. "I should've said something long ago. I am sorry, River. Much time has been lost, hasn't it?"

River smiled, brushing a hand through his hair. Funny, but he almost seemed shy. "Nice thing about having lived this long," he said carefully, "is that time becomes rather meaningless. I wish you'd been truthful with me years ago, but we can get to know each other better now. Starting today."

Nik nodded, his eyes drifting shut even though he wanted to stay awake. "Yes . . . brother."

"You need rest," Mace said, tugging the blanket up over his chest.

He'd have sworn he felt the guy brush a kiss against his forehead. "Not just one. Way, way more than one kiss for you, Nikos."

Juliana held the shopping bag in her hand, swinging it lightly as they walked along River Street. For the first time since her return, it felt safe to see a river—any river. The sun set low over the water, massive ships heading out to sea. She couldn't quite believe how much commerce and industry had grown since she'd last lived here. But she was starting to grow adjusted, even in the few days since they'd returned from Olympus.

"I am so taking you to Leopold's," he said. "Ice cream. Really great homemade ice cream."

"Is that before or after the Thai food, the beers at Pinkie Masters . . ."

He placed a palm atop her head. "Are you saying I'm a Dionysian kind of guy?"

She turned and smiled at him, not even caring that so many tourists bustled past them on the cobblestone street. "I'm saying, sir, that you have . . . let's call them voracious appetites."

"I found a way to indulge them permanently," he said languidly, leaning in to kiss her on the mouth. "A permanent, gonna-live-forever way."

"Do you really believe that's true?" she asked, suddenly unsure. "Do you think that's what Eros meant?"

He cupped the back of her head, kissing her again for a long, thrilling moment. Finally he broke it and brushed his lips against her ear. "I know so. I asked the Oracle after. You're here to stay. Forever. You and me, baby."

She leaned into him, resting her cheek against his broad chest. "Baby. I like that notion." She hoped he'd catch her intention—or, to use his word, *subtext*.

"I want lots of babies with you," he said, kissing her ear, then trailing his mouth down her throat.

The display was so forward and open, she started blushing. "Aristos," she complained, "we are on a public street."

He lifted both arms up high, leaned in for an even deeper kiss, and growled, "Not anymore."

Then, reaching in the pocket of his leather duster, he produced one of his ebony wing feathers, and with a long, sensual stroke, caressed her cheek. "Want to play Eros and Psyche?" he asked innocently.

She took the feather from him and whispered, "Funny you should ask. I've got some ideas about that."

She began walking again, and he kept pace. "I meant right now."

"That's not exactly part of what I'm picturing," she said, and tucked his feather inside the front of her blouse.

"You're gonna keep my feather . . . inside your bra?" he asked incredulously.

"Why not?"

"Because I . . . *I* want to be inside your bra! Not have my damned feather there!" he sputtered.

"It's a corset, actually," she whispered, even though she knew he had made them invisible to the mortals on the busy street. "From that dress shop."

He swallowed, his Adam's apple bobbing. "The black one or the ivory-colored corset?" he asked in a thick voice.

She gave him a coquettish smile. "One you haven't *seen* yet, darling," she said, then lowered her voice. "The girls and I went back yesterday . . . and bought many, many items with your American Express. So you can unwrap me over and over and over."

"Hell, woman, how's a man supposed to wait with a come-on like that?"

He reached for her blouse, but she swatted him away. "No cheating, sir! Where would be the surprise in that?"

"Maybe we should just do it right here on the street," he suggested, making a big show of glancing all around them. "Nobody can see us, anyway."

"Maybe *you* should display a bit of patience. Besides, I'm to meet Shay in a few minutes. She's giving me lessons with the Jeep. I'm going to learn how to operate it, and even get a license, so that I can drive to the shop every day."

"The shop?" His dark eyebrows lifted to his hairline. "Which shop?"

"I'm going to work at the Angels' store. Shay wanted me to help run the place, maybe find ways to generate more customers. She mentioned something called . . . Facebook? I think that was it. And also that Tweeter you spoke of."

"Twitter," he corrected, looking at her with undisguised admiration. "You're already in your groove, aren't you? I should've known it would take you no time at all. Next thing I know, you'll be kicking my ass on Dance Dance Revolution."

"That's for the Wii, right?" she asked, pretty sure that Emma had pointed out the mat for it the night before.

"See? See what I mean?" He pulled her close against his chest. "I can feel my feather through your shirt. Isn't it tickling you?"

"I like feeling you intimately. And I like that it's fine for me to do so. Yes," she declared, stopping and staring at the river again, "I like this twenty-first century of yours, Ari."

"Of ours," he corrected, sliding a muscular arm about her shoulder. As always, his physicality and strength made her feel secure. At peace for the first time since her drowning.

"Aristos, I want you to promise me something," she said softly, and he held her even closer.

"Anything, sweetheart."

"That you'll . . . be careful. About Caesar Vaella. Now that we know he's still alive."

Ari said nothing for a moment, then said, "Jules, my line of work . . . The cadre and I, we're always in danger. You know that. But we're immortal and kick serious ass. So don't worry."

"Perhaps he remains a threat, though?" She studied his handsome profile in concern.

"I'm gonna start looking for him again. Make him pay for what he did to you."

She shook her head. "I don't want you to do that. He's dangerous, Aristos."

"Remember what Eros promised. He said our love would last forever. That having suffered for our love, now we would taste the joy."

She relaxed into his embrace and smiled. He was right; there was nothing more to fear from that demon trader . . . at least not for the two of them. She offered a quick prayer to God and asked him to protect all the others in their circle, to keep them safe and out of that evil man's way.

And then, with a conspiratorial giggle, she retrieved Ari's feather and ran it down his arm. "So, *Eros*, want to know what plan your Psyche has in mind?"

"I suppose you think you've bested me?" Eros's father said in a bored voice. The war god was sprawled on a golden settee, reclining nude as one of his female servants rubbed oil into his shoulders.

Eros fired back, "I suppose you think you're intimidating me. Lying there, being pleasured while we converse."

Ares kept his eyes closed. "What was your purpose, truly, in meddling in your own handiwork? You'd set up the perfect gaming board; all the pieces were in play."

"I would not war against myself. I *am* love."

"I was proud . . . for those few days," Ares admitted. "You were my son, and I was truly . . . proud of you."

Eros had to battle down a swell of pain in his chest. "Father . . ."

"Don't bother," Ares said, cutting off the words of devotion and care that Eros had been so ready to declare. "You and I will remain at odds over this act of defiance."

"Ares, I could make you proud again," he promised his father. "Understand that I can't stop my gift of love any more than you can cease making war and bloodshed. It's in my veins, but I know I can be worthy as your son."

Ares' tawny-colored eyes opened wide, and he fixed Eros

with a hard gaze. "Love and war do not ever mix. Leave. Now. But know that you will not be welcomed here at my palace again. And I will not relent against the Spartans . . . even the pairs of lovers."

Eros shook his head. "I'm sorry, father. Because that means you truly will have war from me."

And with that promise, Eros lifted both hands and removed himself from his father's presence—and hurtled toward home, where he would consider the best way to guard the Spartans and the mortals in their midst.

Epilogue

I t had become their favorite game. Aristos following after
Jules, furtive, stealthy as he tailed her. And she pretending to be unaware of his presence, strolling along the secluded paths that ran from the Angels' house down to the
river, where the palms and live oaks created such a dark
canopy, it felt like a rain forest.

Ari stood poised at the most hidden turn in the sandy
path, bow raised, in his full Spartan garb. His cock strained
against the leather loin covering, the rough texture making
his arousal ache for release.

Jules swung her arms, smiling lightly as she walked innocently in his direction. That was part of the game; she never
knew where or when he might swoop upon her as Eros
himself. With a rustle of his wing feathers, he took flight and
sent his arrow flying. It speared into the path before Jules,
his erotic message fluttering in the light breeze.

She gasped, although surely she'd known he had watched
her leave the house, a plan forming in his mind. Kneeling,
she pulled the arrow from the earth and opened the note
he'd written especially for her.

My Psyche, I have come to claim you!

She smiled, folding the love note against her breast, and
gasped when from the treetops above, her beautiful winged
man came swooping down upon her. She squealed as he
seized hold of her, his feet never touching the ground. Off
he went, higher above the creek, clutching her close, having
captured her most epically.

"My Eros," she murmured against his cheek, the late-
day sun bright in her eyes. "Tell me where you're taking me.
What plan have you devised today?"

A laugh rumbled forth from his bare chest. "You don't

want to get it on up here, halfway to the clouds? Not today, fair Psyche?"

"I thought you said you'd blindfold me this time? That you'd lay me down in the warm grasses by the river, strip me bare, and descend upon me with your god's wings?"

"Ah," he whispered against her ear, "my Psyche demands much from her god of love."

And then he produced a piece of black silk, flashing her an alluring smile. "But you should know that I'd never forget."

"Except," she said, tucking the sash inside her bodice. "I think I have a different plan in mind. Once we land."

"Yes." It was all he said, lips parting. The black satin was tied about his eyes, and he stood there in the woods, feet wide apart. Before blindfolding him, she'd unfastened his loin covering, allowing the cool air to brush across his exposed, heated flesh. His erection had strained even harder then, jutting outward eagerly.

That was when she'd taken that silky scarf and caressed his length with it, back and forth for one long moment. His balls had seized tight, and he'd been halfway to release as she caressed him.

"Not yet, my love," she'd murmured. Then, stepping onto her tiptoes, she fastened the sash about his eyes.

"It was Psyche who wasn't supposed to look at Eros, don't forget."

"I get to change the rules because it's our game."

He smiled, pushing his pants farther down his hips, so ready. Unable to hold back from her. "Tell me what you have in mind."

Her lips brushed against his cheek, the feel of them warm and as soft as velvet. "You're to *feel* everything. Focus on the sensation of my touch."

With that declaration, she stepped away from him, but not before she brushed her mouth against the column of his throat.

"Come back to me," he begged. With a single step, he parted his legs and rubbed himself. "Here. Hungry for you."

She moved closer, sliding a hand along his buttocks; he

shivered, liking that, it was always such a sensitive, reactive portion of his body. "Do you want me?"

"Yes." His voice was tight, urgent. "Desperately."

"Good," she said. "Then, my Eros, my beautiful winged hero, you won't mind me doing *this*."

Ari's cock went rigid, so tight and hard, he'd have sworn he might come there and then, standing blindfolded in the woods. "Jules!" He groaned out her name like the most frantic kind of plea. *"Juliana."* He grunted long and hard, as he urged his hips forward. Eager for more, he tried to reach for her hand. She retreated, causing his whole body to shiver with need.

"Does it feel pleasurable?"

Her voice was tinkling like chimes, and she was fully fucking aware of how hot he was.

"I . . . Please," he beseeched helplessly. "Again. Do it again."

His groin tightened up, his balls clenched, and he knew he was about to let loose like a cannon if he didn't rein himself in.

He tried latching onto every possible image that might keep him from ejaculating this soon but pulled a fat zero. So he pulled off the blindfold, gasping hard.

"That's cheating."

"I'm gonna . . . Jules, I don't wanna lose it so fast." He panted, intensely. "It's too much sensation otherwise."

His balls tightened up harder, and he stared upward at the palm trees. But seeing the fronds only made him think of feathers—which brought him back to *what* Jules was do-ing to him.

She had his full erection in her palm, and the witch was trailing his feather—the one she'd taken to keeping in her bodice—gently across his cock. Teasing a cool sen-sation over his aching flesh, starting with the blunt head, then swiping back down to his base. It was excruciatingly light, the bristling texture unlocking every sensation in that oh-so-sensitive part of his flesh. Back and forth, back and forth she swept that feather, her eyes locked on him with a threatening, daring heat. She was clearly pleasuring herself just as much as him, if that dreamy, half-shut look in her eyes was any indication.

"Again?" she asked, inspecting him like some haughty

headmistress. He pictured her with a whip in her hand, wearing nothing but a black leather bustier and thong.

He had a sudden image of her swatting his hard-on with that feather, and that was it; he just came in thick, pulsing jets right into her hand.

"Oh, fucking . . . fuck . . . oh, oh!" he couldn't stop crying out, his hips surging and pumping as Jules rubbed a thumb to his base, bringing him all the way through.

When his body had finally settled, he was soft in her hand, and damp, and he had no freaking idea how to clean himself up, not out here on the trail. But she didn't seem to mind, because she wrapped her arms about his neck and tugged him down onto the ground with her.

"Now," she said, drawing him into her arms, "let's see how Eros's feather might pleasure me."

As they rolled together, wrapped in each other's arms, he'd have sworn, absolutely sworn, that he heard Eros's laughter ringing through the treetops overhead.

Turn the page for a glimpse of the
next thrilling romance in the
Gods of Midnight series,

RED MORTAL

Coming April 2011 from Signet Eclipse

"I was thirty-five at the Hot Gates. How do you reckon my years now? Forty-five? Perhaps fifty?" Leo strode toward her, favoring his right knee more than she'd ever seen him do before. "I suppose we could call the bet at forty-eight."

"You are so beautiful to me. The lines on your face, the age written across your features—it arouses me. The silver in your hair beguiles me, makes me want to touch it. Touch *you*."

He sighed and stared at his feet. "I was always too old for you." He shook his head slowly. "Ares has now chosen to make that fact quite obvious."

"You are still a young man. Still strong and vital and—"

He cut her off with a harsh laugh. "What were you, eighteen at the time of our bargain?"

She said nothing; he was correct—to a point. . . . She'd been frozen eternally at that age by Zeus and even now was unsure exactly how many years she'd been alive.

"As I suspected. I've always been far, far too old for you, Daphne." He turned and walked slowly toward the window, seeming worn down. But savagely beautiful, still. "In the throes of immortality, we both simply chose to ignore that fact."

"You're wrong."

He glanced back at her, dark eyebrows lifting. "Am I? Wrong that I'm old enough to have fathered you? I think not."

"No—about us. About us being right together. You were never too old for me, and you aren't now."

"I was always almost eighteen years older than you. And now?" He laughed again, a hollow, haunted sound that made tears fill her eyes. "Well, it's anyone's guess how much that gap will widen in the coming days."

"There is only one thing that you have *always* been, Leo, and that is mine. I was a fool to stay away out of fear of my brother, when we could have been together. Ares may have placed this curse upon us—"

"Upon *me*," he corrected in a whisper, sadness filling his dark eyes. "He has touched me eternally once again. But this time . . . my hours are fading."

She searched his face, refusing to back down. "But we still have right now. What more do any lovers ever have? Look at all that Ari and Juliana have endured just to be together. Like them, we must love *now*."

"Now, Daphne? *Now* it is I who must protect you, who must say that we have no future. For I have nothing to offer you, love."

"You're being as cruel as my brother," she cried. "When I stayed away from you, when I said we could not be, it was to save your life."

He smiled faintly, love filling his entire expression. "You think my motives are not the same? You believe that I don't love you?"

She began shaking; she couldn't stop the rush of shock and emotion that engulfed her. "You'd keep me here for whatever time is left."

"I won't have you watch me wither away . . . turn frail and feeble. The change inside me cannot be undone; your brother cannot be thwarted in this attack. But I won't have you see me turn, quite truly, into an *old man*." He laughed grimly. "Perhaps my nickname was always a bit of prophecy."

She moved toward him, hands outstretched. "We don't know how much time we have, Leo. No one in the real world ever does. You once told me that you prayed to claim me. To make love to me. To take me beneath your body and make me yours. I am willing, my lord. I am still—have always been—yours."

His lean body was as sculpted, muscular, and fit as it had always been, and she saw that he reacted to her with the fervor of a very young man. The khakis that he wore bulged prominently in front, betraying how desperately he still wanted her despite all his claims about sending her away. His words were one thing; his visible need quite another.

She stood in front of him and pressed a shy, tentative

hand against his groin, for the first time allowing her fingers to stroke his most intimate place. Leo jolted in reaction, clasping her wrist with a groan.

"Daphne, stop."

"I see how you still react to me. I felt your manhood, your longing with my own hand."

He growled, dark eyes flashing in the semidarkness. "You should not have done so."

"You could still give me a babe, if you wanted. Several, even . . . and live long enough to watch them grow. Live long enough to love me for years, for us to have a family, a whole life together despite my brother's curse."

"We do not know that."

"No," she replied firmly, "we don't know. But all you and I have ever had is the unknown." She fell to her knees, mirroring the way she'd once begged her own brother to spare Leo this fate. "Do not send me away, Leo. Take me as you've long desired. Make me your mate, your wife. Whatever days we have, they will be more than enough. It will be the greatest gift, but take me, please."

Suddenly he was kneeling before her, moving slowly as he favored the leg he'd injured at Thermopylae. When they were face-to-face, knee-to-knee, he slid rough fingers beneath her chin, stroking her slowly. Treating her as his beloved. "Am I to let you watch me die?" He smiled softly, faint lines at the edges of his mouth. "With the way I love you, would I do that to you, sweetness? No. I would not. You must go and be young forever. That is your portion. Mine is to lead my men until I'm no longer able to do so. But not with you watching me." He shook his head firmly. "Not with you suffering on my behalf. I can protect you in this one final way . . . and I will."

"Leo, don't do this." She clutched his arms, tears pouring down her cheeks. "We still have this moment."

He looked at her and instinctively she knew it was for the very last time. That this moment between them, this heartbeat, *was* their forever. "My fate is sealed, but you will always be young. I love you, but I am dying. And you, my beloved . . . you must live."

He rose to his feet without another word. Without so much as a look back, he left her kneeling in the middle of his bedchamber. She heard his heavy footfalls fade down the hallway, listened to the power of total silence that came after.

And still she knelt and waited. Waited and prayed, supplicating every power of the universe that he would return. That he would fall before her and claim her, finally.

But, long as she waited and prayed . . . Leonidas, King of Sparta, did not return.

A THRILLING SERIES FEATURING SEVEN IMMORTAL
SPARTAN WARRIORS PROTECTING MANKIND—AND
CONFRONTING PASSION ALONG THE WAY…

DEIDRE KNIGHT

Red Fire

A Gods of Midnight Novel

Eternity has become a prison for Ajax Petrakos.
Centuries after he and his Spartan brothers made their
bargain for immortality, Ajax struggles to maintain his
warrior's discipline. His only source of strength is his
hope that he will soon meet the woman once foretold
to him—the other half of his soul, Shay Angel.

Ajax searches for his destined mate on the haunted
streets of modern-day Savannah, but he isn't the first to
find her. Shay, the youngest of a powerful demon-
hunting clan, can see the monsters that stalk the steamy
Southern nights—an ability that draws the deadly
attention of Ajax's worst enemy. As Shay and Ajax race
to solve a chilling prophecy—one that could spell Ajax's
death if they don't succeed—a fated passion arises,
threatening to sweep away everything in its path.

S0015

DEIDRE KNIGHT

Red Kiss

A Gods of Midnight Novel

Spartan slave River Kassandros can transform into any
weapon. After a bloody battle he's forever a dagger—
until a mortal can release him. Attracted to this blade,
Emma Lowery draws blood with it and frees River. But
even as they fight off intense passions, a sinister
power arises to destroy them. To protect humankind,
they may have to make the ultimate sacrifice—and lose
their chance at love...

**"A fascinating world of gods, demons,
and immortal warriors."**
—*New York Times* bestselling author
Angela Knight

**Available wherever books are sold or at
penguin.com**

JESSICA ANDERSEN

NIGHTKEEPERS
A NOVEL OF
THE FINAL PROPHECY

*First in the acclaimed series that
combines Mayan astronomy and lore with
modern, sexy characters.*

In the first century A.D., Mayan astronomers predicted
the world would end on December 21, 2012. In these
final years before the End Times, demon creatures of
the Mayan underworld have come to earth to trigger
the apocalypse. But the descendants of the Mayan
warrior-priests have decided to fight back.

**"Raw passion, dark romance, and seat-of-your-
pants suspense, all set in an
astounding paranormal world."**
—#1 *New York Times* bestselling author J. R. Ward

Also Available
Dawnkeepers
Skykeepers
Demonkeepers